A Red Rose

An historically correct romantic adventure story

Tree young Swedish girl's journey to maturity and those who cross their path

Lars Ehrlander

Copyright © 2019 by Lars Ehrlander.

Library of Congress Control Number:		2019908289
ISBN:	Hardcover	978-1-7960-4201-6
	Softcover	978-1-7960-4200-9
	eBook	978-1-7960-4199-6

All rights reserved. No part of this book may be reproduced or transmitted in any form or by any means, electronic or mechanical, including photocopying, recording, or by any information storage and retrieval system, without permission in writing from the copyright owner.

This is a work of fiction. All of the characters, names, incidents, organizations, and dialogue in this novel are either the products of the author's imagination or are used fictitiously.

Any people depicted in stock imagery provided by Getty Images are models, and such images are being used for illustrative purposes only.
Certain stock imagery © Getty Images.

Print information available on the last page.

Rev. date: 06/20/2019

To order additional copies of this book, contact:
Xlibris
1-888-795-4274
www.Xlibris.com
Orders@Xlibris.com
798746

Some of the pictures used in this tale are not necessarily original and are included simply to help setting the mood, although, effort has been made to keep them as authentic as possible.

CONTENTS

PART I

Chapter 1	August, 1939 Sunbathing	1
Chapter 2	August, 1939 - Liseberg	10
Chapter 3	August 1939 - Returning to the ships	22
Chapter 4	September, 1939 - Letters from John and Billy	31

PART II

Chapter 5	September, 1939 - Kurt	39
Chapter 6	October 1939 - Gunnar	48
Chapter 7	August, 1940 Roland and Barbro's crayfish party	55
Chapter 8	December, 1940 - Cecilia	77
Chapter 9	January 1941 Stockholm	85
Chapter 10	January, 1942 Kurt and Eva to NewYork	106
Chapter 11	January, 1942 Kurt courts Annika	111
Chapter 12	June 1942 - John visits Sweden	119
Chapter 13	October, 1942 – Billy's last letter	131
Chapter 14	November, 1942 – Kurt expands to Stockholm	136
Chapter 15	February, 1943 - Kurt and Annika's divorce	148
Chapter 16	April, 1943. Ella and Martin	156

PART III

Chapter 17	July, 1944 - Axel and Alex born	167
Chapter 18	August, 1945 - Yvonne	172
Chapter 19	Oct, 1945 - Eva and Bo Lundgren	177
Chapter 20	August, 1946 - Stellan	182
Chapter 21	August, 1947 - Paris	207

PART IV

Chapter 22 August, 1948 – Camilla, Jodassy 219
Chapter 23 May, 1949 - Leaving Jodassy 236
Chapter 24 July 1949 - Lisa and John.. 244
Chapter 25 July, 1949 - Going to the USA 249
Chapter 26 August, 1949 - Eva and Stellan 261
Chapter 27 March 1952 -- Tina 265
Chapter 28 June, 1954 - Annika moves to Stockholm 271
Chapter 29 February, 1957- Annika and Torsten in Mora 274

PART V

Chapter 30 July 1958 - The boys being boys 283
Chapter 31 1961 - Ali in Salen 292
Chapter 32 1962 - On the road 298
Chapter 33 1964 Axel, Alex and Ann Marie to the US................. 305
Chapter 34 1970 - Sunny, the Wilders and Katrina 312
Chapter 35 1973 – Firefighting, Molly – Tracy, Kurt.................... 325
Chapter 36 Jul. 1973 To Seattle -- Switching rolls 332
Chapter 37 1975 - Back to Fairbanks 338
Chapter 38 February, 1976 Going to Europe................................ 343
Chapter 39 1976 – Lisa and John and Billy 354

PART VI

Chapter 40 1977 Annika and Billy... 365
Chapter 41 1983 Three-day party in Sweden. 378
Chapter 42 1983 Alex meets Corina.. 403
Chapter 43 September, 1983 - The accident 408
Chapter 44 1984 -- Maria 415

PART I

CHAPTER 1

August, 1939 Sunbathing

It was a sunny day at the beginning of fall, in August of 1939, in Longedrag, a suburb of Gothenburg on the Swedish west coast.

"I had the craziest dream last night," said Annika

"What?" Lisa asked curiously, as Camilla turned her head in interest.

"Oh, it was so silly, and the funny thing is that I remember every detail so precisely. Normally I remember a dream for no more than five minutes," said Annika, grimacing. She removed her sunglasses to wipe away a salt stain. The strong midday sun fell on her face.

"I know," Camilla agreed, elevating herself on her elbows. "Usually I can't remember anything from my dreams, and that's all right with me because my dreams are hardly worth remembering."

"Anxiety dreams, huh?" Lisa mused. "So, tell us about your dream, Annika, was it hot?"

"No, no, not like that. But it was fun while it lasted. Another girl and I were rulers of this country . . ."

"What country?" Camilla interrupted

"I don't know, just a country."

"You mean that you were a ruler of a country and you don't know what country it was?" Camilla prodded.

"Come on Camilla, let her tell us about her dream," Lisa chided.

"Well, like I said, we were the rulers of this country in the Middle East, I assume. We were both sitting at a throne, dressed in saris . . ."

"What's a sari?" Camilla inquired.

"You know, the dresses woman wears in the Middle East, India, with the veils and everything," Lisa explained.

". . . and we were being entertained by lightly dressed dancing girls and flame and sword-eating men. While this was going on, people were being brought before us, and we had to decide their fate by showing thumbs up or down. The weird thing about it was that we had no idea why they were brought before us or how our judgment would impact our subjects. We couldn't even understand what they said. Still, we had to proceed. The subjects had a choice of three doors to enter. If both of us showed thumbs down, they had to enter the first door. If there was a thumb up and a thumb down, they could enter either the middle door or the first door; and with two thumbs up they could enter any one of the three doors. Our subjects showed no emotion as we made our choices. The other strange thing was that everyone chose to walk through the first door, making our judgments meaningless."

"So, you didn't know what was behind the doors?" Lisa asked.

"Not a clue. It was almost as if we were sitting in for St. Peter at Heaven's Gate," Annika continued.

"Who was the girl next to you?" Lisa asked. "Were you a couple?" she inquired delicately.

"Lisa, you're getting too personal," Annika scolded her. "No! She was simply my co-ruler. Well, what do you think it could mean?" Annika asked her eyes wide.

"It's hard to tell. It deals with bureaucratic frustration, with uncertainty, with power and wealth, a sense of duty, and just going along with things. I have no clue though how any of that relates to you. In particular, why is your co-ruler is a woman, and why in the Middle East?" Lisa remarked.

"Well it all seemed so real. Do you believe that dreams can come true?"

"Not that one," Lisa chuckled, and Camilla joined in.

"Boy, I can identify with that lost feeling. There is a lot going on around me that I don't understand. I seem to be just muddling through much of the time," said Camilla.

"We're being observed," Annika noted casually, reaching for the sun screen lotion across the hull of the small wooden boat. "Behind the boulders . . . on Sheep Island. Ah, they're only kids, small boys," she sighed, notably disappointed. Ignoring her audience, sitting in the bottom of the wooden hull boat, she proceeded to rub in the lotion. She had developed a deep tan over the summer. Her normally smooth skin was covered with tiny goose bumps from exposure to the wind, light-blond fuzz, bleached by the summer sun, and small white evaporated seawater spots. She tossed her long copper-blond hair back, clear of the lotion. "Whoa!" she squealed, squeezing a little more lotion into her hand than intended. She enthusiastically smeared it over her chest, like a child playing with mud, before rubbing it into a silky gloss. Annika added a little extra lotion on the swell of her breasts. "Your butt is getting red, Camilla. Would you like me to rub on some sun block?" she asked suggestively. Camilla glanced back over her shoulder. Her normally white bottom was indeed blushing, light pink in contrast to her otherwise golden tan. At a distance she appeared to be wearing a light-colored bikini. Camilla could feel the heat.

"Will you, please? I should have already. The sun is so strong on the water. You know, it's deceptive with the wind, you really can't tell how strong the sun is," she mused.

"How about doing me to?" Lisa asked, watching Annika squeeze lotion onto Camilla's back, cheeks and thighs and massage it in.

"Sure, in a minute."

"Oh, that feels good," Camilla sighed. "This is great. I just love lying here listening to the water 'clucking' against the boat and the smell of varnish and the sea. This is living!"

"And having Annika rub your butt, huh?" Lisa added. The girls giggled.

The three girls had lived in Longedrag, a suburb of Gothenburg, the second largest city in Sweden, all their lives. Best friends for as long as they could remember, they did almost everything together. They loved to go camping, even if only in their own back yards, and they were renowned tree-fort builders. They enjoyed playing all sorts of games and sports, often playing on boys' teams, though recently, because of school and work obligations, their sports activities had been reduced to tennis and sailing once a week. At the age of fifteen, they had become "blood sisters" in a sacred ceremony. They pierced the tips of their thumbs with a needle, making blood contact, and pledged to meet every 10 years.

After leaving high school, Lisa, the arguable most intellectual of the three, had continued her studies at the University of Gothenburg. Her original goal had been to become a veterinarian. She had since changed to general medicine, hoping to specialize in obstetrics and gynecology. She preferred to work on healthy people. Her academic commitments had sharply curtailed her social activities. It was a special treat for her to spend this Saturday afternoon sunbathing with the girls, slowly drifting about on the sheltered side of the peninsula where they lived. They knew of several good swimming spots all around the bay. Most of the shoreline in the area consisted of smooth, weathered granite formations, occasionally interrupted by short stretches of coarse sand beaches. However, the boat provided more privacy for sunbathing nude.

"Hey, that's enough, now it's my turn," Lisa whined, elevating her rump to emphasize her point.

"All right, move over girl, so I can reach," Annika coached her. Lisa provocatively raised her buttocks higher as if to dare Annika. Lisa was normally the clown in the group and the one most likely to instigate practical jokes, even though she had mellowed considerably in the last year or two, as she and the other girls matured. Annika refused to let the girls think she was a prude. She began rubbing in the lotion as if it was the most natural thing in the world. "You're so silly Lisa. When you lay like that the boys can see you!" She chided her.

"Oh, that's okay, they have to learn sometime. Let them have a little fun." Lisa laughed mischievously, wiggling her behind to drive home her point.

"All right, cut it out, if you want me to do this!"

"Sorry, I'll behave."

Annika meticulously rubbed in the lotion until only a light sheen remained. "Boy you're hot!" Annika exclaimed.

"It's your rubbing that makes me hot," Lisa informed her, turning around smiling coyly.

"Be that as it may, we should have done this a lot earlier," Annika lectured them.

"Well, you can rub my butt with lotion any time you like," Lisa responded.

Camilla sat up. "We're drifting pretty close to the island. We need to pull out; actually, it's time to call it a day. Let's take a quick swim before we turn back." She stood up, dressed in only the suntan lotion. Carefully she stepped onto the rail and dove into the frigid water, making the small boat rock precariously and splashing water on Annika and Lisa. It was warm, lying down in the boat, protected from the wind, but sitting up, it was chilly. Lisa and Annika quickly joined Camilla in the water.

"What are you guys going to wear tonight?" Lisa asked. "You know, I think there will be a lot of English sailors there. I heard there are two English frigates visiting this week. That should be fun. I don't know what it is, but I love guys in uniforms. They look so handsome."

"Are you going to dance with them Camilla?" Annika asked.

"We'll see. They're so hard to understand above the music," said Camilla, her teeth chattering as she adjusted to the water temperature.

"Anyone is hard to hear when the music is playing," Annika mused.

"I wish that Sven could come along," said Camilla.

"Well, invite him. He's welcome to come along," Annika said. "By all means."

"He's hunting this weekend in Herrljunga, hoping to get a moose." Camilla explained.

"Oh, perhaps next time then." Lisa offered, before vaulting and diving to the bottom, eight feet down.

"At least the British have better manners than some of the country boys," Camilla added.

"Hey, what's wrong with the country boys?" Annika protested. "Come on, there are lots of nice country boys. I think the worst guys come from the downtown crowd. They only have two things on their minds, booze and sex, and not necessarily in that order."

Lisa's head reappeared. "Lisa, I'm sure glad you can come along tonight, to Liseberg. I know it will be fun, for real," said Camilla.

"I wouldn't miss it. It has been ages since I went to any Tivoli or folk park. Liseberg is so pretty this time of year. The flowers are all out and all the lights look so festive."

"And love that Old Spice cologne, huh?" Annika teased, looking up from under her wet bangs, grinning.

The water felt a lot warmer now after the girls had grown accustomed to the temperature. In fact, it felt warmer in the water than being exposed to the air.

"We should probably be getting back, so we don't miss the seven o'clock tram to town. Besides, I think all three of us got a little more sun than what we should of," Annika said, feeling the heat on her breasts.

"Should have," Lisa corrected, wrinkling her nose.

"Yes professor, should have," Annika repeated, grimacing. Camilla and Annika felt nothing but the highest admiration for Lisa's intellect. She seemed to know just about everything. Camilla was gifted too. She was an accomplished artist, studying art at the university and taking engineering classes at the same time, working on a double major.

The girls got back into the boat and put on their robes, hurriedly dried themselves and changed into their street clothes. Camilla was purring audibly to speed up the warming process. She pulled the small anchor they had used to slow their drifting. Remnants of an old fishnet were caught on the anchor. A small crab was tangled in the net, apparently having become stuck while feasting on another crab that had become entangled earlier. It was now too late to save either. "It's a crab eat crab world out there, or rather, down there," Camilla mused.

"Let's see if we can start the motor," Lisa suggested. "I don't trust that old thing. Here's the starter rope." Lisa threw the cord over to Camilla who was sitting in the stern. "Here captain, you drive!"

Camilla wrapped the cord around the rotor, took a firm grip and gave it a good pull. Nothing happened except that she almost snapped Lisa with the cord. "Oops, I forgot to turn on the stupid gas valve."

"It can happen to the best of us," Annika replied.

Camilla primed the motor, pumping the rubber tube on the fuel line, and tried again. The motor started up immediately. It dug into the water lifting the bow, and the boat took off. It accelerated a bit faster than anyone had anticipated, and turned sharply, knocking all three off their feet. No one was hurt. "Oops! Sorry, I think I gave it a little too much gas!"

"You are so modest Camilla. You gave it plenty!" Lisa teased her.

The traffic was heavy pulling into the small boat harbor, and the girls recognized many of the boaters. They waved cheerfully, even to those they didn't know.

"Seems as though there are more and more summer guests here each year," Camilla observed.

"Well, that's okay with me," said Annika, "I love to people-watch, as long as they don't get too drunk and obnoxious, or throw their garbage around."

"Me too," Lisa agreed, "and it's more fun at the Thursday night sailing when there are more boats participating."

"Yes, but you know, those drunk summer guests that got stuck at the shallows last Thursday, in that big fancy mahogany. I don't think they should have pulled them loose. They deserved to sit there. They wouldn't drive a car drunk, but they seem to think that it's all right at sea," Annika complained.

"Are you serious?" Lisa replied sternly. "They couldn't just let them sit there, forever, could they?"

"They could walk ashore when the sea freezes," said Annika, as if she meant it.

"It's been a few years since the sea froze, hasn't it?" Lisa asked.

"Well then they could have swum ashore," Annika persisted, "or walked on the water. They acted as though they could."

"Will Sven be sailing on Thursday?" Lisa asked, changing the subject.

"I think so," Camilla responded, "but he wasn't happy last week when I beat him pretty bad, about 10 boat lengths, and for the fifth time in a row."

"Perhaps you should let him win at least once," suggested Lisa, "after all, what could it hurt?"

"For real? I don't know, it just seems so silly, -- but he's really nice."

The girls had to wait a few moments for an island ferry to pull out and for a commercial fishing-boat with its entourage of screaming seabirds to pull in ahead of them. A couple of sailors had noticed the girls and were waving enthusiastically while throwing kisses and grinning. They acted as though they had been at sea for a long time. The girls appreciated the attention, waving and blowing kisses back.

"Read any good books lately?" Lisa asked.

"Yes, I'm reading Steinbeck's *The Grapes of Wrath*," Camilla responded.

"Is it any good?" Lisa asked.

"I don't know, I just started it, but it got good reviews."

After having tied and tidied up the boat, and loaded their belongings on their bikes, the girls left for home. Camilla and Annika lived next door to one another in typical Swedish middle-class homes, with barn red siding and white trim. The yards were surrounded by picket fences, and their yard featured the typical fruit trees: apple, pears and cherries and a plum tree that more resembled an enormous bush. Flowers bordered the walkways, and red currents and other bushes formed hedges toward the neighbors. A flag pole and a sundial perfected the idyllic scene in both yards. Lisa lived a few lots farther down the road, closer to the tram station.

Annika inhaled deeply as they stopped by a large pink rose bush by her family's gate. "The roses smell so good" she sighed. "Heavenly."

"Yes, just too bad they don't always survive the winter," said Lisa.

"This one seems to be alright though. It's five years now since we planted it, I think. It's a Hansa Rose. It's hardy, but a little bushy. Almost looks like a wild rose," said Annika.

"So, what are you going to wear tonight?" Lisa asked. "Are we going to wear the white pleated skirts? They'll be a little challenging at the funny house. If you will, I will," she dared them.

"Sure, the guys will get a thrill, why not? I think I've got that funny house figured out now anyway," Annika laughed. "Flaunt it while you got it, eh?"

"You guys are too much," Camilla giggled. "All right . . . why not? Well, I can probably think of a few reasons but, what the heck," Camilla agreed. "Those skirts are better for dancing, anyway."

"I'll carry my pumps. They're not exactly made for walking," said Annika.

"You can leave your bikes at my house if you like, or perhaps you'd rather walk. It's easy to get the skirt caught in the chain, or getting it oily. Don't be too late now," Lisa reminded them. "Shall we bring umbrellas?"

"Naa . . . it looks pretty clear. It's not going to rain," Annika said, and Camilla agreed.

Annika licked her index finger and held it up in the air. "It's a west wind," she concluded. "It almost always is. Well, there are some dark clouds to the south, and the wind has been known to change directions. No, it's not going to rain," Annika concluded.

"You're probably right," Lisa agreed.

CHAPTER 2

August, 1939 - Liseberg

The girls caught the tram at its third stop. There were only a few travelers onboard. The seven o'clock tram left at a good time; most of the city folks had already left for home and the evening traffic had not yet picked up. The girls felt at home on the tram; they spent close to two hours there almost every day. They usually chose the same bench up front when it was available, because it offered the best view. The tram brought them down through the residential peninsula where they lived, past Saga, the movie theater, now featuring *The Wizard of Oz*. It traveled across farmlands and down along the industrial harbor, where enormous cranes loaded and unloaded oceangoing freight liners. By then all seats were taken and the tram offered standing room only. Most riders would depart at the shipyard ferry, but the tram would soon fill again as it passed through other residential areas. Even though they saw most of the same passengers every day, the girls seldom engaged in conversations with their co-travelers. Annika enjoyed speculating about the other passengers; imagining how they lived, where they worked and details of their personal lives, mostly based on how they dressed and their hairstyles. In the morning, most passengers sat quietly half a sleep, but returning home, several passengers would typically carry on, chatting, especially the school kids.

The passengers did not have to look up to know when they traveled past the canneries. In fact, all the way down the industrial harbor one could navigate by nose or ears. The coffee roasters, the petroleum refineries, the cracker bakery and the sugar refinery all had their unique smells and sounds.

The large billboards by the sugar factory advertised the opening of the World's Fair in New York.

" That would be something, to get to go to the World's Fair in New York, wouldn't it?" Annika said, dreamily.

"Perhaps someday," Lisa responded, gazing at a discarded Marabou chocolate wrapper on the floor.

"The trip alone on the ship going over there would be quite an experience," said Camilla.

"Yes, if you don't get seasick. The weather on the Atlantic can get mighty rough, especially during fall and winter," Lisa reminded them. She was becoming increasingly fixated on the discarded candy wrapper.

"I know, my Aunt Greta, made the trip last year, and she was in bed five out of six days," Annika replied, straightening the pleats on her skirt after crossing her legs

"That would be such a shame," Camilla sympathized.

The passengers could see the shipbuilding yards and giant dry docks across the harbor. The sparks from the welders glowed bright against the dark hull, even though it was Saturday evening. Clusters of residential high-rises climbed the hillside beyond the ship yards, offering their residents a fantastic view over the city and the harbor. Finally, the tram carried the passengers up a long hill to Slottskogs Parken, the animal park near Gothenburg's central area. They still had a thirty-minute bus ride to the downtown core area.

Lisa picked up the candy wrapper and discarded it properly as she got off the tram. Once downtown, by the central station, they switched back to a tram that took them through the downtown area, across massive stone bridges, down business avenues and past meticulously manicured parks and alleys. They traveled past the downtown Farmer's Market, Botanical Gardens, the State Theater, and Heden with its gravel soccer fields, in the shadow of the tall red-bricked Catholic Church.

The tram stopped at the front gate of Liseberg. It was dark now; however, Liseberg was anything but dark. Chain in bright pastels, pink, green, white and light blue, its facade was reminiscent of a child's storybook castle. About as many visitors were leaving as arriving, as the family crowd was making room for the young-adult evening crowd. In the background, on the hill, the giant, festively lit Ferris wheel turned. Illuminated flower arrangements and musical water fountains lit up the park. Along the slant of the hill stood clusters of illuminated giant mushrooms, creating the illusion of a mythical garden. Visitors occupied park benches watching each other and those passing by. Several nations were represented by their citizens, many dressed according to their custom.

The girls followed the flow of people past the Great Theater and the first class Liseberg's Restaurant, with its popular outside dining deck. The veranda offered a full view of Liseberg's Concert Hall and the main outdoor stage, where world class entertainers performed every two hours.

"It would be fun to go to the Great Theater sometime," Camilla said, "or at least the Revue Theater. They always have interesting acts there."

"Yes, there's a Russian folk-dance group there now that's supposed to be fantastic," Lisa replied.

"Last year I was there and they had a magician who cut a lady in half and made another float in the air. You know that what you see is only an illusion, but still, it seems so real," said Annika. "There was a comedian piano player who was really funny. He would start playing a beautiful classical piece and then he would foul it up somehow. He never finished anything and left you wondering if he really knew the piece."

"What was his name?" Lisa asked, smiling at a group of British sailors who clowned around when the girls walked by. "I think his name was Victor Borge," Annika responded.

"Oh yes, the Dane. I've seen him. He's so funny," Camilla agreed, "and he can actually play really well."

The girls walked past the small pagoda where the band enthusiastically played big band music and old Swedish favorites. At times the audience would sing along. The girls walked through a tunnel of aromatic climbing roses and through the game arcades. Lisa tried her luck at throwing rings around a bottle neck. She came close, very close, but the rings always managed to wriggle off in the last moment, as if they were so designed. She tried one last time but without success. Annika tried her luck at throwing darts at balloons. There was a guaranteed prize every time, and sure enough, she won a pink rabbit foot key chain. The young boy tending to the stand had upgraded her prize from a pencil. Annika was an expert flirt, and it often earned her favors.

They walked past the children's rides, and the many small restaurants. The Tyrolian restaurant seemed especially proud of its yodeling Tyrolean music, which it broadcast at full volume. The girls continued past the Scary House, ending up in front of the Funny House. Predictably, a large enthusiastic crowd was standing there, watching people struggling up the moving stairs and cheering them on. The left and the right stairs moved up and down apparently sporadically, but on closer examination in a pattern. It was particularly amusing to watch the girls, as they reached for the steps, often in rather compromising and revealing positions. Blasts of air would catch the girls unaware and lift their skirts if they were not careful. Many forgot about the air as they struggled with the steps. The ride ended with a swift ride down a slide, again, before the appreciative audience.

"Are you guys ready to give it a try?" Lisa asked.

"Yeah, sure, let's do it!" Camilla agreed. She thought she had figured out how to keep her skirt from ballooning. Not that she cared all that much, but she liked the idea of beating the system. She had tried it several times before and she was confident she knew where the air tubes were located so she could hold down her skirt at the crucial moments. She had not managed in the past, but this time she was sure she would. Little did she know that the air was controlled by the attendant.

Two couples were ahead of them. They did not appear to be familiar with the attraction, and the girls chose the moving stairs, even though one of them was wearing a rather tight skirt. Her escort went first, and it seemed easy enough, once he caught the rhythm of skipping every other step. As the first girl approached the stairs, she was caught in a sudden blast of air and her dress flew up above her head, revealing her long slender tan legs and part of her panties, to the audience's jubilant appreciation. She actually managed the stairs quite well.

The second girl confidently approached the stairs apparently not expecting her skirt to lift, as it was cut rather tight. But she underestimated the power of forced air, and not only did her dress balloon, but also her slip. She made a token effort to press her skirt down, while at the same time grabbing the railing and attempting to rise with the moving steps. It appeared as though she must have lost most of her coordination with her last glass of wine. She was left hanging more or less upside down in the hand rail stretching her legs to the point that it was a miracle that her dress did not tear. The attendant assisted her down and she proceeded up a less challenging stairway, still the good sport. All the while, the audience convulsed with laughter.

Annika, Lisa and Camilla were careful to wrap their skirts around their legs and hold them tight as they took their turns. The girls had no problem negotiating the stairs but were only partly effective in holding their skirts down at the same time. Lisa and Annika waited at the top platform for Camilla to join them, confident they had passed the air zone. Just as Camilla reached the top, the attendant released several air bursts concurrently, right where the girls were standing. Taken by surprise, all three of them had their skirts blown over their heads. The audience roared their approval.

The girls stopped at the Mirror House for a few minutes making silly faces and giggling.

"Hi pretty girl." Lisa heard a deep manly English voice from behind, as she was making a particularly ugly face.

"Now I know that you don't mean that," she said, chuckling in her almost perfect English.

"Well, I was referring to the real thing," said the tall sailor behind her. She could smell his Old Spice cologne.

"Thank you, Sir, you are most kind" she responded. "Where are you fellows from?" Lisa inquired.

"England."

"I sort of realized that. I was more thinking, from where in England?" She smiled, looking up at him.

"I'm from South Hampton" he responded, "or close by anyway." He had a friendly masculine face. "And now I serve in the British Navy," he said with an upward lift of his chin.

"Really" she teased. "I would never have guessed." He actually laughed, joined by the others. He didn't seem affected by her insolence.

"Don't be mean now, Lisa," Annika chided her, turning to the gentlemen. "How long will you stay in Gothenburg?"

"Two more days. Do you ladies live in town?"

"Oh, about an hour's ride out the coast. I saw your ships when you arrived last Wednesday," Camilla replied.

"Yes, about a three-chapter ride in a good book," Lisa added.

Three more British sailors had now stepped up to the group. "I would like to introduce you to my Swedish girl friends," he told his mates. "By the way my name is Billy." He held out his hand.

"John, this is . . . Oh, could you give me a clue?" Billy stumbled.

"Lisa" she volunteered and reached for John's extended hand. "And this is Camilla and Annika." They all shook hands and exchanged names. "It's a pleasure to meet you. Is this your first time to Sweden?" Annika asked.

"For me it is," said Billy, "but John has been here before."

"So, it was worth coming back to?" Annika asked, wrinkling her nose.

"It's very beautiful here, and there are very beautiful girls," he added, raising his eyebrows. "I like it very much. It's so nice and clean," said John, smiling at her seductively, while pulling out a cigarette and tapping it nervously against the package. He held out the package for the others, but there were no takers.

"We were planning on climbing the hill to the Ferris wheel. Would you girls like to come along?" Billy asked.

The girls deliberated in Swedish.

"Cool with me," said Lisa, "they seem pretty nice. Boy! Is that tall blond guy with the three stripes handsome!"

"I like the guy next to him," Annika confided.

Suddenly, John's face turned red. "La a a L a dies, I - I must caution you that I lived in Sweden for two years when I was younger and I do speak some Swedish. I apologize for not speaking up sooner." He tossed a gum-wrapper in a waste basket they passed by.

"Oops," the girls said in chorus.

"I hope we didn't say anything inappropriate." Lisa looked up from under her bangs with her most innocent smile.

"Not at all," John assured her.

"Thanks for telling us. A lot of guys I know would have said nothing, taking advantage of the situation," said Annika. The other girls nodded in agreement. Annika was moving suggestively with the rhythm of the background music instigating a chain reaction amongst the others.

"I'm a gentleman," John said, his British upbringing reflected in his tone. He retrieved a package of gum and passed it around. This time everyone took one. "Would you like me to take that?" He reached for Lisa's empty gum wrapper.

"Thank you, Sir. You're a gentleman indeed."

"I'm impressed at how well you girls speak English. You have obviously studied English in school," Billy complimented them.

"Yes, we had English for five years, as our first foreign language," Camilla told him, fingering her handkerchief.

"We also listen to a lot of English music and watch a lot of English, or American, movies," Lisa added. "Yes, we were about ready to scale the mountain ourselves, and we are forever grateful to the King of England for providing military escort." Lisa affected a somewhat exaggerated curtsy and held out her arm for John to take.

There was barely room for six people in each basket, but all seven were able to squeeze into a basket by the sailors' placing their arms around the girl's shoulders. This was a little too cozy for the girl's comfort, their having just met the fellows, however, they did not feel right about leaving one of them behind. Once the wheel began to turn and the basket began to rock, the girls appreciated the security provided by the men. In fact, it felt nice and a quite romantic. The view from the top was breathtaking. One could see for miles, including Vinga Lighthouse, far beyond where the girls lived.

"One can almost see all the way home from here," said John wishfully, "almost."

Each time the wheel stopped to load and unload riders, their basket would rock back and forth, and each time John would hold Lisa just a little tighter. She looked up at him, smiling softly. The Old Spice fragrance was beginning to work its magic. He bent down and gave her a light kiss on her forehead. She didn't mind.

Annika was sitting tightly squeezed between John and Billy, with Billy's arm around her shoulders. He held her right bare shoulder firmly. "Now I know how it feels like to be a canned sardine," she joked, looking up at Billy grimacing.

"Yes, speaking as one sardine to another, it is kind of cozy, isn't it?" He pulled her toward him a little tighter. "Boy, your shoulders are hot. I think perhaps you have gotten a little much sunshine?"

"Probably. We went swimming today." Annika explained.

"It is. Hmm . . . I hate to have to tell you this Billy, but your fly has come undone. I know you're stuck and can't pull it up. Considering the compromising circumstances, I can do it for you, if you'd like me to," Annika offered.

"That would be appreciated," said the flustered Billy, "please."

"Everyone please look away, I have some personal needs to attend to," Annika announced. Her announcement had the opposite effect. It focused everyone's attention on her task.

"Down boy, down," she joked as she reached over, pulling his tight trousers together over his bulging manhood so she could pull up the zipper. "Oh, no, it's broken. It's not going to work. Let me see if I don't have some safety pins in my purse."

"Safety pins," Billy repeated nervously. "You mean those sharp things."

"Here I have some," Lisa offered. "Let me help you. If you hold the zipper together, I'll try to fasten it with the safety pins." Lisa, who was sitting on the bench across, got down on her knees in front of Billy, and the girls set to work.

"Careful now with those needles, we are talking about the family jewels here." Billy did not appear to mind the attention, but was somewhat suspect of the cure, particularly when the gondola was rocking.

"If you could relax a little, it would make it easier," Lisa advised, smiling up at him.

"That will never happen with two beautiful girls working at my crotch," Billy replied, his cheeks reddening.

The girls had the zipper pinned together just as the attendant opened the gate to let them out, and Annika brushed away a loose thread with her fingers. The attendant looked a little bewildered as Lisa stood up from in between Billy's legs. She glanced at the attendant and blinked.

"What do you think about Jonah?" Annika asked Camilla while the boys placed wages on a chocolate lottery wheel and were out of hearing range.

"Oh. . . he is nice enough but quite boyish, with his freckled face and enormous ears. I can't help thinking about how much nicer it would have been if Sven had been here. How about Billy? He seems real nice.

"He is. I like him a lot. But he doesn't exactly live in the neighborhood. Let's do the log ride down. It splashes a bit but a little water, so what!"

"Yea, and it does a pretty good job getting the bystanders wet as well." said Lisa.

"Well, if they stand close to the rail, I guess they are asking for it." said Annika.

"Wahoo! They all screamed in chorus as the log ride ended with a large splash into a pond, effectively soaking its riders.

Annika pulled herself tight against Billy, seeking protection from the shower.

"Come here baby." John put his arm around Lisa and pulled her in tight as they splashed into the pond.

The damp group strolled past the Mirror House, and the Ghost House. They stopped briefly at a second arcade area next to the large dance floor.

"Here, let's see if I can win a gorilla for you, Lisa. I'm pretty handy with a rifle." John boosted.

"All you have to do is to hit 8 out of 10 ducks, to earn one small gorilla. That doesn't seem like much of a challenge. The boys tried their luck at a shooting range and the girls ended up with a large stuffed, lifelike gorilla each. Lisa was lucky enough to also receive a cuddly teddy bear. John was an expert rifle man.

Liseberg was crowded, as always on a Saturday night. They saw several other British sailors, as well as sailors from all corners of the world, some of whose uniforms the girls did not recognize. John and Billy greeted mates from their ship with salutes and friendly comments. After having strolled across much of the park, having tried a few rides and lost money on various games of chance, the group walked over to the modern dance stage. A popular band played Swedish and American pop music. There was a small fee to dance, and the boys sprang for the tickets. The dance floor was crowded. The girls danced continuously for two hours, mostly with their British friends, but also with a few other fellows who managed to ask them first.

"Hey Annika, you've got the jitterbug down pat," shouted Billy, above the din.

"What?" she yelled back.

"You've got the jitterbug down pat."

"I'm sorry, but I still can't hear you." She leaned closer but kept enough distance to protect her eardrums.

"You dance great," he yelled will full force. This time everyone could hear him as the dance had just ended. Some of the other dancers turned to Annika and gave her a resounding ovation.

"Well, you're really easy to dance with. Do you dance a lot at home?" She asked, smiling and curtseying to her fans.

"I do . . . as often as I can, but not as often as I'd like to. I really enjoy dancing."

"I can tell," she said, breathing heavily from exertion, "and you lead well."

The band announced that the next two dances would be slow. John asked Lisa for a dance. She led the way to the floor and John couldn't but admire her slender figure as he followed close behind. She had a special way of walking, or floating, that he could have watched all day. Now and then she looked back at him smiling. As they stepped onto the floor, he reached for her hand. She responded with a light squeeze and looked up at him with her big blue eyes, as if apologizing for being a little too flirtatious. He put his arm around her waist while they waited for the music to begin.

"Do you have a girlfriend back home?" she asked directly.

"Not anymore," he said regretfully.

"OH, "she said, relieved at his response, resisting the temptation to ask more.

"What about yourself, do you have a boyfriend?" he asked, not sure whether he wanted to know the answer. She probably had a waiting list, he thought.

"No, I don't. I really don't have much of a social life at all right now. School is taking up most of my time."

"Poor baby," John responded, giving Lisa a sympathetic hug. "What's your major?" he asked.

"I study medicine."

"Really, have you chosen a specialty yet?"

"No, not really. However, I have thought about becoming an obstetrician."

AHmm," he murmured, "that's interesting. I'm also studying medicine or am about to. I did my pre-med studies at Oxford and now I'm going to med school through the navy. First, I have to spend three months in active service to become an officer. In exchange the navy will pay for my education." He placed his right arm around her back but rather than accepting his left hand, she put both her arms around his neck. He moved his other arm around her back and pulled her tight towards him. They danced slowly rocking gently with the music. "I like that cologne you're wearing, what is it?" she cooed in his ear, lamenting that she would probably never see him again, but wishing he would kiss her.

"Old Spice," he murmured, resting his cheek on her hair. 'Wow, she is so beautiful; so light and fresh and feminine; so smart, so mature, all in one package. Why does life have to be so complicated? Will she think I'm too forward if I kiss her? . . .'

"I thought so," she said. The band began playing the American hit, Stardust.

"Wow, I love that tune! Whenever I hear this song I'll think of you, Lisa." She looked up and met his kiss.

CHAPTER 3

August 1939 - Returning to the ships

The men had to be back at their ships by two a.m. and the girls were a long way from home, so the group, together with many others, began to head toward the exit gates. Suddenly a flashing light brightened the park, followed a few seconds later by a roaring thunder that shook the ground. A few seconds later the sky opened up and rain poured down. Another large flash hung in the air for seconds, flickering, immediately followed by a series of sharp, crisp, and almost deafening crashes. Suddenly it turned pitch black. The contrast between the thousands of bright lights and loud music and seconds later it was pitch black and semi silence, was striking. People called out names of their friends, their voices filled with anxiety.

"How would you like to be sitting up in the Ferris wheel now?" Camilla asked.

"Yes, and how about the roller coaster?" Annika countered.

"Actually, you would not get stuck in the roller coaster," Billy explained, "unless you were on your way up, because once you reach the top the ride is powered by gravity."

"Yes, as long as they don't have electric brakes at the bottom, then it could get ugly," Camilla joked.

"That is a nasty thought," Billy agreed.

The thunder could now be heard in the distance, but the rain had intensified, hitting the pavement hard, splashing up, and drenching its victims a second time. Small emergency lights came on, helping visitors to navigate toward the exits. A small group sought shelter under a large tree, but the rain poured too hard for the tree to offer much protection.

"Let's just run!" Lisa shouted. "We're so soaked now, it really doesn't matter anymore."

"You have a good notion for describing the reality, Lisa. We have to be back on the ships at two," John responded.

The thunder disappeared as suddenly as it had begun. The girls were completely soaked, their dresses having turned transparent, clinging to their skin, and leaving little to the imagination, as the fellows' eyes adjusted to the darkness. Their dark tanned skin made their bodies shine through the light, soaked, cotton dresses. The crowd was thick at the exit gate and the tram at the stop was not moving. There was no electricity.

"Oh no," sighed, Bill. "How are we going to get back to the ship on time? How about a cab? Are there any taxies around?"

"Follow me!" said Annika and took off down the street. Just a block away, a cab was dropping off a patron at a nightclub. Annika had the door open before the arriving passenger had a chance to get out. Ten seconds later they were all seated tightly in the back of the rather large Russian-made Volga cab, with Jonah and Camilla on the fold down backrest seats.

"Oh boy," sighed Annika. "I must be a sight, soaking wet, looking like a wet wash rag."

"You look mighty fine to me." Billy assured her, looking at her with a sly grin. He pulled her closer kissing her forehead.

"Where to?" the driver asked, flipping over the timer. The windows in the cab were already fogging up.

"Would it be all right if we get dropped off first? We have to be back in thirty minutes and then your fare home is on us," Billy explained.

"Sure" said Annika, "that will be fine, but you don't have to pay our way. We live too far out, but thanks anyway." The other girls agreed, nodding their heads.

"We insist" said Billy. "We're not professional sailors. We signed up recently because of the German aggression. We can afford it, besides, what could be a worthier cause to spend your money on than on some beautiful girls?"

"What do you guys think about Hitler?" Lisa asked. "Do you really think that he will invade Poland?"

"Well if he does, he knows that both the French and the British will declare war against Germany. You know, we have guaranteed Poland its independence," Billy explained.

"That man is completely insane, in my opinion," Annika declared. "Can you believe he just announced that Germany needs '*lebensraum*?' He seems to think that the world is there for his pleasure and that when he needs more space, he can just go and take it," she said disgustedly.

"Yes, and then he annexed Austria and invaded Czechoslovakia. What is he going to do next? I don't trust him for a second. He should have stayed in jail," said Billy. He held Annika's hand tightly.

"True, but I guess the Austrians actually invited Germany in. Unbelievable," said John, shaking his head, Abut that is his home country, where he was born . . . and really, the Russians aren't much better. It was only five to ten years ago when the Russians simply slaughtered thousands of Kulaks to get their land. They took all private property and turned it into collective farms," John continued, "and now they can't understand why their farms are failing . . . after they killed all the experts."

"That just goes to show you." Billy's wet hair clung to his forehead, and water dripped down his face.

"Who are the Kulaks?" asked Annika.

"Oh, they are Russian-peasants that own, or rather owned small farms." Lisa explained. She opened a tube of breath mints and passed it around.

"And the Japanese, invading China, killing thousands. . ., acting like barbarians." Billy said. "I think the whole world has gone bonkers."

"This is too depressing a subject. Let's talk about something else," Camilla suggested.

"You know, tomorrow, on September first, there will be an open house on the ships. It will be open for the public and, of course, it's free. It would be great if you gals could come. We'll be working, but we can still give you a private tour of the ship. How about it?" Billy asked hopefully, sounding particularly British.

"I don't know," said Lisa. "I have a lot of school work. I'd love to. It would be great fun, but I don't think it will be possible."

"Let's wait until tomorrow to decide, and if we can come then we will, for sure," Annika promised.

"Well it would be great fun if you could," said John, "very nice."

"t sure would," Billy agreed.

It was strange to travel through the downtown area in the dark. Only a few automobiles were on the streets. The cab pulled up to the pier just ten minutes before liberty ended. Moments after they arrived, the street lights came back on. The cab had stopped next to a hotdog vender on the pier.

"I just have to have one of your Swedish hotdogs before we go onboard. I had one yesterday. It was absolutely delicious, the way they serve it with creamy mashed potatoes. They must use a ton of butter and cream in the potatoes to make it taste so good," Billy said. "Anyone else for a hotdog?"

"Sure, I'll have one," said Annika. "A half special with mustard, ketchup . . . and sliced pickles, please."

"What's a half special?" John asked.

"A hotdog in a bun topped with two scoops of mashed potatoes, like the one in that picture. A full special would be with two hotdogs. That's quite a meal," the vendor explained in his accented English.

"Oh, what the heck, I'll have a full special please. The smell makes me hungry." John explained.

"Hey listen" the hotdog vender called out and increased the volume on the radio. They're talking about unusually strong German troop movements, close to the Polish border.

"This is not looking good. Not good at all," John sighed.

They exchanged addresses, and the girls promised to try to join the fellows the following day.

"Ah! The sleeping beauty is coming alive. A rough night ah, said Bo, her older brother, as Annika came down the stairs?

"Smells good! You have some coffee ready."

Her parents, younger sister Kristina and older brother Bo were talking animatedly. The strong aroma of freshly brewed coffee greeted her as she stepped into the bright kitchen. It was a spacious room with windows offering a view of the veranda and the street beyond. It had the customarily low ceiling of chain white wood. Her mother stood at the sink, pumping water for the dishes. Kristina was adding wood to the large cast-iron stove, and Bo and Mr. Bengtson sat at the large, worn kitchen table, Mr. Bengtson cleaning his pipe more by habit than of need.

"Good Morning! What's going on?" Annika asked.

"Germany has invaded Poland, and now England and France are going to declare war against Germany, like they said they would. It's hard to believe that Hitler can be that stupid," Mr. Bengtson muttered, shaking his head.

"Oh no!" Annika exclaimed. "This can't be true."

"It's true all right," Mrs. Bengtson said. "The question now is what will happen next, and whether Sweden can remain neutral. Is this the beginning of a new world war?"

"Yes, and will Bo be called into the service?" asked Mr. Bengtson.

"Don't tell me about it. I was just in. That was enough for me. That Hitler, I could kill him," he declared.

"It looks like you may get a chance to do just that," said Kristina.

"Well, let's not assume the worst. Maybe if England and France stand up to him, he'll realize that they were serious and maybe he'll pull back," Mr. Bengtson speculated.

"What about America, what do they say?" Annika asked. She helped herself to some of the porridge on the stove.

"Nothing yet," said Mr. Bengtson. Mrs. Bengtson refilled his coffee cup. "Thank you."

"Do we have more lingonberry jam?" Annika asked.

"I would hope so, I made fifteen liters this fall," Mrs. Bengtson reminded her. "I'll get another jar from the cellar," Mrs. Bengtson offered.

"No, Mamma. I'll get it myself."

"They're already talking about issuing ration cards for food and gasoline," Mr. Bengtson informed her when Annika returned from the root cellar. He reached for his pipe paraphernalia.

"Who, the Americans?" Annika asked. She scooped a generous helping of lingonberry jam onto her porridge.

"No, no. Heavens! Here at home, in Sweden," Mrs. Bengtson clarified. "They expect shortages on just about everything."

"Will you please pass the jam," Bo asked.

"Can't believe you were too lazy to get a new jar, so you were going to do without," Annika teased, raising her eyebrows in mock disgust.

"What can I say?" Bo shrugged.

"As long as we have potatoes, I'm all right," said Mr. Bengtson, trying unsuccessfully to make light of the situation. He ran a pipe cleaner through his pipe soaking up the stale smelling pipe oil.

"It's difficult to tell whom we should fear the most; the Soviets or the Germans," said Kristina, helping out with the breakfast dishes.

"It's pretty much for sure that I'll have to go back in," Bo sighed. "They are calling for 10,000 navy and coast guard service men right now." He reached for a sweet-roll. The thought of going back into the service made him hungry for his mother's home cooking.

"I was hoping that we would be able to tour one of the English warships this afternoon. The girls and I were invited for a tour by some Englishmen we met at Liseberg last night. I guess we can forget about that now. Oh boy!" Annika sighed, dreamily. "And he was so nice."

"Yes, they said on the news that the British frigates left early this morning," Mr. Bengtson said. He unrolled his tobacco pouch, took a pinch of fresh tobacco and worked it into his pipe.

"What's that? You got a slice of apple in your pouch?" Annika said. "You don't smoke apples . . . do you?" she asked with disbelief.

"No, no," Mr. Bengtson laughed. "I only keep it in there to keep the tobacco fresh, so it won't dry up."

"I have to run" Annika declared.

"Where do you have to go this early?" Mr. Bengtson asked.

"I just want to ride to the cliff for a few minutes."

Annika biked to a spot on the sea side of the peninsula, where she had a good view of the boat traffic, destined for Gothenburg's main harbor. She could see ships leaving, eventually disappearing beyond the horizon. She noticed some coast guard soldiers working on concrete bunkers. She sat down on a park bench staring westward, chewing on a strand of grass. "Oh Billy, may God be with you," she whispered.

Annika got back on her bike and rode to Lisa's house. Lisa was getting ready for a christening ceremony.

"I guess . . . you've already heard," Lisa greeted her. "Can you believe it, and Billy and John? Shit!" Lisa added in a rare display of rage.

"Let's write them a letter," Annika suggested.

"We have to go now. We'll write as soon as we get back from church, okay?" Lisa suggested.

September 1, 1939

Dear John,

Dear John seems such an inappropriate greeting for this letter, as I'm really writing to let you know how much I enjoyed meeting you last night. I'm so sorry that I didn't get a chance to see you again before you left. Thank you so much for a wonderful and exciting evening. I enjoyed every moment, including the downpour. You know, I was talking about myself most of the evening, and I hardly found out anything about you. I'm so worried about the war and your safety. I'll pray every day for you. I'll keep the gorilla in my bed. I call him Johnny.

Please write me and tell me a little about yourself. Tell me about your favorite things, about your family and friends and about what you're doing now. Write about anything you'd like to share with me, important or insignificant. I will think of you whenever I hear Stardust played. I would love to hear from you. I wish you the best with your studies. I hope this letter will find you.

*Warm regards,
Lisa*

September 1, 1939

Dear Billy,

Thank you so much for a wonderful time last night. You know, I was really looking forward to seeing you again, and to getting to tour your ship. Maybe I can have a rain-check. Talking about rain, that was one of the worst showers I have ever seen, but it was kind of fun. You're probably used to heavy rains. I hear that in England it rains all the time, although, you probably think the same about Sweden and it really doesn't. Do you think that your ship will return to Sweden again? I hope so.

I'm so worried about the war. Please write me and let me know how you are doing. Stay away from those Germans now so you can get home safely. I hope that you will receive this letter and that you'll write on your own. I would really like to hear from you. I walked down to the sea to see if I could catch a glimpse of your ship as you were pulling out, but you were long gone. Take care of yourself and I hope we can meet again.

Love, Annika

"You don't think that signing the letter with Love, is a little forward for your first letter?" Lisa asked her.

"I don't care. Besides, I think the British use love more genetically, not necessary meaning that you are in love with the person in question.

I liked Billy a lot and we will probably never meet again. So, that's just fine."

The girls read each other's letters, put a drop of perfume on the envelopes and rode their bikes down to the tram station where they mailed them.

CHAPTER 4

September, 1939 - Letters from John and Billy

"Hey Billy! A penny for your thoughts! What's that grin all about?"

"Oh, I was just thinking about last night, what a good time I had. You know, I really enjoyed meeting Annika. She was so full of energy, and funny, but without being silly like most girls. She was so very easy to look at, and easy to talk to and . . ."

"Yeah, because she did most of the talking," John interrupted, grinning. "Just kidding, she did like to talk, but she was entertaining. I liked her too. She was a lot of fun, and boy . . . what a build," he added, raising an eyebrow.

"And that sweet face. You know, I think, no I know I'm in love." Billy paced the floor.

"What about Lisa though?" Billy asked. "She wasn't exactly a dog either. And I tell you, she's one smart cookie. Maybe someone who lives up to your standards, eh?" he asked John.

"Yes, I liked her a lot, a lot. . . but I'm not sure that it makes a lot of sense to get involved with anyone now when we don't know what could happen from one day to the next," John replied. "But yes she was very nice and I liked her a lot. But I just don't know . . ." John sighed, trailing off.

"Well I'm going to compose a line to Annika and see if she'll write back," said Billy. "You know John. . . I can hardly read the address. The rain got the best of the paper. Do you have the address to Lisa and I can ask her to give it to Annika?"

"Sure, here it is," John responded, pulling the neatly folded paper out of his left breast pocket.

September 2, 1939

Dear Lisa,

Thank you so much for a lovely evening. We had a great time. I'm sorry about our abrupt departure, but I'm afraid that it was nothing we could do anything about. I know you heard about Germany's invading Poland.

I'm writing to ask you for a big favor. Unfortunately, my note with the address to Annika got ruined in the rain. I was hoping that you wouldn't mind passing on my letter to her. Thanks a bunch. John is asking me to say hi, and to thank you for a great time. He is half asleep now from having been awake for almost 48 hours, but he says that he will write later. Thanks again for a great time and for the help with the letter.

Your friend, Billy

Three weeks later when Lisa came home from school, her younger sister Rosemarie greeted her enthusiastically waving a letter in her hand. "You got a letter from England! I bet it's from John," she called gleefully. "Aren't you going to open it, and read it?"

"Later," Lisa said, taking the envelope from her sister, "after dinner."

"Oh, how can you?" Kristina demanded.

After dinner and when the kitchen was cleaned up, Lisa took the letter and walked down to the old cherry tree swing. She made herself comfortable and looked at the envelope. There was a return address but no name. Her name was neatly printed on the front of the envelope, and even though the street address was slightly wrong, it had found its way. The mailman had been delivering mail there for many years, and he knew everyone. Lisa detected a hint of Old Spice as she opened the letter. She slowly pulled out the letter to Annika and the note to herself from Billy.

First, she was happy to learn that they were all right, but when she noticed that the letter was written almost three weeks ago, her concerns reemerged. She was glad to hear from Billy, but she had been hoping that it was from John. After a moment's disappointment she ran over to Annika who joyfully read her letter aloud.

September 3, 1939

Dear Annika,

Thank you for a great evening last Saturday. I can't remember the last time I had such a good time. I also enjoyed meeting your friends very much. I'm so sorry that we had to leave so early. We were back for less than an hour when we took off. We even left behind two men who did not make it back in time. I'm not sure what will happen to them. They probably get to go back on a luxury liner or perhaps they get to work at the British Embassy in Stockholm for some time. I'm jealous. I hope you don't mind my mailing this letter through Lisa, but I couldn't read your address after my note had gotten soaked.

"It's going to be really nice to come home again, even if it will only be for a few days. My older sister Jenny just had a baby daughter whom I have not seen. So, I'm an uncle. Also, I have some business to tend to. When I'm gone this long, I feel that I lose control over everything and that's not a comforting feeling. Right now, I'm involved in promoting a knitting machine, one that can knit transparent nylon stockings for ladies. I don't know if you have heard about it, but they are doing great in the States.

It's difficult right now to predict the future. With Russia and the Nazis signing the Non-Aggression Pact last month, it's going to be very difficult for anyone to stop them, when these two bullies put their resources together. I hate to tell you this, but I think that it may not be long before either the Nazis or the Russians will take over Scandinavia. If that should happen, the Swedish currency will be useless. I would strongly recommend that you take whatever you can and exchange it into US dollars. You can't go wrong no matter what happens if you take my advice. I hope I don't sound too pessimistic now and the battle isn't lost yet. One can still hope that both the Nazis' and the Soviets' ambitions will get in the way of a lasting relationship. Also, there is the American wild card.

The trip back to England went without incident, but the weather was rough most of the way and several of us got quite seasick. I don't think that I'm a born sailor.

You know, I really enjoyed meeting you. I have to admit that I have thought of little else since. I hope that you get this letter, and that you write me back. I would love to hear from you. I know that it's asking a lot, but if you have a picture of yourself that you could send me, I would treasure it forever. I know you felt a little embarrassed about getting soaked in the rain. Let me assure you that to me it just made you real and as pretty as can be. I hope you don't mind my saying so, but I thought you were quite sexy, soaked like that. I still remember your scent of Lilac. I thoroughly enjoyed your sense of humor. That joke about the beauty contest was great. It was especially funny because it was so untrue. I would really like to get to know you more and I hope you'll answer this letter.

Friends, Billy.
P.S. I know John had a really good time with Lisa and that he really likes her. However, I'm not sure he will write. I know he is concerned about getting hurt again in a relationship with a girl and in particular, a relationship

that goes against the odds. Maybe you could ask Lisa to write. John is a great guy and my best mate."

"What beauty contest joke?" Lisa asked.

"Actually, that was Camilla's joke and I didn't hear the whole joke. I'm not sure," she admitted, "however, if he wants to give me credit for the joke that's fine with me. Oh, hi Camilla. We were just talking about you."

Camilla dressed in her short white tennis dress came up the stairs to Annika's room. "Hi, ladies," she greeted them. "What's up? What could I possibly have done that is worth talking about?" She moved Annika's violin off the bed and sat down next to Lisa.

"Oh, we got a letter from Billy. . . or rather, Annika did," Lisa explained.

"For real! What did he say? and what did it have to do with me?" Camilla asked curiously.

"Nothing really . . . Billy said he enjoyed the 'beauty contest joke,' and Annika told me that it was actually your joke. How did it go?" Lisa asked.

"Really, you guys know that silly old joke. You know. Who won the Norwegian beauty contest? No one! Well, it's only funny if you make it personal so . . . I made it the Swedish beauty contest."

"Well, Billy appreciated it, and it earned me some brownie points," Annika said. "He thought it was I who told the joke."

"Tell me what he wrote," Camilla pleaded.

"Here, you can read it yourself," Annika handed her the letter and continued to brush her hair.

After having read the letter she looked up smiling, "Hey, I think Billy's in love."

"Oh, that's silly," protested Annika, "I've only met him once . . . but who's complaining?" She pulled her hair back into a ponytail.

"I was going to play tennis with Sven this afternoon, but he had to cancel for some family emergency with his grandma. I have the court reserved. Do you girls want to join me?" Camilla asked.

"You girls go," said Lisa. "I have to do homework. Have fun." Lisa left the house, but rather than going straight home she rode her bike back to the bench with the ocean view.

PART II

CHAPTER 5

September, 1939 - Kurt

Will you be okay for a while Annika? I have to finish the head phones at the hospital so we get paid." Mr. Bengtson asked, gathering his tools.

"How are you coming along with that project, Dad?" Annika asked.

"Another week and I should have it nailed down. It's going pretty smooth now when we got the conduit installed. We better, because the regular work load is catching up with us. By the way, I'm really proud of you for handling things here in the shop so well, Annika. You'll have to close up yourself. I'll go straight home from the hospital"

"See you tonight for dinner then, Dad. It's Friday so it will be pea soup and pancakes. Or perhaps the flounder I caught last night."

"My favorite." Mr. Bengtson closed the door behind him, the door bell ringing.

While waiting for the regatta to start, she had dropped down the herring pilk for less than a minute when there was a sudden strong pull. First, she thought that the hook had caught the bottom. She could see something white move slowly below, through the clear water. A full-size flounder, perhaps thirty pounds emerged at the surface. The pilk was only designed for small herrings and it was a wonder that the fish did not chose to take off. One flip of the tail and he would have been nothing but an unbelievable fish story.

Annika then faced the problem of not having enough room in the small sail boat for both herself and the flounder during the race. She had no choice but to bring the fish back to the dock which made her ten minutes late. She decided to skip the race, the last race of the season. Still, she was excited about bringing home the prize catch. It was quite unusual for a flounder of this size to come this far into the relatively shallow water of the bay. It was almost as though it had been on a suicide mission. It looked sad, Annika thought.

"Hi, can I give you a hand pulling up your boat?" Annika heard an unfamiliar man's voice offered from behind her. "Throw me the line and I'll pull you in." The deep masculine voice came from a well-dressed man standing in a shiny mahogany motorboat tied to the dock.

"Thanks," she said, tossing him the line.

"What happened? Did you have to break the race?" he asked. She told him her fish story.

"By the way, my name is Kurt. Kurt Nobel," he offered, "I take it you live around here?"

"Yes, just down the road some," she responded, grinning into the sun. She was curious about the stranger. He didn't look bad. Not bad at all. He had an average build. His blond wavy hair was perfectly groomed, although slightly receding in front. He was clearly a man with a touch of class. He wore white trousers, white shiny dress shoes, and a blue club jacket, topped off with a captain's cap sporting the emblem of the Royal Swedish Yacht Club. Perhaps he was a little overdressed, considering the size of the boat he captained. It was a nice boat, but not exactly a royal yacht. "You have a nice boat," Annika remarked as she put away her rig.

"Thanks, I just got it," he said proudly. "I haven't even tried it out yet."

"No?"

"Can't get it started," he confessed.

"What's wrong?" Annika asked.

"Don't know, she simply doesn't like to start. She's full of gas, I choked it and the start motor runs, but she simply doesn't want to start," he repeated, frustrated. "I suspect she has an attitude problem or that she doesn't like me."

"That's hard to believe." Annika smiled at her own forwardness. "Do you mind if I take a look? Do you have any tools?" He handed her a tool pouch. Annika raised the motor cover, and removed the spark plug. "Looks like you might have choked it a little too much, flooding the engine," she concluded. She wiped the spark plug dry and screwed it back into its socket. "OK, try to start it now," she said, "NO WAIT! Put the gear in neutral first!" she cautioned, laughing heartily at his near fatal mistake.

"Thanks that could have been ugly." He turned the key, pushed the starter button and the motor started right up, with a gentle hum. "Hey, thanks a million. I had just given up. How about a test ride, and to check up on the regatta?"

Annika felt a little uneasy about going out in the boat alone with a perfect stranger, but he seemed nice enough, and how often did one meet a perfect stranger? Perhaps he could use a little coaching on boating. They puttered out from the docks towards the finish area.

"It's a nice evening for boating. The sky is clear and the sun is setting on the horizon. It's so red," said Kurt.

The mild west wind blew Annika's hair back highlighting the stark contrast between her blue eyes and her sun-darkened skin.

"I'm surprised how many onlookers still come this late in the season." said Kurt.

"I think most of them are from town, on an evening tour." Annika speculated.

People scattered along the shoreline watched the sail boats and the sunset, while listening to the symphony of boat engines, the water rolling against the shore and the seabird sopranos. Most people had their sweaters tied around their waists or hanging over their shoulders. The outside dining deck of Longedrag's Restaurant was filling up, and so were the tables at The Bakery's terrace. A steady flow of pleasure boats returned from their outings or fishing trips, their engines puffing enthusiastically, or their crews pulling the sails.

Kurt choked the engine, so they could hear themselves and enjoy the tranquil clucking sound of the water against the boat. They drifted slowly while waiting for the racing sailboats to return.

"Kurt, what do you do for a living?" Annika asked.

"Oh, I'm a business man. I do whatever brings me the best return on my investment. Right now, I'm putting together a deal selling cobble stones to the city. In fact, I'm getting them from the northern district where they are tearing up a stretch and selling them to the west district where they are adding on. That's the way to do business," he boasted.

"You must be doing quite well. This boat is very nice." Annika let her hand slide across the shiny wooden dash board.

"I traded it for a 1937 De Soto. I recently ordered a new Ford Mercury from America and I think I got a better deal trading the De Soto for the boat than selling it outright."

"You're quite a wheeler-dealer, are you," Annika said with admiration reflected in her voice. She took up her sunglasses from her shirt pocket and put them on.

The sailboats were now approaching the finish line.

"Go Camilla! Go!" Annika cheered. Camilla was third, and Sven was just a nose ahead of her. Camilla clearly was doing everything she could to slow her pace. She made no attempt to straighten the boat and she was even dragging a foot in the water.

Alright Camilla, you don't have to be so obvious. Get your feet out of the water." Annika murmured. Unfortunately, her boat was blocking the wind for Sven, so despite her effort, she beat him by half a boat length.

Annika was awakened from her thoughts by the rattling door announcer as to her surprise; Kurt entered the shop and stepped up to the counter. "Hi lovely," he greeted her. "I was in the neighborhood, so I thought I'd stop by to say hello."

"Oh, so you didn't make the trip just for my sake?" she asked, smiling coyly.

"Well, I guess that was the reason why I was in the neighborhood," said Kurt, returning her smile. "The truth is that I came to see if you would consider going out for dinner with me after work. I really appreciated your helping me out with the boat yesterday, and I figured I owed you a dinner."

"So, you're not asking me out because you would like to. You're doing it because you think you owe me a favor. Did I get that right?" she continued teasingly.

"No, no . . .," he stammered, looking bewildered.

"Well you don't owe me anything. I was only glad to be able to help out." Annika, turned finding some busy work on the counter.

"Oh, no, please, I didn't mean that. Can I please start over again?" he asked, as he pivoted around and walked out of the shop.

Kurt reentered the shop and removed his hat as he closed the door. "Hi Annika, I'm glad you're here. I was hoping that you would be."

"Hi," she responded. "By the way, how did you know where I work? I can't recall giving you the address."

"Annika, you know, I really enjoyed meeting you yesterday so I took the liberty of asking Camilla where you work. I was really hoping that you could join me for dinner after work. It would be a great honor . . . and I got the new Merc. today, a Mercury," he clarified, his eyes glowing with excitement, as a child at Christmas. "They called this morning and told me it had arrived, and fifteen minutes later I was out at the Free Port. One hour later I drove it home. It has to be converted to gen-gas, because private cars can't use gasoline, you know. They gave me a week to get it done. It's unbelievably comfortable. You'll just love it," he promised.

"Why do they call it 'the Free Port?' "Annika asked. "Don't you have to pay for things there?" she asked, deliberately taking the risk of sounding dense.

"I wish. No, it's called that so merchandise from other countries can be reloaded to other ships without the owner having to pay duty in Sweden. It's a transfer hub," he explained. "Well . . . what about it? Please say yes."

"I would like to, if it doesn't get too late, but I can't close the shop for another hour. Also, it can't be too fancy of a place, because I don't have any nice clothes here to change into."

"I'll be back in an hour," he said and left, whistling Marlene Dietrich's hit song "Falling in love with you".

"Mom! I just calling to tell you to go ahead and eat without me. I have been invited out for dinner by a fellow I met the other day at the races. His name is Kurt Nobel."

"Be careful Annika!" Mrs. Bengtson cautioned.

"He seems quite nice."

"I will leave the light on for you. It is getting quite dark in the evenings now. I hope you have a nice time and don't be too late."

"Ok. Mom. I will turn it off. Don't worry, I'll be fine."

Annika freshened up as best as she could in the small shop sink. Luckily, she had no late customers. Kurt came back exactly on time, as she was about to close the shop. He handed her a package. "Here . . . for you. I hope you like it." He was grinning nervously, in anticipation of her reaction.

She eagerly pulled off the ribbon and opened the box that featured the name of a stylish downtown boutique and pulled out a cream colored two piece suit. "Oh no!" she exclaimed.

"This is crazy. I can't accept such an expensive gift. I just can't."

"You'll be doing me a favor," he insisted. "I have always dreamed of owning such a nice car, and then to have such a beautiful girl at my side. It would be a dream-come-true for me."

"But one can't wear a dress like that with tennis shoes," she protested.

"Look again. . . in the box," he suggested.

Annika pulled out a bag and inside she found a pair of high heeled pumps in the same color as the suit. "Oh, it's so beautiful I've never had anything like this. But it must have cost a fortune."

"Don't worry about it, it's only money, and you're worth it."

"Well thank you very much. I can't believe you did all this . . . in one hour." She reached up and placed a kiss right on his mouth. "I'll go and put it on right now. I'll be right back." She strode back into the store like a model, one foot in front of the other, pivoting in the middle of the floor. "Well, what do you think?" she asked, taking a model's pose.

"Stunning! Absolutely stunning, and the dress looks nice too. It fits you perfectly. You look like a movie star, a very beautiful movie star at that . . . totally amazing . . . absolutely perfect . . . like a million crowns!" He sat down on the edge of a small table. Both her reaction and the overall effect had exceeded his expectations.

She glanced at the prize-tag that was still attached. Three hundred crowns! "Did you really pay three hundred crowns for this outfit? That's more than I make in a whole month! How did you know what size to get?" she asked, walking back and forth in the shop to get the feel of it and to adjust to the high heels.

"I looked for a sales girl who had your build and I asked her to try it on. And the shoes, well, I only guessed on those. But it looks like I guessed right."

"You sure did. They fit perfectly. They are a little bit higher than what I am used to, so it may take a little getting used to. Actually, they're quite a bit higher," she admitted. "You're making me feel like Cinderella, with the shoes and all. I still can't believe you got this for me, and you hardly know me."

"I'm glad you like it." He stood up, taking her in.

"Like it, I love it" again she reached up and kissed him, but this time she also put her arms around his neck.

"Let's go!" he said. "I have a lot planned for tonight."

As they stepped out of the shop, Annika could hardly believe her eyes when she saw Kurt's new Mercury.

"That's your car? It's beautiful." It was huge, a dark red convertible. And it was so shiny. She carefully touched the door to get a feel of it.

Kurt opened the door for Annika and she slid into her seat. Kurt sat down behind the wheel and Annika moved over next to him. He started the engine with a powerful sounding Broumm.

"You're something else, Kurt." She felt as though she had known him forever and she felt as good as she looked.

"Then we make a good couple, because so are you. I hope you don't mind, but I need to make a quick stop at the office before we go out. Is that okay?" Kurt asked.

"Of course, I'd love to see your office."

"Great! Then I get to show you off at the same time."

"Is anyone going to be there? It's after five," she reminded him.

"I think so, I hope so, we have a special project they're working on." He turned on the car radio. The deep base in Old Man River made it vibrate slightly. Kurt tried to sing along. He had a nice baritone voice but struggled to reach the low base tones.

"You have a great singing voice, Kurt. I love that song."

"Yes, from the American musical Showboat. Next time I go there, I plan to see that show."

"You've been to America?" she asked, in awe.

"Twice," he boasted. "I was in New York only two months ago at the World's Fair. Boy, was that impressive! In fact! I will probably go back in March again when the fair reopens for the summer."

"I can imagine." Annika's imagination carried her off on an excursion to New York, on the luxury packet with all the bells and whistles.

Kurt's office was still open when they got there. Kurt raised the roof of the car by pushing a button.

"Annika, I'd like you to meet Eva. Eva has been with me since the beginning of time . . . "

"Come on now! I'm not that old," Eva protested, her warm smile progressing to indignant laughter. Eva always smiled.

". . . and she keeps it all together. I don't know how I would manage if I ever lost her."

"Oh, that will never happen. Nice to meet you, Annika," said Eva her cheeks blushing.

"Nice to meet you, Eva." Annika smiled awkwardly.

"Miss Karin, Miss Margareta, Mrs. Petterson, please meet Annika," Kurt continued.

Kurt showed Annika around his modest office. There was a dominant picture of the ocean liner Gripsholm on the wall centered between two pictures of Kurt standing next to American cars. "It's nothing special, but it's conveniently located. It's only a couple blocks away from the central station, and the main post office is across the moat, over there," he pointed through his picture window, "I have a pretty nice view of the Botanic Gardens. It suits me quite well."

"It's lovely, really great, I'm glad you showed it to me. Eva sure seems like a nice, attractive girl. May I ask why you are not dating her?"

"I would love to. Unfortunately, she's already spoken for." He continued after a pregnant pause, "but we're very good friends. Her parents have a small farm and furniture shop in Lindome and I often go out there to see them. Eva's dad, Jonas, has been doing some work for me. . . In fact, he made that picture window."

Kurt signed a stack of papers Eva handed him, without reading any of them. "Here, this is my private room where I can take a shower, and stay over if I don't feel like driving home at night."

"Pretty convenient," said Annika.

"It's functional," he responded, pushing down on the overstuffed couch to demonstrate its firm springs. They returned to the car.

"First I'd just like to cruise through town. I just love to drive this car . . . with you in it.

Then, I know a nice restaurant not far from here that has a terrific seafood menu, and a nice atmosphere. Do you like sea food?"

"Love it, I like all foods, unfortunately," she added. "I would have had fish if I had gone home, the flounder I caught last night."

"There's also a terrific view of the harbor and the boat traffic from there. Then, how about the Botanic Gardens for dessert and coffee? They always have nice music, and there should be lots of people tonight, on a Friday. And if you feel like it, we can go into the restaurant for a while and dance a couple numbers. Maybe we could do the Samba?" Kurt took a few samba steps showing off his dancing skills.

"Let's do one thing at the time, okay?" Annika suggested. She felt slightly overwhelmed. "And with these high heels . . . I'll be doing well if I can walk."

CHAPTER 6

October 1939 - Gunnar

Annika and Gunnar Grundin had been dating occasionally for some time. Gunnar was a classmate of Lisa at Gothenburg's University School of Medicine. Annika had met Gunnar when Lisa arranged a double date for a New Year's party, two years ago. Gunnar lived on a small farm south of central Gothenburg. They had agreed to meet at the party. Gunnar and Annika had connected instantly. Gunnar was tall, blond and muscular. He had a gentle unassuming demeanor and he was a good listener. He was generous with compliments and possessed strong social skills, for a country boy. He oozed self-confidence, but was perhaps a little quiet. Even though Annika did not reach the intellectual sophistication of his school friends, he appreciated Annika's energy, innocence, free spirit and sense of humor and, of course, her figure. In addition, Annika was well informed on social and political events, and she was quite street smart.

Gunnar rode a small motor-scooter to school. It was nice when the weather was agreeable, but less so when it was wet and cold. Annika rode the scooter a few times, riding sidesaddle behind Gunnar. She wasn't entirely comfortable with Gunnar's leaning into the curves, but at the same time she enjoyed the thrill; it was rather like riding a roller coaster. Gunnar would take the curves, perhaps a little deeper than needed, prompting Annika to hold on really tight.

Like Lisa, Gunnar did not have much time when he was not studying, and he was therefore not able to satisfy all of Annika's social needs. They still dated whenever time permitted, but both were free to see others.

Besides his studies, Gunnar also had chores to tend to at the farm. After his father had passed away, two years earlier, he had sold their cattle and the pigs. Gunnar leased out most of the land and had now only one horse left, some chickens that his mother cared for, and of course, he had a dog and a few cats. Until last summer he still grew potatoes, but now, he only grew feed for the horse, and fruit and vegetables for personal use. He did not have any use for the horse, but he didn't have the heart to get rid of the old mare that had been part of the farm for as long as he could remember.

"You don't miss the animals, the cows and the pigs?"

"No not really. They took up so much time. It was alright as long as dad was here. It is obviously too much for mom and I don't have the time as my studies takes all my time."

Annika had visited the farm a few times, and so had Lisa and Camilla. Last summer they held a "bringing in the hay party" and several friends showed up to help out. Afterwards, everyone walked down to the sea and went for a swim, in their under wear. Unfortunately, several of the bathers lost their attire during the swim, as the swim turned into a game where the winner had collected the most garments.

It was October 1939 and Annika had come out to the farm to visit Gunnar. "What is that book you're reading?" Annika asked, lifting it off the table. *Native Son*, by Richard Wright," she read. AThat doesn't look like a school book. Do you have time to read novels?" she asked.

"Not really, but sometimes you need a break from school books."

Gunnar and Annika would often engage in philosophical discussions. They both enjoyed discussing current events. Their opinions were normally not significantly different, and both of them were able to discuss issues without becoming annoyed. Annika would often try to provoke Gunnar with her questioning, but Gunnar would always respond calmly and rationally. Gunnar walked over to the wood stove, stoked the fire, and took the coffee pot. "Would you like a refill Annika?"

"Yes, please." She slid her cup across the old kitchen table toward him. The aroma of the freshly brewed coffee filled the kitchen. Annika carefully sipped on her hot brew. "Hm, this is not bad coffee. Is it mixed with rye?" Annika asked.

"I'm not sure, but they do mix it with some grains, to make it stretch. Another sweet-roll?" he offered.

"I would love to, but I have to watch my weight."

She reached for a cookie but changed her mind on second thought. Annika stood up and collected the dishes for the sink. She walked over to kiss him goodbye.

Gunnar's mother was out feeding the chickens. "Let's leave next Sunday open on whether we can get together, ok?" Annika suggested.

"Are you sure you don't want me to give you a ride home?" Gunnar asked.

"I'm sure. I don't mind taking the bus, and you don't have the time, regardless."

"Thanks for coming." He smiled at her and she smiled in return. I'll call you on Wednesday, otherwise the operator will have nothing to gossip about. They are putting in a new switch down town now where one doesn't have to go through an operator. It is all automatic, except for long distance of course."

"Well that won't help us any since our calls are all long distant."

"Oh well"

Annika was not comfortable speaking with Gunnar on the phone and rarely did, because of the operator listening in on their conversations. The intervals between Gunnar's and Annika's meetings grew longer and longer.

"You look fantastic Lisa, and your apartment looks great too! Your decorations are so festive. Happy New Year!" Annika gave her a firm hug and a kiss on the cheek, which Lisa returned as she greeted Annika at the door.

"Oops, you got my lipstick on your cheek. Let me rub it off," Annika offered.

"That dress, wow, the guys will go wild. What keeps them from falling out?"

"Gravity." Annika replied.

"And your shoes, you look so tall. Sexy-sexy," Lisa added.

"Believe it or not, Kurt bought me this outfit on his own," Annika responded.

"Really! Well, if you're going to look that sassy, I'll change some too." She took the lace that she had added to the front trim of her dress and simply ripped it off, exposing the swell of her breasts, pushed up by her bra. "Well, what do you think?" she asked, finishing off by picking off a few loose threads.

"Smashing, Lisa. Absolutely smashing," Annika repeated. "I'll get the door. Happy New Year Camilla, Sven!" Annika greeted the two, hugging and kissing them both welcome. "Doesn't worry about my lipstick on your cheeks, everyone else will have it too." She made a short turn from the newly arriving guests, while looking back over her shoulder and winking suggestively.

The dining table looks so festive. The hibiscus - can you get them this time of the year?"

"Yes, I'm sure they grow them in greenhouses."

"You will have to show me how you fold the napkins into swans like that, cool. And the party favors, nice touch I must say."

The tables looped through the living room to make seats for sixteen guests. Soft classical music from the radio filled the room.

Something smells really good from the kitchen. Baked chicken I believe." Sven noticed.

"Kurt, meet Gunnar. Gunnar, meet Kurt. Gunnar goes to Gothenburg's Medical, same school as Lisa," Annika announced.

"Gunnar is a special friend of mine whom I met through Lisa and we've gone out on occasion," Annika explained, as a matter of fact.

"It's nice to meet you Kurt." Gunnar extended his hand.

"Likewise," said Kurt.

"For real, Lisa, you look like a million, and Annika, wow!" Camilla exclaimed.

"Yes, for real," Sven mimicked Camilla. "You ladies look great, and boy, does it smell good in here."

"From what? The dinner or me?" Annika asked coyly.

"Both, for sure." Sven leaned forward and inhaled deeply by Annika's ear. "Hmmm, nice. Very nice. Good enough to eat."

"Thanks, but you'll have to wait for the chicken," Annika informed him.

"Here, take a ticket for the seating game. It's to find out who will be your table partner for tonight. Each ticket has the name of an animal written on it. When you hear your animal, you have found your partner. You may only communicate with the sound or special demeanor your animal is known by until you find your partner. In other words, if you approach someone rubbing your beak and your subject responds with picking flees, you would probably want to move on, unless you are into that kinky stuff," Lisa explained. "Please help yourself to the sherry, find your partner and we will be ready to sit down to eat in just a few minutes," Lisa announced.

Most guests were friends of Lisa and Gunnar from their medical school and had never met Annika or her friends.

"You are one of Lisa's class mates? Annika asked.

"Yes, we take a few of the same classes," he explained. Annika was paired up with a medical student from Ystad, at the southern tip of Sweden. He was bright and charming, but difficult to understand with his strong southern dialect.

"Turtle, hmm," Annika said in an effort to sound dismayed. "Who has ever heard a turtle speak?"

"Your turtle gate was terrific though," said Nils. "I could easily tell that you were either; a turtle, crab, spider or a sloth."

"Thanks, that is the nicest thing anyone has said to me in a long time," she replied.

"I meant that your performance was terrific," said Nils.

"Ladies and gentlemen," Lisa tapped a spoon against her glass. "Ladies and gentlemen, thank you again for coming, and bringing in the new-year with the rest of us misfits who were not invited to a more prestigious event. Oh well, we are going to have a fun time tonight, I'm sure. I have planned a few games for during and after dinner . . ." She was interrupted by cheers and applauds. "After dinner we'll clear the floor for dancing and bring in the New Year with a glass of champagne. On a more serious note, I'd just like to remember the struggle that our neighbors have to endure because of the German and Russian aggression. May God save them, and may God save us, and may He keep us out of the path of war and destruction. Now let's forget all the misery in the world and have a good time tonight! Cheers!" The men downed their Aquavit in one gulp. The women sipped on their sherry.

"Whew," gasped Nils, after downing his Aquavit. "Wow, I needed that. It feels so good when it tears up the old throat," Nils announced.

"I'm not sure I can identify with that," Annika remarked, shaking her head at the men's seemingly senseless custom.

Spirits were high and guests took turns telling stories, making brief speeches that ended in toasts for various worthy causes. They also sang the customary drinking songs that predictably ended in toasts. After dinner, coffee and dessert, they cleared the floor, and game time began.

"All right!" Lisa called out. "We are going to stay with the same partners for the games. First, we'll see how well you can recognize your partners. We will blindfold the guys, and they must find their ladies by simply feeling their faces. No talking or heavy breathing permitted, of course." Lisa instructed them. Hearty laughter ensued.

"That's Lisa," the young man guessed, after having closely examined and run his fingers all around Annika's face, smearing her rouge some. She had closed her eyes, relaxed and was enjoying the gentle face massage.

"Don't stop! Try again, that felt so good. You'll get it eventually." Her comment brought another round of laughter.

"Now we're going to try something a little different," Lisa announced. "Each couple must cross the floor, the same way, but different each turn. Okay? If a manner of crossing is repeated, that couple is out. The last remaining couple wins."

The game started with the most basic gaits, such as walking, running, trotting, skipping, jumping and the gaits repeated, but with perhaps both hands above their heads or holding hands or kissing, while crossing. Lisa was a tough judge and disqualified couples when both partners didn't make the same moves. As the game proceeded, the couples had to become increasingly innovative. One couple somersaulted across the floor. The more daring the crossings the more appreciative was the audience.

"It's five minutes before midnight," Lisa announced. She turned on the radio to monitor the last minutes of the year. They could hear the sonorous ringing of church bells at a distance, ringing out the old year.

"Wow!" Lisa cried, as the champagne oozed out of the bottle. Lisa and Camilla filled champagne glasses with the sparkling wine. Lisa asked one of the fellows to help her open the bottles, but there was still a good pop and they had to hurry to fill the glasses, to avoid losing the bubbling liquid. "Nine, eight, seven, six, five," everyone joined in the count down, Afour, three, two, one, HAPPY NEW YEAR! Happy 1940!" Everyone shouted, blowing whistles and paper trumpets and throwing paper-serpents, all about each other, kissing whomever came near, while chirping Happy New Year. Lisa turned up the radio to its loudest as the band played Auld Lang Sine. After the customary New Year's poems were read, the band returned to playing dance music. The couples resumed dancing, often breaking in and changing partners.

At 4:00 am, Lisa brought out the Swedish specialty, *Janson's Temptation*, an oven-baked dish of potato strips, anchovies and onions. This dish required acquired taste, which possibly went back to the beginning of the century, or before, when potatoes and sardines or herring was a basic food for Swedes.

CHAPTER 7

August, 1940 Roland and Barbro's crayfish party

Lisa, Annika, Camilla and Sven arrived together. Kurt arrived on his own.

"Thanks' for inviting us. This is really a great place," Annika complimented Barbro.

"Well what's really great is to be able to party on the boat dock and there's no one close by for us to disturb," said Barbro.

"For sure," Camilla agreed. "So, this is where you spend your summers. This summer home is nicer than most people's city homes."

"It belongs to my parents, but they don't come out here that much anymore," said Barbro.

"Stig, meet some of Lisa's friends. We met at Lisa's New Year Party. That was such a nice party. Lisa sure knows how to entertain."

"Nice to meet you Stig. So, you are Barbro's boyfriend?" Annika asked.

"I should be so lucky! No, but I'm working on it," he grinned. He reached over and hugged Barbro.

"Shame on you Stig! He's dating Monika," Barbro explained.

"You caught all your crayfish yourself?" Kurt asked. "I understand you did."

"Every single one . . . down at the lake. We have a pretty good lake not too far from here where they are abundant."

"The paper-lanterns look so festive. Did you do all the decorations yourself?" Camilla asked Barbro.

"No, no I had a lot of good help. Some of us spent the night here."

The girls were given a screw and the guys got a nut and they were all asked to mingle around to find their table partner by matching nuts and screws. There were thirty some guests at the party. Camilla was matched with Barbro's younger brother Roland. Lisa and her partner sat across the table from Annika.

"We sure lucked out with the weather. This is gorgeous, beyond expectations. The full moon, it's warm and the sky is completely clear," Camilla observed. "I wish I could freeze this moment so I could paint it when I get home."

"You paint?" Roland asked.

"Yes, I like to. It's one of my majors," Camilla explained.

"One of? You mean you have more than one major?"

"I also study engineering. I might like to become an architect someday. It's actually not that far removed from my art studies."

"That's true. Michelangelo is proof of that," said Roland.

"Well that would be a stretch to compare my work with that of Michelangelo, but I try" Camilla giggled.

"I wish I could paint better. I try a little sometimes, but unfortunately wishing can't always make up for lack of talent. I can do landscapes passably, but I can't do people worth a hoot, especially faces."

"It's mainly a matter of technique. Did you ever take a class in drawing?" she asked.

"No, not other than in elementary school, but from a non-artist teacher." He shrugged his shoulders.

"Well I would be happy to share my limited knowledge if you have time sometime," Camilla offered.

"That would be great. I might just take you up on that. I couldn't do it right now, because of school, but I'll definitely keep your offer in mind," Roland assured her.

"What does your dad do, that allows him to have this nice summer home?" Camilla asked.

"He is, or was, an orthodontist," Roland informed her. "He has retired now."

"And you, are you also going to become a tooth fairy?" Camilla teased.

"I'm not sure about the fairy part, but a dentist, yes. That's my goal. I don't think that I'll get much business from you, though. Your teeth are beautiful, straight and bright white."

"Thank you," she smiled, revealing her perfect bite. "Do you have any paintings here that you have done?" Camilla asked.

"Nothing worth looking at, but yes I have several up at the house that I've started."

"Can I see them later?" Camilla asked.

"Sure, if you'd like." Roland stood up with his glass raised. "Ladies and friends," he began to chuckle. "Let me take this opportunity to welcome everyone, our old friends and our new friends. I'm glad that everyone could make it. I can't remember the last time I got to go to a sleep-over party. Unfortunately, we don't have enough hot water out here for everyone to take a shower before going to bed, so we are pretty much stuck with these three options. One, you simply don't go to bed. Stay up and party all night. We have no close neighbors here, so we won't disturb anyone. Or, you go to bed dirty. That would not be the first time out here. Your last option is to take a bath in the fjord. Those Vikings amongst us who choose option #three need to be reminded of house rule # six. After intense negotiations with our insurance carrier, we have stipulated to adhere to rule # six at all times. It reads as follows: 'Any permanent resident or valued guest,' Barbro insisted on including the word 'valued' to provide for a little legal wiggle room, 'staying at these premises must never go swimming alone. Nor may anyone incapable of walking . . . go swimming.' That clause may be especially applicable tonight. I'd also like to extend this cheer to whoever is responsible for the terrific weather we are enjoying tonight. While I have that line open I'd also like to ask for a little compassion for our occupied neighbors to the east and south. The German occupation of our neighbors will be remembered as a blatant violation of human rights. Clearly our Danish and Norwegian brothers and sisters do not deserve what they have had to endure from the Germans. Nor do our Finnish neighbors deserve the treatment they're getting from the Russians. Further, a thanks to our leaders who have been able to keep us out of armed conflict thus far, even though we've had to deal with the devil himself . . ."

"Amen"

"I also would like to thank Barbro for all her effort in putting this party together. Thank you, Barbro, you're the greatest, and thanks to Lisa for bringing her great friends. And a special thanks to Mother Fortune for placing me next to Camilla. Please join me in a toast for peace, and let the games begin. Skål!"

"Skål!" Everyone responded, raising their glasses.

"Well," said Roland turning to Camilla. "I also think we owe a lot to the British air force, for holding off the Germans.

"Yes, were it not for them, Germany would have invaded Britain by now, and that would have been the end of Europe," said Lisa.

"With France's falling, there would be no one left to stand up against Germany," Annika added.

"Yes, and with Russia in the Baltic States, and taking part of Finland, it looks like there are only going to be two countries in Europe, and we'll be part of Germany," Lisa mused.

"It's a pretty scary thought," Roland agreed.

The girls had brought their fiddles. Annika had played since she was six years old and knew her instrument, even though it had been a while since she had played. Lisa and Camilla played the fiddle as a second instrument. Lisa was first a pianist and Camilla a clarinetist. Both Camilla and Lisa had picked up the violin in high school and they sounded good playing together with Annika. The girls got their violins ready and played a few Swedish favorites, including *Järdeby låten* and the theme from *Värmlänningarna*, while the others finished their crayfish. They concluded their "dinner concert" with Evert Taube's *Havs Örnens Waltz* and the *Beer-Barrel Polka*. After a few more shots of Aquavit, more speeches and bawdy jokes, they cleared a dance floor. The girls played a few polkas, fox-trots and waltzes until two other guests who had brought their guitars and a third who played the accordion, took over the musical entertainment.

Most guests stayed over at the cottage. The girls had brought their sleeping bags. When the party neared its end, the guests moved inside and Roland took the opportunity to show Camilla his art work. "I'll show you mine if you'll show me yours," he offered.

"Sure, drop by any time and I'll show you mine," she responded coolly.

Roland had set up a studio upstairs, and had several of his paintings on display throughout the house. The wall toward the bay was glazed from ceiling to floor.

Wow!" said Camilla with awe. "If you don't get inspired here, it's not going to happen. This is great."

"Yes, it's nice," Roland agreed.

"Do you sculpt too? Hey, that's nice. Who modeled your bust? It looks so familiar," Camilla asked.

"It's Greta Garbo," he replied.

"She must have been an expensive model?" Camilla mused.

"I just did it from some pictures . . ."

"Oh," she said, thinking "I'd never have guessed," and continued "It's a little difficult to see now with the oil lamp. I'll have to take a better look at it tomorrow."

"We were going to get electricity here some time ago, but then they decided to change the old system to a 220-volt system and that slowed everything down," Roland explained.

Roland started a fire in the fireplace, especially for those who went swimming after the party and were now coming in shivering. The guests were filling up much of the floor space with their sleeping bags. Most of them had changed into something better suited for sleeping. A few characters that had drunk too much to go swimming never made it that far, falling asleep in precarious positions and in various state of undress.

Roland's bed was occupied, so he rolled out his sleeping bag next to Camilla's. Sven spent the night by his "table date," oblivious to rest of the world.

Annika had been matched with Bertil.

"What do you do? Annika asked.

"I'm a promoter."

He had come as the date of one of Barbro's friends.

"I manage a few convention centers, in Sweden and in Norway, Oslo. I organize industrial conventions of various kinds, along with sporting and artistic events. I'm 34 years young and I stay here in Gothenburg most of the time. What about yourself?"

"Not very interesting. I live in Longedrag and work in my father's electric shop. I was in Lillehammer on a ski vacation a few years ago and that was quite nice."

"I go there at least a few times every year. I have relatives that live close by." Bertil explained.

"Relatives, then how come you don't speak with a Norwegian accent?" Annika asked.

"Oh, they are in-laws on my brother's side."

Annika was intrigued by his apparent "worldliness," and she was fascinated by his active life. At thirty-four, he was several years older than anyone Annika had ever dated, and he had a lot of stories to tell. His maturity actually fascinated her. He talked about his travel adventures and about some of the more interesting promotions that he had been involved with. He was humorous and had a heart melting smile. Bertil had grown up close to Annika's family home, although, given their age difference, they had never interacted. They both knew of the colorful people from the area and had fun exchanging memories. Bertil used to go sailing, when younger, but did not much anymore. Annika was impressed with the way he dressed and his gentleman's demeanor. He was not completely self-absorbed, like some of Annika's male friends. He would ask questions and actually listen to the answers. He was articulate, and he was quite handsome.

"It's ironic that we never met before when we live so close together, and we both sail!" she added. I guess it's because I don't normally interact with the older crowd. Well I mean the more mature crowd. I'm not sure that is much of an improvement but what I want to say is that maturity can be quite good."

"Thank you, I think."

By 5:00 a.m. everyone was asleep.

"Tell me about Bertil," Camilla persisted, she had dropped by where Annika worked, while shopping. "He looks like quite a charmer."

"He's really nice. I like him a lot. It seemed like we danced all night. He really knows how to dance. He has such a strong, firm lead. He even knows how to do the mazurka."

"Sounds promising," Camilla giggled, "are you going to see him again?"

"Tonight."

"Really, that soon?"

"I couldn't think of any reason not to," Annika explained.

"There is a boat show that Bertil is promoting at Mässan, and he invited me to stop by for a private tour and we'll have dinner afterwards."

"Alright, Annika, that goes to show you!"

"Tell me about Roland. He's such a sweetheart! How did it go?" Annika pried.

"Yes, he is. He's really sweet. It was funny. He showed me this bust that he had made of Greta Garbo. Although it was a pretty nice bust, there was no resemblance what-so-ever! It looked more like a man. He would make a good impressionist, like Picasso." They both laughed.

"Are you going to see him again?" Annika asked.

"I don't know. He's a medical student, dental student, so he is quite occupied right now. I offered to help him with his painting, so it's up to him now, if he wants to call me. But yes, I liked him a lot, but I like Sven a lot too."

"I know. I feel the same about Bertil and Kurt. I like them both. Of course, I don't really know Bertil, but somehow it seems like I do. We both went skinny dipping last night at the party. . . I didn't see you," Annika recalled, "Where were you?"

"Roland was showing me his art."

"It was fun. The water was a little cold. It was dark in the water so it was difficult to see who was who. Then some prankster took our clothes and brought them inside, so we had to run around in the buff before we could find them."

"Really? That's why so many came running inside naked? I thought there was a streaking party."

"That's why."

"Did Bertil have a nice body?" Camilla asked.

"Yes, he did . . . but he was awfully hairy."

"I like hairy chests. That's so sexy," Camilla said.

"Well, I like hair on a man too, but not too much, or hairy backs."

"Yes, not too much. Too much is always a little more than just right. Isn't it?" Camilla giggled.

"Well, I'm not sure one can have too much money, or that there can be too much love," Annika speculated.

"Maybe not money, but too much love can be a bad thing, because it would probably bring out jealousy and possessiveness," Camilla responded.

"You're right. Too much is probably a little excessive," said Annika.

"Yes. Who needs someone who gets upset every time you talk to another guy?" Camilla asked.

"I know."

"What about Kurt?" Camilla asked.

"Well he seemed pretty taken with that little floozy he was paired with."

"Do I detect a trace of jealousy?" Camilla asked.

"No, he can do what he likes. We're not dating seriously, and we probably never will. Talk about a guy who's self-absorbed."

"But you still like him, don't you?"

"Yes, I do. I'm not sure why, but I do. I guess, perhaps we're quite alike. There's something about being able to domesticate this guy. He is attractive because he sometimes acts so indifferent. That's probably difficult to grasp. Kurt feels the same way about me. When I withdraw, I become a challenge again who needs to be concurred."

Bertil waited for Annika at the door of the shop. He was smartly dressed in a dark suit. He greeted her a warm hug and a light kiss on her cheek, and they drove over to Mässan in his Citroen, pulling the gen-gas unit.

"I'm really glad you could come, Annika. Thank you again for a lovely evening at Barbro's. I had a wonderful time, thanks to you." Bertil held the door open for her. Annika was dressed in a tight navy suit with white and red stripes. She had on a matching hat that resembled a bowed scarf. The suit accentuated her figure, narrow waist, and lifting her chest.

It was a large show, with perhaps five hundred boats on display. Most were indoors. There was everything from rowboats and dinghies to luxury yachts. Annika's skirt was a little tight to climb into the boats, but she managed. Bertil had arranged for fruit and cheese snacks and a bottle of red Alibassi wine in one of the nicer yachts, and they had a nice time talking and people watching.

Bertil confided to Annika about his brother who had married a Norwegian girl, and their effort to stay ahead of the Germans, removing anything of value from Norway before the Germans arrived. Annika got the feeling that he was more involved in Norway's resistance than what he professed to be.

They finished the evening at Liseberg's restaurant dining and dancing. Bertil's Citroen, pulled the gen-gas attachment behind. He drove her home and they agreed to meet again the following day, Saturday.

It was shortly after noon when Bertil arrived to pick her up.
"It's about an hour's drive."
"That's alright."
They drove south to a summer house of Bertil's friend Karl Johan.
"You'll like this place, I'm sure. It used to be their family farm, but after his parents passed away, all the land, including the barns, was leased out to a farming co-op and the family only kept the farm house as a vacation home," he explained. It was in an ideal location next to the water, protected from the weather.

"The apple trees provide for some protection from the ocean winds. That's mostly why we keep them. They are a little overgrown admittedly.

It is also nice to have own fruit orchard." Karl-Johan explained while giving them a tour of the yard. "The water is a little too shallow to bring the bigger boats close to the shore, but it's great for swimming. We keep the bigger boat anchored further out during the season, but now it's stored for the winter."

The main building was shielded among several large fruit trees that provided wind protection from the sea. Karl Johan was an engineer for the local electric corporation. His girlfriend Monika was a news reporter, and they both lived in Gothenburg during the week.

"We just finished bringing electricity to the building, mainly to run a well pump and for light. The kitchen stove had been our only heat source, but now we also have an electric heater." Said Karl Johan.

"We both like to work in the garden. We probably got a little carried away, but the flowers are so pretty, and they smell so good." said Monika.

Their garden was meticulously maintained, and flowers greeted guests everywhere.

"This is where we eat. The table is protected by the building. We just finished this court yard." Karl Johan explained.

"Seems like a perfect place to enjoy some shrimps. Here we just happen to have brought some." Bertil handed over the package to Monika.

Karl Johan was a short-wave radio enthusiast and all his equipment was set up in the building, he liked to listen in on marine conversations.

It got cold quickly when the sun went down, and the group moved inside for coffee, wine and to play cards.

"You guys are welcome to spend the night here so you can have some wine. We have an extra room upstairs," said Karl Johan.

Bertil looked at Annika with begging eyes, "what do you say?"

"Sure, why not?" Annika agreed. The wine was partly effecting her decision.

For a week Annika saw Bertil every day. Then he disappeared as suddenly as he had appeared. He had told her that he would be gone for three days, but Annika never heard from him again.

Kurt's annoying habits diminished Annika's enjoyment of his company. Kurt did not seem to mind spending a lot of money on extravagant things, but when it came to mundane things he could be quite stingy. He would only tip what he thought he could get away with, and he would take home things from the table that was not his to take. He would normally order the least expensive dish on the menu, or order a nice dish for Annika but then ask that she share. Annika found it embarrassing at best.

"I don't understand what you see in Kurt, Annika, when you could be dating Gunnar. Gunnar is smart, humble, considerate, the totally opposite of Kurt. Gunnar will stick to one woman, while Kurt is a womanizer, if I ever saw one; he even came on to me once, your best friend." Lisa told her.

"Kurt is a friendly guy. You can't fault him for that. I think he just like to talk big." Annika responded.

Annika, Camilla and Lisa were chatting over coffee at Lisa's.

"Did Billy write anything about John?" Lisa asked.

"No, I'm sorry. I asked him in my last letter, and he said that he had not seen or heard from John since John began medical school." Annika responded.

"What about that Roger fellow you told us about last week, the one who fainted during the autopsy class? Didn't you say you liked him?" Camilla asked Lisa.

"I don't know. I don't really have time for any guys yet. He was all right, and you know, I don't really think that he fainted from seeing the blood. I think it was more from exhaustion, from standing up too long and from staying up so late," she added. "Yesterday we were practicing feeling for abnormal growths, including detecting lumps in a breast. We were working in teams of two, and Roger was on my team. It was almost comical how shy he was when touching my breasts. That is something that he will have to get over if he wants to be a doctor, and especially a gynecologist."

"Do you mean to tell me that you can sit there with an attractive guy and flip your boobs out for him to feel and squeeze, and you don't feel anything? That is abnormal for sure!" Annika declared.

"Oh no! I couldn't say that. It takes a little time to get used to it. I know . . . it feels strange when you are not used to working on nude bodies. It's especially weird when you're being examined by an attractive guy, who you can tell is getting turned on from doing the examine. One has to concentrate on the task at hand, telling oneself that this is what doctors do and one just has to get used to it. You have to focus on the clinical aspect of what you're doing. We are eight students in our group, three girls and five guys, and we do a lot of practicing on each other. Well, sometimes there are volunteers that we work on also. It's almost like . . . it becomes as if we are all married. We get to know each other really well," Lisa revealed.

"I'll say you do. You mean the guys examination you girls?" Camilla asked.

"Sometimes. If you are intimidated by nudity, you can't be in this business," Lisa explained.

"How are the guys in your group, any hunks?" Annika asked.

"They're actually all really nice. But frankly, we don't have the time or energy to think about personal relationships. Our biggest challenge is to get enough sleep. If we can get five hours in a night, we're doing well. A couple weeks ago I was so nervous. I had to give a full physical to my instructor. It was a . . . well, like a chapter progress test. It was intimidating, for sure. You know, the most difficult thing we have to do though, I think, is to draw blood."

"Really?" Annika asked in surprise.

"Yes, you have to stick this rather large needle into someone's arm and sometimes it's hard to find a good vein, so you end up doing it again, and you feel really bad for your patient. One can't help but feel incompetent. For me that is much worse than the nudity. At school, bodies are just something we work on and there's nothing sexual about it. There is nothing sexy about an injured or sick body, and you know, I don't really think that it's all that important where you touch someone. . ."

"What? You're trying to tell . . ." Annika interrupted.

"Let me explain," Lisa cut her off. "I think what makes touching exciting, is that someone you find attractive, is letting you enter their private space, to do something that is reserved for special people, towards whom you have strong intimate feelings."

"Yes, I think you're right," said Annika nodding her head. "Like, the Arabs that hide most of their bodies would probably get turned on from touching a girl on her face or arms."

"Yes, or get shot, or stoned," Camilla injected. They all laughed.

"Exactly my point," said Lisa. "And I know that in some African tribes a man greets a woman by touching her breast, and I'm sure they think nothing sexual of it."

"That would be quite cozy, wouldn't it . . . if we adopted that custom?" Annika suggested and the girls joined her giggling.

"My point is that whether we get turned on or not is pretty much up to us and how we have been socially programmed. Besides, falling in love is essentially a chemical reaction. We arbitrarily chose, or perhaps deliberately, how intimately we pre-classify specific parts of our anatomy," Lisa explained.

"You're such a romantic fool Lisa," Annika teased her.

"Well, I'm not casting judgment on whether being in love, when we act without our rational faculties, is good or bad. I'm simply stating the fact." Lisa defended herself.

"That's not so strange," commented Camilla. "Like that day when we went sunbathing in the boat and Annika was rubbing my bottom with sun screen, I remember being turned on. I even got turned on watching you do that to Lisa. It was so sexy somehow. In fact, I'm getting turned on now, from just thinking about it."

"That was kind of nice, wasn't it?" Annika recollected. She reached over giving Camilla a light swat on her behind.

"It was great," Lisa responded. "I also think that partly what made it exciting was that we knew that we were being watched, even if it was just kids."

"I told Kurt about that, and he got so turned on that he was ready to make love right there in the car," said Annika. "It's kind of funny; most guys will get turned on by hearing about girls making out, while at the same time most of them can't stand the thought of two guys making out."

"Well that's our culture that has shaped us. If you take a place like Hawaii for example, before the white man arrived, it was natural and customary for both parents and siblings to have sexual relationships. They had to be taught that this was wrong," Lisa told them.

"It's funny, we often have nude models in the art class, both males and females, and it seems so natural." Camilla reflected.

"Well that further supports my point," said Lisa. "It's because there is nothing personal between you and the models. There is no foreplay, no intimacy and no personal interest. They come, do their job, and then they're gone. The models simply become a tool that you use for your artistic expression," Lisa explained. "Now, if the model should do something personal or act flirtatious, the situation would change and you would most likely become aware of, and be affected by, his or her nudity."

"By the way Annika, will you be able to model for me on Friday?" asked Camilla. "I need to make some charcoal drawings for my class on Saturday. You can have them after I show them to my professor."

"Nude?" she asked.

"Yes, but it will be in my apartment, so it won't be cold like the last time. I'll turn up the heat."

"All right, but you'll owe me one," Annika responded.

"Isn't it weird how nudity and sex are supposed to be something bad?" Lisa added. "Still we all look pretty much the same. We all enjoy sex and that's how we were created. I realize the practical aspects of limiting casual sex, but isn't it a shame to make taboo what most of us like the most?

"I agree with you. Sex is fun and it makes us feel good. It's not something that hurts others and what consenting adults do is no one else's business," Annika added firmly.

"I'm not sure I agree, though, that we all look the same. I would give a million for the boobs that you guys have. I'm basically flat." Camilla grabbed her chest as if to feel if her breasts had grown.

"Oh really, I think you have a great body. Your long slender legs and tight little butt are the envy of most girls. . . of me for sure. I think big boobs are overrated. The most essential factors regarding sexuality are how a person acts and interacts, one's attitude. A smile is worth more than big boobs any time. Little things . . . like friendly touching, taking someone's hand, or giving a friendly hug when you meet someone is worth a lot more . . . just a little basic flirting. Actually, Camilla, you give some of the best hugs of anyone I know. You snuggle up and actually hug a person as if you really like the person you are hugging. I tell you, a person feels good after one of your hugs," Lisa flattered her.

"Thanks, I love you too," Camilla said, smiling warmly, although not totally convinced.

"Anyhow, other factors are, of course, hygiene. Is there anything more inviting than a fresh clean body that has just stepped out of a bathtub? It is also important to show interest in the other party. Sex is a two-way activity and you are only going to get out of it what you put into it. I think I got a little bit off the subject, though, sounding like a lecturer, but we are studying human sexuality in school right now, and I find it really fascinating."

"It is!" Camilla encouraged her.

"Second that, carry on Ma'am," Annika joked.

"Anyway, small boobs are just as sexy as big ones. After all, if you have a hand full, why would you need more? Besides, any guy that is shallow enough to only care about big boobs is not likely to be worth pursuing for a long-term relationship," Lisa elaborated.

"I wasn't suggesting that the boobs were the only asset, only an essential asset," Camilla interjected.

"Well that's true, of course, but all I'm saying is that big boobs are overrated and that there are positive aspects to having smaller boobs."

"That's right, and big boobs can be quite a strain on your back." Annika said, speaking from experience. "They are not exactly light to carry around."

"Besides, it's the nipples that matter the most. They are what turn a guy on and that's where we are the most sensitive to touch." Lisa continued, "Besides, you can feel just as much pleasure with smaller boobs as with large. Most of the sensation comes from the area around the nipples. Like I said before, most guys are turned on simply by your permitting them to enter your private space. Besides, your breasts are not that small."

Annika began spending more time with some of her old friends. She and Camilla and Sven went dancing a few times, but Camilla was now seeing Sven on a regular basis, and Annika felt like she was intruding, going out with them, even though they assured her that they enjoyed having her come along. She still saw Gunnar from time to time.

"I hope you can join us tonight, Annika. Sven and I are going to Rondo. We haven't really had a chance to dance for some time." Camilla prompted.

"Are you really sure you want to drag me along. You guys are always so nice and bring me along, but I feel a little like the fifth wheel. Don't you really rather have some time alone with Sven?" Annika asked.

"Don't be silly Annika. You are the third wheel. I hope we don't make you feel that way. We really like it when you come along, both Sven and I. We have plenty of opportunities to be alone. We don't need privacy when we go dancing publicly." Camilla ensured her. "Why don't you bring Gunnar, he is nice."

He is studying for a quarter-final test on Monday."

Camilla was working in a woman's dress shop part time while pursuing her studies. It was a small shop and she had time to study in-between customers. She played the violin and clarinet, and she took voice lessons, besides taking her painting and engineering classes. Painting was her great passion, particularly in oil. Sven had registered for some of the same evening classes, mainly to be with Camilla, but did not lack on artistic talent and enjoyed painting. He did well in the class, perhaps because of the personal coaching he received from Camilla. Sven worked full time on a housing project, as a carpenter, during the days.

After she began to date Sven regularly, Camilla moved closer to the city center. She rented an apartment on the fourth floor of an older building. It was a penthouse apartment, and had a charming roof-garden balcony, but it had only one room, with kitchen and bath. The rent was affordable and the flat was conveniently located, not counting the four flights of stairs she had to climb to get there. There was no elevator, so she got good exercise climbing the stairs.

"At least one gets a good workout visiting you Camilla." Annika was breathing noticeably audibly. "You live on the fourth floor and have no elevator!?"

"I know." She shrugged her shoulders. "Fortunately, I have lot of helpful friends that helped me move in. "I hope you don't mind if Sven is here, Annika. He needs to do the same project."

"If you don't mind, neither do I. What would you like me to do?" She asked while taking in the room. She took a deep breath.

There was a large overstuffed couch on one wall that also turned into a bed. An old door served as a coffee table. The opposite wall was mostly glass looking onto the roof garden. A few large plants filled one corner of the living-room and on the opposite side of the kitchen, some of Camilla's large illuminated oil paintings decorated the wall.

"You got a dog? When did that happen?" Annika asked, surprised.

"Oh no. Lazy there belongs to my neighbor. I volunteered to doggy-sit tonight, so she could go on a date. I hope you don't mind, he is really friendly."

"What is it I smell? Is it some kind of chocolate or incense?" Annika asked.

"Oh, no, it's Sven's new pipe-tobacco. Yes, it does smell a little like chocolate, doesn't it?" Camilla agreed.

Sven and Camilla had set up their easels in the open kitchen, and they had spread out a few blankets on the hardwood floor and several pillows were tossed in the middle. The room had a rather strong odor of paint from several paintings that were drying. Camilla turned on the radio. Henry Miller's big band was playing Chattanooga Choo-choo.

"Why don't you put your clothes over there on the couch, and then we'll have you pose over here on the blankets? You can use my robe if you like," Camilla offered.

"Oh, I don't see what difference it makes if I'm going to pose nude for you." She proceeded to undress moving very lightly with the music. Sven was watching her with fascination as she removed each garment. He had seen her nude before, a few years ago, skinny dipping at Gunnar's 'bring in the hay party' but it was at twilight and in a group of several people splashing in the water. The third time he saw her was at Barbro and Roland's crayfish party under similar circumstances. Here she was undressing in bright light and for him to study. Lisa's theory that if a model strictly modeled, that she would have no arousing effect on the artist, proved flawed. Of course, Annika was much more than a model, much more. Annika was a good friend whom he had admired since he first laid eyes on her. She was exquisitely beautiful, built like a model, but more developed, much more. She had a sense of humor and she was a natural flirt. All she had to do was to smile to melt the heart of any man. This was a treat for Sven. "Would you like me to try different poses or do you have something in mind?" she asked.

"Go ahead, just move around until we say stop," Sven instructed her. Annika got down on her knees, spreading her legs slightly apart, she leaned backwards, her hair hanging down behind, her breasts pointing almost straight up.

"Stop!" Camilla and Sven called out at the same time.

"It will have to be a pose that you can hold for ten minutes or so," Sven advised her.

"Three minutes," Camilla corrected him. "We can only spend three minutes on each pose. These drawings are not supposed to be portraits. The idea is to catch the balance in the image and to play around some with shading and contrast. We'll do several. It will almost be like an old movie screen . . . if you look at them all, fast."

"All right, three minutes. Let's try a few different poses. Perhaps a few when you sit on a chair, and even a few when you have your blouse on but hanging open in front."

"Sven, why don't you let me draw a few sketches of you and Annika, and then you can do some of Annika and me if you like."

"I'm not sure that would work out very well. I have never posed au natural, and I doubt that I could stand there without getting aroused," he explained. "I have a hard-enough time looking at Annika, no pun intended."

"Oh, that's silly. You're just going to have to get used to it. You're going to have to model for me often and we don't want to have to deal with this every time. Let's just do it now when only Annika's here. She won't care."

"I've seen you nude before, when we all went skinny dipping at Lisa's crayfish party. It's no big deal," said Annika. "Perhaps we could also include Lazy"

"Yes, but then I had a few drinks, and it was dark outside. This is a little different, but if you can, so can I."

"Here, I'll get you a glass of wine if you think that help. Annika, do you care for one?" Camilla offered.

"Sure . . . thanks."

"Do you care for a cigarette?" Sven offered, as he lit one for himself.

"No thanks, I don't smoke."

"I'll have one," said Camilla, although she rarely smoked. Perhaps she intended more to make the point that she was also there.

"Oh! I'm sorry!" Sven apologized.

Sven removed his clothing and walked over to Annika. Annika studied him as he undressed, with amusement. She had never seen a guy seeming so shy before. She was convinced that Kurt would be happy to have sex in the middle of a public place if she would go along with it. Sven's shyness had the opposite effect on Annika. It prompted her to relax even more and to be a little bolder than she might otherwise have been.

"What can I say?" He took the pose of a body builder momentarily forgetting his shyness.

"You certainly don't have anything to be ashamed of, old boy. Your body should be on display at a museum of art," Annika continued.

"All right, let's not overdo it. It'll go to his head," Camilla chided. "Okay, let's have both of you sit on a chair, back to back, each posing like 'the thinker.' . . . Now let's have both of you sit on one chair as if you were riding a motorcycle, Sven in front, and Annika behind and leaning your head onto his shoulder. All right that will have to do." Sven took a short break filling the wine glasses and lighting another cigarette.

"That wasn't so bad, was it?" Annika asked him, looking up innocently.

"You made it easy," he conceded.

Lazy appeared to sleep through it all.

"Okay, it's your turn Sven. What would you like us to do? Let me rephrase that question. How would you like us to pose?" Camilla asked as she disrobed. "You'd just as well stay nude, Sven, so you can get used to the idea of working nude around other people," Camilla coached. "Besides, I kind of like it when you're strutting around in the buff. What do you think Annika?"

"Yes, I like it too. It's nice."

"Annika's right, you have a gorgeous body and you have every right to be proud of it. Is it getting hot in here or is it just me?" Camilla asked.

"No, it's not just you. It's really hot in here. I can feel it too," Annika agreed.

"How is it going with you and Kurt?" Camilla asked. "Are you getting serious yet?" Camilla continued.

"I don't know. I like Kurt, but he seems so occupied with his affairs, his business. I'm not convinced that he is ready to settle down yet. And Gunnar essentially studies all the time."

"Do you ever see Bertil, anymore? It seems as though you were pretty hot on him . . . for a while." Camilla prompted.

"I don't know what happened. He seems to have disappeared from the earth. I hope nothing bad has happened to him. It's so out of character with him to not even call and let me know what's going on."

It was a difficult time for Annika. She doubted Kurt's sincerity and intentions. Gunnar didn't have much time for her, and her long-distance relationship with Billy did not promise a future. She had received several letters from him, and she had answered them all, but then they stopped coming. The last letter she had received was in November.

November 2, 1940

Dearest Annika,

Thank you so much for your warm letter. You do not have to apologize for your English. You write better English than many Englishmen I know. I love to hear from you and nothing you say is boring or unimportant. I love to read about what you do, minute by minute. I pretend I'm with you as I read about your activities. I keep all your letters under my pillow and I read them over and over. I'm sorry to hear that it is not working out well, your working for your dad. I know exactly what you mean. I used to work for my dad too. He had a sea food shop that he had started himself, and he expected me to have as much pride in the shop as he did. The problem was that one always smelled like fish, and that was difficult for me to overcome. Annika, I know that it would be too much to ask, that you should come here now. We have only met once, but somehow it seems as though I have known you for a long time, and I would like to extend that time to eternity. You seem so perfect for me, and I would never rest seeking to make you happy. As you know, I'm not at liberty to leave now, and I don't know how much time I could spend with you, even if you came at this time. There is no telling how long this war is going to last. It appears as though things are only getting worse. As much as I would love to have you come here right now, I can't bear the thought of something happening to me and your being left alone, away from everyone you know and love. Also, I'm concerned about your coming here at this time. We are constantly subject to German air raids, and who knows if the Germans will invade Britain. I feel more comfortable knowing that you are safe in Sweden, even though it breaks my heart to be away from you. I think of you every minute of the day, and I often dream of you. The other night I dreamt that we were dancing together just spinning and spinning while floating in the air. We were spinning faster and faster until we had merged into one body with two minds. I know it was a little strange, but perhaps it was some sign that we are meant to merge someday. I have to go now. The supply ship is pulling up and I want to mail this letter now, so you can get it sooner. Who knows when I will be able to send the next one. I will write a longer letter tonight.

With all my love, Your Billy.

Not having heard from him for so long Annika feared the worst. She carried that letter with her at all times and when she felt a little down or unappreciated, she would read the letter once again.

CHAPTER 8

December, 1940 - Cecilia

After a cooling down period when Annika and Kurt only dated sporadically, Kurt was now picking up Annika from work on a daily basis. Normally they would have dinner together, either at a restaurant, or in Kurt's apartment.

"I heard that Sweden have worked out an agreement with the belligerents, permitting Swedish vessels free passage to New York.

"I will be leaving next week for New York and I will be gone for five weeks. I will bring home a new car."

"You are crazy Kurt. I wouldn't count on a trigger-happy captain noticing that little blue and yellow flag."

"I'm sure they look twice. They wouldn't want to trigger the 'north man's rage'. I hope you like mackerel because that's what we are having for dinner. I fried them right before I came to get you, so they should still be warm."

"It doesn't matter. It smells so good. Mackerel taste good either warm or cold."

"The potatoes look ready so let's eat."

"What's that, spinach?

"Spinach is supposed to be good for you. It makes you strong, like Pop Eye."

They would take turns cooking, and often they would see a movie afterwards. On a rare occasion they would go to a theater or to a night club. Kurt liked to take Annika for a drive to the smaller towns up and down the coast, sometimes to stroll down the board walk, to people watch, or to go dancing in a folk-park.

"There is a Charlie Chaplin movie playing at Vågen, shall we go?" Annika asked

"Sure, it could be good." Kurt agreed.

In December of 1940, Kurt left for New York. There was still a great risk in traveling, as a nervous U-boat crew could mistakenly sink the ship, but Kurt was eager to go and willing to accept the risk. He planned to return in five weeks. Annika was disappointed that she never heard from him while he was away, and he had not told her exactly on what day he would return, but she knew when the Gripsholm was returning to Gothenburg. The Gripsholm was Sweden's largest merchant ship and took up to fifteen hundred passengers. Kurt thrived on the service and luxury onboard.

Annika arrived at the Stigbergs' Landing wearing the dress that Kurt had bought her for their first date. She had been to the hair salon and she had chain her nails and lips bright red. She had brought a bouquet of flowers. She was ready.

Annika saw Kurt walking across the landing, toward the customs area, but he was not alone. He was escorting a woman off the ship. Annika turned around, confused and returned home. A week later she saw Kurt driving his Mercury with the same woman next to him. Kurt attempted to call Annika several times, but she had told her family that she was not available if he called.

"Dad, can't the Svensons come and get their own radio? It's so hard to get it on the bus." Annika asked.

"No, we have to bring it. That was one of the conditions for the sale."

"Then we should get a truck if we are going to deliver everything."

"Someday perhaps."

"Well dad, you are going to have to do something. Do you remember the nanny job I told you about in Stockholm? They called and said that they would like me to start as soon as possible."

"Well, you are going to have to wait a couple weeks, so I can find a replacement, OK?"

"Bo could work here for some time, or Kristina. Bo have 3 months before he has to report in, and Kristina is old enough to work."

"We'll see."

Annika felt that she was being taken too much for granted. She especially resented having to deliver heavy radios by public transportation, which entailed carrying those long distances.

Mainly she took the job in Stockholm to get away from Kurt.

"Hi gorgeous!" Kurt stepped into the Bengtson's Electric shop. "What's going on?" he asked. "Why are you avoiding me?"

"I saw you get off the ship with that woman. I was there to welcome you home." She could feel her cheeks flushing with anger.

"Oh no, you didn't!"

"Oh yes I did," she responded.

"I meant, oh no . . . you didn't think that she was with me, I mean, she was with me, but not 'with' me. That was Mrs. Greenberg from New York. She's married and she runs a small travel operation for me there. She was only here for two weeks. She should be back in New York by now. I'm sorry you didn't get to meet her. She's very nice and very capable," Kurt explained.

"You have an office in New York?" Annika asked, clearly impressed. "Well I'm sorry, but you didn't have time to send me even a post card? I wasn't even sure on what ship you would return. Is that asking too much?" She demanded. "And then I see you walk off the ship with that glamorous lady on your arm . . . do you understand how it looked?" Her previous anger had dissolved into a state of relief and joy to see him back. She approached him, laid her arms around his neck and kissed him. "Welcome back," she said. "I'm sorry I didn't trust you."

"That's okay, I understand. You know, I was thinking about writing you, but then it seemed a little silly because I figured that the post card would probably go back with the same boat as I did. So, you would most likely see me before you would get the card." He wiped a tear off her rosy cheek with his thumb.

"Ship" she corrected

"Ship what?"

"You said boat. It is a ship, not a boat. Boats are small." They both laughed.

"A few days later she spotted Kurt in his car driving down the 'Allee'." Kurt's red Mercury was easy to spot. The view was partly obscured by the trees and she saw him at some distance; still, his passenger looked a lot like Mrs. Greenberg.

Mrs. Greenberg's younger sister Cecilia had come from New York with Kurt and Mrs. Greenberg. If Annika had waited a little longer by the Gripsholm when Kurt arrived, she would have seen her too. Cecilia looked very much like her older sister. She was planning on touring Sweden, and perhaps Denmark, depending on how safe it was at the time.

"I'm sure glad you could come, Cecilia, I seriously need help with merchandizing my apparel shops. Perhaps you can add a little American flair. I think that will sell here. After all, the American stuff is continuously being fed to us in the movies and the papers."

"I'm ready to go to work. By the way, the apartment is really nice, and right down town. I couldn't have asked for a nicer place."

"Well, let's start with the four shops I have here in town, and then let's go up the coast for a few days and do those there in a couple of days."

Cecilia was also going to help Kurt, advising him on merchandising his apparel shops. Cecilia was a marketing expert, and Kurt was interested in adding a little American flair to his shops. Kurt had twelve apparel stores, along the Swedish west coast, four of them in Gothenburg. When Mrs. Greenberg had left, Kurt and Cecilia went to work. They spent a couple days in Gothenburg before they left, traveling north to Udevalla, Fiskebäckskil and Strömstad, where Kurt had shops. They traveled in a small truck, bringing merchandise along. Cecilia was in her late twenties, and she had her own consulting business in New York. She was recently divorced and was happy for the opportunity to get out and see some new faces. She had met Kurt in New York, by chance, when she was visiting her sister, and she accepted Kurt's invitation to go with him back to Sweden. She was tall, with a slender build and lovely face. She was also friendly and outgoing. She had Kurt in her spell, but she hesitated to get involved with anyone so soon after her divorce. She had had to pay her husband for her freedom.

"Imagine, if you had not been visiting your sister when I was there, I would most likely never have gotten to know you and about you're consulting business."

"It's a small world."

"And I'm grateful that you could come on a moment notice."

"For you Kurt it's a pleasure. After I left my husband, I decided to get out a little more, and to expand my business. So, it worked out perfect."

Kurt and Cecilia spent the night in Strömstad. They had not made reservations. It was out of season, so Kurt assumed that a reservation would not be needed. However, many places were closed for the winter. They found a small hotel close to his shop that had one room available. Cecilia agreed that they should take it. Kurt offered to sleep in his shop, on the floor, hoping that she would see the cruelty in such arrangement. She did. There was a couch in the room and she invited him to use the couch. They had a nice dinner together. The restaurant was small but homey and reflected pride in ownership. They had Antelope steak for dinner, with red wine.

"This is the first time I have eaten Antelope," Cecilia told him. "It's good, quite lean. I didn't even know that people ate Antelope." Cecilia had worn her hair in a ponytail all day, while traveling, but she had dressed up for dinner and let her hair down and then rolled up in the back, held in place with a come. It was difficult for Kurt not to stare at her. He enjoyed watching her eat. She had gotten meat stuck in her teeth and was working her lips, trying to get rid of it discreetly. She looked exceptionally attractive when she smiled her soft seductive smile.

"We eat just about anything here in Sweden; reindeer, buffalo, gazelle, moose, crocodile . . .. If it can be eaten, we'll eat it. Did you like the Alibassi wine?" Kurt asked.

"Crocodile? That must be tough on your teeth."

"Well, perhaps not crocodile," he conceded.

"Yes, it's very good. Not too dry. It's just right for me."

"You prefer sweeter wines?" he asked.

"Normally, yes, I do."

"So, what do you do when you're not consulting?" Kurt asked.

"Lots of things. I love to travel. I like to read . . . and I like to cook and to garden. I like to go sailing and I like to dance."

"Me too, I love to dance, and to travel."

"The last couple of years before I got divorced, I tried a few different things to stimulate our marriage, so I took lessons in belly dancing," Cecilia continued.

"Really? There's a Greek restaurant in Gothenburg where they have belly dancers. The girls are very attractive, and very lightly dressed, and they come up to the tables dancing. The only thing is that it's difficult to know where to look. One doesn't want to look like a pervert, staring at their assets, but then again, one doesn't want to look like a prude only looking at their faces, especially since they are doing these seductive dances using their bodies."

"Well, they don't mind if you look at their bodies, you're expected to."

"I know, but it still feels a little funny. It seems so sexual somehow, intimate. Too bad they don't have dancing here, but tomorrow night we'll find a place where they have dancing," he promised.

"Somehow you don't strike me as someone who would be intimidated by a little intimacy."

"Well . . ."

They returned to their room and Kurt brought an extra bottle of wine with him. The room was spacious and pleasantly decorated. One side featured a sliding glass door to a deck, with a view of the ocean.

Kurt ordered a pot of tea to the room. The Inn was out of coffee. They sat down on the couch chatting and sipping their wine and tea.

"Would you consider doing a little belly dance demonstration for me?" he asked.

"I knew you would ask that when I told you, but I can't, because I don't have a costume, and I don't have the music." She finished up her wine and Kurt was quick to fill it up again.

"Oh, no I shouldn't," she protested. "I can feel the wine already."

"Tomorrow we'll get you a costume, so you can dance."

"Really? They're not cheap, and you need several chains and beads." Cecilia's speech slurred just slightly.

"We'll find them, don't worry." Kurt assured her.

"Boy, I'm not even sure I remember how. It's been some time."

"I know, let's find you one of those baby doll outfits. We have some in the shop. I will run down and get you one, and we have beads there too. I'll be right back." Kurt was only gone for ten minutes, but Cecilia was out cold when he returned. She was sound asleep on the couch and did not wake up from a gentle shake, or from a rather desperate one. Kurt was careful not to give her too much wine after that.

The following evening in Uddevalla, Kurt planned ahead and reserved a room at the Tourist Hotel. It featured dancing in the evening. He had also called ahead to his shop and asked the manager to fix him up with a costume. Unfortunately, they had car problems in Lysekil and ended up spending the night there. Cecilia did not ask for a separate room. After dinner, she was eager to demonstrate her belly dance routine for Kurt. He had found a drum and had brought some baby doll lingerie to the room, and she easily chose one. He had also brought several long silk scarves in various colors. Kurt offered her some more wine.

"You know you don't have to get me drunk to do this. It'll be fun. I've never done this for such an appreciative audience that's willing to go to so much trouble. I look forward to dancing for you, and I don't mind if you stare at my . . . assets, as you put it. You're supposed to." She smiled at him coyly, shaking her assets.

She used a scarf for a veil and she tied several beads and a few chains around her waist. She tied the short transparent jacket up under her chest. She wore nothing underneath and the jacket provided only minimal coverage. She instructed Kurt how fast she wanted him to play the drum, and she began moving with the rhythm, humming as she danced. Her legs were shaved and she had also shaved under her arms, something Kurt found very sexy. She was beautiful, exotic, and sensuous. She began by moving her hips in a rolling motion and then her stomach began to undulate, as she smiled at him seductively. She moved her supple body like a well-trained gymnast. Cecilia completed a couple dances before they turned on the radio and continued dancing together.

CHAPTER 9

January 1941 Stockholm

Two weeks after Cecilia's departure, Kurt stepped into Annika's shop. "How have you been gorgeous?" he asked, giving her a light hug and a kiss. "I'm sorry I haven't seen you for a while, but I've been really busy with work."

"That's all right. I've been quite busy myself. I'm getting ready to go to Stockholm," said Annika bluntly, but it went past Kurt whose mind was elsewhere.

"I'm currently negotiating buying myself into a coffee import business partnership. It's something new for me, and it appears promising, but it's taking a lot of my time. But the longer that I'm away from you, the more I realize how much I enjoy being with you. I'm going to be totally honest with you. . . .."

"That would be refreshing," she interrupted.

"You know, my parents want only the best for me, and they were hoping that I would marry someone of a higher social status. They weren't really thrilled when I told them that we were dating. You don't have to say anything. I agree with you totally. They're snobs and unreasonable, but the fact is that they are still my parents and I have to deal with them somehow. They're not going to stop me from doing anything, but I have to deal with this in a gentle way. Dad has been ill for some time now and there's no telling how much time he has left. Anyway, I was hoping we could have dinner together tonight."

"Well there's something that I must tell you that will probably give your parents some comfort. I've accepted a position in Stockholm," she said, "as a nanny to a little girl. It will be for at least four months until the end of the school year. Mr. Liljekrona is a director at Stockholm's opera house. Mrs. Liljekrona sings and they both have to travel frequently and sometimes we, their daughter and I, will go along and sometimes not."

"Why? Don't you like it here?" Kurt asked, sounding perplexed.

"I do, but I want to get away from everything for a while. It will help me to sort things out. I need to figure out what I want to do with myself. I also think that it would be a great experience to get out on my own . . . and my mother wants me to meet a millionaire."

"Touché!"

"If you still want to go to dinner, it would be nice," said Annika.

"Now more than ever. I can see that I'm going to have to do some fast talking to change your mind about leaving."

"It's too late for that, I'm afraid. Everything is already arranged. I'm leaving on the fifteenth. I have a few things to finish up here. Could you come back and get me at five?"

Kurt was back ten minutes before five, but he waited outside until it was exactly five o'clock.

"Hi gorgeous!" He held out a bouquet with twelve red roses.

"They're beautiful. Thank you. What did you do, stop in the park on your way here to pick these?"

"Let's be nice now," he said.

"I'm sorry. I just couldn't help myself," she giggled. She walked up to him, leaned forward and pouted for a kiss. He met her half way. "Ah," she took a deep breath, smelling the roses, "they smell so good."

Mr. Bengtson came into the shop. "Hi Kurt, how are you?"

"Fine thanks, I just take one day at the time. How about yourself?"

"Fine thanks, busy, busy. It is so oppressive with the Germans in Denmark and Norway. One has to wonder when it will be our turn," Mr. Bengtson said with melancholy voice.

"What will be will be. There's nothing we can do about it, so there's no point in thinking about it," Annika interjected philosophically.

"At least the British Royal air Force trounced the *Luft Waffe*," Kurt added.

"Yes, God only knows what would have happened otherwise," said Mr. Bengtson.

"God . . . right," Kurt said with some hesitation. It was clear from the tone in his voice that he was not impressed with God's handling of international affairs. "You know if it wasn't for the supply routes open to the Allies, our industrial production would be down the creek, and so would our defense. We wouldn't be any better off than our neighbors."

"You can't fault the Allies for being unhappy with our iron ore transports to Germany. Of course, France wouldn't mind a little fighting up north to divert some pressure from Germany. You know, I think Sweden is worse prepared now than when the war broke out, because we've depleted our resources, especially in helping the Finns," said Kurt, leaning back on the counter.

"How long do you think the cease-fire between Finland and Russia will last?" asked Mr. Bengtson.

"Unfortunately, I believe that it's only temporary, permitting Russia to prepare for a major war, but probably first against Germany. At least it relieved us from the Allied pressure of permitting troop movements across Sweden to assist Finland, which would have placed us smack in the middle of the war," said Kurt. "Then again, Russia would probably love to wait for the capitalists to destroy each other before they step in."

"You know, the Soviet communism is actually an extreme form of capitalism. About 6% of the people own just about everything, and the rest work for them in some way. Yes, I'm afraid you're right," Mr. Bengtson agreed. "However, I don't believe that their system has a future. With no middleclass to speak of, to buy things, and I also think that people will not accept being explored and oppressed for very long. One of the problems though, is that with their governments control of media and speech, most Russians are not aware of them being worse off than people from other nations."

"Yes, and the Japanese aren't any better, wreaking havoc in their neck of the woods, invading Indonesia last September. So many people have been killed," said Annika.

"Yeah, it's unbelievable! Yes, but at least they are not killing their own people, so their system may last a little longer, and I believe, they do have a middle-class. I think the whole world's gone mad. Let me take care of the roses so you kids can get going. I'll bring them home and put them in water," Mr. Bengtson offered.

"Thanks dad," said Annika, with a tired sigh, and gave him a quick kiss on the chin.

"Where would you like to go?" Kurt asked.

"Well, how about Paris? Or Rome, or Chicago or . . .?"

"Okay, okay. I was more like thinking for tonight; where would you like to go?"

"Paris, Rome . . . actually any place is fine with me." She moved close to him, placing her arm in his while looking up at him, as if to say; "let's go, I'll follow you anywhere."

"I was thinking that maybe we should go and see '*Gone With the Wind.*' I heard that it's supposed to be really good. It has Clark Gable in it. The only thing is that it's quite long."

"Maybe it would be better to do that some other time. The line to the movie is going to be long today, since its Friday, and with that movie . . ." Annika suggested. "Why don't we stop by your place first Kurt, so I can have a quick bath before we go out?"

Annika freshened up quickly which was a good thing, because it was difficult for Kurt to control himself when he knew that Annika was lying naked only a few feet away from him, taking a bath. She had left the door slightly open, so they could continue their conversation while she was bathing. He could hear the water trickling down her body as she squeezed the sponge. He could smell the fresh cent from her lotion, carried out with the escaping steam. She came into the room wrapped in a towel. Her skin was red from the hot water, and from rubbing herself dry. Her hair was fluffed up from the drying process, reminding Kurt of a shaggy mop. She looked delicious and Kurt couldn't stand it anymore. He walked over to her, put his arms around her and kissed her, first gently.

In June 1941 Swedish intelligence confirmed Germany's invasions of Russia. Most Swedes were not happy with Finland's jumping back into the war as Germany's co-belligerent. Germany pressured Sweden for various concessions, and Sweden avoided the war by practicing double blackmail. To the Allies Sweden maintained that without the transport connections to the west, the US and later South America, Sweden would be easy prey for Germany. For Germany Sweden maintained that its industrial production would cease, if trade routes were not maintained; that is, Sweden would end export of products essential to maintain the German war machine.

Annika and Kurt had a late dinner at the Botanical Garden Restaurant. They had a good view of the dance floor from their table. The lights were dimmed and a trio was playing lively dance music. An older couple danced a Vienna waltz, exhibiting a grace that could only have been developed through years of dancing together.

"What would you like for dinner, gorgeous?" Kurt asked.

"Oh, I don't know. Why don't you surprise me and order something for me?" Annika asked, mostly to avoid the awkwardness of considering prices.

"I realize that this place is most famous for its seafood menu, but it does have a lot of other good things too. I think I feel like having a steak. Does a Tournedos sound good to you, with parsley butter?"

"Super, sounds delicious." Annika moved her legs so that one touched Kurt's. Kurt smiled at her enthusiasm. "Fine, that's what we'll have." He signaled the waiter. Kurt was not the type who could quietly sit and wait for things to happen. "Waiter, we'd like to order please."

"Would you like to see the menu, Sir?"

"No, that's ok. I know what we'd like to have. I had it before, here, and it was great."

"Thank you, Sir, what would you like, then?"

"We'd both like to have the Tournedos with parsley butter and we would like to substitute the boiled potatoes for the wedged fried potatoes you serve with your chicken. Ok?"

"Fine Sir."

"We'd like the steaks well done and we'll take the asparagus with Hollandaise sauce." He looked over at Annika for approval, and she nodded.

"Thank you, Sir, boiled substituted for fried, and steaks well done. Sir, our chef is going to cry when he sees this order. He thinks that to cook a steak more than medium rare compromises its quality."

"You will have to hand him a handkerchief then," Kurt responded unsympathetically. "I don't want my steak still kicking."

"Alright, Sir . . . I'm sure he'll get over it. Will there be anything else, Sir?"

"Annika? . . . No that will do for now, thank you."

"Anything from the bar, Sir?"

"Since we're having steaks, please give us a small carafe of your house burgundy."

The restaurant was filled to capacity. Several couples had taken to the dance floor as the band was playing the Charleston Swing.

"You know, the Charleston Swing brings back memories. It actually originated back in West Africa and in the Caribbean, by the Negroes. I saw the musical, *Running Wild* where it was first featured, some fifteen, seventeen years ago, in New York. I was a sailor then, working on a freighter, going around the world. It was the first musical I ever saw. The year was 1927. A penny for your thoughts," Kurt offered, bringing Annika back to the present.

"Oh, nothing special," she smiled. "That must have been so exciting to travel around the world . . ."

"Actually, then it seemed mostly like work, and I couldn't wait to get home."

"Imagine that. Anyway, I was only thinking that I really like this place, the decor. Everything is so perfect. It makes you feel like you're on top of the world. What are you thinking about?"

"You! . . . How beautiful you are . . . and how much I always enjoy your company." He leaned over the table slightly, looking deep into her large blue eyes.

"Thank you, Sir. You are most kind. I like you too!" She winkled her nose and placed her hands on top of his. "I'm glad we came here. In fact, I wouldn't mind staying here for the rest of the evening. The band is great, and we always go to those other places."

"Then so be it. That's fine with me. I like it here too. When you're at a place like this you can almost forget about the rest of the world and its problems. The world would be so perfect if people could only get along." Kurt said dreamily.

"I know what you mean. You're preaching to the choir." Annika rubbed her leg gently against his. "We are so lucky to live in a place like Sweden. Things are so civilized here. We have good schools, healthcare and we can come and go as we please. We can say and just about anything. We have freedom of religion and of art . . ."

"I think most countries have freedom of art," Kurt reminded her.

"No that's not true. I read that in the Soviet they control what people can do. The state censor just about everything."

"That is true, in the Soviet they do that, but in most counties . . ." he argued.

"They are not the only country to do that. China even tells people how many children they can have. The US is another country that likes to tell people how to live their lives."

"The US? They probably have the least restrictions of all." Kurt offered. "What do they restrict? One can even drive a car there when only sixteen years old."

"I read that one can get arrested there for sending nude photos in the mail. How imposing is that? They have a list of things one can't do in one's own bedroom. One can't cross someone's property for picking berries, or their beach to go swimming. They have a history abusing their black people. They can get arrested if they don't sit in the back of a bus or use the white's bathrooms. They can't even go in to most restaurants. I don't see how a country can be more restrictive than that. They censor movies and books and art and there surely is no freedom of religion there. It is more like it used to be here in Sweden in the old dark ages when the priests told the people how to live." Annika took a deep breath.

"Perhaps they don't treat their blacks so well, but white people are doing quite well," he countered.

"Yes, if one is not involved in the arts or a Native or a Chinese . . ."

"Well, the natives and Chinese are not white."

"Somehow I can't see how that improves on anything?"

"I can't get over Germany's occupying both Denmark and Norway, and we aren't doing anything about it," Kurt said disgustedly, changing the subject.

"But what could we do, really? Everyone is better off if we remain neutral. Then at least those who need a place to hide have somewhere to go. But I know what you mean. Did you hear in the news that Germany is demanding free access across Sweden for transporting their troops?" Annika placed her napkin in her lap.

"I'm not sure why, because I'm sure they would do it with or without our permission," said Kurt, taking a deep breath. "n my opinion, I think the main reason why Germany has not taken over Sweden is that they're afraid that we will sabotage the iron ore shipments and the ball bearing shipments that they need desperately for their war-machine."

"The King is trying to pressure the parliament into permitting it. He thinks that if we don't, we'll also become occupied. It's difficult to watch German trains going through our country though," said Annika. "The way they block off all the windows, you know they are up to no good."

"You have to tip your hat to little Finland, holding out against giant Russia as long as they did. It's really amazing and admirable that they have done as well as they have against those odds." Kurt sipped on his water.

"And in record cold weather, often minus forty," said Annika

"It's a good thing that the Russians have to protect their eastern border against China and their western borders against Germany. I think that's the only thing that's stopping them from bringing more fire power against the Finns.

"Perhaps all our fake wooden tanks, sitting everywhere are working after all, keeping those bullies from taking Sweden. Do you really think that they are so stupid that they can't see the difference between a wooden tank and a real one?" Annika asked.

"Who knows? I guess we just have to take one day at a time . . ."

"I think we are pretty lucky to live in Sweden," said Annika. "For however long it lasts."

"Today we closed the deal on the coffee business I was telling you about. It's pretty exciting. With the war going on coffee prices should stay high," Kurt explained.

"Good for you. You're such a wheeler dealer, you are," Annika complimented him.

Their dinners arrived, and the meals presented beautifully on the large wooden plates set Kurt's stomach growling.

"Do you serve seconds if I'm still hungry when I've finished this?" Annika asked the waiter.

"Yes miss, I will guarantee that if you finish this, and are still hungry, you can have a second serving without charge," the waiter promised.

"Great, does that go for me too?" Kurt asked, grinning.

"I'm sorry Sir, the offer is for the lady only. You will want to save some room anyway for one of our special desserts. We have several choices. Today we're featuring baked Alaska. It has a minimum of two servings."

"Baked Alaska, what's that?" Kurt asked.

"It's ice cream covered in meringue and baked for a short time in the oven, topped with swirled chocolate sauce, whipped cream and cherries, it's rather special," the waiter explained.

"Seems as though the ice cream would melt in the oven," Annika pointed out.

"Only enough to get soft, Miss, the meringue protects it. Will there be anything else, Sir?"

"No thanks, not for right now."

"I hope you enjoy your meal. Thank you."

"Thank you."

"I'll never be able to finish all this you'll have to help me Kurt." Knowing the price and scarcity of meat she couldn't think of leaving anything behind, even if it would mean stuffing themselves.

"No problem, but make sure you leave some room for dessert."

"Alright, but I don't think so. Thanks anyway," Annika replied. Her hair fell on her bare shoulders in golden waves. The thin straps from her light-yellow dress contrasted with her golden tan complexion that had not faded much from the summer. Her scent of lilac was just noticeable. It was warm in the restaurant. Kurt had unbuttoned his suit jacket. He did not take it off even though some other guests had shed theirs. The dance band was taking a break, but in its place musicians were walking amongst the tables playing gypsy music on violin and mandolin.

"Annika, I've been looking for a place where I can build a summer home someday. I've been working on a plan for one and I think it's going to be pretty nice. I have yet to find a place that I'm really happy with, though. Do you have any ideas about where you might like to spend the summers?"

"In Southampton."

"Excuse me?"

"Oh nothing, just a private joke. I wouldn't know where. There are so many beautiful places around here."

"My main concern is that it can't be too far from town and it has to be close to the water so I can go fishing and boating."

"There are so many great places . . . Marstrand is beautiful, with the old fortress and everything. There are lots of interesting people to watch."

"Yes, I love Marstrand, if it weren't for having to wait so long for the ferries. I would have to get up in the middle of night to get to work on time. I know there's been talk about building at least one more bridge there. Perhaps then I would reconsider."

"Yes, but the ferries are part of its charm. Then how about Kungsbacka, Särö, Tjörn or Stenungsund? They're all neat coastal communities, and with their own special charm."

"You're right, and that's what makes it so hard to choose. I think that I could be content with any of those places."

"I would." Annika concluded. "Särö is a little expensive, but it could be fun to have royalty for neighbors. Kungsbacka has everything, but there are a lot of people there. The Kungsbacka Fjord is nicely protected for boating, even though it's a little shallow for fishing and sailing, unless one goes further out, like to Gottskär."

"It's nice, but the road out there is quite narrow and curvy. If you get stuck behind one slow car, it's almost impossible to get around," Kurt pointed out. "It is one thing for woman to be . . ."

"Funny, funny," she interrupted him. "It's kind of weird that all the old roads curve back and forth. Why didn't they realize that going straight is shorter?" Annika mused.

"Too much Aquavit probably, that will do it to you," Kurt replied. "I'd like to show you the plans of the house and see what you think about them."

Kurt signaled for the cigarette girl. He purchased a large cigar, ogling the girl's deep cut dress. His focus moved to her behind as she walked away.

"Be careful so your eyes don't pop out when you stare at her like that," Annika chided him.

"Do I detect a trace of jealousy? You have no reason to be jealous. ou have everything that she has and better proportioned. You don't want the poor girl to have to go through the trouble to dress up all sexy like that, and then not have anyone notice, do you? Have a heart." He grinned reassuringly at Annika.

"I wouldn't lose any sleep over it if I were you. I'm sure she gets her fair share of attention."

"You're probably right. I guess I'm just an old softie." Kurt was now responding to Annika's advances with her legs.

The band was playing again and the dance floor was filling up. Kurt and Annika had finished their dinners. No seconds for Annika but Kurt ordered the Baked Alaska for dessert, coffee and a glass of Cognac for himself and Green Chartreuse for Annika.

"I'm surprised you like that liqueur, it's so strong. I don't think they make anything stronger," Kurt said.

"I love it, but you're right, it is very strong, so you can only take a tiny sip of it at a time."

"How about a dance?" he asked. "It would probably help to settle the dinner and make room for the dessert."

"Sure. I'd love to," she said smiling warmly at him.

Kurt stood up and assisted Annika, pulling back her chair. He followed her out to the dance floor, taking a chance on what sort of dance music would come next. The dance was slow and Kurt appreciated Annika's resting her head on his shoulder. He held her firmly as they moved about the floor. A feeling of contentment washed over Annika. It felt right to be in Kurt's arms. Kurt enjoyed the intimacy of Annika's warm body against his own. He liked the sweet fragrance of her perfume. After a second dance they returned to the table as the dessert arrived. It was huge, decorated with marzipan flowers and waffle wafers. However, there were no cherries as promised by the server.

"I think that if we finish this, we'll both get sick. This would have been enough for dinner!" Annika exclaimed.

"Alaska, I wouldn't mind going back to America pretty soon again, and spending a little more time there, but not as far as to Alaska," Kurt said dreamily. "But, it would be much more fun to have some nice company."

"Alaska, that's not part of America is it?" Annika asked.

"Well it's a territory of the USA, but it is not connected to the continental USA. Canada comes in-between. It's a nice place if you are into wild things. No, I was more thinking of the east coast. I would like to visit New York and perhaps even Canada. I have a friend who lives there, in St. John, Canada. It's a nice area. He's a captain for the Swedish - American Line."

"As long as I don't run into any polar bears . . . I guess, I could enjoy that too."

"Good. There's a ship leaving tomorrow afternoon. Can you be ready by then?" Kurt asked her enthusiastically.

"Are you serious?"

"Absolutely! Why not?"

"Even if I had not obligated myself to go to work in Stockholm, which I have, I couldn't get my pass and visa in order that fast."

"How about the next one, in seven more days?" he persisted.

"No, no thank you. I have an obligation to work for the Liljekronas, and that's what I'm going to do for the next four months, at least. It will help me sort things out about what I want to do with myself. Also, I couldn't leave my job at Dad's shop just like that. He needs enough time to find someone else to fill my shoes."

"That will probably take at least two people."

"Maybe so, because I have such big feet."

"No, no, you don't and that's not what I meant," said Kurt, slightly flustered.

"I know, but you know, I'm really looking forward to going to Stockholm for a while. I think it's going to be exciting and I expect that I will learn a lot. But I will miss you . . . a lot." Annika reached over and took his hand.

"Are you going to pick up that silly Stockholm dialect by the time you get back?"

"Oh, I doubt it," she said, looking a little indignant.

"Annika, I care a lot for you. I can tell that your mind is made up, so I'm not going to press my point . . ."

"However," she smiled.

"However," he repeated.

"I'm really going to miss you. You know my mother wants me to marry a rich girl, and I realize that marrying you would probably alienate me from her, but I feel so strongly about you that I'm willing to do that, and from the rest of the world too, if that's what it would take to have you. You know that I have done quite well for myself financially, and I'm only getting started. I'm going to own this city before I'm done. I could take good care of you."

"And you're modest too," she added. "I don't need to be taken care of. Last year I won ten thousand crowns at the state lottery," she lied.

"Really? What did you do with all that money?" Kurt asked.

"I gave it to my mother so she can have a little nest egg if something should happen to Dad."

"I'm not going to apologize for being successful. I'm proud of it. I just wanted you to know that you will have it well with me and that . . . that I love you."

"That's the first time you told me that you love me," Annika said in wonder.

"I don't use those words lightly, but now I know that I love you."

"I think I love you too, but I still have to go. I've promised."

"Okay, but why don't you call them and tell them that you'll start there on the first day of 1942. Then I can ride there with you, and we can celebrate New Year's Eve together. You can work for a while and then I'll come and get you when you're ready."

"Okay."

"You said okay?" Kurt said in astonishment.

"Yes, I did." She smiled at his confusion.

"You mean that I can ride up to Stockholm and we will celebrate New Year's together?" He still couldn't quite believe that he heard right.

"I have always loved you Kurt, but at times you haven't exactly acted as though I meant that much to you. I don't want a one-sided relationship. I think you've changed. This was the first time you actually told me that you love me. And . . . you chose me over your mother. I hope you meant it."

"I do, I really do." He reached under the table for her hands which he grasped firmly, resting their joined hands on her knees.

"You've made me very happy, Annika."

In July 1941, a German train exploded in Krylbo at the railroad station. Sabotage was suspected. The deed likely was a response to Sweden's acquiescing in Germany's crossing Sweden with troops from Norway to Finland. That controversial government decision was a clear violation of Sweden's neutrality status and risked bringing Sweden into the war. The King lobbied strongly for permitting the transports, and the Swedish government did not feel it had a choice. That same month, Sweden's military draft was extended from 175 to 450 days. Sweden's industry was closely tied to Germany's. They cooperated on several industrial projects, and their banking systems were closely linked, as well.

"Welcome to Stockholm. How do you like it so far?" Kurt greeted Annika as the train was pulling across a small bridge into the Stockholm's Central Station. The bridge amplified the da - dunk, da - dunk sound from the train.

Annika had dozed off for a few minutes. "Are we there?" she asked, a little sleepy eyed, sittin up quickly.

"No, not there, here," he teased her. "I concede that it is a beautiful city. Look over there! You can see the Parliament Building and Grand Hotel, over there, right next to the Opera House. That's where we'll be staying . . ."

"We'll be staying at the Opera House?" It may not be that easy to sleep there."

"Actually, it's quite easy to sleep there. I went there once, and I slept like a baby through the whole performance. Anyway, it says here, 'Stockholm, the capital of Sweden, its largest city, has a population of six million. Hmm . . . That can't be right. I understand there are only six million people in all of Sweden.'" Kurt was reading from a travel book. "Stockholm was founded in the year 1252 by Birger Jarl. To aid in its defense it was built on an island. Stockholm includes 62 major islands, connected by 40 bridges. It is located on the east coast of Sweden, on the Baltic Sea, 300 miles northeast of Gothenburg . . . with completely different terrain. The west coast has salt water whereas the east is half salt and half fresh water. The west coast is smoother with the east being more rugged and forested. Bla bla bla. Stockholm has the Royal Palace, the seat of the government and the Supreme Court among its many attractions. There are numerous old structures that have been painstakingly renovated, and preserved. It's beautiful castles, parks and museums are enjoyed by people of all ages," he continued.

"Are you trying to sell me on Stockholm or what?" Annika asked, wondering at his enthusiasm.

"No, I was just reading from the travel guide. But I don't have anything against Stockholm other than, perhaps, it is full of stuck-up snobs."

"Well we have our fair share of those in Gothenburg also, don't we?" said Annika, responding with a left hook to his jab.

"Be that as it may, let's just try to have a good time while I'm here, okay?" Kurt extending an olive branch. "Let's check into our room first, and we can go from there."

The first item on their agenda was to check into their hotel room. Annika stood behind Kurt as he registered.

Mr. and Mrs. Noble." Kurt signed in and got the keys. She felt a little uneasy when he introduced them as Mr. and Mrs. Nobel, whether from guilt or excitement, she wasn't sure. She did like the sound of "Mr. & Mrs. Nobel" though. She repeated to herself Mrs. Annika Nobel. It was a beautiful old hotel with extensive details in carved wood, crystal chandeliers in the high ceilings, and exclusive art. The bell boy showed them to their room. Kurt handed him a tip and they were alone.

"What a beautiful place!" said Annika. "I could live here forever. This place must be quite old. They don't make wood carvings like that anymore."

"Yea, it's probably the best that Stockholm has to offer." Kurt informed her.

"Look here! One can see the harbor from here, the Royal Palace, the City Hall. One can see everything from our window."

The room was comfortably furnished with a king-size bed against the back wall. A round table and matching stuffed chairs faced the picture window.

"Look, the island shuttles, and two large sail ships."

"I read that they use them old ships as school ships for naval officers," said Kurt.

"Over there, is the Tivoli. You can see the roller coaster from here, wow," said Annika. She began to pull the curtain closed.

"You can leave them open Annika. On the sixth floor it's not very likely that anyone can see in."

The fruit bowl on the table included a few candy bars. Kurt and Annika faced each other, both feeling slightly awkward. He gently pulled her toward him, kissing her first on her forehead, then the tip of her nose, and finally their lips met in a warm and tender expression of their mutual attraction.

It is getting dark outside." Annika pointed out. "We should probably get going." Kurt rested on the bed while Annika put away her clothes. She had the radio on low. She had removed her skirt and blouse and wore just her slip and under garments. Kurt pretended he was sleeping while he watched her every move. His growing arousal would soon give him away. As she walked near the bed he reached out, grabbed hold of her arm and pulled her down to him. He could feel her heart beating rapidly, her warm body pressing against his. He reached around her, slowly massaging her back, kissing her desirously.

Annika moved his arms and stood up. "I'm not ready for babies yet, so we better slow down. We should get ready if we are going out," she reminded him.

"Turn up the radio, quick," Kurt directed Annika. "Hurry!"

"Swedish radio has learned that today, December 7, at 7:55 a.m., Pearl Harbor, Hawaii, was subject to a massive Japanese air raid. There was substantial destruction. Several US war ships were trapped in the harbor. Nineteen US ships were sunk or damaged. More than 3000 military personnel were killed. The US fleet appears to have been taken in bed, despite several warnings of the attack. Stay tuned for further information."

"Oh my God! We are really in it now. How can the Japanese be so stupid, thinking they can take on the US?" Kurt began pacing the floor.

"What's going to happen now?" Annika asked, bewildered.

"Well, we're in the middle of a world war. Maybe now when the US is forced into it, this could be the beginning of the end . . ."

"You don't really mean that?" Annika asked in disbelief.

"No, no. I didn't mean the end of the world," he said, mustering a smile, "I meant the end of the war. I don't see how things can get too much worse, just about everything is prohibited and there are shortages of everything."

The following day the US declared war on Japan, and two days later Germany declared war on the US.

Kurt took a cold shower and they left. The tram took them along the tree lined shore walks. They rode through an upscale business district, passing several foreign embassies, all with impressive facades.

They drove past the Opera House and several museums, which easily could have been taken for Royal Palaces.

Riding past the British Embassy, Annika could not help but think about Billy for a moment. What was he doing? Where was he? Was he all right? Why had she not heard from him for so long?

"A penny for your thoughts," Kurt offered, startling her slightly.

"Oh, I was just thinking about all the people walking out there, what they do for a living and how they fit into this world. That will be a penny please," she said, holding out her hand. Kurt playfully bit into it.

"We are getting off at the next station," Kurt warned.

"What? Is it inside the animal zoo where we are going?"

"Yes, it's on top of the hill with a pretty impressive view. You will like it." He assured her.

They stepped off the tram at Skansen, on Djurgården, a peninsula with several impressive museums, the Tivoli, estates of dignitaries and royalty and a recreational park. They thoroughly enjoyed themselves, the company and the grandiose setting. he restaurant had been decorated with balloons, paper streamers and party favors at each plate. The place was full, and a live band stood for the entertainment. At midnight they were dazzled by fireworks launched all around the city, brightening up the sky in a cascade of sparkling and snapping lights. At the stroke of midnight hundreds of church bells all over Stockholm began ringing in the New Year, simultaneously. For a few moments all inhibitions were lost, and kisses and Champaign flowed freely. "Happy New Year, happy 1942."

Kurt put his strong arms around Annika, sliding his hands down her back and placing them firmly on her buttocks, pressing her body tightly against his. Annika, feeling lightheaded from the wine and the atmosphere responded willingly to his advance.

"Have you had enough dancing for tonight?" he asked nuzzling her ear. "Are you ready to go back to our room?"

"Mm-hmm," she murmured.

Outside the park, Kurt hailed a cab. The driver had two near collisions driving them back to the hotel, having difficulty concentrating on his driving with Kurt and Annika carrying on in the rear seat, which was visible through his rear-view mirror.

The streets were still crowded, many in lavish costumes, having attended masquerade parties, blowing their horns, singing, laughing, dancing and making spectacles of themselves. Sporadic fireworks were set off all around them, echoing against the house facades, but Kurt and Annika were obliviousto their surroundings.

Back at their hotel, Kurt guided a rather tipsy Annika into their room. Annika had never experienced this sensation before, of floating on a cloud. She was enjoying the attention it brought her and she was determined to play the role to the hilt. Annika had Kurt sit on the bed while she poured them each a glass of the complimentary champagne that had been brought to their room. She tuned the radio to Louis Armstrong playing his *"Wild Man Blues."* In tune with the beat, she began to move around the room seductively moving her arms and caressing her sides. She worked her way over to the bed, leaned over, supporting herself on her palms, her breasts nearly escaping their confinement. "Are you enjoying the entertainment?" she asked seductively, slurring noticeably. Kurt reached out for her, but she quickly retreated . . . undulating . . . moving in rhythm with the music.

"Love that perfume you're wearing. Is it Lilac?" Kurt asked, finding it increasingly difficult to control his growing desire.

Annika turned around, inviting him to unzip her dress. Hands shaking, Kurt complied, again seeking to pull her down on the bed. Annika insisted on first finishing her performance. She turned around, moving to the beat of the music. She unbuckled his belt before unbuttoning his pants. Feeling Annika's fingers working his buttons was almost unbearable for Kurt, and his excitement only hampered her efforts. After what seemed like an eternity to Kurt, Annika removed his trousers, methodically placing them on a hanger. She proceeded with taking off her dress, and hung it in the closet. Her slip followed. Facing Kurt, she placed one foot at a time on the edge of the bed, unrolling her stockings. Taking the champagne bottle, she walked over and sat down next to Kurt. She refilled Kurt's glass, raised the bottle and gulped the bubbly wine straight from the bottle, spilling half of its content down her chin . . . onto her breasts . . . soaking her stomach and panties. "Oops!" she giggled, "I think I missed," her speech slurring. "Not fair . . . that I'm the only one that's wet," she said, and before he could stop her she poured the rest of the bottle over him.

"Oh no, don't waste that good champagne!" he cried out, attempting to stop her.

This was more than Kurt could take. He grabbed her arm and pulled her down on the bed, despite her half-hearted protest, before she willingly and enthusiastically pressed her partially opened mouth against his.

"I sure love you Annika," Kurt said with conviction, "you're something else."

"Thanks . . . I think."

"How about getting married? Forget about the job and come back with me."

"Thanks for asking. You say you love me now, but what about after we get married? Will you love me then? Maybe someday? I'm just not ready right now."

"You don't need to worry about whether I will love you when we're married; I've always loved married women."

She ignored his tease.

Annika started her new position in Stockholm. Her duties were to look after the Liljekrona's daughter Annette, to do some light housekeeping chores and to prepare supper. Annika enjoyed working for the Liljekronas and met a number of interesting people from their social circle. Her salary was modest, but it included room and board. The experience was of greater value to Annika, than the monetary reward.

The Liljekronas lived in a modern home a few miles northeast of Stockholm. It was clearly the home of an artist. The unique home was molded into the hillside, high enough to offer a spectacular view of Lake Mälaren below and far enough down the steep slope to make the beach accessible. Mr. Liljekrna was tall and slender and in his mid-forties. He had a full, but well-trimmed beard. He could easily have been mistaken for Abraham Lincoln. He was friendly and easy going, somewhat eccentric and clearly of high intellect. Mrs. Liljekrona was a large woman and shared her husband's easy-going disposition, most of the time. Mr. Liljekrona would strip down to a robe as soon as he got home. He spent most of his time reading, playing his instruments or listening to classical music. The Liljekronas had an impressive collection of instruments from every corner of the word and Mr. Liljekrona appeared to be proficient in them all. They had a large music room with picture windows facing Lake Mälaren. The focal point in the room was a white grand piano. Annika would on occasion make music with the Liljekronas and they encouraged her with her playing.

The Liljekronas were gone most of the day and often for several days at the time. The yard was naturally protected from insight, other than from the lake side, and Annika and Annette spent most of their time down by the water swimming and sunbathing, in eider their own large pool, or down at the dock. On one occasion the Liljekronas came home while Annika was sunbathing on the dock. She had the radio on and did not hear them until they were standing right next to her. She sat up quickly and shielded herself with her arms.

"Oh, sorry we startled you," Mrs. Liljekrona apologized.

"Don't mind us, I'm going for a swim," Mr. Liljekrona added. He walked over to the diving board, dropped his robe, took a few quick steps and jumped, before catapulting into the brownish lake water, making a terrific splash. Mrs. Liljekrona joined him but with a less dramatic entrance, climbing down the stairs. After that day, Mr. Liljekrona would walk around the dock in the nude most of the time, even when boats puttered by or Annika was there. Mrs. Liljekrona would only lie in the nude on the dock, but she didn't seem to mind or even notice her husband's exhibitions. Annika would sun bathe topless when Mrs. Liljekrona did. Like all small Swedish children, Annette did not wear a swimsuit when playing by the water.

CHAPTER 10

January, 1942 Kurt and Eva to NewYork

Kurt returned to Gothenburg the following day, and he was scheduled to leave for New York the same day. He had to rush as the Gripsholm was scheduled to depart four hours after his arrival at the Central Station, and he had to stop by the office for a fresh change of clothing, a shower and then be at the dock two hours before departure. Eva was there to greet him at the train station. She helped him pack his bags while she filled him in on the latest news. Kurt placed an envelope on the desk of Mrs. Peterson as they headed off to the dock, where the magnificent Gripsholm was waiting. Kurt cleared the Swedish customs, a simple process for those leaving the country, and then invited Eva to tour the ship.

"Come on Eva let me show you Gripsholm. You'll love it."

"Do we have time?" Eva asked apprehensively.

"There is plenty of time, and they always warn you by blowing the whistle before they leave." Kurt calmed her. "There is plenty of time. We aren't leaving for another two hours. They got delayed some."

"Well okay then."

"We'll do the top deck first, with the movie theater, bowling alley, exercise room and the swimming pool. Then we'll do the shopping and dining decks. They also have a health center, a dentist, a salon and a massage parlor with manicure there." Kurt bolstered as if the ship was his.

Of course he also showed her his cabin. It was neatly crafted in wood and had the basic furniture, one couch, one desk and chair, a stuffed chair and two single beds.

"This is so nice. I can understand now why you always speaks so highly about Gripsholm, why the Gripsholm is your favorite ship and why you enjoy traveling so much." It was all about luxury and being pampered. Eva laid down on one of the beds.

"It's so comfortable that I could go to sleep here," she said.

"Just a minute, I have to take care of one matter. I'll be right back," he said, as he closed the door to the cabin. He returned momentarily. "Okay," he told her. "Do you remember last year when we got your passport?"

"Yes" she shuddered, anticipating what he had done.

"I just cleared it with the purser. You're coming along."

"Oh no I can't. I don't have my passport with me. It's in my desk, and tomorrow . . ."

"Tomorrow will come and go without you. I gave all instructions to Mrs. Peterson about what to do, and regarding your passport, unless I took the wrong one, here it is. Also, they do have a telegraph onboard, as you know, so if there is anything I've forgotten, then we will deal with it as it comes. This will be fun, and you always ask me when I'm going to take you along. Well this is it, so enjoy."

"Kurt you're crazy. I don't have anything to wear, or my toothbrush," she protested.

"They have everything we need here onboard and when we get to New York we can get all the things we don't need."

"Oh Kurt! You're absolutely crazy! For sure? She no longer protested. As they pulled out from the cheering and flag-waving crowd, Eva and Kurt were shopping. By the time they dropped off the harbor pilot, Eva was at home on the vessel.

"That was a pretty nice crossing," said Eva. "That constant rolling though will get you eventually. I should have been more careful with the sun. The burn isn't helping anything."

Eva was glad when they pulled into the New York's harbor. The constant slow rolling back and forth had finally gotten the best of her and she had had to spend the last two days in her cot.

In New York they had a suite on the 44th floor with a view of the harbor, the Statue of Liberty, the Empire State Building and some tall-mast ships in the harbor. Yet, Eva was still so under the weather by the time they arrived at their hotel room, that she took a rest while Kurt went exploring on his own.

Cecilia was just on her way out when Kurt called, but she agreed to join him. Thirty minutes later she pulled up in her red Volvo outside the hotel. Kurt got in and twenty minutes later they pulled into Cecilia's driveway. Her home was huge, with cedar siding and large windows. It was tucked away in the trees, next to a golf course.

"Your house is stunning!" Kurt exclaimed.

"Yes, it's nice, but it gets a little lonely here at times in this big house. It was okay when I was married and we entertained a lot. Now it's really too big, just for me. I've been thinking of moving to an apartment I have next to the office, but it is hard to get rid of this home. I have a lot of good memories from here, and some not so good."

"Boy, in Sweden you would have to be the King, to get to live like this. I can't believe though that you are driving a Swedish car, when there are American cars all over the place," Kurt said in wonder.

"Well, that's why. The American cars are so common here that they're nothing special. A Volvo, however, I don't think you saw another one on the road. They're special here."

"All the same, I'm bringing a Chevrolet with me home. Maybe next time I will bring a Volvo here."

"Maybe I can be of some help. I have connections," she offered, returning Kurt's hug.

"Thanks for your warm hospitality when I was in Sweden, by the way. I had a wonderful experience there. I hope you can stay for supper. It will be good, and perhaps there will be some entertainment after."

"I guess I can, but I have to call my secretary, Eva. She is with me on this trip but wasn't feeling good so she stayed behind at the hotel to rest. Let me make some arrangements and we'll see." Kurt called the hotel and ordered up dinner for Eva. "Eva, I'm going to be a little delayed. You should go to bed early anyway so you will be ready for tomorrow, and don't worry about anything, get some rest okay."

Cecilia was a good cook and Kurt enjoyed his steak, which was about as big as he had ever seen. But he finished it all, along with the baked potato and beans.

"That was a great steak. Apparently you remember that I like my meat well done."

"Glad you liked it."

Cecilia's home was filled with artifacts from all over the world, including several from Sweden.

After dinner Cecilia put on the coffee and they moved into the living room.

"Why don't you sit here and I have a little surprise for you."

She excused herself and returned a few moments later in an authentic belly dancing costume. "How do you like it? It's one of my favorite costumes. A little bold perhaps, but you should appreciate that."

She turned on the music and began her routine. First, she danced a little at a distance, but then she moved closer and made Kurt part of her act. Even though the air conditioner was turned on, Cecilia was perspiring heavily and again excused herself to take a shower. This time Kurt followed her into the large bathroom.

About four in the morning Kurt returned to his hotel. He was still tuned to Swedish time.

"I feel much better this morning. Did you say that we were going shopping this morning?" Said Eva as Kurt was trying to sneak into bed.

"Let's rest a few more hours, have breakfast and the stores should be open by then.

They spent the morning together before venturing out on a shopping spree, visiting some warehouses that appeared to have everything, and in large quantities. Kurt purchased Eva several outfits and accessories. He helped her pick out some negligees, and Eva helped Kurt pick out some presents for home.

"Kurt, you are going to have to excuse me but I'm getting really sleepy again. It's difficult to get used to the time change."

Kurt and Cecilia continued to work some more on her belly dancing. Cecilia had actually taken some more classes since her rusty performance in Sweden and was eager to show off her new moves. She had intentionally left off a layer of her costume, so her top was now transparent. It had the intended effect on Kurt.

CHAPTER 11

January, 1942 Kurt courts Annika

Annika had not been gone long before Kurt missed her. He called frequently and pleaded with her to come back to Gothenburg.

"Annika, I have great news. I brought home a new Dodge on my last trip to the US. It's gorgeous! You'll love it!"

"What color is it?"

"It's blue and white with blue seats. You'll love it, and it has lots of room for a large family."

"Family? You are only one."

"Well I've been thinking about that. I think it is time for us to move on."

"What do you mean? To break up?"

"No, no, heavens no. I meant that we should get married and make some small Annika's and Kurt's. I need someone to take over the business when I'm gone."

"So you want me to provide you with some heirs for your business."

"No, well yes but I want to marry you because I love you very much and I miss you very much. I now feel that I'm prepared to settle down, have children, and I promise you that I will be a devoted husband and father."

"But I don't have a job there . . ."

"My dear Annika, you don't have to work. I'll take care of you, us. You can do whatever you like during the day, besides taking care of our kids. Besides, you are so beautiful that you could get a job any time you like, on that asset alone. I just read that Zara Leander is the highest paid performer in Europe. I think mostly because of her sexy appearance."

"You mean Goring's girl friend."

"Well, yes, so? She might be the reason for why Sweden is still neutral."

"She's very good. Her deep voice is so sexy." Annika said.

"Perhaps, but not even close to you." Kurt complimented her.

"What do you mean? I can't even hold a tune."

"So? You are still many times sexier than Zara, and you can play the fiddle."

"I'm not sure that being sexy is enough to base a relation on?" Annika concluded.

"Well, it doesn't hurt; besides, you are also one of the most talented people that I know. You seem to be able to do anything and I'm sure that you will be a super mom."

"Cut it out! You're embarrassing me. I'm not that great . . . am I? I'm getting a little old perhaps."

"No, Annika. You are most certainly not getting old." Kurt insisted adamantly.

"Well thank you."

Annika was hesitant, but Kurt persisted. He had focused on her weakest link . . . motherhood . . . the prospect of having their own family . . . children.

"Well I was thinking in terms of starting a family, and dad is getting worse."

Given her father's failing health and Kurt's persistence, Annika decided that it was time to return home. In early April Kurt came up for a visit. They dined and danced at Cicel's the day before Easter Sunday and Annika accepted his marriage proposal there. They exchanged engagement rings which in Swedish tradition, they placed on their left hands, since the left hand has a vein that leads directly to the heart. The rings represented the dowry given in the old days. The bride would then receive a wedding band during the wedding ceremony to be worn with the engagement ring. The man, if judged by his rings, would remain only engaged.

Annika quit her job and two weeks later she returned to Gothenburg to join Kurt. She moved into Kurt's small apartment behind his downtown office. Soon he had another suggestion.

"Annika, I have an apartment that just became vacant. It's in the older part of town but it's in a very charming building. I think it will be perfect for us until we can find something better."

"Really?" Annika looked up from reading a magazine.

"The only thing is that it will need some work. What do you think? Are you up to it?" he goaded her.

"Sure. It won't take all that much to beat this place," she responded eagerly.

"Well, it will take quite a bit of work," he admitted. "You don't mind?"

"Let's go!" Annika said.

"It sure will be nice when this war is over," Kurt sighed. " With Germany invading Russia . . who knows what will happen? I'm not even sure who we should support, though I guess that the Germans are still better than the communists. Let's take the truck; it's simpler, since we can't use gasoline in the cars." He continued.

"Didn't you just buy a new gen-gas trailer, so you could use the car any time you please?" she asked.

"I did, but it's too much work to start the fire in it and to keep the fire cool enough so it leaves some exhaust for the motor to run on," he whined.

"Well, you have to do what you have to do."

"That big ugly gen-gas attachment spoils the look of the car anyway. I've ordered a unit that is mostly hidden in the trunk. Then at least you don't have to look at it."

"Then where are you going to store the wood chips or the coal, if you fill the trunk with the unit?" Annika asked.

"There is still enough room for the coal. It doesn't take that much coal to make it work. They've improved on them so it takes a lot less smoke now to make them run."

Kurt had not exaggerated the need for repairs, but the apartment did not lack in charm. They had to walk through the wrought-iron front gate and through a vaulted opening into the court yard, before negotiating three flights of stairs to reach the apartment. The building faced a town-square that hosted a farmer's market twice a week. The main highway to Stockholm ran behind the building and beyond it was the main railroad yard. The apartment's high ceilings, sculptured cornices and beautiful parquet floors charmed its residents, but all the walls needed to be re-papered or chain.

Annika removed her street clothes and slipped into one of Kurt's old dress shirts.

"I'm not sure that I can concentrate on painting with you running around looking that delicious," Kurt confessed.

Annika pranced over to him with a mischievous smile and kissed him. "First comes first. We have to get this place in order first," she reminded him.

She knew how much she was tempting Kurt and took every opportunity to tease him further. She found pleasure in his frustration and enjoyed the power her sexuality gave her. She would step up on the stepladder and reach up when she knew that Kurt was watching her.

They spent all day and most of the evening working on the apartment. Kurt ran down to the hot dog stand and picked up their dinner, which they consumed sitting on the floor.

Despite a mountain of protests from Kurt's family, Kurt and Annika were married three weeks later by a judge in a civil ceremony.

"Lisa and Camilla thanks for coming."

"Are we the only ones?"

"Yes, for now. We will have a party later on when things have calmed down some. We are taking my side out for dinner on Friday. Of course, you guys are invited. 18:00 at Leksands Gården. I hope you can make it. I hope Sven can also come and Lisa you can invite anyone you like." Annika offered.

"Thank you. I will come alone," said Lisa.

"So, you are the only invited guests tonight. Because of Kurt's parents' resistance, we decided not to invite any relatives. Not even from my side. Like I said, we will do it later."

"What's the matter?" Annika could tell that something bothered Kurt.

"Dad died. He passed away this morning from pneumonia. He never got over the cold he caught in the park, sitting on a cold bench to long. Who would think that would be deadly."

"Perhaps he died from old age. He was almost 100 years old." Annika offered.

"Perhaps."

The relationship between Annika and her mother-in-law deteriorated even further, if possible, after Mr. Nobel's passing. Kurt was the last son of eleven children, including four sons, to move out. He was the youngest and the most spoiled, and his mother had not planned on losing him. When she learned that Kurt had married Annika, she was furious and set out to wreck their marriage, with the eager assistance of other members of the Nobel family.

Not long after their marriage, Kurt began thinking of a trip to the US again, he told Annika.

"You must be insane!" she exclaimed. "Do you know that last year 24 Swedish . . ." she emphasized, "ships were sunk from being torpedoed or from hitting mines? You can't possibly mean what you say," Annika declared in disbelief.

"That was before Sweden entered into a safe passage agreement with the fighting parties." Kurt explained. "Germany needs our iron ore for their war machine and they are paying well in gold. I don't know of any passenger ship that has been sunk."

"Yes, with gold that they have stolen from occupied countries and from the Jews," Annika responded.

"Well that I can't do anything about. It would make little sense to stand up for principles, in this case, and be wiped out by the Germans in the process. Besides, was it not for the Germans, Finland would have been lost to the Soviets a long time ago, and so would Sweden."

"It still doesn't seem right to deal with Hitler," Annika persisted. "And it's more or less suicide to travel on the open sea now," she added. She walked over to the window to water her flowers. She was blessed with a green thumb and her window overflowed with a variety of vigorous plants.

"I saw the letter you were drafting to the German government guaranteeing that you were an 'Arisk merchant'. What does that mean?"

"You know the Germans are obsessed with the Jews and they don't want to do business with anyone that works with Jews. I have to do business with the Germans. They control all transit and I couldn't import coffee or anything if I didn't cooperate with them. It isn't like . . . like I'm laying off any Jews. I never had any Jews working for me in the first place, except for Mrs. Greenberg in New York. But that is a completely different operation."

"It's not right," Annika insisted.

"I agree with you, 100 percent. But at the same time . . . I also think that one should be permitted to do business with whomever one chooses or doesn't choose. But I agree. It's not a simple question. We'll see."

"I've been thinking about volunteering with the Swedish Women's Driving Regiment or with the Red Cross. They are both recruiting for help," Annika said.

"Why don't you hold off on that, at least, until you can confirm if you actually are pregnant?" Kurt cautioned. "I've invested a fortune in war-bonds and we put war-stamps on all our mail-deliveries, so we're doing our part," Kurt assured her. He squashed his cigarette.

"How would you like to see a movie tonight? I saw they're playing *Ninotchka* with Greta Garbo at the Saga Theater," Annika said. "it's a comedy making fun of Russian communism."

"So much for our neutrality," Kurt smirked.

"Yes, if it was about Germany it would have been censured, like they did to Charlie Chaplin's Dictator movie. "Annika added.

"Yes, and like with the Karl Gerhard's play. The Stockholm police chief prohibited them from singing the number *Mein Kampf* because it had the same name as Hitler's book, but it also has the under meaning of an old worn out horse." Kurt shook his head. "It didn't even help to appeal to the government," said Kurt.

"Yes, it doesn't appear as though anyone cares about what's right anymore. There is also a Zara Leander movie playing at Vågen, but that's probably mostly German propaganda," Annika speculated

"You know, it's kind of interesting . . . did you hear about the scientist Leo Kall, that invented a truth serum?" Kurt asked.

"No, I can't say I have," Annika admitted.

"Can you imagine the consequences if everyone always spoke the truth?"

"Doesn't sound like a major problem to me."

"When we saw someone we didn't care for, it would be no more 'nice to meet you.' It would be something like, 'oh no, not you again, you boring, self-centered slob.' It could lead to all kinds of problems," Kurt assured her.

"Yes, that could get ugly," Annika agreed. "You would stop asking for people's opinion, that's for sure."

"I don't know. I don't care much for all this superficial stuff anyway. Maybe it could work. Wouldn't it be refreshing if everyone spoke the truth all the time?" Kurt proposed.

"You would only ask for someone's opinion if you really wanted it."

"What would you do if the government asked you if you barter with coffee and whatever else, and you had to tell the truth? You would end up in jail for sure," Annika reminded him.

"Did you hear that they lowered the allocations for alcohol to only three liters a month?" Kurt asked. He patted her behind as she walked passed him.

"Yes, but that ought to be enough. Besides, my mother will not use up her allocation. I'm sure she would be happy to trade her coupons for some coffee," Annika said. "It's Tuesday today and we have hot water. Do you want me to fill the tub for a bath?"

"That's probably the worst thing about living in an apartment building, that we can only have hot water two days a week. I like my hot baths. I think I may take my showers at work, there are no restrictions there," Kurt said. "We also need to go up to the loft and make sure there are no burnable items there, in case of a bombing raid, I was informed this morning. I think Sweden is becoming just as communistic as Russia. The government is telling us everything about how to live our lives."

"Come on now, there is still a great deal of difference," Annika argued. "You can own your own business here and you get to keep the profit. You couldn't do that in Russia. . .."

"True, but the Swedish government makes sure there is no profit to keep," Kurt sighed.

". . . and we don't have a bunch of government spies running around checking on everything we do."

"We hope we don't. But we don't know for sure," Kurt countered.

CHAPTER 12

June 1942 - John visits Sweden

The war escalated. By mid-1942 Japan's red and white flag with its rising sun flew over most land in the western Pacific Ocean. German submarines effectively attacked allied convoys. The main Allied forces in the Pacific were the Americans and the Australians. They stopped the Japanese move toward Australia in the crucial five-day battle of the Coral Sea. US Hornet warplanes attacked Japanese soil for the first time in sixteen air-raids. In June the Battle of Midway played out. Americans had broken the Japanese code. They knew of Japan's intent to take Midway and were able to stop the Japanese fleet, destroying 322 planes, 4 carriers and several other ships. The battle of Midway ended the Japanese threat on Hawaii and turned the tide of the war.

Two weeks after the wedding Lisa stopped by. "I got a letter from . . . guess who?" Lisa asked. She was breathing heavily from running. "From John!" she shouted. "Can you believe it?! He's coming to Sweden in one month. He's going to attend a seminar here in Gothenburg for three months, and he wants to see me. Can you believe it?" Lisa danced with excitement.

"Really? You're kidding!"

"No, cross my heart. Here . . . you can read it . . . and he has seen Billy, and Billy's fine. Here, you're not going to believe this."

"Here, let me read it." Annika grabbed the letter from Lisa's hand.

June 15, 1942

Dear Lisa.

I don't know if you remember me, but we met at Liseberg almost two years ago. I was that British naval officer that you met, together with Billy Jones. That evening we had a terrific thunderstorm and all the lights went out. It was also the eve to the morning when Germany invaded Poland and our ship had to leave immediately.

"All right already, I know who you are," Annika injected impatiently.

"I have often thought about you and I now wish that I had written you sooner. My girlfriend had broken up with me when I joined the Navy. Considering how far away you live, and the war escalating, I was afraid to get involved again at that time.

I don't know if you are interested in seeing me again. Perhaps you are dating or even married. I'm hoping that your studies have kept you too busy for any social life. I know you were attending medical school in Gothenburg, and I know, first hand, that there is no time for a social life while studying medicine.

I'm coming to Gothenburg on October 15, and I'd love to see you. I'll be attending a seminar on insemination and I'll do some other research there for three months. I'll also attend some classes while I'm there. Perhaps we will be class mates.

I have been doing little but studying since I saw you last. Last week I saw Billy. He was admitted to the hospital adjoining my medical school. We get a lot of military personnel here. I had not seen him for over a year, and I had no idea how to get hold of him. Well it turned out that his ship had been sunk by a German sub. He was picked up by a German supply ship. He was a prisoner of war for four days when the German ship was sunk by a British destroyer. He had to spend two weeks on the destroyer before he was sent to a hospital in London where he had some corrective surgery done on his back. Apparently, the force created by the torpedo lifting the deck compressed his vertebrae. He's all right now and has been discharged from the navy. By total coincidence I ran into him at our outpatient clinic about two weeks ago where he had gone for a checkup. I don't know if I'd have recognized him. He had lost some weight. He saw me first and boy was that a nice surprise. You can tell Annika that he lost all his belongings when his ship went down and he has not been able to get in contact with her. I told him that I still had your address and that I intended to write you and that I would ask you for Annika's address. I sure hope that you're doing well. I would love to see you again. I really treasured the short time we had together. Please write and let me know how you are doing and whether it would be possible to see you again when I get there. It was wrong of me not to write you right away and I deeply regret that I didn't. Perhaps it's not too late to make up for lost time.

Please pass on Billy's address to Annika and please write me soon.

Love, John

"One more thing . . ." she pulled out a note from Billy to Annika. "I got this at the same time."

"Oh God! I can't believe this. I thought the worst had happened to him when I didn't hear from him for so long." Here let me read it," she said her voice breaking as she grabbed the letter with shaky hands. She ripped open the envelope. She recognized Billy's bold but meticulously neat hand writing.

Dearest Annika.

If I knew where to look, I would come to Sweden to look for you, but I have no clue where to look. I just ran into John totally by coincidence. I had not seen him in over a year. I had a few mishaps including our ship being sunk by a German U-boat. In the process I lost everything I had with me, including your address. I tried to write to you from memory, but apparently, I never got the address close enough for my letters to reach you, because they all came back address unknown. After I recovered from my navy mishaps, I was discharged, or rather put in the reserves. I've been working on the knitting machine that I told you about before. It is now in production and it's doing well, beyond expectations. I have also developed some other equipment that appears promising.

I have thought of you every day and it helped me through the four days I had to spend on a German ship as a prisoner of war. Actually, we were treated well by the Germans.

I will keep this short until I know that I have found you again. I pray that this letter finds you well and that I hear from you soon.

Affectionately, Billy

Dear Billy

I could not believe it when I got your letter, and Lisa got a letter from John at the same time, and he's coming here. I'm so happy for her. I know she was very impressed with John and wants to see him again. I was so glad and grateful to hear from you. I had feared the worst when I didn't hear from you for so long. I have thought of you, too, and I often wonder if you are okay and what you're doing. I have a lot to tell you about what I have been doing during this time. I'm not sure how to tell you this but I just got married, only two weeks ago, to a man named Kurt Nobel. He is a local businessman who is involved in a little of everything. I would love it if we could still be friends. I'll always have a special place in my heart for you. One more thing, I'm going to have a baby. I hope you will still be my friend . . .

Dear John.
Thank you so much for your letter. Of course, I remember you. Like you, I haven't had time for any social life either. Of course, I'd love to see you again. I'm really looking forward to your visit. Let me know all the details of what you've been doing and about your arrival so I can meet you. I have . . .

"Can you believe that two weeks after I married Kurt, I hear from Billy? Life is not fair. Kurt is nice but I don't think he knows what love is. Or rather, I think he loves everyone," Annika sighed deeply. "I'm so happy that Billy is safe."

"Isn't it unbelievable?" Lisa jumped with glee. "YEAH!" Annika looked on enviously.

John arrived on October the 15 on the Swedish passenger ship Saga. All three girls and Kurt and Sven were there to greet him. Lisa had a bouquet of mixed flowers that she handed to John as he stepped out of the customs gate. They embraced and just stood there while the others patiently waited their turn to greet John. Tears of joy filled Lisa's eyes and spilled down her cheeks. Annika and Camilla walked over and joined in the embrace. John was smartly dressed in dark trousers and a tan suede blazer with the elbows reinforced in darker suede.

"Boy, you look even better than I remembered," he said to Lisa.

"I'm so happy you made it here safely. After what happened to Billy, I have to admit that I was concerned, and with all the mines floating around patiently waiting for their next victims." Lisa sighed deeply.

"Traveling under a Swedish flag made it quite a bit safer. We saw some German warships out there, but they left us alone," John explained.

"I'm sorry, John, this is Kurt, Annika's husband."

"Nice to meet you, John. I've heard a lot about you. I thought that perhaps you would be wearing a halo."

"Really. Well some of us always appear better from a distance," he responded lightly.

"This is Sven, Camilla's boyfriend," Lisa said.

"My pleasure."

"Boy, you took a risk traveling right now," said Sven, shaking his hand.

"How was the trip? Did you have good weather?" Lisa asked.

"It wasn't bad, even though the ship rolled quite a bit. But considering the time of year it is, it could have been a lot worse. It's great to be here though. I had a strong incentive to make the trip . . . I've been really looking forward to this trip, and especially to seeing Lisa again."

"I'm just so happy that you made it all right." She gave John another light hug. "How about taking your things to your quarters and then if you care to, Annika and Kurt have invited us to dine with them tonight. Do you feel up to that?" Lisa asked.

"I'd love to, thank you very much. You are most kind. Billy asked me to give you his best, Annika." John told her while Kurt went after the car.

"I'm so glad you're here. I know Lisa thinks very highly of you," Annika told John.

"Well the feeling is mutual, I can assure you." John said, smiling.

"We just moved into a new apartment that none of our friends have seen. This will be the first time we entertain there," Annika told him.

"Well, I appreciate your hospitality," John said.

"It's so nice to see you again, John." She gave him a second hug, warm enough to last.

Kurt and Annika's new apartment was near the maritime museum with a magnificent view of the Port of Gothenburg inlet. They could view the departures and arrivals of the navy-escorted ocean liners. The ships were welcomed with congratulatory whistles after their successful voyages, having negotiated through German mine fields and submarine infested waters to safety at Stigberg's pier and awaiting crowd. Annika contented herself with tending to their new home. She made curtains and darned their socks. Annika enjoyed crocheting and knitting and she had even begun to hook, a Rya Rug, a shag carpet for the living room. She was a meticulous house keeper, vacuuming and dusting daily. The abundant flowers and plants in the apartment reflected the great pride and care given them by Annika.

"Thanks for inviting us over. Your apartment is beautiful. And the view, breathtaking," said Camilla as she stepped out on the balcony. "Maybe I could come up here one day and paint the harbor from your balcony," Camilla suggested focusing in on prospective motifs. She looked fresh and vibrant standing there in the sun, subject to the moods of the wind.

"You're welcome here any time Camilla," Kurt offered gallantly.

"Yes, we like it, but we're not sure how long we will stay here if we'll have a family. It's not the best place for small children, but it will do for now," said Kurt

"Europe is so unstable nowadays that the US is looking pretty good. I heard that the US sent a bunch of warships to the British as a 'loan.' At least that makes it crystal clear what side they are on," said Camilla, looking towards the horizon.

"Yes, 50 destroyers," John confirmed.

"What is this I hear from Annika? You too are thinking of moving to the US? How did this come about?" Kurt asked genuinely interested.

"Well they say that the US is the land of opportunity, so why not give it a try? I inherited some money from my dad when he passed away and we thought that we could start an art studio there, or perhaps an apparel shop, perhaps in the Chicago area. Camilla knows all about that, or an art supply store, or perhaps an art gallery," Sven rambled on.

"Did you hear about John's friend Billy, who lives in England?" Kurt asked.

They returned to the living room where Annika was serving coffee and homemade cake.

"Yes, I know him," responded Camilla. "Wow! The coffee smells so good, Annika."

"Yes, thank you, its real coffee."

". . . I met him when he was in Sweden some years ago. He was in the navy, a really nice guy," Camilla continued, dreamily, reminiscing about the evening at Liseberg.

"Well, he has invented a knitting machine that can knit ladies' nylon stockings. They were such an unbelievable hit when they went on sale in New York not long ago." Kurt informed them. "I tell you guys, I'll make a deal with you. If you want to go into business for yourselves, if you guys invest in one of those machines – I understand they run about seven thousand dollars each – if you buy the machine, I will go into this venture as an equal partner with you and I'll provide everything else we need for an equal value. What do you say?" Kurt asked eagerly.

"Do you always have to do business Kurt? Can't we just relax tonight for once?" Annika asked.

"Of course, but you know, last year when nylon stockings went on sale in US department stores, 72,000 pairs sold out in eight hours. There was a limit of two per customer. Think about it. The offer stands for five days," Kurt added.

"We are definitely interested. I see two outcomes of this war; the Russians win or the Germans, unless the U.S. takes on a leading role. I'm not as concerned with Russia being a communist country, Sweden, being socialist, is not that far away. But there are major differences. I don't think most people cares about who owns the place of their employment as long as they are being treated fairly. The Soviet communist party seems o have little concerns for human rights and welfare. They are more like a police state, controlling everyone and limiting everything; speech, art, information, travel, religion . . ." Sven elaborated. "The Germans seems to follow a similar pattern. Moving to the U.S. may be the safest thing to do? We will get back to you, and appreciate the offer, regardless," Sven concluded

"I'm so glad to see you here again, John," said Lisa, putting her arm around him. "You'll have to tell me everything that's happened since I saw you last. I'm also interested in your work here, what specifically you're studying."

"Well, we have plenty of time. You know, since Zworkin invented the electron microscope last year, it has opened the door to so many new discoveries. Despite all the fighting going on, I think there are a lot of positive things going on and I have a lot of hope for the future," John mused. His warm smile prompted Lisa to reach for his hand.

"Well, well, the new positive John. I like the new John even more," Lisa said, giving him a warm hug.

"I'm glad to be here." John put his arms around Lisa and they stood there for a few moments simply enjoying each other's company, being close.

"Annika, your apartment is beautiful, and all the flowers, I'm impressed," Sven told her.

"Well, I'm not doing so well with that umbrella tree. I've learned that if the leaves turn yellow at the bottom of the plant it means that it is under-watered, whereas leaves turning yllow at the top are an indication of over-watering. That plant doesn't seem to know that. I have tried everything. I have soaked it in water to where it almost drowned, and I have let it go without water for weeks, but nothing seems to help." Annika raised her arms in surrender.

"Perhaps that's the problem? Maybe your plant would like a little consistency, moderation?" Sven chuckled, everyone else joining the laughter, and then quieting down, only to burst out in a hearty laughter again after having digested his comment. The evening continued in the same light-hearted mood until Annika's and Kurt's guests finally departed at 1:00 a.m.

Annika was an excellent cook and entertained masterfully. Her parties were always memorable, partly because of several novel ideas she incorporated into the evening.

"You colored the ice cubes with food color or fruit juice. It looks so nice. How do you get the sugar to stick to the rim of the glasses?" Lisa asked.

"Oh, I just wiped the rim with a lemon rind. That works pretty good."

Her flamboyant desserts were pieces of art. Yet, despite her many talents, Annika was plagued by insecurities, especially relating to her lack of higher education. She seized upon opportunities to point out Kurt's shortcomings, attempting to boost her own self-esteem. She constantly needed reassurance and affection, but Kurt grew less and less sympathetic to her needs.

"Lisa, I'm going to have to go to Stockholm for a seminar at Salgrenska Hospital." During his visit to Gothenburg, John stayed with a family, arranged by the University, but he spent most of his free time with Lisa.

"Relly? I was actually awaited the idea of attending myself. Now I will for sure. We'll go together." Lisa confirmed, giggling like a school girl.

"Alright Kurt. It's a deal. We will contact Billy tomorrow and order a knitting machine, and we'll have it delivered to the Freeport for now." They shook hand, signed an agreement and were now partners. Camilla contacted Billy and ordered a knitting machine. Thirty days later, Kurt received a wire from the shipping company, informing him that the British vessel which was bringing the knitting machine had been sunk by the Germans. They expressed their regret that they would not be able to make the delivery now or in the foreseeable future. Kurt closed the store he had opened for the Kurt-Sven venture and moved all the merchandise back to his other store before he told Sven and Camilla. Kurt stopped over to see Sven and Camilla in the evening. They had just finished dinner and invited Kurt for a cup of coffee.

"Sven," Kurt began. "I have some good news and some bad news."

"Yeah, what is it?" Sven asked.

"I got a wire from the British shipping firm Sea-lane in response to my inquiry. They said they had located the machine and that it was on its way here."

"Was on its way here?" Sven repeated.

"Yes, the bad news though, is that the ship that carried the machine was torpedoed and sank." Kurt held back a nervous smile, thinking of the clever way in which he had announced the tragic news. "I'm really sorry," he continued, "that our partnership should end on this note. You know, a few years from now you will have forgotten that this ever happened."

Camilla walked over to Sven and put her arms around him. "So how are we going to settle up, then?" she asked.

"I'm not sure what you mean. We have a deal. You were responsible for the machine and I was to take care of everything else.

"Yes, but that was assuming that the machine would get here. It would only seem fair that we split the loss. After all, we are fifty – fifty partners and we could just as well have invested in cash."

"We could have, but we didn't, and a deal is a deal," Kurt insisted.

"I don't think that's fair and as you always say, 'It's only small potatoes for you,' anyway," Sven argued. He was standing now, the color in his face raising. What I have, or don't have, has nothing to do with it," Kurt responded indignantly, his voice rising.

"Do you really think this is fair Kurt?" Camilla interjected.

"Business is business and this was our deal. I'm sorry that it didn't work out, but that is all I have to say about it." He strode over to the door and grabbed his coat and hat. "I'm really sorry, but it wasn't my fault. Blame the Germans, not me. I'll see you tomorrow at the store, Camilla." He walked out and closed the door behind him.

"I'll see you in hell," Camilla shrieked, her voice carrying through the door. Sven was speechless.

"So, you're going there too, huh Camilla?" Kurt mused, relieved at finally having told them, and rather pleased with his performance.

"That was a really rotten thing of him to do . . . but it showed us his true side and we're probably better off for ending our venture now. I have insured the machine so we should be alright financially," Sven comforted Camilla.

Camilla quit her job the following day. Besides Sven having insured the machine, Billy had done the same from his side, insuring the shipment. On top of that, Sven and Camilla also received compensation from the insurer of the ship, thereby being compensated three times. They sold everything they had and four months later they left for the United States. Camilla did not speak to Annika until the week they left for America. It was Lisa who finally convinced Camilla that Annika was not involved in Kurt's businesses and should not be held responsible.

Meanwhile, Annika and Kurt were drifting further apart and Kurt was spending longer periods away from home, ostensibly attending to his many business affairs.

CHAPTER 13

October, 1942 – Billy's last letter

Annika had just received a letter from Billy.

October 14, 1942

Dear Annika
 Thank you so much for your letter. It was so nice to hear from you and to learn that you are doing well. I'm really happy for you. You have found a nice husband and congratulations on the baby. I'm also getting married. I finally got snared. Her name is Diana. She is a nurse and I met her at the hospital when I first got back. She also trains dogs for the National Guard. She is a wonderful person and she is excited about planning the wedding.
 Work is going well. I'm really sorry about the machine that Camilla and Sven lost, but at least the insurance should cover any monetary loss. The insurance company is not willing to cover a second shipment, which is understandable, so Sven and Camilla will have to do something else for now.
 I hope all goes well for you and wish you the very best.

Your friend always, Billy.

"What does he say?" Lisa asked impatiently.

"He's getting married. Well I'm happy for him. Here read it yourself," Annika responded flatly. "I hope that she will make him very happy . . . He deserves the best," she said sincerely.

Annika came down with a virus, she thought, and she struggled with it for a couple days when Lisa insisted that she check herself into the hospital immediately. Lisa called for the ambulance and Annika checked in a few minutes later with a highly inflamed appendix. It was removed two hours later.

"I have some really great news," Lisa announced. "I bought you a lottery ticket in the state lottery last week, as a late wedding present, and I couldn't believe my eyes when I looked at the drawing list this morning. You won one thousand crowns on your ticket. Congratulations!" she added.

"You're kidding! I never win anything."

"For real, as Camilla says. You won one thousand crowns. Would you like me to get it for you? I have to go there anyway. I also won, but only fifty crowns," she told her.

"Wow! I can't believe it. That will come in so handy right now with papa being sick and everything." Thank you so much Lisa." Annika gave Lisa a hug. Her smile resembled one of those days when the sun shines and it rains at the same time.

"Well . . . my part was quite modest. I only had to fork out one crown for the ticket. But I'm sure glad it worked out."

Annika remained at the hospital fourteen days recuperating. On the thirteenth day her sister Kristina came to visit dressed in black. Annika was not alarmed as she knew that Kristina's father-in-law had died a month earlier. She did look terribly forlorn, though, and upon Annika's probing, she tearfully told Annika of the death of their father three days earlier.

The German troops was moving in through Russia and in late October Mrs. Bengtson sold the family home and moved to a small one-bedroom apartment down town, at her children's urging.

"Flowers for Mrs. Nobel," the delivery boy announced as Annika opened the door.

"Really, well thank you." Annika removed the paper from the twelve long-stemmed dark red roses. The fragrance was strong and invited her to raise the bouquet to her nose and take a deep breath. 'Wow that smells wonderful,' she thought. She opened the attached card.

"Dear Annika, this is for you personally, your special friend," she read. She looked inside the envelope and pulled out a check for one thousand crowns. The name of the flower shop was printed on the wrapping paper. She looked up the number and called. The store had no information on who had sent the flowers. They had received the order by mail and there was no return address, the woman explained. Annika called the bank that had issued the check, but she received no information. The bank teller told her that the bank could not reveal any information on their customers. He assured her that the check was good and that the only restriction was that she had to open an account in her own name. She decided to go to Lisa for advice the following morning.

"The strangest thing happened to me yesterday. You're not going to believe this."

"What?" Lisa asked. "Here, why don't you make yourself useful and help me rinse the shampoo out of my hair." She was leaning over the wash bowl slightly blinded from shampoo seeping into her eyes. "What happened?" she repeated.

Annika added some hot water to the canister from the pot on the stove and gently poured the warm water over Lisa's head while working out the lather. "I got this beautiful bouquet of twelve red roses delivered to the apartment yesterday, and there was a card stating that it was from 'my special friend', and . . ."

"It must be nice to have admirers. I can't even remember the last time I got twelve red roses from anyone. Actually, I can, NEVER!" She raised her soaked head, the water dripping down her face.

"That wasn't all. There was a check for one thousand crowns in the envelope. One thousand," she repeated. "I don't know what to do. I called the flower shop and the bank and neither could tell me who sent it. It's kind of creepy, don't you think?" Annika asked.

"Have you told Kurt?" Lisa asked.

"No, h's gone for two days." Annika took the towel that Lisa had wrapped around her shoulders and began rubbing Lisa's hair.

"I have to hurry to work, but I don't think you have anything to worry about. There is obviously someone who has decided to take you under his wing for whatever reason, and I think you should be flattered. There are a lot of nice people out there and someone chose you. It could be for a lot of reasons. Some shy person could be infatuated by your charm, which is understandable, or perhaps you were picked at random." Lisa slipped into her dress, walked over to the mirror and quickly brushed her hair before rolling it into a knot in the back. Regardless, as long as all he wants to do is to share his good fortune with you, I would just say 'thank you very much'. Also, I would do as he asked, open an account in your name and don't tell Kurt anything about it. Not that he would be jealous, but he would figure out a way to spend it for you. I have to go, but I can stop by tonight." Lisa picked up her purse, extracted a tiny perfume bottle, shook it, and rubbed a drop behind each ear instantly filling the room with the fragrance of pansy. "In fact, now that you're rich, why don't you have me for dinner and we can talk some more, Kurt is gone, and everything?

"Okay, see you at six."

Lisa arrived a few minutes early. Annika was still in the tub when Lisa rang the doorbell. She opened the door wrapped in a towel. "Oh, is this how you greet all your guests?" Lisa asked ebulliently.

"No, only a few selected ones," she responded, smiling suggestively.

"I got out a few minutes early so I thought I'd just as well come on over," Lisa explained.

"Oh, that's fine. I have the dinner in the oven and I'll be ready in a just few minutes."

Lisa followed her to the bathroom. "Well, did you open an account in your own name as your friend asked you to?"

"Yep." She hung up the towel and slipped into a house coat. She didn't bother with underwear.

"Are you going to tell Kurt?" Lisa asked.

"I will tell him about the flowers, just to see how he reacts. It's not inconceivable that it was him, even though I doubt it. If it was him, I'm sure that he had an ulterior motive. I won't tell him about the money unless he asks. If he doesn't say anything then I know it wasn't him. Who do you think it could possibly be?" Annika asked, dumbfounded.

"You said the check was drawn on a local bank, right? Well that narrows it down some. Do you have an old relative who might regard you as their favorite niece and like to give you a little help?" Lisa asked.

"No one I can think of."

"You will have to make sure you pick up the mail from now on, in case there is a bank statement, and you will have to do your own taxes. You know, I'd be happy to help you with your taxes if you'd like," Lisa offered. "Really? Lisa you're such a good friend, I'm embarrassed." Annika walked over and hugged her. "Thank you, Lisa." Annika buttoned rest of the coat as they moved into the kitchen. "I always get the mail anyway so that shouldn't be a problem. How's John? Have you heard from him?"

"Yes, he's back home in London, and the trip went fine. I'm so glad he was able to come here. I know him so much better now. You know, I miss him already. Mmm that smells good, dill meat, my favorite."

"I know." Annika drained off the water from the boiled potatoes and put them back on the stove to steam off. "It's almost ready," she announced.

Lisa helped with the condiments. "We've talked a little about my going over there. We haven't decided yet. It would have to work out with school and everything, but I think it's fun to just think about it."

"I would miss you," said Annika.

CHAPTER 14

November, 1942 – Kurt expands to Stockholm

Annika felt guilty about not helping her mother more, and it caused several arguments between her and Kurt, but Kurt ruled the roost and Annika accepted her lot. Kurt had made it clear that he had married Annika and not her family. He had not forgotten his mother's warnings, and he was not about to make her prediction come true. Kurt visited his family twice a week and always brought a bag of coffee, a rare commodity during the war. Annika was not welcome so she did not accompany him. She visited her own mother once a week, but she could not bring anything from Kurt's stores. However, Lisa learned of a trust fund that paid the rent for elderly widows. Lisa helped Mrs. Bengtson register. With the rent taken care of, her mother had some money to spend on herself each month, which relieved Annika's guilt.

"Annika. You know I have been thinking about expanding the business to Stockholm." Kurt began pacing the floor. "After all, 20% of the population lives there."

"That's a true story," Annika responded.

"Given the family issues we have to deal with here, I think the time has come to give Stockholm a try."

"You mean that you would like to open a shop there?" Annika asked.

"Yes, a shop or a restaurant."

"That would take some time. How long will you be gone?"

"Actually, I was thinking that you will come along. We get an apartment and stay there . . . at least for some time. I have talked to an old friend that lives there and he thinks that Stockholm is pretty nice and lots of things is going on there. He found a remodeled apartment in a central section of the town. What do you say? Are you ready for a little adventure?"

"Well yes. That could be fun. Both Camilla and Lisa have moved so I guess now it's my time."

"Lisa has? I just saw her," Kurt asked.

"Well, almost. She is thinking about it, and I have a gut feeling that she started packing her bags."

Annika took the train leaving Friday night and arrived in Stockholm early on the first Saturday morning in November. Kurt planned to ride up on Saturday morning with one of his chauffeurs in a truck filled with coffee surrogate and Kurt and Annika's personal belongings. Most goods were rationed by then, except for potatoes, milk and fish. Kurt had made arrangements so Annika could go straight to the apartment when she arrived. Kurt and Annika were the first tenants to move in after the work. Annika walked from the train station carrying her luggage.

When Annika arrived at the apartment a red rose awaited her along with a short note. "Direct deposit, your special friend." Annika was dumbfounded. She could think of no one that knew where she was. She waited all day, but Kurt never arrived. Finally, about 5:30 in the afternoon, she lay down and fell asleep on the hardwood floor.

A dog sniffing her face awakened Annika. She jumped up, horrified, when she saw a man in the room. "I'm sorry I startled you. I knocked but there was no answer so I came in. I'm Jan Karlson, I'm a friend of Kurt. He called and asked me to come and tell you that he's been delayed. They were having problems with the truck, but they're on their way now. He should be here in a few hours. You're welcome to come home with me tonight if you like. You can't stay here without a mattress or blankets."

"I appreciate the offer, but if Kurt is coming soon, then I want to be here."

Jan Karlson left, and after another hour Annika dozed off again. Kurt arrived the following morning, exhausted. He had loaded the truck too full, too high and too heavy. Buying new tires had taken them the better part of the morning, given their scarcity during the war. Then they had to unload half of the load in order to lift the truck. It was four o'clock in the afternoon before they departed Gothenburg. Having no way to call Annika, Kurt had called his friend Jan and asked him to contact her. The journey took them straight across the country from the west coast to the east coast. They passed through beautiful scenery. The rolling hills were often dressed with sparse pine forests and junipers. Large boulders sat intermittently amongst the greenery as if they had been scattered by giants. In fact, they had been left by a giant ice mass about fifty thousand years before. Fences surrounded pastures with grazing sheep, horses and cattle were constructed of rocks collected from the fields, and stacked neatly. A beautiful setting was thus created for the many farm houses, chain red, white and occasionally yellow. Houses were often set on top of low hills or by one of the many lakes. In strategic areas huge concrete barriers had been placed to hinder the movement of tanks.

They drove through several small towns and villages. The well-maintained mansions, were visible reminders of the "good old days," many, now being used as museums and parks. Other reminders of the past were the beautiful stone churches. Some were built as early as the eleventh century, not only to save souls, but also to protect the people from invaders and they were still in use.

Kurt and his driver could have enjoyed the trip, which under normal circumstances would have taken eight hours, but Kurt had loaded the truck too high to pass under five overpasses, forcing them to unload and reload the truck and trailer. The trip took fifteen hours and they arrived at the apartment in Stockholm at 7:00 the following morning.

When Kurt walked into the apartment, he found Annika sitting on the floor, leaning against a wall, sound asleep.

"Annika," he whispered. She jumped up and flew into his arms.

"Kurt, what happened?" she exclaimed, tears in her eyes, "what took you so long?"

Kurt sat down with Annika on the floor relating the troublesome events of their trip. They unloaded their personal belongings, the driver left, and Kurt collapsed on the bed. Annika spent the rest of the day unpacking and getting settled in the apartment. They spent most of the following day organizing and decorating. In the late morning they paused for a stroll to Haga Parken. Haga Parken lay on the shore of Mälaren. Located in the park was Haga Castle which had been a favorite home of the Swedish royal family. The four Princesses, Margareta, Birgitta, Desiree and Christina were all born there. There was no motor traffic in the park making it an ideal spot for a daily Apromenade."

Monday morning Kurt and his driver left for Slussen, in south Stockholm to pick up a load for the driver to take back to Gothenburg. Kurt should have returned by 10:00 in the morning, but Annika waited all day for him. At two in the afternoon Annika walked over to the Karlsons, who lived close by. Solvej Karlson suggested that she go back to the apartment and leave a message telling Kurt where she was and then come back and stay with the Karlsons until Kurt returned.

Following Solvej's advice, Annika returned to the apartment where she found a note which had been slipped under the door. It read: "Call Maria Hospital."

Annika rushed back to the Karlsons and called. She learned that Kurt had made it to Slussen, a multilevel traffic intersection in the center of Stockholm, and when the driver had negotiated a sweeping turn, Kurt's door had flown open and Kurt, who was leaning against it, flew out head first. He tried to brace himself with his right arm as he landed on the hard cobble stone street. He sustained a compound fracture and five ligaments pulled lose from his rotating cup, in the shoulder.

Slussen was a busy key intersection with heavy traffic all hours of the day, including fast-moving trams that would not have been able to stop going downhill, so he was lucky to have sustained only injuries that would heal with time.

Kurt would have to stay in the hospital. Owing to complications three days stretched into six. Unfortunately the fracture didn't heal properly and the arm had to be re-broken and realigned which meant three additional days in the hospital. Annika took the tram to see him every day. Kurt had a private room and enjoyed the pampering he received.

When Kurt recovered, he went out prospecting for new business ventures. He discovered a coffee shop at Nybro Plan that seemed ideal. It was well established and centrally located, close to movie theaters and the Royal Dramatic Theater. The restaurant belonged to a Jewish couple who wanted to sell out and move to England where they planned to join in the fight against the Nazis. The restaurant was close to their apartment and the price was right, so Kurt signed the papers and the place was his. It had not occurred to him to consult Annika.

Wine had been served in the restaurant in the past. However, the liquor license was not transferable. Kurt would have to operate without alcohol for some time while the city monitored his performance. Shortly after he took over the establishment, the city also informed him that he would have to close one hour earlier, at ten o'clock in the evening. This was a hard blow, as most of his business derived from the after-movie and theater crowd which he would lose with the new hours. Shortly thereafter Kurt learned that he could not serve the popular *smorgasbord*; it was prohibited by law.

Annika and Lisa wrote once a week. Neither had heard from Camilla for some time. Every month Annika received a red rose, and always with the same short message; direct deposit your special friend. Each month an additional one thousand crowns was deposited to Annika's private account. Annika did not tell Kurt, but she did not dare to spend any of the money, should it turn out to be a mistake. Lisa encouraged her to use the money, but to no avail. Of course, with almost everything rationed, there wasn't much to buy and especially if she didn't want Kurt to know.

Annika worked full time in the restaurant and they hired a girl to tend to the apartment and help out with their social gatherings. Kurt did not seem overly concerned with the slower business at the restaurant, at least he was not losing money on the place and it kept Annika occupied. Kurt had placed an ad in the paper that brought more than twenty responses. The first woman who came was an older lady. She had experience and came with good recommendations, but Kurt didn't want to hire the first applicant without giving the others a chance. The second applicant, Bella, was only twenty-two years old. She was neatly dressed in a smart khaki trench coat and a small brown hat that defied gravity, on the side of her head. She was cute, with large expressive brown eyes. She told them her boyfriend was in the service, so she had no time restrictions. Kurt and Annika hired her, though Annika felt a little uncomfortable having such an attractive young lady move in with them, knowing Kurt's weaknesses. She was comforted by Bella's having a boyfriend. At the same time Bella fascinated her, with her simple charm. After all, Annika had been doing something very similar not too long ago with the Liljekrans family. Kurt saw no reason to waste time interviewing others when Bella was obviously the perfect choice.

Bella's duties included to keep the apartment clean, do the laundry, prepare meals, when the Nobels did not dine in the restaurant, and help out with social events and shopping. She would live in, have the run of the house, and of course, have her own room. She would be free after dinner, but if she wanted to earn a little extra, she could knit Lappish ski hats that Kurt sold in his stores. Textiles were being rationed, and the yarn that was available had wood fibers mixed into it making it coarse and hard to work with.

A week after Bella moved in, Kurt came home at eight o'clock. Annika was still at work in the restaurant. As he walked past the open door to the bathroom, he noticed the tub was filling. Bella enjoyed taking a relaxing and soothing bath in the evening. Hot water was rationed but she could heat water on the stove. Kurt continued to the kitchen where he found Bella standing at the stove, waiting for the water to heat, with her back to him, completely naked. The radio was on and she had not heard him enter. Bella's long blond hair covered most of her upper back. It swayed as she moved gently with the music. Kurt's eyes followed it to where it grazed the small of her back, feasting on her firm white buttocks sharply contrasted by two dark tanned slender legs. He was sure he could reach around her small waist with his hands.

"Hi Bella . . . I like your outfit. What are you doing?" he asked her.

She swung around, startled by his appearance, but was relieved to see that it wasn't a stranger.

"I'm sorry I frightened you." He smiled, lifting his eyebrows apologetically.

Bella was trapped, she had to walk passed him to leave the kitchen. Noticing the arousing effect, she had on Kurt, her initial panic turned into amusement. She nonchalantly crossed her arms and strutted past him to her waiting bath, smiling at him as she went. "Sorry," she said, "I didn't expect anyone home this early."

"Don't mention it, it was my pleasure. Do you need help scrubbing your back?" he offered.

"No thanks. I'm a big girl; I know how to bathe myself." She closed the bathroom door behind.

"Big indeed," Kurt sighed.

Kurt and Annika visited the Liljekronas just once. Their good friends were the Karlsons. Kurt had known Jan since school. They had attended the same university in Gothenburg, after which Jan had moved to Stockholm where Solvej was born. Jan and Solvej had met on a ski vacation a few years earlier. With their busy agenda Kurt and Annika did not have much time for socializing. Kurt would frequently leave on trips, often for more than two weeks at the time.

With Kurt gone so often, Annika became good friends with Bella. The two talked about nearly everything, including Kurt's advances towards Bella. Annika knew that Kurt was freewheeling at times. She had come to accept this, given that there was nothing she could do about it. Leaving Kurt was out of the question; she still enjoyed Kurt, the social status he brought and their affluent living standard. Annika's secret account was growing quickly although she was still not looking at the money from her special friend as hers. Upon Lisa's advice she invested some of her funds in securities that quickly shot up in value.

When Kurt was away, Annika and Bella would turn on music, get their hand work projects out, and crawl up in the large bed and talk until they fell asleep. They enjoyed each other's company and the closeness they felt for each other. During the night Bella would snuggle up to Annika and put her arm around her. First Annika had removed her arm, not being totally sure of how to react to the intimate gesture. After a while Annika got used to it and liked to feel her touch.

"You know Annika it was so funny last week. I was getting ready for my evening bath just as Kurt came walking in through the door. He seems to have figured out that if he comes home around eight then he can catch me taking my bath. Well I was in the tub when he asked if he could pee. He said that he had to go really bad. He asked me not to look. Well I was nice enough to let him in but I was not nice enough not to look. My God, what did he expect? How often does a good-looking man come in to pee while you're taking a bath? I asked him, 'boy, do you always have such a hard on when you pee?' He was standing there for some time not being able to go because of his erection." Bella confessed.

"Tell me, what do you really feel for Kurt? Are you attracted to him?" Annika asked.

"Sure, he is an attractive and interesting guy, and he's a man. I love that deep voice of his, its so sexy."

"Yes, and he knows it," Annika responded.

"What about you? Don't you get turned on sometimes, by other guys, ones who come on to you? I see you flirt with guys all the time."

"Yes, I do, and you know what, this may sound a little strange, but I even get turned on hearing or fantasizing about Kurt's affairs," Annika confessed.

"Would you ever go to bed with another guy if you knew that you could get away with it?" Bella asked, putting away her knitting.

"If I knew for sure that I would get away with it?" Annika repeated the question to buy a little more time to respond. "I'm sure I could get away with it. What is good for the goose is good for the gander, or vice versa. It doesn't seem to bother Kurt that he is second string to all those other females he sees, so I don't think he would mind, as long as he gets his time. But I don't know. I have to admit that I have fantasized about doing it, a few times, but I don't know." Annika put away the embroidery she had been working on. "It depends," she conceded.

"Depends on what?" Bella insisted.

"Depends on how much I had to drink," Annika giggled. "No, but . . . it would depend on a lot of things . . . but if the question implies someone that is gorgeous, intelligent, humorous, understanding, romantic and filthy rich, I would definitely entertain the idea. . . . in fact, one of those qualities wouldn't be bad."

"What about a girl? Have you ever fantasized about having sex with a girl . . . or taking part in a threesome?" Bella asked boldly. She moved a little closer to Annika and began playing with her earlobe.

"Having sex with a girl?"

"Well I don't mean having real sex, I just mean getting a little extra friendly, intimate, exploring a little?"

"I guess I've thought about that too." Annika could feel a shiver go up her spine and she could feel her heart beating stronger.

"How about me? Do you think that I'm sexually attractive?" She suddenly got up on her knees, in the bed. She was dressed in an oversized pajamas top.

"Well yes, of course, I think you're very attractive, and sweet," Annika added.

"Yes, but sexually attractive? Do you think that I'm sexy?" Bella asked, letting her top slide off her shoulders exposing herself from the waist up.

"Yes, I do find you sexually attractive, very much. I often include you in my sexual fantasies," Annika confessed. "You are gorgeous."

"Really . . . tell me a fantasy that included me," Bella asked, settling back down on the bed sitting in front of Annika with her legs crossed and without making any effort to cover herself. She listened intently.

"Oh, the other day I had a dream, after you had told me how Kurt caught you naked in the kitchen. We were living in a mansion and you were walking around cleaning the house, essentially naked, except for a pair of high heeled shoes and a bow in your hair and a small white apron. Then we were sitting down to eat supper and you were serving us in that same outfit."

Bella moved over and lay down across Annika's lap. Her dark red nipples were standing straight up. She reached for Annika's hand and placed it on her breast. "Do you like that? It feels really nice to me."

"Yes, it feels nice, very nice." Annika bent down and kissed her softly on her lower lip.

"You know, I was thinking, if you are up to it, tomorrow, being that it's Kurt's birthday, what if I serve you two dinners in my blue apron only, I know you'll love it, we know Kurt would love it, and I think it would be hilarious."

"Sure . . . you don't mind? I will have to come up with something sexy to wear too," Annika proposed.

"I know, I have this little outfit that you can wear that's hot, hot. It can't get much sexier than that." Bella laughed. Boy, this is going to be some birthday party."

Annika greeted Kurt at the door, dressed in a deeply cut, long black velvet dress, split up her left leg. She wore high heels and a white pearl necklace. This was Kurt's favorite outfit. She handed him a glass of sherry and raised her glass.

"Happy birthday sweetheart!" She raised her chin to kiss him. "We're going to have a special dinner tonight, just for you. Please don't go into the kitchen. We have a surprise there."

"We?" he asked?

"Yes, Bella's going to join us tonight. I hope you don't mind. Get yourself ready and we'll have dinner when you're ready." Annika turned the gramophone on low and dimmed the lights. The only lights in the dining room came from two lit candles on the table.

"Why are there only two plates on the table? Didn't you say that Bella would join us?"

"She will, you'll see." Annika began singing Happy Birthday and the kitchen door swung open and Bella entered dressed in high heel shoes and her apron, and with a towel hanging across her arm. She carried a tray with soup bowls. She went to Kurt first, set his bowl in front of him and wished him happy birthday.

"Wow, you girls are something else! How did you come up with this idea? I love it, but why don't you join us for dinner Bella."

"OK, but like this, Annika?" Bella asked.

"Absolutely. I know this is for Kurt's birthday, but I have to admit that I'm enjoying having your strutting around like that," Annika conceded.

Bella refilled the wine glasses before joining them at the table. She looked especially sensuous with the soft flickering candle light reflecting against her chest. From the rear, she was totally naked.

Annika felt herself getting warm. She was not sure if it was because of the wine, because of Bella, or because of the anticipation of her wearing Bella's outfit during the dessert. Regardless, she was ready and eager to do her part.

After they had finished their meal, Annika asked Kurt to leave for a moment, while they prepared dessert.

"All right, then I will run down and get some cigars. I will be right back."

On his way back, he ran into the Karlsons, who were stopping by with a birthday present. Kurt invited them up for dessert. When they arrived, the table had been cleared, and a large meringue cake, covered with whipped cream and chocolate dipped strawberries sat on the table. Annika was now also dressed in one of Bella's small aprons and heels; the apron covered even less of her than Bella's did. She held a server knife in her hand, ready to serve dessert.

"Wow!" For a few seconds Kurt stood speechless in the doorway, forgetting that Jan and Solvej were standing next to him. The kitchen door swung open and Bella came in still dressed in her apron and heels.

"Oh, I didn't know that we were having guests for dessert," she said, as if it was her daily routine to serve dinner half naked. She returned to the kitchen and brought back two glasses of wine for the Karlsons.

"Hi guys!" Annika greeted them. "Looks like you came just right to have some dessert. We're putting on a little adult show for Kurt's birthday," explained the slightly tipsy Annika.

"Boy, you sure know how to entertain. Why don't you ever think of things like this Solvej?" Jan asked.

"What do you mean? I went with you to the nude beach last summer, didn't I? . . . twice."

"True, but there was hardly anyone there. If you're going to feel like a free spirit there have to be other people around."

"Well that wasn't my fault, and what do you expect in late August? It was cold."

"I think I might have screwed up," Kurt mumbled, "but . . . what the hell, have some dessert folks."

CHAPTER 15

February, 1943 - Kurt and Annika's divorce.

Annika and Kurt remained in Stockholm over winter, and in late February of 1943 they moved back to Gothenburg. It had been the coldest winter on record. Minus thirty-five was registered in Ystad, at the southernmost tip of Sweden. Bella had met a new boyfriend and stayed in Stockholm. Camilla and Sven had settled down in Chicago, USA. Lisa was doing an internship at a children's hospital in Gothenburg. John was back in England working at a naval hospital outside of London. John and Lisa corresponded regularly. Lisa contemplated taking a trip to visit John, but not until the end of the year.

Annika and Kurt moved into another of Kurt's apartments in Gothenburg, not far from where they lived earlier. "This is about the same view as we had before." Annika noted.

"It's not bad. There is always something going on in the rail road yard. On the hill over there, the old fortress Three Crowns, built almost a thousand years ago. I think that might be the oldest building still standing in Sweden, and we have a lot of old buildings." Kurt reflected.

"I just wish we wouldn't have to look at the German trains passing through, with their windows covered. They are supposed to bring relief personnel to the occupying fores in Norway, and bring back soldiers on leave. Then why do they have to cover the windows?" Like most Swedes,

Kurt and Annika resented the trains; some Swedes would shake their fists defiantly as they passed by.

The location of Kurt's and Annika's apartment was convenient, within walking distance of Kurt's office, Ullevi Stadium, Liseberg, and good shopping.

In early April, Kurt came home one day and announced that he had purchased the building where he had his headquarters. He explained to Annika that since he was getting into higher finances, they would be incurring more risks, and in order to protect her if anything should go wrong, he thought it best if they would divorce, on paper oly of course. No one would have to know, and they would continue to live together as before, but Annika would have the home and everything in it in her nme. The business would be his, along with its potential risks. Kurt assured Annika that the arrangement was for the safety of the family. Annika loved her beautiful home, the classic furniture, oriental rugs, crystal chandeliers and several valuable art objects.

"So, everything here at home is mine, and my alone," she said firmly. Annika thought of her treasured jewelry that she could not imagine losing.

"Everything. The war seems to escalate every day. Who knows how long I can stay in business. I heard that the Americans just built a super large airplane, the "Super Fortress" B-29, I think they called it. It can fly at 33,000 feet, a bomber. They also announced that some physicists in Chicago had made a first nuclear reaction, whatever that means. They said that now they can build much bigger and more powerful bombs."

"So now they have a bigger bomb and a bigger plane to deliver the bomb." Annika shuddered.

Naive and trusting Annika went along. Kurt agreed to give her a modest living expense each month. Annika consulted with Lisa first, as she did on all important matters, and Lisa encouraged her to go along with it, knowing of Annika's secret bank account that was steadily growing and now would be beyond Kurt's reach. Of course, Lisa had never liked Kurt in the first place.

On April 19, the British began the bombing of Berlin. In May Allies broke German code and could trace its communications. German

U-boats could be detected, using radar, and were sunk in groves. The Germans were losing one sub a day. In September Italy was defeated and Hitler lost at Stalingrad, 400,000 Germans died.

In July of 1943, Lisa moved to England to be near John. She entered the same teaching hospital where John was working, close to London. She continued her research on infectious diseases. Lisa was supposed to set up a rendezvous with the three blood sisters in 1943. However, Camilla now lived in the US, and Lisa in England, so the girls agreed to postpone their reunion for five more years.

Annika continued to receive a red rose every month, and the thousand crowns kept coming to her account, like clockwork. She still had no idea from where, and she still did not dare to use it. She could think of no one, friend or stranger, who could possibly know her as well as her special friend, so she suspected Kurt. He knew her the best, and he would be capable of sending the roses as a joke. Yet, she couldn't imagine his sending the money without taking credit for it. Mr.Liljekrona from Stockholm? Very unlikely. He lived in his own world. Jan? Not possible because the roses began arriving prior to her meeting him. Billy? Not possible. He knew nothing about her and the sender appeared to know where she was going to be even before she got there. For instance, when the rose awaited her at their Stockholm apartment. No one knew about that, unless it was one of Kurt's friends. It would have to be a perfect stranger, but who? Annika thought that it was highly unlikely that it was from someone she had never met. Stellan, Kurt's friend was a possibility. He was always gone, but he did have some contact with Kurt and could have learned from Kurt where she was. Annika knew that he had a crush on her. He was single and made good money. She also had some old boyfriends whom she had not seen for a long time, like Bertil, who had suddenly disappeared. Annika suspected that he had something to do with removing the Norwegian treasurers before the Germans arrived. He could possibly have the money, but then it wouldn't be his to give away. Perhaps it wasn't even a man?

Kurt was spending more time away from home again, visiting his mother or taking care of business. Annika felt left out and decided to make an extra effort to please Kurt and to bring some romance back into their relationship. It was late 1943, and Annika was expecting Kurt back any minute. He had been at a trade show in Malmö for two days and was returning on the 7:30 train. Annika had prepared a candle light meal for the two of them. She had put on one of Kurt's favorite dresses. It was black with tiny red polka dots and the skirt was split in front with an overlap. The plunging neckline revealed and accented her soft curves. The dress fit snugly on top and snugly down to her thighs, before flaring out at her knees; it was clearly Spanish inspired. "Annika, I'm home!" Kurt called as he entered the door.

"I'm in the kitchen," she answered.

"Smells good - what's cooking?" he asked. He handed her a bouquet of red roses. Kurt knew of the roses Annika received every month, but he didn't mind. In fact, he liked the idea that someone else wanted something that was his.

"Thank you so much, they're beautiful!" She put her arms around him squeezed him tight and kissed him. "Did you eat on the train?" she asked.

"No, all they had where some dry sandwiches."

"I better make you an extra crepe then. I thought you would have already eaten. How was the trip?" She handed him a glass of sherry, kissing him invitingly. "Welcome home," she said softly. She put the roses in water.

"Thanks, I needed that, but what's the occasion? Have I forgotten something . . . again?" He shook his head, puzzled.

"Not at all," she smiled at him, amused at his confusion.

Kurt put away his things and returned to the dining room shortly thereafter and sat down at the table. "That dress, it makes you look Spanish. I like it."

"I know you do. I like it too."

Annika walked over to turn on the record player. "Do you remember this song?" she asked.

"Old Man River, of course I do." Kurt began to sing along.

"Do you remember anything special about it?" she asked.

"Should I?"

"They played this song on the car radio the first time you took me out."

"Oh, yes, I remember. I remember it well." Kurt stared into the air, reminiscing. "I really like you in that dress, you look great."

"I know, you've told me that before. Just one of those little things I do for my favorite husband." She brought the food to the table, fully aware of how her movements affected Kurt.

"What's this?" Kurt looked at the creeps with suspicion.

"They are crepes, filled with stewed liver and mushrooms. I used real cream so it should be good."

"It looks like pancakes to me; shouldn't we have jam and whipped cream on them?" He lifted his fork and carefully gave one a poke in the side. Annika smiled somewhat amused, but disappointed in his lack of refinement.

"Don't make up your mind before you've tried it. There is nothing there that you don't like, so why not give it a chance?" She gathered some toast and a bottle of dry white wine from the counter.

"I'm not sure about the mushrooms, if I can eat that?"

"What do you mean the mushrooms? Last month after we had been out picking mushrooms in Lindome and I fried them that evening, you couldn't get enough of them."

"Those were chanterelles. I love chanterelles, but these. . ."

"Agaricus ardencies," she interrupted; proud of herself for remembering the Latin word from a class on mushrooms she had attended a few years before. "Or prairie, or horse mushrooms or *champinjoner* or Agaricus, as they are also called."

"Whatever. Those I'm not sure of." Kurt took a bite. "Hmm, not bad, not bad at all. Do you have more?"

"There's one more," she said, thinking she would give him her second crape. "Why don't you first finish what you have before you take more? They're very filling."

"I'd still like to know what the big deal is. Do you need money for anything?" Kurt asked suspiciously.

"Well, now that you mention it, I could use a new swimming suit. My old suit is so old that I'm wearing holes in the knees" He looked up at her. "Just kidding."

"Funny, funny," he said, unable to stifle a chuckle.

"I have no ulterior motives. Is that so hard to believe? I just thought it was nice to have you back and thought I would do something special. It's been so long since we sat down alone, just you and me. I thought that maybe if I tried a little harder to make it nice for you here at home, that maybe you would stay home more. That's all."

Kurt finished his crepes and Annika's too, along with a piece of toast. Still hungry, he made himself a cheese sandwich on a thick slice of homemade bread. Kurt's high metabolism allowed him to eat as much as he wanted without putting on weight.

After they had finished the wine bottle, Annika straightened up the kitchen and put on coffee. She could hear Kurt singing Old Man River, in the bathroom. She turned the phonograph on low and turned off the ceiling light, leaving a couple table lamps on low. She served cake with the coffee and a glass of Dom Liqueur. Kurt, after having finished his meal, along with the wine and liqueur, felt relaxed and leaned against the armrest.

"I like that dress. You should wear it more often. It makes you shine."

"Thank you. It's a little too low-cut to be worn in public, but thanks. I'm glad you like it. I tried to make it a little sexier for you."

As Annika snuggled up close to him on the couch, her skirt slid open. As she moved closer yet, her dress opened a bit farther. Kurt noticed the scent of her lilac perfume. He placed his arm around her back, his other hand resting on her thigh. Moving his hand up and taking the dress with him, he felt for the edge of her panties.

"Your naughty girl" he admonished. "You're not wearing any panties."

"Oh, I forgot. I hope you don't mind." She kissed his neck moving up his cheek to his earlobe. "Shall we dance?" she asked. They stood up embracing and Kurt guided her through the Blue Danube Waltz.

Slowly caressing her back as he nibbled on Annika's neck, Kurt lowered her zipper.

"Did anything interesting happen on your trip?" Annika asked, her heart beating rapidly, as she pretended not to notice his action. She could feel his excitement growing against her.

"Nothing that would interest you," he said, clearing his throat. He slid her dress off her shoulders and let it fall to the floor while they continued dancing. "Why don't you dance for me? I love when you do that." He sat down on the couch, poured himself another glass of liqueur and watched.

Annika, clad in only her black heels and a strand of pearls, and holding her freshly refilled liqueur glass, began her seductive routine, sending Kurt into frenzy. She walked over to the window and pulled the curtain wide open. Facing out, she continued her seductive dance. It wasn't likely that anyone would see her, as their apartment was above the normal line of vision for the traffic below, with the exception of a viaduct. Slowly she worked her way over to Kurt. Sitting on his knee, she unbuttoned his shirt, leaning over to kiss his erect nipples. He pulled her down in his lap and decorated her breast and belly with the cream and fruit from the cake, after which he sampled his work.

"This reminds me of Stockholm. Annika, do you remember when the Karlsons dropped in on my birthday party in Stockholm . . .?" Kurt asked.

"Of course, I do. How could I ever forget that? That was the biggest turn on in my life. I still dream about it. Yes, I remember," she responded.

"No kidding! I wonder what the Karlsons are up to nowadays. I haven't heard from Jan since we left. They were great friends . . ."

"I miss Bella too, a lot. She was precious. I would never have thought that I would enjoy getting so close to a girl, but I really enjoyed sleeping with her."

"Sleeping or fooling around?" Kurt asked teasingly.

"Both," she said wrinkling her nose at Kurt. She knew Kurt loved when she talked dirty. "I loved snuggling up to her and putting my arms around her and feeling her, so warm and soft. And I loved when she came on to me. She seemed to get satisfaction from making me feel good. It's too bad she didn't come with us here."

"Yes, she was a jewel," Kurt agreed.

"We need to, or I need to, get out more. We've moved around so much that I haven't been able to make lasting friends anywhere. I don't mean that I don' have friends, but they all live hundreds and thousands of miles away. Everyone I have run in to here seems so stiff and preoccupied. What's Eva doing? Do you think that we should invite her over?" Annika asked.

"I'm not so sure that that would be a good idea. I don't see you two getting along that entire well. I've noticed the jabs you take at each other." Annika didn't dispute his observation.

"I've been thinking of taking classes so I can see some people, or perhaps join a band and get back to my music," Annika said.

"You should. Why not?" Kurt agreed. "Actually, if you'd like to meet some free-spirited people, I have some friends that I know that you would enjoy. There's this girl I know who runs a catering business, Ella. Your birthday's coming up in September, right?"

"What, you don't know for sure?" Annika challenged him.

"Of course, I do. I'm going to talk to Ella about arranging a party. She's the expert on wild and crazy parties. I have known Ella for a long time and we have dated on occasion."

"Kurt, I think the liquor is getting to me."

"Let's go to bed," Kurt suggested.

"Alright," she murmured.

She finished undressing him and they proceeded to the bathroom where they bathed together, taking their time, and each washing the other. After toweling themselves dry, Kurt carried Annika to the bed to resume their love making.

CHAPTER 16

April, 1943. Ella and Martin

Besides Kurt, Annika, Ella and their dates, a dozen other couples were invited, all strangers to Annika. Kurt knew the girls, but none of the men. It was not going to be a sit-down dinner party but there would be plenty of food and refreshments, American style. The party was held in one of Kurt's warehouses. Ella and her assistants had spent the afternoon decorating the place, covering the walls and the floor with black plastic and taping large paper flowers and silhouettes of people on the walls. Some also hung from the ceiling. Balloon laden strings crossed the room, creating a dropped-ceiling effect. Blue lights made light colors appear fluorescent. A perforated tube with blades hung over a ceiling lamp, and the lamp's heat caused it to spin, creating a cascade of moving light dots in the room. The room looked both mysterious and festive. Besides the serving table there were no furnishings in the room, except for several pillows thrown about the floor. Ella's sense of humor was expressed in placing the skeleton of a mermaid as a decoration on the serving table.

It had not been promoted as a birthday party, but after all the guests had arrived Ella made that announcement and when it came time to do the customary "finding your partner for the evening game," the men first had to audition for Annika to win her approbation and to become her evening partner. The men tried to outdo each other in creativity generating outbursts of laughter from the onlookers. One man tried to impress her with his waltzing, another with telling risqué stories and another with his kisses. One fellow claimed to give the best massages and another boasted of his ability to satisfy three women at the same time. One claimed to be the best looking in the bunch while another claimed that he could hold his breath for one minute. After the audition the girls were allowed to eliminate two of the men that Annika could not choose. Eventually Annika chose Ella's date Martin. He was actually her second choice. Her first choice, the guy that claimed he could satisfy three women at one time had been eliminated by the girls. Martin was tall, muscular and had a warm smile. He had auditioned by walking on his hands and whistling at the same time.

Everyone except Annika and Martin was blindfolded and had to spin around three times. Under Annika's and Martins supervision they now had to find a partner by hugging someone, making sure he or she was of the opposite sex, removing his or her blindfold, and stepping over to the side. The last subjects were permitted to call out their whereabouts so they could find each other.

The dinner was consumed half sitting, half laying on the floor, Roman style.

"Martin, how long have you known Ella?" Annika asked.

"Oh, I have known her for a couple of years now. I'm a photographer and I did a wedding that she catered. That's how we met. We are more friends than dating, but I do like Ella. She's great company. You never know what will happen next when she's there. The problem is that she's never there, always working."

"Are you a freelance photographer or do you work for someone?" Annika asked.

"I'm a freelance photographer. I have a studio by Heden. I do a lot of weddings and family photos. Occasionally I work for magazines too, and for an advertisement agency, but not full time."

"How do you become a professional photographer?"

"I have a degree in photo journalism, but to take portraits you only need a camera and a studio. I'd love to do a photo session with you. You are so classically beautiful and your body, wow!"

"How much do you pay?" she teased.

"I'm sure we could work something out to your satisfaction. Of course, photos for men's magazines pay the best, and with your body you'd be well compensated."

"Something to think about. Anyway, if you need a model for advertisements keep me in mind, okay? I just learned that I'm pregnant, so it will be sometime before I would be available, but I wouldn't mind getting out a little more."

"You bet I will," Martin responded enthusiastically.

The following morning both Kurt and Annika slept in.

"Good morning Annika. Well, what did you think about the party last night? Was it another one of those that you'll remember?" Kurt asked.

"It was great! Thank you so much!" She leaned over to kiss him.

"You're quite welcome. I had a great time," Kurt grinned.

"Oh, yeah. I knew you would. I saw you, and you looked like you were doing just fine. It was fun, and I enjoyed meeting Ella and Martin. Martin was really nice. They were all just great."

"I lucked out with my partner too. She was quite something."

"I told Martin that I might pose for him. He's a photographer. He said that there was a lot of money to be made modeling for men's magazines, what do you think?"

"You mean that next time I look at one of those magazines, you might be on the center page?"

"You never know."

"That would really be something."

A few days later a police officer came to Kurt and Annika's door. Someone had reported them for having been pleasure driving with a gas engine, which was still against the law. Kurt took the policeman out to his car and showed him how he had mounted the gen gas kit in the trunk, which was permissible.

The Allies invaded Europe at Normandy on June 6, 1944. There was still no ending in sight for the war even though the Allies had scored major victories and the German, and Japanese troops were retreating. Annika joined the Swedish Women's Motor Corps, a volunteer organization that delivered supplies to the regulars. Annika looked sharp in her brown uniform, the same uniform used by the cavalry, with boots and riding pants. She wore a tan shirt and tie under the stiff jacket and a wide leather belt crossed her chest. A boat hat topped it off. She had to quit with the Corps, when she could no longer fit into her uniform because of her pregnancy. US and its allies invaded Europe, landing in Normandy on June 6, 1944. A long-range German V2 Rocket, accidentally landed in Sweden. It was sent to Britain for scrutiny, against German protests. Germany no longer posed a threatening force.

Annika, I think we should move again. I know it's a big hassle, but with the baby coming."

"Oh, you aren't getting an argument from me. I have been thinking the same thing."

"I know of some pretty nice apartments available in Johanneberg and they are designed for families. It is right next to where my dentist lives. It is close to the central business area, but protected from the traffic with green-belts and parks and enjoy bus service at the doorstep". Kurt didn't own this building. His property was concentrated in the central core area, with the exception of some older apartment buildings.

"There is a large fenced in backyard where children could play safely and it is within walking distance of schools, hospital, church, stores, movie theaters and Liseberg's sport facilities. The view is breathtaking, of central and eastern Gothenburg. It's a five-story building with several conveniences. The tenants can beat their rugs on a roof balcony and do their laundry in a modern laundry room in the basement. Each apartment had a storage room in the basement and a room for bicycles. The building has an elevator. Each floor had a garbage drop and a small compartment by the doors, where milk and other delivered products can be placed, and each door has mail and newspaper delivery slots.

The rent is one hundred crowns a month, including everything but electricity and telephone."

Take it before it is gone. It sounds perfect." Annika prompted.

Sweden was on high alert. All able-bodied men, including Kurt, had to take their turns serving in the defense of their country. Kurt was sent to Uddevalla, a ship building city and naval base a couple hours' drive north of Gothenburg, where he spent January and February. Annika came to visit him for two weeks during that time, staying at the post guest house. Kurt had an office job, which suited him well, and he didn't have to familiarize himself with the trenches

While Kurt was gone Annika decided to stop by Martin's studio to say hi. She had to wait a few minutes while he finished a shooting.

"Annika, how great to see you again! Thank you so much for a great time! I've been thinking a lot about you, and I was just about to give you a call." He walked over to her and greeted her with a kiss on her forehead. She responded with an extended hug.

"Thanks! I had a good time too. So, what's up, do you have a photo shoot lined up for me?" she asked.

"As a matter of fact, I do. I have a new contract shooting for a lingerie manufacturer. Interested?"

"Well, yes!"

"You'll get paid fifty crowns for each picture and we'll take several. How does that sound?" he asked.

"But I'm pregnant, as you can see. I wouldn't be able to do it for about four more months," she explained.

"I know you're pregnant. It does show. That's what makes it perfect. That is exactly what I need. There will be other shoots later."

"Really? You want to take my pictures with this belly?"

"Yes, I do, and if you don't mind, I'd also like to take some nudes for an exhibit that I'm working on. I will pay you 1000 crowns for the session."

"When would you like to start?"

"Right now, . . . would be fine with me."

"No, I'd like to shower first and freshen up."

"I have a shower here. In fact, it would be perfect to take a few shots in the shower. I'm expecting Ella to come here in about two hours. We could work until then and then you could join us for dinner if you like."

"Are you sure? You don't think Ella would mind."

"Mind? She will love to see you again. She was just telling me yesterday, when I told her about doing some shots of you, how much she liked you."

They were just finishing up when Ella arrived. Ella walked straight over to the set to hug Annika.

"Hi Annika! It's great to see you again. How are you? Boy, you're big!" She gently patted her stomach.

"Thank you so much for putting together that party! I had a wonderful time," Annika bubbled.

"It was fun wasn't it? They are great people, the whole bunch."

"Annika is going to join us for dinner."

"Great, I always have lots of leftovers that I take home from work. I can fix something in a few minutes."

Ella's house was quaint and meticulously cared for. Its large kitchen had been remodeled into a commercial kitchen. "I used to make all my food here at home when I first started catering, but as we grew, I had to get a larger kitchen and in a commercially zoned area," she explained. "I still use this sometimes for a backup kitchen." Martin and Annika took a stroll in the garden while Ella prepared dinner. Martin had brought his camera and kept taking pictures of Annika against various backgrounds. Annika enjoyed modeling, and having posed for Camilla and Sven before, she knew what was expected of her. Shortly they went inside, when the sun set, as the evening was chilly.

"Dinner's almost ready. I hope you don't mind eating in the kitchen," said Ella.

"Of course not, this is great. Thanks' so much for inviting me. It's nice to have company for a change. Kurt's gone so much," said Annika.

"Well I'm glad you could come. I love to entertain."

"I noticed the piano in the living room. Do you play?" Annika asked.

"Yes, I love to play whenever I have time, which isn't too often. Do you play an instrument?" Ella asked.

"I used to play the violin, but that was some time ago. I've tried the piano a little but I can't say that I play it. I worked as a nanny for the director of Stockholm's Opera House not so long ago and he tried to teach me a little, but I wasn't there long enough to become a Maestro. Maybe you can play a little for us after dinner."

"Sure, I'd love to. You know, I have an old violin that I inherited from my grandmother. I don't know if it's any good, but maybe you'd like to check it out."

"Sure."

Martin kept taking pictures and Annika kept posing.

"It's going to be expensive to develop all those pictures you're taking," Annika reminded him.

"Oh, I develop them myself. I have a dark room at the studio."

"It's going to get more expensive to go dancing now," Ella informed them.

"Why is that?" Martin asked.

"The government has passed a new dance pleasure tax, of all things. Seems a little silly," Ella commented.

"It's probably the morals police at work. The conservative prudes are not very impressed with the new American jitter-bug, especially when the girls sometimes split their legs across the guy's hips," Annika commented.

"Yes, some people have nothing more important to worry about," said Ella,

"Yes, but in some ways the government's getting more liberal, like . . . the parliament just decriminalized homosexuality amongst adults," Martin told them.

"About time. Seems pretty crazy to make criminals out of people for something as stupid as that," Ella agreed.

"This is a nice violin," said Annika as she stroked the bow over some resin before bowing a few notes from *Värmlänningarna*.

"I love that song," Martin told her. "I saw the play last summer performed at the Marstrand fortress, by a touring theater group. It was fantastic, but oh so sad. I fell in love with that poor girl, wasn't she named Annika?

"Anna."

"Huh?" Martin said.

"Anna, her name was Anna, the girl you fell in love with," Ella said.

Martin kept taking pictures as Ella served the food and even as they dined.

"Are you making a documentary? A day with Annika Nobel." Annika asked.

"No, but that's not a bad idea"

They moved into the living room for their concert. Martin staged a few pictures before the concert began. Annika and Ella sounded good together and played several tunes.

Ella put on the coffee and they moved over to the sofa corner for small talk. Ella told stories about Kurt and some of the funny things that he had done. Like when Kurt used to have a key to her house, and sometimes he would come over late at night and just slip into her bed. Well, one particular night she was awaited another man in her bed, a particularly bearded and hairy gentleman when Kurt arrived. They could hear him come and Ella told her friend that they were going to teach him a lesson so they pretended to sleep, her friend covered up by the quilt when Kurt came into the room, undressed, and slipped into the bed. "You can probably imagine what happened after that," she giggled. "Kurt got the shock of his life. He rushed out and it was the last time he came over without first calling," she told them.

"I would have loved to have been there then," Annika laughed.

"The worst thing he did though must have been when he came to show me one of his fancy American cars that he had just imported from America. It was an absolutely beautiful car, a burgundy-colored convertible. Well, we ended up driving out to a pier somewhere around Särö where we parked to make out. Well, I'm not completely sure what happened next, if the pier was not strong enough . . ."

"Oh, no!" Annika shrieked.

". . . to hold the rocking car, or if we accidentally released the parking brake, or a combination of the two, but a few seconds later we were both sitting in a slowly sinking convertible."

"I remember that car very well. He had just gotten it when we first met. It was a beautiful car."

"Well, they were able to clean it up, but I tell you, it all happened so fast that we never had time to get scared, but then we had to walk quite a distance to a house where we could call for a cab. It wasn't easy to explain to those people how we had ended up in our dilemma." They all laughed heartily.

"Kurt will be Kurt," Annika sighed, fascinated to learn more about Kurt's former life.

"Heard anything from Kurt?" Ella asked.

"No, he never writes when he travels," Annika explained. "He's too busy," she added.

PART III

CHAPTER 17

July, 1944 - Axel and Alex born

Dismayed by her enormous proportions and depressed by her lack of energy, Annika grew increasingly short tempered and emotional as spring approached. Kurt suggested they hire a nanny. Annika knew it was merely a matter of status for Kurt and that he enjoyed having another woman living with them, but she was appreciative of the help and the company, regardless of his motives. Perhaps she could be another Bella, whom they both had enjoyed?

Eventually Kurt chose Ingrid Grundin, with Annika's approval. Ingrid came from one of the smaller islands in the Gothenburg archipelago. She was the oldest of seven children whom she had helped to care for. The Nobels knew that Ingrid was used to hard work, having been raised on the islands. Perhaps she didn't possess the most refined social skills, but she had an inviting smile, and was attractive in a natural way. Perhaps her most appreciated skill was her training as a masseuse.

Ingrid had not oversold herself on her skill as a masseuse and Annika appreciated her service as she grow increasingly uncomfortable. Kurt was also one of Ingrid's frequent patrons. He enjoyed his sessions so much that he purchased a special massage table. He would start with a hot bath, wrap a towel around his waist, lay down on the table while he was still warm and listen to the radio while Ingrid gave him the treatment. Annika got her massage on the bed as she could not lay comfortably on the narrow table.

Most foods were being rationed. Trying to buy meat meant several hours waiting in line with no guarantee that there would be any meat left by the time one progressed to the front of the line. Milk was easier for the Nobels to come by. Because Annika was pregnant, she was allotted extra rations. They could also get milk and eggs from Jonas and Signe Berg, Eva's parents. The Nobels were more comfortable than most, because Kurt could barter for just about anything he wanted with coffee. Bartering was illegal, of course, and at one occasion, Kurt had to sweat out a couple of days when a man with whom he had been trading was arrested and Kurt feared that he would turn him in. Luckily for Kurt nothing was said.

From their windows, Kurt and Annika could see the search lights scanning the sky at night. Occasionally a German plane had to be chased out of Swedish air space with the assistance of ground artillery.

They saw several wounded planes struggling to reach the safety of Torslanda airport. One evening when Kurt and Annika were sitting on their balcony drinking coffee, they saw a German plane coming in really low over the city, smoking badly. The following day they heard on the news that it never made it to the airport. It crashed a few hundred feet short. Luckily no one on the ground was injured; however, the pilots were killed.

Annika developed a close friendship with Ella and Martin. She did several modeling assignments for Martin, for which she was well compensated. Annika also helped Ella hosting a few banquets. She didn't need the money, but she liked getting out of the house and she enjoyed the work.

Annika was due to deliver her baby in July. She was scheduled for a caesarean delivery. Knowing that she would not have to endure the torturous labor relieved much apprehension for Annika, especially since it was obvious that she was going to have a very large baby. On July 11, her water broke, and Kurt drove straight to the hospital. Annika went into surgery at 8:00 a.m. and at 8:25 the doctors were amazed to discover that there were not one but two fine baby boys. Kurt was delighted. The prospect of having two sons to carry on the family name was more than he could have dreamt of.

Annika opened her eyes to the nurse standing over her. "Good morning Mrs. Nobel! How do you feel?" the nurse asked.

"Okay, I guess," She didn't feel much of anything yet.

"I'm afraid you want not be getting the two hundred and fifty crowns one normally gets for having a baby," the nurse joked.

Annika was a mixture of panic and confusion. "Why . . . is something wrong?" she asked nervously.

"Oh no, you will be getting five hundred crowns for having twins. You had two healthy and handsome boys," she responded quickly, realizing how her joke had scared Annika.

A lovely smile brightened Annika's face and she drifted off to sleep. Two hours later she awoke from a beautiful dream of her two little boys playing in the garden. It seemed so real, could it have been? The nurse came to her bed side. "Hello again Mrs. Nobel! Are you back with us again?"

"How is my baby?" Annika asked cautiously.

"Baby, don't you remember? I told you that you have two little boys. Your husband is beside himself. I don't think I've ever seen such a proud papa."

So, it was true. Two babies . . . two boys. It was a miracle. Annika was for one of the few times in her troublesome marriage truly happy. Ironically, she and Kurt weren't legally married then.

The average stay for a mother and baby was eight days but Annika had to stay for two weeks again because of the caesarean section. On the third day Annika was encouraged to get up and walk some. She participated in a crash course in baby care, although she would have competent help at home.

All hospital expenses were paid for by the state. As was the law, Annika received a bonus of 500 crowns, half of which she had received three months early so she could purchase supplies she would need, when the baby arrived. In addition, the state would pay the Nobels a sum each quarter until the children were 18 years old, regardless of need. Swedish families also received assistance in paying their rent based on number of children and income.

Ingrid took care of Kurt while Annika was at the hospital. Although, for the first three days she returned to her island home to see her parents. When she returned to the Nobels' apartment, she found Kurt at home and Eva was taking a bath.

"We had to work late so Eva stayed over in the guest room", he explained. "I would appreciate if you didn't tell Annika that Eva was here while she was gone," he said. "She might not understand."

"I won't tell," she promised, smiling sympathetically at him. "She probably wouldn't understand." Ingrid walked past the guest room and noticed that it did not appear disturbed.

When Kurt came home for dinner that evening Ingrid waited with her own dinner so she could dine with Kurt. She had made fried flounder, one of his favorite meals. She was dressed in her house coat that she always wore around the house, leaving a few buttons undone, both up and down, making it more comfortable for working. The housecoat revealed enough to distract Kurt from his supper.

"Another great meal, Ingrid. I want you to know how much we appreciate you around here. You've exceeded our expectations."

"Thank you, Mr. Nobel, I enjoy working here. Both you and Mrs. Nobel have been most kind and generous, and I appreciate the opportunity," Ingrid replied shyly.

"Please, there's no need to be so formal. Please call us by our first names. We want you to be part of the family and feel at home here.

"I'm glad to hear that you're pleased with me. I try my best, and if there's anything I can do for you, feel free to call on me at any time, Kurt."

"Well thank you, and the same goes for you. If there's anything I can do for you, please let me know."

"Thank you, Kurt."

"I could use a massage after dinner if that's all right? You give the best massages of anyone I know," he said. He selected a cigar from the box and prepared to light it.

"Oh, thank you, I enjoy doing it. It's nice to be able to make people feel good and appreciative," Ingrid replied, as she began to clean the table.

Kurt's eyes followed her as she moved about the kitchen. "Well, I appreciate you a lot. You know how to get rid of that tension. Your hands are magical."

"Why don't you take a hot bath while I clean up and then I will tend to your tensions?" Kurt liked his bath hot and he submerged himself, but for the nose, to soak. Ingrid had to heat extra water on the stove to reach the desired temperature.

She knocked softly on the door and walked in without waiting for an answer, bringing in another pot of steaming hot water." Pull your legs back so you don't get burned," she cautioned. "I thought we'd start in the tub today, with a good scrubbing." Again, without waiting for approval she took a semi-soft scrub brush and worked in the soap before scrubbing his shoulders and back, reaching deep into the water. "Does that feel good?" she asked.

"Like magic," he responded almost purring.

"Oops!" she exclaimed, as the soap slipped into the tub. She had to reach deep down to eventually find it after several failed attempts.

She continued to scrub his lower back, sides and legs. She teased him, scrubbing under his feet as he quickly pulled them away. She grabbed a large bath towel, pulled the plug to the tub and asked him to stand up. She was already aware of his excitement, having searched for the soap and scrubbing him down. She was still surprised of how large he was.

"I'm not sure of how good a job I'm doing. I was supposed to release your tensions, but it appears to me as though you are tenser than ever," she said, smiling at him. "But I'm not done yet."

She rubbed him down well, with the towel and invited him over to the table. She began rubbing in oil on his back methodically first working on his shoulders, kneading his muscles with her strong fingers. She continued down his back, buttocks and down his legs to his feet. She rubbed the balls of his feet and the toes, individually.

"Are you feeling more relaxed now?" she whispered.

CHAPTER 18

August, 1945 - Yvonne

The tension between Kurt and Annika grew and arguments became more frequent. Those arguments often related to their family feuds or Kurt's insisting on doing all the shopping for the family, providing Annika with a minimal pocket allowance.

While the boys were infants, Kurt played the devoted father and came home after work on a daily basis. He would take the family for drives and strolls in the park. However, after a couple of months Kurt began spending more time away from home than ever before. Besides his busy business schedule, he was active in several organizations which kept him out in the evenings. He made frequent trips up and down the coast selling coffee, mainly to hotels and restaurants and bringing merchandise to his boutiques. His several rental properties also demanded his attention. Kurt now decided to fulfill an old dream, to build a summer home. The house was being constructed outside Stenongsund, a popular summer community one to two hours' drive north of Gothenburg, depending on traffic. The drive included crossing two lift bridges and a one-lane bottle neck controlled by a slow traffic light going through Kungälv, a picturesque medieval town.

Kurt had chosen Stenongsund, mainly because several of his friends lived in the area, in particular Yvonne, a seamstress. Yvonne was one of Kurt's several casual girlfriends as well as being a supplier of apparel for his shops. Yvonne was a tall slender girl. At six foot, she was close to two inches taller than Kurt. She operated a sewing shop from her home business, a converted farm. Only twenty-six years old she had rapidly grown her business from nothing to now having more than twenty seamstresses working for her. She specialized in making luggage and in making women's undergarments, but also produced a variety of other products. She was attractive and used her femininity to her advantage. Kurt was not her largest customer but an important one nevertheless. He received the full VIP treatment whenever he came, perhaps partly because Yvonne enjoyed his company. She knew that Kurt was married. She had met Annika on a couple occasions but she saw Kurt as a customer and friend with needs. Kurt would stop by her place every time he traveled north, and again on his way home. He enjoyed Stenongsund's tranquil setting and spent many hours strolling along a shoreline trail. Yvonne's business was tucked away from the main streets, although, it was relatively close to the city. It was a treat for Yvonne to get a visitor, and in particular, a man's man, like Kurt.

"Hi Kurt! I'm so glad to see you, sweetheart," Yvonne greeted him as he stepped into her small but functional office. "You should appreciate this. We just got our pre-show presentation ready and are going to do a dress rehearsal in a few minutes."

"I'm sure I will. So you have everything ready for the big show in Borås on Tuesday?" he asked.

"Oh God, I hope so," she sighed. "It's been a madhouse here the last few days . . . or weeks actually. It will be so nice when this show is over and we can concentrate on the one in Malmö in two weeks."

"Here, I brought you some coffee."

"You're an angel Kurt." She stood up and greeted him with a hug and a kiss on the lips.

"Thanks a million sweetheart!" Yvonne called most men and women "sweetheart". She continued, "There are a few other guests that I've invited too. Why don't we go into the loft so I can introduce you?"

There were eight other women in the loft. Four of them were models getting ready. Lisbeth was a customer, a boutique owner from Strömstad. Lisa dyed fabrics. Fredrika was a designer, and Martha was Yvonne's assistant. Kurt already knew Lisbeth from Strömstad and Martha, but the others were new acquaintances. Each was handed a glass of wine, and they took their seats in the makeshift showroom. The lights were dimmed and spotlights lit the short runway. Music was turned up behind Yvonne, who narrated the show. They began showing coats and jackets, with the girls displaying luggage at the same time. They continued with a line of hats and finished with the undergarments. To Kurt's dismay, the girls wore leotards under the undergarments.

"Well, what do you think, sweetheart?" Yvonne asked when it was over.

"Very nice. You've come a long way since you got started here, what is it? Five years ago," he replied. "Very nice indeed. Too bad only that you had to cover up those beautiful girls with leotards."

"Well, yes, you know. We have to, in Borås, and I wanted to get a feel for how it will be tomorrow. But we don't have to here. Ladies and gentleman she announced we are going to put on a special private show only for you, modeling some of our undergarments the way they are intended to look without the leotards. Are you girls ready?" she asked the models behind the curtain. They could hear the girls giggle behind the stage. First the girls modeled more conventional white and black undergarments. Next came a line of suggestive undergarments that emphasized being sexy over practical.

"This is where I was hoping that I could get some input from you. This is a new concept that I would like to venture into. I think it's just as important to wear sexy undergarments as it is to wear sexy street clothes and beach clothing. Perhaps even more so. You're all my best friends and you are knowledgeable on the subject. I think we can have some fun here, go a little crazy and break some rules this weekend. What do you think? Kurt, I was hoping you could help us by offering a male perspective. Lisa has brought us some fun materials that we can play with, and Fredrika has drawn some basic sketches that we can work from, or we can start from scratch if you'd rather. I have a couple girls ready to sew up whatever we come up with . . . What do you say? Are we ready?"

They spent the first hours coming up with basic designs that they tried out on the models, before they drew features onto the garments, or carefully pinned on details such as lace or ribbons or little bows or hearts. Then they made the alterations and tried again. Martha, Yvonne's assistant, was the expert on support-related issues. The girls all had to try out how comfortable and functional their garments were. They spent most of the day working on various designs and Kurt was treated as one of the girls.

The following day Kurt continued his trip up north, but he stopped by a few days later on his return trip. Yvonne was eager to show Kurt the new garments and had Martha model for him.

After dinner Kurt joined Yvonne in the main house while the other guests retired to the guest cottage.

"Why don't you model a little for me?" Kurt asked.

"Oh, I can't do that; I'll call for Martha if you like!"

"No, no, I want you to model for me, not Martha. I would like to see how they look on your body. You have a beautiful tall slender body, very sexy," he added.

"You really think so . . . I don't know. I would feel silly."

"Well I think you should feel silly if you don't. You have an absolutely stunning body and have absolutely nothing to be ashamed of. Why don't you just start a little slowly and put on this bikini. It doesn't reveal much skin. If you expect other women to wear your creations, you must be comfortable wearing them yourself," he lectured. "Come and stand in front of the beach photo so it looks as though you're at the beach.

"Alright I will, that is not much smaller than my regular swim suit. But promise not to laugh."

She was gone for more than fifteen minutes, and Kurt had to call on her.

"I'll be right there," she answered. He called again after another five minutes and she slowly opened the door. "It looks nice," she told him, but she would not come out.

"Well, come out of there so I can judge for myself," he urged.

"Its so small. It hardly covers anything," she complained.

"Well, that's the whole idea, isn't it? We tried to make it sexy."

She came into the room, standing by the door. "Well, people can't wear this in public."

"Good thing then that you're not in the public, besides, it's not intended to be, but let me see." He walked over to her. "That's not that small. I think we could cut even more, right here." He reached over and pulled back the top of the bra a little. Yvonne stood still, frozen. She was breathing heavily but determined not to back out.

CHAPTER 19

Oct, 1945 - Eva and Bo Lundgren

In August 1944, Eva began seeing Bo Lundgren, a teacher, who lived in an apartment in the same apartment building where Eva lived, and which Kurt owned. Earlier they only met when Bo came to pay the rent or when he saw Eva on her knees cleaning the stairway. Their relationship sparked when Eva went up to his apartment to fix a leak under his bathroom sink. Bo had complained several times about the leak but to no avail. The regular maintenance man had been called into military service and Kurt was away on a trip to the US. After having tried unsuccessfully to find someone else to do it, Eva decided to have a look at the problem herself. Actually, Eva was curious about Bo and did not mind having to go up to his place.

Bo opened the door, surprised to see Eva. "Hi, your local plumber at your service. I brought home some tools from work," she explained. "I thought I'd give it a go. I had to replace a washer in my own sink not too long ago and chances are that you're having the same problem," she explained confidently. Having been raised on a farm, Eva was quite resourceful.

"Are you sure you can do that?" he asked doubtfully, while at the same time admiring her spunk.

"Well, we'll soon find out, won't we?" She said, slightly miffed. Eva sauntered across the living room through his bed room and into the bathroom. It was apparent that the drip came from the connection between the supply tube and the faucet. To be able to reach up under the cabinet she had to crawl up inside. Only her hips and her legs remained outside the cabinet. She realized that it was not really a lady like position, but she couldn't quit now, especially since Bo had expressed some doubt as to her credentials.

Bo couldn't resist appraising her slender body half way tucked into the cabinet. Her dress had slid up, revealing most of her legs.

"Oh no!" Eva shrieked. Having tightened the nut too tight, the worn-out washer together with the supply tube popped out, spraying water all over, completely soaking her.

"The valve!" Bo spotted the turnoff valve in the back of the cabinet. He quickly crawled into the cabinet atop Eva. After several turns, he succeeded in turning off the water. Suddenly he realized that he was laying right on top of a soaked but unflustered Eva.

"Thank you," she said smiling at him, "I'm sure glad you noticed the valve before the whole apartment got flooded. I couldn't get to it with the drain trap in the way."

"It was my pleasure." He smiled back at her.

They crawled back out and stood on the floor looking at one another soaking wet. Eva's hair was hanging straight with water still dripping from the ends. Her dress was clinging to her skin. Bo took down a bath towel. "Here let me wipe you off so you don't drag the water out on the parquet floor in the living room. It would get ruined."

"I'd just as well put in the new washer now before I clean up in case something else goes wrong." She slid back into the cabinet to finish the repair. Her soaked dress was now transparent. Bo admired her shapely figure all the while she worked under the sink.

After she completed the task, as she was gathering her tools, Eva turned to Bo.

"You know, I put a chicken in the oven before I came up. How would you like to come down and join me for dinner in . . . let's say thirty minutes . . .? so, we have time to put on some dry clothes?"

"I'd love to, although, I like the way you look right now."

Precisely thirty minutes later Eva greeted Bo at her door.

"How is my favorite plumber?" he asked.

"I did get it done eventually, didn't I?" she responded. "But not before I got the both of us drenched. Oh well, it could have been worse."

"It sure could. I'm actually glad that it happened or I wouldn't be here for dinner now, with you. Oh, here, I didn't have time to get you flowers, which you fully deserve, but I brought a bottle of wine."

"Thank you. You didn't have to bring anything, but I'm glad you did because I didn't have any wine to go with the chicken. I put my last drops in the sauce"

"I saw in the paper that the Soviets have now joined the US and Britain in fighting Japan. This war is making strange bedfellows, isn't it? I wouldn't have guessed that the US and Soviet Union would end up on the same side for any reason," said Bo.

"Well, the Allies seem to be doing pretty well regardless, with the US taking Okinawa and everything," Eva said. "It seems ironic that it would happen on fool's day."

"What a blood bath though, 100,000 Japanese killed. That's so many that it doesn't seem real." It was Bo's first visit inside Eva's apartment and he was looking around the apartment, noticing the female touch in its decorations.

"Yes, it's as if a whole city perished, unreal," she agreed. "What do you think will happen now after Roosevelt passed away? Do you know anything about Truman?" she asked, pulling the cork from the wine bottle.

"Here, let me help you," Bo offered, taking the bottle. "I really don't know that much about him. Perhaps we should give him a chance before we judge him. At least he has some experience; being vice president under Roosevelt."

"Cerebral hemorrhage at the age of 63," Eva reflected. "Seems too young to die. What a catastrophe for the US. They must be in shock, with losing their President so suddenly and right in the middle of the worst war in history."

"He seems to have been a great president. They reelected him four times."

"Kurt said that he really liked him, but then again, Kurt likes anything that's American."

Eva looked fresh in her white pleated skirt and pink angora sweater. Her hair was still wet and she had tied it into a ponytail. She had also replaced the white wet blouse. "Boy! . . . you look nice, so young in that outfit . . . like a teenager. You're a woman with many faces. In the mornings you're always dressed so properly in a business suit . . ."

"When did you ever see me in the morning?" Eva asked.

"Lots of times. I can see you from my window . . ."

"Now wait a minute . . ."

"When you wait for the bus," he continued. "And I've seen you as the cleaning lady doing the stairways here in the building."

She showed him around her tastefully decorated apartment.

"Wow . . . This is really nice! You have excellent taste."

"Thanks, I like it here." She guided him into the kitchen and finished off the final touches of their dinner. "And now I have also met you as my favorite plumber, and master chef. That is quite a repertoire. Do you have any more faces that I should know?"

"How about a farm girl? I grew up on a small farm in Lindome. But enough about me. Tell me about yourself. Who is Bo Lundgren, the virtual stranger that I soaked just half hour ago?" She looked at him mischievously, smiling. "I know that you're a perfectionist. I have seen your apartment. I know that you are a school teacher and that you always pay your rent on time. I know that you're a gentleman," she concluded, smiling at him.

"I think you pretty much got me covered. I'm afraid there isn't much more to know. As you noted, I'm a teacher, a wood craft teacher. I was raised on a farm in Värmland. I teach school during the winter and during the summer I go back to the farm to do forestry work, and I love children." he added.

Bo and Eva spent the rest of that evening together, and he moved into her apartment shortly thereafter. They were married in December, 1945, one week before Christmas. Kurt did not attend the wedding, but he gave Eva a generous gift certificate to any of his stores. He couldn't help feeling jealous of Bo. He had long been strongly attracted to Eva, and they had been intimate more than once, but both knew their relationship would not lead to anything more. Eva appreciated the gift. Eva had always admired Kurt but she was not willing to accept his womanizing. Kurt did never understand why Eva choose Bo over him, although he did not choose Eva.

Bo and Eva applied for a state home starter loan, to get some new furniture, but with their combined income they earned too much to qualify. They weren't really disappointed. They didn't need furniture, other than possibly a larger bed. The newlyweds had planned on using the money to buy a car. For the time being, Bo's motorcycle would have to suffice.

With Eva less available after her marriage Kurt found her even more intriguing. He pampered her with generous bonuses and gifts, and made a point of involving her in his business dealings so he could spend more time with her. On the weekends he would go out to visit her parents in Lindome, hoping that Eva would be there. Kurt's indulgence of Eva possibly contributed to the failure of Eva's and Bo's marriage, after less than four years that was plagued with difficulties between them. The largest hurdle was perhaps Eva's inability to bear children.

CHAPTER 20

August, 1946 - Stellan

Kurt was not one to give early warnings. He could call home in the afternoon and tell Annika that he was bringing company for dinner. Or he could announce that he was getting on an America liner that night and would be back in perhaps three weeks. He always brought home nice gifts to the family, in general, although, frequently without much forethought. On one occasion he brought home a very nice electric train set for the boys with moving bridges and several other elaborate details. When it was all put together and plugged in with great anticipation, the transformer burned up instantly, as it was designed for the much weaker electric current used in the US. However, the children appreciated the American chewing gum sticks and other candies that he always brought them. On each trip, he would bring home a new American-made car, often to sell almost right away. He made good money with his car dealings, but he would have made the trips regardless.

Kurt was infatuated with the US and often dreamed about moving there, even though things were improving by leaps and bounds in Sweden as the welfare state expanded. Not only did the government provide free public schools, but school supplies and school lunches were provided without charge. Child support was provided for all children until their 18th birthday. In October of 1945, Sweden joins the U.N, and the America liner Stockholm is completed, the largest ship ever built in Sweden. The Swedish Crown Prince Carl Gustav is born. Plastic is invented, and Sweden begins research with atomic energy.

In August of 1946, the Nobels' summer home in Stenongsund was completed. Kurt had designed the house himself and hired a local builder to construct it. The large white structure sat on a granite rock foundation, a hill, that was surrounded by a wide deck and rock gardens. Picture windows overlooked fields of grain, with the ocean visible at some distance. It was a ten-minute bike ride to a favorite swimming spot where the Nobels kept a wooden pleasure boat.

To get to the beach they had to cross a cow pasture. The cows would often come running when they saw the bathers, hoping for a treat. They especially loved sugar cubes. It could be rather frightening, with ten, fifteen cows coming running towards them. However, the cows always stopped when they came close. Bathers had to take special care not to step into a cow-pod.

The beach was ideal for small children. They could wade quite far before the water became knee-high. On the other side of a rock pier the water dropped off rapidly, making it ideal for swimming, fishing and boating.

Annika and the children moved out to the house as soon as it was completed. Two days later when Kurt arrived for the first time since Annika had settled in, he was greeted by a fresh scent of Lilac as he stepped into the house. Besides wearing the perfume, Annika liked to place a few drops on the light bulbs, which quickly carried the fragrance throughout the house.

"Did you notice anything new?" she asked hopefully.

"What do you mean? . . . in the house?"

"Anything, at all?" she urged.

"Why don't you just tell me?" Kurt asked impatiently. "You cut your hair," he declared.

"No, try again," she urged.

"I'm too tired to play games. Just tell me or forget it."

"I got a permanent. Can't you tell? Do you like it?"

"I liked it the way it was. How much did that cost?"

"It's the latest style. I did it because it's the same style that the girl had that we saw the other night at Stats Hotellet. You said that you really liked her."

"It's okay. How much did it cost?" he repeated.

"I thought it would be nice if I looked good tomorrow when we go out with the Bergs."

"I'm sorry, I totally forgot about that. I'm not going to be able to come. I was going to tell you. I'm going away for a few days on business. I just decided this morning and I'm leaving tomorrow morning."

"Where are you going?"

"To New York"

"To New York, America?" Annika asked, astonished.

"The one and only."

"What about me and the kids? That will take more than a few days and you know I don't like to sleep alone in this big house." Annika's voice was rising. "Ingrid isn't coming back for another three weeks."

"Don't worry. I've thought of everything. Stellan is going to come and stay here while I'm gone. I'll only be away a little more than three weeks all together. I'll bring you back something nice."

"What? You mean Stellan Strand your friend who was here last year?"

"Yes Stellan. He's in town. I saw him this morning and he needs a place to stay for three weeks, so I thought it would work out perfectly if he stayed here while I'm gone. He's a great guy so you should be all right."

The fact that he was going to be gone for some time did not bother Annika so much. Kurt was rarely home anyway. But it irked her that he made such decisions without even considering consulting her. She consoled herself with the thought that she did have this beautiful summer home, and Stellan was going to keep her company so she wouldn't be afraid at night. It could even be fun. Stellan was Kurt's childhood friend. He was a seaman, a navigator and had been a mate of Kurt's on a trip to Brazil. He was single, made good money and had no apparent sense of time. He could drop in to visit at any time of the day, but was away at the sea most of the time. Annika had not seen Stellan for over a year. Annika was curious about why Kurt had invited him to come and stay now, when he was going to be gone for three weeks. Stellan had always had an eye for Annika and Kurt knew it. It was as if he intentionally was asking for trouble.

"He came into the store this morning. He's going to stay ashore until the fourth of September which will work out perfectly. The Stockholm is leaving tomorrow morning for New York and I was able to get a ticket with Stellan's help. He'll come out tomorrow night after he drops me off first. Then he can have the car."

Stellan was always a prankster and Annika was never really sure of where she had him, but she was fond of him all the same. He told the most unbelievable stories about his journeys. She had dinner ready when Stellan arrived. She didn't hear him come. He walked right in and put his arms around her, standing by the stove, and gave her a warm hug, kissed her on both cheeks and squeezed her a little longer than necessary, but Annika didn't resist.

"Hi Annika you look smashing as always. It's been a long time." His skin was dark brown from spending long hours under the ocean sun. He smiled warmly. He was tall, perhaps 6'2", with a strong but slender build. He was smartly dressed in a white loosely fitted suit and a bright colored necktie, and shiny white shoes. He wore a fresh rose on his lapel, the same kind that Annika had in her garden. A handkerchief occupied his breast pocket and he held his white straw hat, with a band matching his tie in his hand. His blond hair was combed back and held in place with a generous helping of Brill Cream. Annika breathed in his manly cologne. He had not changed.

"It sure has. You should drop by a little more often." She returned the smile and the hug.

"I don't want to wear out my welcome. I'll make up for it this time, though," he said with a broad grin. "Three weeks straight. Do you think you can stand me that long?"

"Really, Stellan, I appreciate your doing this for me. I would have been scared stiff staying here alone at night. The only close neighbors we have are the Bergs and they only come out on the weekends. You're a life saver. Otherwise I would've had to move back into town, and I love it out here. Soon enough we'll have to move back to town anyway. It's nice to be able to stay here as long as possible."

"Don't mention it. I had to pay Kurt good money for this arrangement," he chuckled.

"Oh yeah, and how much were I worth?"

"More than I could ever come up with, that's for sure, "he responded. He lifted Alex with a pair of muscular arms, to the boy's delight. "You must be Axel, what a handsome lad you are. And have you ever grown from the last time I saw you."

"I'm Alex," Alex corrected him.

"I'm sorry, that's what I meant to say. For sure that was going to be my second choice." Turning to Annika he asked, "Can you tell them apart when you dress them the same as that? I don't think I can. All the same, it's amazing how much you have grown. And you're getting heavy too," Stellan said as Alex smiled shyly.

"Oh yes, when you get to know them, you can tell. Maybe you children can speak some English now with Uncle Stellan. They are debating over switching from German to English as the second language in school now," she explained, "even if it will be a few years yet before we'll be affected, I wish they do."

"Let me show you your room so you can put away your things, and dinner will be ready in just a few minutes."

"Fine, it smells terrific. What are we having? Lilacs . . . my favorite flowers?"

"No, that will be tomorrow. Today I was trying to think of something that you may not get at sea that often. We're having fresh fried mackerel. You know it sounds so funny that you don't get fresh fish out at sea, but that is what my grandpa always used to say that he missed the most."

"You're right, we don't usually have the time to stop the ship and go fishing. Nowadays, though, we have freezers onboard and we can have anything that can be frozen. But frozen is not fresh, and our meals were not prepared with loving hands, like yours. It smells great." Stellan spoke with a strong Gothenburg accent that Annika would have found unpolished if spoken by others, but she found it quite charming on Stellan.

The dinner was as delicious as it was enjoyable. Meringues topped with fresh strawberries and whipped cream, which Annika had prepared, topped off the meal.

"The strawberries are from our garden, and I helped pick them," Axel informed him.

"And you did a great job at that," Stellan flattered him. After not having visited the Nobels for so long, there was plenty to talk about, especially with Stellan's having traveled to several exotic places.

Stellan took a walk out in the yard with the boys while Annika straightened up after dinner. They showed him their white play house in the back corner of the lot. It was a smaller version of the large house. A tire hung from the big oak tree making an ideal swing. Axel and Alex, only two years and three-month-old, needed some assistance in getting up on the swing. They appreciated being gently pushed. They continued to the back of the house and climbed the small mountain from where they had a good view of the ocean. The yard was surrounded by a chain link fence, not so much to keep the children safe, as there was little traffic there, but to keep the rabbits and the deer from feasting in the yard. They had dammed up a crevice in the mountain in a corner of the yard, where the boys could splash and play with toy boats.

Annika announced that the coffee was ready. She served it on the veranda, together with her homemade cookies and liqueur.

"I don't think I paid Kurt enough. This is a better deal than I bargained for," Stellan teased her.

Annika gazed at him with a soft smile, and then wrinkled her nose, looking cute as only she could. "Yeah, a real bargain, huh?"

While Annika put the children to bed, Stellan went to his room to unpack his bags. Afterwards they went back out to the deck. It had grown dark and Annika lit a candle that flickered slowly in the light, warm breeze.

"Here Annika, I brought you a couple of small things. Why don't you look at this first?"

She opened the package he gave her with suspense. One could never be sure, when it came to Stellan, that it wasn't some prank.

"Chocolate! Just what I needed. If anything, I should be dieting."

"You don't need to go on a diet. You are absolutely perfect just as you are."

"You're just being kind, but I appreciate it."

"I mean it." He looked straight into her large blue eyes. "I can't think of anything that could improve on you, except for one thing."

"Yes, and what is that?" she asked.

"If you were mine," he sighed. "I guess we always want the most what we can't have.

Annika opened the chocolate box. "I bet you use that line on all your girls, you smooth talking son-of-a-gun. I can't resist. This looks too good! She popped a piece into her mouth, prepared to enjoy the delicious chocolate. "Yuck . . . it's soap! I should have known! You never change!" She rushed into the kitchen to rinse out her mouth. "I'm going to get you for that," she cried out when she returned. "I've plenty of time and I'm going to think of something really good. I promise, I'm going to get you!" She ruffled his hair as she walked passed him, coming away with a somewhat sticky hand from the Brill Cream. He handed her the other package.

"I don't know if I dare to open it," she said, turning the package several times, shaking it and squeezing it, like a child examining a Christmas present.

"Go ahead, I promise it won't bite you. If I'm not telling the truth, I agree to be your sex slave for three weeks. How is that?" he asked grinning.

"Somehow I don't find that all that comforting." She opened the package a little bit at the time. Her eyes widened as she pulled out a black negligee, trimmed in red. Annika stood up as she held it up in front of herself. "It's really beautiful. Thank you very much." She walked over and gave him a quick hug.

"Shouldn't you try it on to see if it fits?" he asked.

She smiled at him seductively. "Later."

They spent most of the next day at the beach, until it began to cloud over. A wall of black clouds moved their way and the wind grew chilly and picked up. They returned home, put on some music and relaxed until dinner. For dessert Annika swapped Stellan's whipping cream for shaving cream, causing a good laugh for all, including the children. Upon retiring he discovered that Annika had sneaked into his room and short-sheeted his bed. Light thunder rumbled during the night, but at a distance.

The following day it rained all day so they stayed inside. The children ran out to their pond a couple of times, but the rain was cold so they soon came back inside. When Annika went to bed that night, she noticed that Stellan had been in her room and removed her night gowns and robe. The only nightgown left was the black negligee. She put it on and looked at herself in the mirror. It followed her body, hiding little. She toyed with the idea of modeling it for Stellan but decided against it. The wind was increasing, as she lay down in bed. A shutter on a basement window began slamming and the thunder moved closer. Axel showed up at her door, crying. Annika took Axel and walked over to Stellan's door and knocked.

"Come in!" Stellan sat up.

"Can we come in until the thunder has passed? We're scared," Annika said, having forgotten for the moment what she was wearing.

"Of course. My room is always open to you. You look lovely," he said.

"What have you done with my robe?" She asked playfully.

"What robe? . . ." Lightning suddenly lit up the sky, flickered for several seconds.

"One thousand, two thousand, thr . . ." The thunder crashed as if a series of cannons had been fired in the room next door. "That was less than two hundred meters away. It sounded as if it hit something." Her voice shook with fear.

"Come here and sit on my bed. I won't mind."

Annika did not need a second invitation. "I can't believe that Alex can sleep through this noise," she said. There were another four or five strong flashes of lightning before it moved past their house. Annika helped Axel back to his bed. The rain had now intensified, and it was hammering the roof, too fast for the gutters to handle, and they overflowed. "I wonder what's going to happen to my pretty flowers, with this heavy rain." she said. "And all the fruit will be knocked off the trees."

"Maybe you can make us one of your special apple cakes that I still remember, and dream about, from the last time I visited you. All this talk about food . . . How about another cup of coffee, since no one seems to be in the mood for sleeping anyway?" he asked.

Now the storm had passed, so Annika put the children back to bed and put on the coffee pot. "I think I can use something to calm my nerves. Boy, was that a strong thunder storm!"

The rain stopped almost as fast as it had come, but the wind was picking up again, and the shutter was beginning to slam against the window again. "Stellan, would you mind running out to close that shutter? I'll never be able to go to sleep if it keeps on banging like that. You can wear Kurt's raincoat."

"Of course, for you Annika, I'd do anything," he replied. Annika followed him with her eyes as Stellan dressed in only his pajama bottoms crossed the living room, walking toward the door. She took in his muscular build, thinking he must work out regularly. He discarded the idea of putting on Kurt's clearly too small raincoat and merely held it over his head when he ran out. The door slammed behind him. Annika went back to the kitchen to get something out to serve with the coffee. She just had the liqueur bottle in her hand when the lights went out. Annika felt her way across the kitchen and found a couple of candles that she lit. She poured two cups of coffee as Stellan returned soaking wet and looking cold.

"Thank you so much. I think the coffee got warm enough before we lost the power. Otherwise I do have a camping stove if you like it hotter."

"No thanks it'll be fine. I'm sure it's fine."

"Let me see if Kurt's pajamas won't fit you. They're pretty large, I think. You can't go to bed with those wet pants."

Stellan returned in Kurt's blue, which fit him good enough.

Annika held out the platter with coffee bread. "Here, help yourself. Is there something else you would like with the coffee?" She asked.

"Yes you," he said softly.

"Don't forget that I'm married, and to your friend," she reminded him.

"It's OK. I know that you and Kurt are divorced. He told me."

"That son of a bitch." Annika muttered. "I can't believe that he told you that. It was supposed to be a secret. We only did that on paper to protect me and the children, if Kurt should run into economic problems." Annika stiffened in anger. I can't believe he did that." Tears filled her eyes. "I wouldn't be surprised if his mother knows too."

Stellan moved closer, took her hand and rubbed it gently. "Whose idea do you really think that was? You don't have to get a divorce to protect your private property. Kurt is incorporated, and no one can touch his personal stuff," he explained. He wiped away a tear from her cheek, put his arm around her shoulder and gently pulled her toward him.

Annika rested her head on his shoulder. "That arrogant woman . . . that bitch, she finally did it." Annika's anger turned on her mother-in-law now. "She always knew how to wind baby boy Kurt around her little finger."

"You have a right to be angry. I would be too, if I were you," Stellan comforted her.

"I hope that old witch chokes on her success." Annika finished up her liqueur.

Stellan leaned over and kissed her on her forehead.

"She looked up at him and smiled. "You're so sweet, and that damned Kurt." She took a deep breath, slowly calming down, thanks to Stellan's comforting. "Would you like a drink? I sure could use one." She poured them both a glass of sherry and sat back down next to him. She had completely forgotten any discomfort about her nearly transparent negligee. She lifted Stellan's arm and placed it back around her shoulder. "When did Kurt ask you to come here and stay?"

"Oh, about two months ago."

"I should have known. This is part of some scheme he's up to. I know he has girls all over the place. He has Eva at his office and God knows who else. That's no surprise to me. Kurt's been freewheeling ever since we met. It isn't as though we've lived like a married couple. We have both had our separate lives for some time, but for the sake of the children we have agreed to officially stay married. Well, if he wants to be divorced, then let it be. He probably thinks that if you are here, then I won't complain about him being gone so much. I wouldn't be the least surprised if I should find out that he's seeing someone in the US. He travels over there all the time. By the way, how come you've never settled down and gotten married?" she asked. "I bet the girls would be standing in line for you. You're everything that Kurt is not."

"Well it just never happened. I guess I never met the right girl. The one I wanted was not available, and who would want to marry a sailor? I'm gone most of the time.

"You wouldn't happen to know something about roses being delivered here, would you?

"Roses, no I can't say that I would."

"It's so strange, I get these roses at least once a month, and I have no idea who sends them."

"Well, it's not me, although I might have if I had thought of it first. You certainly deserve to be pampered with flowers. It is a little strange though, that the sender doesn't seek recognition. To get back to your question about my getting married, I have to admit that I have thought about settling down and having a home and a family. There is a position open right now as a harbor pilot in Gothenburg."

"Oh, my brother is a harbor-pilot, as you might remember."

"That's right. Your brother Bo."

The power suddenly came on, flickered a few times and remained on. The whole house lit up. Annika jumped up, startled from the bright light. She walked around turning off all the lights again but leaving the radio playing soft music. Stellan followed her with his eyes from the couch. She was breathtaking. The sheer material of her gown was nearly transparent in the bright light. He walked over to her and placed his arms around her. "Would you like to dance?" he asked.

She nodded.

The following morning the sun was back out and it was a beautiful day. Everything looked green and fresh after the rain. Stellan, Annika and the children spent most of the day, and several to follow, on the beach. The days were peaceful and care free, but despite everything, Annika began to look forward to Kurt's return.

"Hi sweetie! I'm back."

"Hi darling! Where are you?" Annika was surprised at the joy she felt at the sound of his voice.

"I'm in Gothenburg, at the office. I have quite a few loose ends to tie up before I can come home. In fact, don't make dinner for me, and go ahead and put the kids to bed. I'll see them in the morning."

Annika tried to not let the disappointment she felt show. Why did something or someone else always have to come first?

"Okay, Darling, I understand. But I'll fix a nice snack for you when you come home."

"Sounds good. I'll see you about 9:00 this evening then."

It was September 2, 1946, the day Kurt returned. Stellan had left in the morning. He had four days left before he had to go to sea again, if he did not get the pilot job. He needed the time to get ready, and he did not feel comfortable staying at the summer house when Kurt was back.

Precisely at 9:00 Annika saw Kurt drive up the driveway in a brand new dark blue, shiny automobile with wide white sidewalls on the tires. She ran outside to greet him. Kurt stepped out, dressed in white pants and shoes, a dark double-breasted club jacket and a blue captain sailing cap. The cap bore the emblem of Gothenburg's Royal Yacht Club, and the same emblem was sewed onto his breast pocket. Kurt always made a point of dressing up. Actually, he did not own any casual clothing.

"Hello sweetheart!" he greeted her, and from the car he pulled out a big bouquet of red roses. For my beautiful and devoted wife," he said, bowing melodramatically. "How do you like our new wheels? It's a Buick, Roadmaster, straight from Detroit and it runs on gasoline. Isn't she a beauty?" he asked proudly. He demonstrated all the special features of his new pride to an equally admiring Annika. "And It's not for sale . . . at least for now. Let's get it unloaded first, and then I'll tell you everything."

"Welcome back," Annika said, giving him a quick smooch. She had prepared warm crab sandwiches on toast, smothered in a cheese sauce and served with a sweet white wine. Kurt gulped his down as if he had not had anything to eat in days. Afterwards they went into the living room for coffee.

"It feels awfully good to be back again. That was a long trip." Kurt began taking out some packages from his suitcase. The boys, having heard Kurt's animated voice, had gotten out of bed. They sat on the floor in front of him with big eyes and expectations.

"It sure is good to have you back," Annika purred.

She had decided not to mention anything about what she had learned from Stellan. After all, she had two beautiful children with Kurt, she lived in semi luxury, and she had the freedom to do pretty much as she pleased. Kurt frequently showered her with gifts, whether he did so because of guilt or to gain social status was not important, as long as he kept doing it. After all, Kurt was usually quite nice to her. Annika had decided to get the most out of her relationship with Kurt and accepted their living separate lives on the side. She would fulfill her need for intimacy with her extended family.

Kurt gave the boys various cars that ran on batteries, and, of course, American candy. Kurt had bought two elaborate cowboy outfits for the boys that would probably fit them in another three years or so. Finally, he brought out a large box and handed it to Annika.

"What do you think about this?" he asked her. "I told you I would get you something special, didn't I? What do you think about this?" He pulled out a full-length black Persian coat from the box.

"Wow! It's beautiful!" she exclaimed. She tried it on immediately and pranced around in it, twisting and turning in front of the mirror, trying to get the feel of it, hardly believing that it was actually hers. "Thanks a million, Kurt! Hey, you can be gone as much as you like, if you bring me presents like this when you get back!"

"Good I'll remember that. How did everything go here at home?" he asked. "Did Stellan behave?"

"As well as can be expected." She was looking for any trace of jealousy. "We had a really nice time with Stellan, really nice," she emphasized.

"Yes, that's what he told me too. I saw him this morning."

"Yeah, and what else did he say?" she asked cautiously.

"Oh, just that he had a terrific time and that he would be happy to 'wife-sit' any time I needed him. I'm glad you made him feel welcome. Oh yes, he also said that he had got a new job as a harbor pilot and that he will be living in Gothenburg permanently from now on."

"Really! He got the job?" Annika could not conceal her enthusiasm.

"That's nice, because he seems to be the only really good friend that we have together. In fact, I know he likes you a lot. He always tells me how lucky I am to have you, and that I should appreciate you more. I do appreciate you though, a lot."

"Yes, I know he does. Well I like him a lot too. He's a lot of fun, and he's so sincere. The kids love him. I hope he'll come over to see us often now that he'll be living in Gothenburg."

"I'm sure he will. You know, actually I think he's doing this because of you. He's a sailor and sailors never stay very long in one harbor. You must have left a lasting impression on him, for him to settle down now."

"Don't be silly. He told me when he first arrived that he had applied for the job . . . that he was tired of always being at sea. Did you see Sven and Camilla?" she asked.

"I sure did. They live at a nursery where Camilla works. Sven works there, part time too, but he also does carpentry work on the side. Camilla is still painting, and she's very good at it. I bought one of her paintings." Kurt rolled out a canvas featuring a nude painting of Annika lying on a couch. "What do you think? I think it's great. I thought I'd have it framed and hang in the dining room in town."

Annika's eyes widened. "I remember when I posed for that. Wow! It's quite nice, isn't it? She is good; she can make even me look good." I'm not sure the dining room is the best place for it, but we'll see."

"Actually, she gave me, or you, this one. Here is the one I bought." It was a painting of Sven working in a flower bed with Lake Michigan in the background. It was done in soft pastel colors and Camilla had captured the mist in the air perfectly.

"Boy! That's amazing! I knew that you got this one. Camilla writes me perhaps once every two months, and I heard from her two weeks ago. She must have written the same day you were there."

"Well, they're doing all right. You should have heard the stories they told me. Sven doesn't speak English worth a damn and that can really get you into situations."

"What did they say when they saw you? I'm surprised they wanted to talk to you at all."

"Why? They came out smelling like roses on that deal. They have no reason to be mad."

"Maybe so, but no thanks to you."

"They knew I was coming. I called them from Detroit and warned them. When you live that far away, anyone from home is good company, even me," he grinned smugly, "and they were dying to find out what was going on here in the old country. They live right outside of Chicago and there are a lot of other Swedes living there too. It's a really nice place. Evanston, it's called, and it's right next to Lake Michigan. Now, if she writes you all the time did she tell you anything about Sven?"

"What about Sven?"

"About him being ill?"

"Is Sven ill? Camilla didn't mention anything in her letter."

"Then do you know that she is going to have a baby?"

"Camilla, she is going to have a baby? When?" Annika squired.

"They just found out so you will probably get a letter from her now with my ship. Did you know that they already have a son? Well you must."

"Of course, the same time we had the boys. Perhaps you were gone then? That is so exiting. Camilla is going to become a mother again. What about Sven though? You said he is ill, what's the problem?"

"They are not sure. He's in constant pain and his remedy is, to not be sober. They are even talking about going back to Sweden so he can get better medical help. America is great, but their Medicare stinks. It is too expensive, all private. Then I drove up to see Peter and his family in Quebec. It was fun, but I had to leave the car at the border since I had temporary US plates on it. I took a bus up from the border. Peter drove me back down when I left. I tell you Annika I'm in love. I'm really in love."

"Did you meet someone over there?" Annika asked dryly.

"Oh, no. I meant I'm in love with America. Everything is so big over there. I went up to the top of the Empire State Building, the tallest building in the world. There was a restaurant there and they had a music studio so you could sing a song and they made an instant record while you waited. It was really something. I made a record and I sang a song especially for you, but I have to find where I put it. When you look down at people below from the top of the building, they all look like little ants running around.

"I thought you just said that everything in the US was big." She teased him.

"Everything else. Peter, lives in a nice home on the beach," Kurt told her. I can't believe how nice he has it. He's a captain on a Swedish-flagged merchant ship. He works one month on and one month off, what a life! They have this enormous tide where he lives. At low tides the water disappears several thousand feet out, and it was so much fun to walk on the beach where lots of fish, crabs and other creatures were left behind in small puddles. This happens twice a day, and then the water comes gushing back. And the ships! That was worth the trip alone! They pamper you all the way. There was a swimming pool onboard, a movie theater, a massage parlor, several exclusive restaurants, and in the evenings, dance and all sorts of entertainment. It was the new ship, the Stockholm, and she was really something."

"When are you going to bring me along?" Annika asked.

"Perhaps next year. I'm even thinking we might move over there for good. You'd love Chicago!"

"I wouldn't mind going there on a trip, to visit. I think moving there, though, would be going a little too far. You can read in the papers daily about all the kidnappings and murders that happen every day of the week. That doesn't sound like such a great place to raise children.

"We'll see."

"Poor Camilla. I can't get over what you told me about Sven. I feel so bad for them"

Ingrid still lived with Annika and Kurt, not so much because they needed help, as because a nanny was a status symbol. It did, however, give Annika a little more time to spend with Stellan. She still helped

Ella occasionally and the same was true for Martin. Kurt and Annika officially lived together, because of the boys, and on occasion they entertained together, but otherwise they lived separate lives.

Annika had eagerly awaited Kurt's arrival, not necessarily because she missed him. Their sex life was unemotional and mechanical, but also unconditional. Annika knew that Kurt spent time with Eva, and others, especially during all his travels. They talked about it openly and Kurt encouraged her to see other men. Nevertheless, Annika still enjoyed Kurt's company. He was entertaining, full of energy and always up to something. Perhaps most of all, he always brought back presents from his travels. Ironically, Kurt and Annika were closer now, as good friends, rather than as a conventional married couple. As their relationship was based on convenience and mutual respect, it did not trigger jealousy. Annika actually enjoyed listening to Kurt's stories about other women. And Kurt enjoyed listening to Annika's stories, even though she made up most of them. Kurt did not mind that Annika spent time with Stellan. He liked the arrangement of Stellan doing most of the fatherly things, for which Kurt had little interest. It was like having his cake and eating it too.

Annika had never been in love with Kurt as a person. She had loved what he brought her, the social status, the carefree living style and the excitement he brought to her life. Kurt was the father of her children, but this relationship represented social status more than anything else. Children were to be seen and not heard. The Noble boys dutifully bowed for friends of their parents, displaying their upper middle-class social skills. Neither Annika nor Kurt was especially close to the boys.

"September 2, 1945, remember that day," Annika shouted as she opened the morning paper. "Japan surrendered!" she exclaimed jubilantly.

"No kidding?! Well it's about time. I thought they would have surrendered sooner, especially when the US dropped the bombs over Hiroshima and then Nagasaki," said Kurt.

"They probably would have pretty soon regardless, with the Soviets declaring war against them, in August."

"It says here, that there are more than a million Japanese in Soviet prison camps. How can they fit them all?" asked Annika.

"Well, they're probably not first-class quarters," Kurt quipped.

"'US General Douglas McArthur takes over supervising the Japan effort, it says.' I think the Japanese are probably lucky if the US takes charge. They'll probably get humane treatment from them, even though Japan bombed Pearl Harbor," Annika said.

"Who was it on the phone?" Kurt asked.

"It was Stellan. He was telling me about his new job and asked me if I'd like to see his apartment. It's up by the Masthugg Church and has a panoramic view of the harbor area and beyond. He says that he can see all the way to England from there, but that's probably a slight exaggeration." Annika smiled, thinking of Stellan's tendency to embellish.

"Why don't you invite Stellan to our party next week?" Kurt suggested. "He'd definitely add some life to the party,"

"Yes, I was planning to. And why don't you invite Eva? I wouldn't mind getting to know her a little better."

"Are you sure you don't mind?" Kurt asked cautiously.

"No, I don't mind. Thanks to her, I get to spend time with Stellan. Frankly, I don't think that you would have been quite as permissive, had it not been for you seeing Eva," Annika added, pointedly.

"Perhaps not," Kurt admitted. "Also, the Falks, my dentist, and her husband."

"What about Doctor Falk?" Annika asked. "Are you seeing her too?"

"No I just meant to invite her and her husband to the party. Will you please invite them to the party?" Kurt asked. "Dr. Falk is quite an amusing and talkative lady. At least she likes to chat a mile a minute while she has her hands in my mouth so I can't respond."

"I know. I wonder why dentists always insist on asking a lot of questions when they know you can't answer," Annika reflected. "By the way, if you want to invite any other women friends, feel free to do so. I'd enjoy meeting them," Annika offered daringly. "How about Yvonne, the seamstress?" Annika was curious to know if she was as great as Kurt had suggested.

"No, Eva wouldn't stand for it. She can accept you because you're my wife, but she's not very tolerant of others." Kurt stated matter-of-factly.

"Imagine that," Annika commented. "Well you can invite them as my friends if you like. Will there be enough room for them all?"

"We'll see, and feel free to invite any of your male friends too, if you like."

"All of them?" she asked.

"Perhaps we should hold the party at Ella's banquet hall," Kurt quipped.

Annika made appointment with her beauty shop for a manicure and to trim and bleach her hair.

Stellan had not exaggerated the view from his apartment much, it was breath taking. "Go on out on the balcony and I'll bring out some hors d'oeuvres," Stellan suggested.

"Oh, let me help you," Annika offered. "Wow! The sandwiches look delicious. Brauthinghams, eat your heart out! I didn't know you had such refined culinary skills, Stellan! Hey, you can cook for me any time you like!" Annika offered slyly.

"I'd be happy to. When you've been a bachelor all your life, necessity takes you all possible places. I like to cook and I'd love to fix some of my specialties for you," Stellan offered.

"You're on," Annika responded, taking the wine bottle and two glasses with her out on the balcony.

The apartment was tastefully decorated with pictures and memorabilia from all over the world. There were unusual African instruments and weapons, several oriental rugs and unique furniture. A large white polar bear rug, including head and paws, lay on the floor. On one wall hung a painting of a full size African beauty dressed in a necklace of seashells. She had round stones inserted into her earlobes stretching them grotesquely.

Romonda used to belong to me. She was given to me as a present by her husband, the King of Butbuttsi. He gave her to me some ten years ago when I took part in an expedition in Butbuttsi collecting exotic furs. We traveled up the Nile to pick up skins. This was before they became extinct. Anyway, we spent a year in this village and it turned out that our host had a serious problem that I was able to help him out with. He had eight wives but no children, no offspring. This was a real problem for obvious reasons. Well, by the time I left all his wives had children and they were pregnant a second time. The host was so pleased that he gave me one of his wives as an expression of appreciation. I was also awarded the Locust award, the highest honor that can be given to a civilian, for my fertility achievement."

"Alright, and you expect me to believe that," Annika responded dryly. "And what happened to Romonda?"

"I gave her back to her husband when I left as a gift to show him my appreciation for his hospitality," he explained with a serious face. "We didn't have that much in common, Romonda and I, but she could whip up a terrific poj-poj, and she could grill a monkey like no one else."

"Yuck! That's disgusting!" Annika shuddered. "You know, I didn't even think the Nile ran through Butbuttsi, in fact, I'm not sure there even is a country called Butbuttsi"

"Well it was a long time ago. Perhaps it changed channels. Rivers will do that now and then, you know. Then again, perhaps it wasn't the Nile, but it was a large river," he admitted.

"And perhaps it wasn't the King of Butbuttsi, but a large guy?" She speculated.

"Perhaps . . . you better keep your coat on, even though it's pretty warm outside right now. As long as you stay out of the wind and in the sun you should be all right for a few minutes." Stellan joined her with a tray full of small sandwiches. He had cut each one in the shape of a heart, with a cookie cutter.

"Oh, your romantic fool," she teased him. "How many people have you invited? There are enough sandwiches here to feed a whole regiment"

"That's all right. I don't mind eating leftovers," said Stellan. "Here, let me pour you some wine." He put his arm around her, to keep her warm. Annika was wearing her black Persian coat, a tight yellow jersey and a rather tight black dress, split on the side, to where a row of buttons took over. She looked quite cuddly.

"Let's go inside," Stellan suggested. We can see the sunset from there." He had put his arm inside her coat and around her waist. He gave her a light squeeze.

"Yes let's," she responded looking up at him, and meeting his lips half way.

They returned inside, removed their coats and Stellan showed Annika around the apartment, explaining the story behind many of his things. Annika knew well Stellan's tendency to make up amazing stories, but his tales fascinated her nevertheless. Sometimes he carried on ridiculously, though, such as the time he was shipwrecked on a tropical island and some mermaids took him under their flippers.

Stellan set the coffee on to brew and put a Jussi Bjorling record on the phonograph. He poured them each a glass of Chartreuse and they sat down on the couch. Annika sat close to Stellan, and he put his arm around her shoulders.

"Are you doing anything next Friday?" she asked. "We're having a dinner party. Would you like to come?" She pulled her legs up on the couch, snuggling up against him.

"Sure, I'd love to. Wow, you smell so good. I always think of you when I smell lilac."

"Great! I told Kurt to invite Eva and his other women," Annika told him, smiling smugly.

"You two have the strangest relationship of anyone I know. But I'm not complaining," he added.

"It's really not that strange. Our marriage didn't work out, so we decided to find our happiness elsewhere. It happens all the time."

"Yes, but you live together as if you were still married. That's what makes it a little unusual." He pointed out.

"Well, it's in both of our best interests. We're just being practical about it. After all, we do have two beautiful children together, and it's in their interest that we live as a family until they get a little older. We still live our separate lives and see whomever we like, so . . . It's not that we dislike each other, I'm very fond of Kurt. He's nice, clean, and he always dresses sharply. He's generous in most ways, and I think he's quite sexy, although he's a little selfish, egocentric and too fast for me," she smiled. "But let's talk about you instead, tell me something about you."

'Like what?"

"Something personal and intimate."

"Oh, let's see."

"Tell me how your perfect girlfriend would be."

"That's easy. She'd be exactly like you . . . I can't think of anything that I would change."

"I wasn't looking for a compliment. I really want to know. What if you had to change one thing then what would that be?"

"Are you trying to get me in trouble or what?" he asked, smiling at her. "What I told you before is actually true. Comparing other girls to you, no one ever comes close. So, it's actually your fault that I'm single."

"No, I just want to know. Come on, one thing," she persisted, ignoring his flattery. "Tell me one thing that would improve on me."

"All right, I'll tell you one thing, but remember that I'm not complaining. I only say it because you insist. Well, I would like it if you dressed and acted a little sexier toward me. But I do understand the awkwardness. You're still Kurt's wife, even though you're not married. And my being his friend adds to the awkwardness, although, I know that he encourages us to see one another so he has more freedom to see Eva." He leaned over and kissed her, as if to ask for forgiveness for his frankness.

"More sexy! I think I dress quite sexy." She looked down at her tight yellow jersey that showed every detail of what was underneath. "What do you think is sexy? Clothing that reveals more?" she asked.

"You do dress sexy in a subtle way and that's fine when we're out with the children, but when we go out alone, or stay at home you could be a little sexier," he suggested

"How can you say that? When you came out to Stenungsund I was running around in that negligee you got me that concealed absolutely nothing."

"True, but that was only once. I'd love to see you like that more often. There's also a difference in whether you dress sexy because it's what you happened to wear at the time, like the negligee, or whether you dress sexy intentionally, for my pleasure."

"You guys are all the same. All you want is to see more skin. You like a girl who is conservative in raising the children, but a prostitute at home."

"You got that right. Remember, you asked. Well when a girl has a body like yours. . . Why it's a national treasure, it should be a crime not to show it off."

"Well, that's nice to hear, but if I was running around naked all the time, you'd get bored and soon you'll be off to greener pastures."

"I could never get bored with you," he protested. "In fact, when I was going through some boxes yesterday I found this camera that I bought in Singapore. It's a really nice camera and I was thinking I would take some pictures of you. Would you mind?"

"No go ahead. Would you like me to put on something hot for you now?" she asked, rhetorically. "I'll put on anything you like, or . . . let me go into your bedroom and find something that I think you will like."

"You won't get an argument from me! I'll sit here and wait, but don't take too long." And it did not take long for Annika to return, dressed in one of Stellan's shirts. It hung loosely on her, and she had left a few of the top buttons open. She spun around, revealing that she was wearing nothing beneath it.

"Oh Annika, if you knew how beautiful you are, and sexy," he added.

He stood up and started to walk toward her, but she stopped him. "No, not yet! I'm not done modeling yet. She returned wearing a loosely tied bath towel and began dancing to the music. "Is this hot enough for you?" she asked in her lowest and sexiest voice. She made a twisting move and the towel fell to the floor. Stellan's camera was going hot. "I will be right back," she promised. This time she returned dressed in only her panties and one of Stellan's T-shirts. She did a striptease routine that she had done for Kurt many times, one that drove him crazy every time. At this point she would not have been able to refuse Stellan if she tried. She didn't.

Stellan never missed an opportunity to see Annika, although he did date other girls on occasion. He would come with Annika to school functions, and he would take her, Ingrid and the children ice skating and to other family events. Stellan got along great with the children. They adored him and would never tire of listening to his stories. Stellan also took Annika to the theater and the opera, which Kurt never did. On occasion, Ingrid would join them. Stellan loved classical music and was well informed on the subject. Annika shared his interests and enjoyed the time with Stellan. They talked about Annika's leaving Kurt and marrying Stellan, but with the children, such a move seemed overwhelming at the moment.

Annika did several modeling assignments for Martin, for which she was well compensated. Annika also helped Ella hosting a few banquets. She didn't need the money, but she liked getting out of the house and she enjoyed the work. She felt wanted and desired strutting around naked before the camera, submitting to Martin's whims.

Stellan could not stay away from the sea even on his time off, and he purchased a 30-foot Sea raider. It was a two mast, blue, fiberglass sailboat and he named it Ingrid. He was hoping that it would raise a little jealousy in Annika, but apparently, she liked the name.

"Hey, thanks for helping me scrape the algae and paint it. I hope this poisonous paint will keep them away a little longer," said Stellan.

"After all, she bears my name." Ingrid lifted her nose some.

"Well, it's a dreadful job." Stellan kept "Ingrid" at the prestigious small boat marina in Longedrag. It had comfortable sleeping for six and a small kitchen/dining room. The stern also featured an open sitting area where they dined, weather permitting.

"Will you be able to take her out for a spin next weekend? I'm working one day on and two days out now so it will work out for Saturday if you can make it? We are supposed to have good weather through the weekend."

"I should be able to. I would love to," said Annika. They would explore the archipelago around the marina. They also make excursions up and down the coast and spend the night out, if Stellan was not on call, often stopping at a coastal town shopping, or visiting a folk park for evening dancing.

"Let's go to Marstrand. We haven't been there for a while. They have such a nice restaurant there." Annika suggested. Perhaps next time we can bring Ingrid and the boys and go to a little more child friendly place."

When the kids came along, they would have to go further into the inlets where the water was shallow. The boat needed twelve feet of water, but they always carried a small lifeboat that they used for a shuttle craft. It was not completely safe, on occasions they would spot dud mines that had drifted ashore, and they read in the papers about these mines sometimes exploding, but that was a rare occurrence and the boys knew not to get close to them.

CHAPTER 21

August, 1947 - Paris

The red army, largest in the world in1947, March through Moscow in their Mayday parade. Secretary of State George Marshal spoke at Harvard University explaining the need for economic aid to rebuild and stabilize Europe. US provides fifteen and a half billion for fourteen countries in the 1947 Marshal Plan, to assist recovery in those countries

Annika and Stellan still spent time together, but the relationship became increasingly awkward. Annika still modeled for Stellan now and then but Stellan didn't do anything with the pictures and Ingrid preferred that they stopped meeting. Stellan was ready to settle down with a wife and children of his own. He could not convince Annika to leave Kurt, because of the boys. Annika felt that the benefits of their peculiar relationship outweighed the problems with interruption and changes in the children's lives. Stellan began spending more time with Ingrid and much less with Annika..

Kurt had returned from a trip to the US, and Annika was eager to travel some place. Kurt decided to take the family along on a European tour that would include a trade show in Paris. They gave Ingrid a month off while they were traveling.

The Nobels took the train to Hälsingborg where it was loaded onto a ferry boat. It was a pleasant 45-minute trip across the sound to Hälsingör, in Denmark, just enough time to have a light lunch.

"Four roast beef sandwiches, two orange juice and two Tuborg beer," Kurt ordered at the sales counter.

"We have to rush a little," Annika nudged him, "so we have time to shop in the duty-free shops."

Why don't you and the boys go to the candy shop and get some chocolate, and I will get the cigarettes and liquor."

"Doesn't seem like we need cigarettes. Neither one of us smoke." Annika reminded him.

"You know I like to have some at home for guests. I also like to give some to Eva's dad. "If you are buying a gift for Eva's dad, then I'm going to buy something for my mother." Annika announced.

"You have your allowances; you make your own choices." Kurt replied.

The train took them south along the coast of Denmark, traveling through some of the most affluent residential districts in Denmark, offering a grand view of the sound and Sweden beyond. The family spent two days in Copenhagen, enough time to visit the famous Tivoli Gardens.

"Alright, be careful now boys so you don't spill the mustard and only dip your hotdogs very lightly in the mustard, I it is extremely strong and your nose will burn if you take too much. Oh no, Axel. You can't eat the bread after it has been on the ground." Annika admonished him.

"Here son, have another bun," The vendor offered.

"Thank you. Why are they red Mom? At home they are not red," Axel asked.

"Well that's how they make them here. They are pretty good though, aren't they? Annika asked.

"Yeas," the boys managed, with their mouths full.

The boys were thrilled by the giant waffle ice-cream cones they got at Tivoli Garden.

"How's everything Annika?" Kurt asked as they took a break on a park bench while finishing off their ice-cream cones. Kurt wiped off the damp bench with his napkin.

"Not bad for a rather unorthodox couple," Annika responded, smiling up at him. "The flowers smell so good." There had been a short rain shower freshening up the park and bringing out the flowers' sweet fragrances. Fog was now rising from the ground. Annika tossed the last of her cone to some friendly birds. They attacked the cone fiercely and not so willing to share with others.

"I think you would like to live in North America, be it Canada or the USA," he ventured.

"Perhaps, but I like it fine at home. That's where all my friends are, with a few exceptions. It seems to me that even though there are a lot of fun and interesting things over there, there are lots of negatives, too, like all the crime you continuously read about. Everyone seems to carry guns, and as soon as there is a disagreement its bang- bang. And then it's the colored people, the way they treat them, like if they weren't real people."

"Well, that's because America's so big, and because of its zealous press it sounds like there's a lot of crime, but if you spread out the incidents over the whole country, I think you'd find that it is as peaceful there as most everywhere else. Also, a lot of your perceptions of the US come from watching American movies and they are not exactly documentaries."

"I don't know. It seems to me as though most Americans are like big happy dogs with long wagging tails in a small room filled with expensive porcelain. They seem immature, self-centered, and self-important only focusing on short term gratification."

"Well that was a rather stern assessment of Americans." Kurt could not help smiling at her firm stereotypical perspective. "That's why I want to take you there, so you can see for yourself. I think you'll like it," he repeated.

"To change the subject, an article I read the other day stated that everything we do, every action we take, including the food we eat, is based on sexual gratification. What do you think of that?" she asked.

"Hormones, huh?" he responded. "Well that wouldn't surprise me a bit. I know that I base most, if not all, of my decisions on what I think is sexy," he added.

"Yes, I'm sure you do, but I'm not equally sure that everyone else does. It said that males like to have sex twice a day but a woman is happy with sex once a day. They must have been interviewing a bunch of newlyweds to come up with those statistics. If that's the norm, I should be able to sue for breach of contract . . ."

"For frustration of exuberant expectations . . ." he helped her. "I guess the question then is whether we have an inherent right to 'exuberant' expectations," he smiled, chuckling at the concept.

Annika and Kurt had more Danish beer, and next, the family watched the changing of the guard at the Royal Palace. The soldiers were impressive in their red and black uniforms and their tall round fur hats, and the children loved watching the soldiers march in goose step.

They boarded the ferry to Travemunde, from where they continued on a train to Paris. It was a depressing sight to see all the devastation from the war. Whole areas of the cities were leveled to the ground.

"Can you believe that they still live in those ruins? They look like they could tumble any minute. It must be windy up there. There are no walls." Annika observed.

Most of the outside walls had collapsed, exposing apartments like beehive combs. It was a relief to enter Paris, which was less scared, even though Hitler had done his best to level Paris during his last days. Luckily his orders were not fully obeyed.

"Alright, now we have seen the Eiffel Tower and the Louvre, perhaps it's time to do a little work. We have two more days in Paris so perhaps we can do more later?" Kurt offered.

They stayed at a small Inn on the Seine, and close to the Arch of Triumph and to where the trade show was taking place. The Inn belonged to an older couple, the Foughts, who kept it neat and clean. Meals were provided for their guests and the Foughts agreed to babysit the children. They even took them to the zoo. It was a perfect arrangement for Kurt and Annika, so they were able to go out at night and enjoy the night life.

They spent the third day at the fashion show. By chance, they ran into Yvonne there, from Stenongsund. She was easy to spot, given her height. She joined Annika and Kurt for the rest of the day and she invited them out for dinner in the evening. Kurt and Annika stopped by the Inn to check up on the children and to freshen up before they left for Yvonne's hotel. After a pleasant evening, Yvonne insisted that Annika come with her shopping the following day. "Annika you have to," she insisted. "How often do you have a chance to go shopping in Paris? And I can bring someone with me to the fashion show for lunch. Say you will."

"You go Annika. There is an auto show here that I wouldn't mind taking a look at." Kurt prompted.

Kurt and Annika saw two night shows and enjoyed the good French dining, even though Kurt had some difficulty getting his meat grilled well done. Neither Kurt nor Annika could speak much French, which limited their activities. Kurt could converse well in German, but most Frenchmen would refuse to speak German even if they could.

"Let's stop in Amsterdam for a couple days on the way back." Kurt suggested.

"Let's" Annika agreed. I would love to visit one of those tulip farms. I have seen pictures of some and they have tulips as far as you can see," said Annika.

"I'm not sure that this is the season for that, but we'll see what they have. At least we can get some clogs and hike on the wall, the dike, and I have to admit that I'm somewhat curious about the red-light district." said Kurt.

Kurt and Annika visited the red-light district one evening to satisfy their curiosity. It was just as they had read, girls displayed in glass windows in various state of undress, promoting their services. Kurt and Annika left the area feeling sorry for the girls.

The ship from Amsterdam took them all the way back Gothenburg. Their journey made Kurt and Annika realize how blessed they were to live in a country like Sweden. They returned to their summer home in Stenongsund and stayed there until late fall, when the weather turned cold and windy, and Kurt got tired of commuting to work.

Ingrid would help out with the children, but she was no longer working full time. She had moved to her own apartment and was now exclusively dating Stellan.

Now that Annika and Yvonne had become friends, Annika and Kurt included her in their dinner parties. Yvonne stayed the night with Annika a few times, when she was in town. They went to the theater together and they made a couple trips to Uddevalla. Occasionally Annika accompanied Yvonne when traveling to trade shows. At one Copenhagen show, Annika helped out modeling when one of the scheduled models had turned ill.

Annika fascinated Yvonne with her free spirit. Even though Annika could be a little naive, flighty at times, she was always genuine, straight forward, resourceful and acted from her heart. Annika could have any man she chose, yet, she stayed with Kurt, a fascinating and awaited man, but normally not the kind of man one married. Annika had a helpless side that apparently needed Kurt as a safety net. She also had a strong independent streak and took what she could from Kurt, without suffering from a misplaced need to fill the role of a model wife. She had a desire to please, but she also had a strong need to be loved, to be appreciated, desired. Her sensuous moments with several of her girlfriends showed an adventurous side, an untamed side; she was someone who was not afraid of stepping on virgin ground, not afraid to experiment and to explore. Annika told Yvonne about Ella and about Bella and the intimate moments they had shared. They both shared stories about Kurt.

"Whatever happened to the Karlsons?" Yvonne asked, "Do you ever hear from them?"

"No, not really. We exchange Christmas cards but that's about it."

"Bella sounds really neat. I admire people who have the guts to do what they feel like, without inhibitions." Yvonne mused.

"She was fun," Annika agreed.

"I admire you too Annika. You're not afraid to do anything."

"That's flattering, but a gross overstatement," Annika responded.

"Sweetheart, you play the cards you were dealt, without a lot of fuss and wining," Yvonne continued.

"Well thank you for that vote of confidence," Annika said, smiling coyly, "but if anyone should be admired, it's you. You got your business going against all odds and now there's no stopping you."

"Well, I wasn't talking about that . . . I was talking about having the guts, the self-confidence to do whatever you want. Like posing naked. I could never do that." Yvonne confessed. "Kurt showed me a magazine that featured your pictures. I didn't know that you were famous."

"Well, I'm not sure that having nude pictures in a magazine qualifies as being famous." She giggled. "Don't you like it when people. . . men, look at you with desire?" Annika asked.

"Well, of course I do, and I like to dress sexy, but I'm way too much of a chicken to strut around in my underwear in front of an audience."

"It's something one have to get used to. I've only done it a few times, but it's quite a turn on. Skinny dipping, modeling, whatever. When I was little, we were three siblings in our family, and we always played in the nude on the beach with our friends, like everyone else. It was as natural as . . . as sleeping. I didn't start wearing a swimming suit in public until I was, perhaps, ten years old. And I would go swimming nude with my friends until I was . . . well, I guess I still do."

"Well, I am the only child and I always wore a swimsuit, as far back as I can remember, even when only my parents were around."

"But you recognize that that's fairly unusual, don't you? I guess it's all what you're used to."

"That was well done. I loved the music," said Annika. Yvonne and Annika had returned from the theater.

"It looks a little funny when the guys stuff the crouch in their leotards like that. No guy is that big," said Annika giggling.

"I know. But it is kind of sexy I think," said Yvonne. Let's stop by Valand on the way home and have a glass of wine and an open-face shrimp sandwich. It's my treat."

"Yes, but no way will you pay again. You paid for the theater, now it's my turn." Annika insisted. Kurt was in Stockholm for the weekend and the boys were sleeping over with neighbors' children.

Two young men who had a little too much to drink tried to engage in a conversation with the girls, but they were not interested and returned to Annika's apartment.

"Ingrid has the weekend off, so I'm by myself." Annika explained. She poured a couple glasses of cold white wine and put on the coffee.

"This is an excellent wine, but it's like drinking a soft drink, one can hardly tell that it has alcohol in it," Annika commented.

"Yes, it's deceptive," Yvonne agreed. Annika turned on the radio for background music, and sat down on the couch, in the living room, pulling her legs up underneath herself.

"I can see that it could be difficult to be excessively bashful in your business," Annika sympathized.

"Yes. I think perhaps one problem is that I'm so tall, you know, over six feet. It makes me feel like I'm standing in the spot-light all the time."

"Yes, I can understand that, but there are a few things that you have to concentrate on. First you have to remember that we all look almost the same, all of us, men and women. The differences are minor. Now, you're a beautiful, sexy woman, and sure . . . people are going to look, but with admiration. Most girls would love to have your slender body, and your beautiful face. I know how you feel though. It took me some time to get used to people always staring at my chest. I was developed at a rather young age, and you know how young boys are. And, I wasn't comfortable the first times when Bella snuggled up to me. I didn't know how to deal with it . . . until I got used to it and then I began to like it, and missed her when she wasn't there."

"Do you think that I could snuggle up to you tonight Annika?" Yvonne asked shyly.

"Of course, you can," Annika responded warmly. "I can make it easy for you. Just do exactly what I tell you to do, and you'll see . . . your confidence will come by itself. First, go ahead and finish up the wine. Then I'll fill the tub with hot water while we have a cup of coffee and . . . how would you like a glass of banana-liqueur?" Annika asked.

"I would love some, thank you."

"Then I'll help you get undressed, we'll have a bath, and then we'll go to bed. If Ingrid were here she could have given you one of her massages. She has magic fingers," Annika said.

"That sounds nice. I've never had a massage in all my life."

"Never? You have dated, haven't you? I mean . . . I know you have been with Kurt."

"Yes, but Kurt isn't exactly known for his great massages."

"That's true," Annika agreed, and they both giggled.

". . . and neither is anyone else that I've been with."

"Kurt is probably best known for his speed record," Annika chuckled.

"No doubt," Yvonne added.

"Yes, I'm afraid so. I guess you have to be fast if you are going to serve the whole Swedish west coast . . . make that the western world," Annika responded. "We'll take this slowly," she promised. "We'll start with the top and let you get used to it. I'll remove my top too, so you don't have to feel alone. Or, perhaps you'd like to remove my top?" Annika offered. "At least I think it is super sexy to get to undress someone."

Yvonne took a deep breath . . . "'ll do it." She removed Annika's blouse after fumbling some with the buttons, and her bra. "You're so lovely," Yvonne sighed deeply.

"Would you like some more wine, or liquor? Or would you like a cigarette? "Annika offered.

"You don't smoke, do you?" Yvonne asked, taken aback.

"No, no, but Kurt does now and then and he has some. Besides, we always have some at home for our friends. How does it feel to be topless?" Annika asked.

"A little strange, but it feels nice at the same time." Yvonne's breasts were rather small, but her nipples were large and erect.

Annika stood up and slowly swayed with the music. Yvonne did her best to do the same. Annika's eyes moved hungrily over Yvonne's beautifully toned body. "That's great, really nice," she said, to encourage Yvonne. "Now, swing your hair around too, rolling your head," she coached her. "That was great. That wasn't so bad was it? It's no difference if there is one or one million in the audience, you do the same thing."

"No, that wasn't bad, but I think that's because it was only you here. I would have been scared stiff if someone else had been here too, and of course you're a woman."

"Let's get ready for the bath," Annika said. "Here, let me remove the rest."

Annika urged Yvonne to dance for her. Annika sat back down on the couch while Yvonne began moving slowly, a little more sensuously than before.

"What if someone came in?" she asked nervously.

"No one is going to come. Just relax. Close your eyes if that helps, but don't lose your balance," she cautioned." Alright, let's get into the tub." Annika had added a package of bubble bath to the tub. She also lit a couple candles. Annika scrubbed Yvonne's back first with a soft-bristled scrub-brush.

"Wow, that feels so nice," Yvonne sighed.

Annika continued scrubbing her and then sponged her off well.

Then she spread out a beach towel on the floor. "Here lay down here and I will rub in some oil." She began working her shoulders first, just like Ingrid did, and worked down to the small of her back, to her firm bottom, her thighs and down to her feet. She continued to work in the lotion on her feet, rubbing each toe individually.

"It feels so good. You're spoiling me Annika." Yvonne murmured.

"Alright, now roll over. Here, you can put your towel over you for now, if you like." She placed the towel across her abdomen while she again began with her shoulders and worked her way down. It wasn't the first time Annika gave someone a massage. It had almost become a routine in her lovemaking, not this elaborate a work out, but a little back massage and foot massage. They traded places and Yvonne rubbed Annika with body oil. Annika was surprised at how intimate Yvonne dared become as she massaged first her back and then her legs.

PART IV

CHAPTER 22

August, 1948 – Camilla, Jodassy

Camilla and Sven returned to Sweden in the fall of 1948. Sven's condition had worsened and Camilla wanted to finish her degree in architecture. They could accomplish both goals cheaper and easier in Sweden. They found an apartment close to the Nobels. Annika and Camilla renewed their friendship and met for a short moment daily. Camilla's schedule was brutal. Besides her school work, she still painted to support the family. Sven only complained about his pain and stayed away from home sometimes several days at the time. The doctors could not find anything wrong with him other than his drinking problem. Camilla had to take care of the children but Annika was able to step in when needed or Ingrid the house keeper.

"Annika, before the new semester starts, what do you think about if you and me was taking a vacation to Majorca? They have a tour that leaves in one week and it is really not that expensive. It would do us both good to get away for a while. Perhaps we could meet some handsome fellas that would treat us a little nicer than our guys do. It shouldn't be much of a challenge."

"You're crazy Camilla, Kurt would never pay for me going away like that."

"Well it doesn't hurt to ask, does it?"

During dinner Kurt again raised the issue of moving to the States. "I think the boys could learn a lot if we did, and there are much more opportunities to succeed there. You know I would still keep my activities in motion here. Eva knows how to run everything on her own, so it's not like we would cut all ties with Sweden. We'll keep the summer house and the apartment for now."

"So, you would have two families then. Eva here and us there. Pretty convenient for you. I know how much you want to move there, so here's the deal. If you let me and Camilla take a vacation to Majorca for two weeks first, then I will not object to going to the U.S."

"Alright, you've got a deal. Then I'll make a quick trip myself when you are gone, and we will be ready to sail in four weeks on the MS Stockholm. You will love that ship. It's fabulous!"

Annika was not concerned that this would be a final arrangement. Kurt had talked so many times about moving, but he always came back.

Traveling by ship to Majorca was possibly just as much fun as being in Majorca. The Stavanger was a sizable ship that had all the comforts that could be found in most respectable resorts on land.

"Woo!" Annika screeched as she entered her cabin. A red rose lay neatly across her cot. "This is impossible. No one knows that I'm here."

The Norwegian vessel featured both a movie theater and a swimming pool. It had three restaurants, several shops, bars and a cabaret at night. Each meal was a culinary experience, worth the trip on its own merits.

"I like Sigrin, the tour guide," Camilla told Annika. It looks like most guests are our age. This will be fun," said Camilla.

The package included tour guides who made sure that the travelers were continuously occupied and enjoying themselves. The guides organized games to make sure no one was left out and everyone got to know one another.

After dinner and a few dances, mostly with a gentleman apparently of Middle Eastern decent, Camilla disappeared outside, and Annika didn't see her again for several hours. Just when Annika began to get seriously concerned, Camilla came back, alone. Her cheeks were flushed and she was smiling. Her long blond curly hair bounced against her bare shoulders as she strode across the room toward Annika.

"You'll never guess what happened!"

"I'm afraid to guess," Annika responded.

"I've met a real Arabian prince. A Real Royal Prince! He has a home, or palace, on Majorca and he invited us to come and have dinner with him there. Can you believe it?

"Wait a minute! You mean to tell me that you have accepted a dinner invitation for the two of us to the home of an Arab prince that we don't know?"

"Yes! Isn't it exciting? Isn't that what you've always dreamed of, but knew would never happen to you?"

"Well, I'm not sure I have, but tell me, what do you know about him?"

"He's wonderful, so romantic. He thinks that I'm sent by Allah. He appears to be financially independent. He's traveling with eight of his wives. He offered me the position of his first wife if I chose. Unbelievable, isn't it?!"

"Have you lost your mind? Don't tell me that you are considering moving into his harem!"

"No, no. He was schooled in England and he said that he is prepared to live according to western culture. He would support his other wives, of course, but he would live with me only," Camilla explained.

"You must be insane, thinking of marrying a complete stranger after only knowing him for a couple of hours. Hey, wake up girl!"

"I don't have to decide tonight. I'm just thinking about it."

"What about the children?" Annika asked, "and Sven, what about him?"

"Sven . . . he probably wouldn't even notice if I left. The kids, they would be all right. I would take care of them. Perhaps they could benefit from this," Camilla speculated. "It seems to me that I can either continue to support and sit home and wait for Sven to show up, for the rest of my life, or, I could marry this enormously wealthy, gorgeous, romantic prince. Ali, his name is Ali. . . . something, but I call him Ali. I can live in a palace and be waited on from morning to night. Also, someday Ali will be King of his country and guess what will happen to me then?"

"You will become the Queen." Annika couldn't but smile and shake her head at the same time. "This can't be real. Tomorrow morning when we wake up, we'll realize that this was only a dream, and we can return to our regular lives. However, since it's only a dream, does he only need one more wife? After all, he only has eight," Annika asked, giggling.

"Twelve, he actually has twelve," Camilla responded, "but only eight are traveling with him on this trip. It's not really like having wives the way we know it, he told me. Most of them were 'assigned' as a social favor and duty. He does not have a wife whom he chose himself nor an offspring for his estate," Camilla explained.

"Don't you think that you're getting a little too old to start having children again? What are you, thirty-two?" Annika asked.

"Well barely. I don't think that's a problem, though. I know of women who had children into their mid-forties, with no problems. To me the problem is more whether I want to step into a different century and culture and how it would affect the children." They returned to their cabin. "I'll introduce you to him tomorrow at lunch. You'll like him when you meet him, I know it. By the way, here I'm totally absorbed with myself. How was your evening, anything exciting?" she asked.

"Nothing that can even closely compare with what happened to you. I did meet a really nice guy from Stockholm though. A true gentleman. He is the vice president of a plumbing supply company. He's married, but semi-separated, just like me. He has three children, all girls. His name is Torsten Farin. He's down here on a working vacation, but he would like to see 'some more of me,' as he put it."

"Well who wouldn't? Look at you."

"I'm not sure if that's what he meant. Regardless, perhaps a little forward, but what a charmer, and he danced like a god."

"Looks like we are going to have quite some vacation, Annika."

The following morning Annika and Camilla slept through breakfast. They were scheduled in arrive to Majorca that afternoon, so they organized their belongings before they went up for lunch. On the floor they found an envelope that had been slipped under their door. It was addressed to "Princess Camilla." Camilla ripped it open.

Dearest Camilla

Thank you so much for the most wonderful evening of my life. Unfortunately, I have to return to Jodassy on a political emergency tonight and regretfully I will not be there in the morning. However, I hope to be able to return within the next few days. In the meantime, I hope you will accept my invitation to stay at my home in Majorca. Maida, my senior wife, will help you with all arrangements. I want you to feel comfortable and therefore I expect you to invite your friends to stay with you. We can accommodate up to twenty-five guests at the villa. If there is anything you need or want, please tell Maida, and it will be done. I will contact you at first opportunity and I hope to see you soon again.

Love, Ali

Camilla looked outside the door and saw a young woman sitting there waiting. She stood up quickly when Camilla opened the door.

"Princess Camilla?" she asked, bowing deeply.

"I'm Camilla," she responded, "and you?"

"I'm Princess Elli Alibassi, wife of Prince Modan Alibassi. I'm sorry that Ali couldn't be here today. He would have been here in person if it was within his power. I can take you to Maida or she can come here if you prefer. She has additional information." The girl spoke perfect Oxford English.

Annika stood behind her in the doorway. Camilla turned around. "Let's go and see Maida," she suggested.

"All right, let's go." They followed Elli to the first-class deck. Maida had her own suite there and part of it was arranged as an office. She greeted them when they entered. Elli stayed outside. "So very nice to meet you, Princess Camilla." Her eyes wandered back and forth between Camilla and Annika, trying to discern which of them Camilla was.

"I'm Camilla, and this is my good friend Annika." Camilla introduced her modest entourage.

"Please accept my apology on behalf of Prince Modan, or Ali, as his friends call him, for not being able to be here in person. Ali told me all about you, and I can tell you that he is very impressed with you, and I may add that he did not exaggerate your beauty. You're as lovely as he described. He has asked me to do whatever I can to make you feel comfortable. If there is anything you want at all, money is not an issue, it will be done." She invited the girls to sit down on the overstuffed couch. "Between you and me, I've never seen Ali act like this over any woman. I believe that he is head-over-heals in love. Ali has asked me to explain anything you want to know about him, our family, our country and our customs. When we get to Majorca we will have transportation available for you and your party. How many will there be?"

"Annika?" Camilla implored.

"Alright, why not? Let's do it." Annika smiled, shaking her head in wonder at Camilla.

"There will be two of us for now, but if possible, we would also like to have Mr. Torsten Farin join us for dinner. He is a passenger on the ship and a close friend of Annika." Camilla was sliding straight into her role as Princess Camilla, without any adjustment problems.

"We will take care of your luggage. You will not have to go through customs, being part of Ali's entourage," Maida explained. "Would you like to go straight to the villa, to settle in, or do you prefer to stop somewhere first?" she asked. "Perhaps you would like to go shopping?"

"Let's go to the villa first and get settled in," Camilla requested.

Four limousines awaited them at the pier when they arrived. They departed the ship through the crew exit, straight onto the pier. Each limousine had two small flags, one on each front fender. One was the flag of Spain and the other was the flag of Jodassy, that featured a black rearing stallion on top of a red field. They were escorted by four motorcycle police.

"It's not a long ride, fifteen, twenty minutes," Maida told them. "It's a pretty ride. I hope you will be comfortable. If there is anything you need or like to know please just ask. The villa is molded into that smaller hill at the base of the large mountain over there." Maida pointed out.

"It's so beautiful. What a magnificent view of the ocean." Camilla noted.

A large wrought-iron gate swung open and four guards in military uniform saluted as the party entered onto the property. The convoy climbed the hill on a serpentine road, driving through a beautiful park, with exotic shrubbery and flowers, many unfamiliar to Camilla and Annika. Marble park benches were scattered throughout the park. Parallel to the road was a trellised riding trail, partly shaded by a blanket of purple bougainvillea. Maida, and on Sonja's request, Elli, rode with Camilla and Annika. They were amazingly well informed on the history of the island, buildings and the botanic gardens, explaining everything they saw.

The convoy pulled up in front of the villa after first circling a water fountain. A black marble statue of a nude woman riding a lion, accompanied by two male soldiers, dressed in only their crossbow arm shields, stood in the center of the fountain. Everything else was painted bright white, and flowers grew everywhere in abundance. A long-terraced stairway led down to the pier, which was bordered with marble statues. Most were fictional half animals and half people. Several small boats were tied to the pier, including the royal yacht.

The women were shown into the main lobby, a rotunda in white marble. This part of the building also served a dual purpose as the Jodassy Embassy. The pictures of the royal family were displayed between the pillars that supported the upper level. Maida explained that the large picture in the center was of Ali's father, and two smaller ones on each side were of his sons. Ali, like the other males, was dressed in uniform.

"He is handsome indeed." This was the first time Annika saw Ali. He's the poster boy image of an Arabian Prince. His black wavy hair was combed back. His cheek bones were chiseled, very masculine, Annika thought. His face was tan and featured a well-groomed mustache, not obnoxiously big, but big enough to add character. He looked confident. His smile showed dignity, with a hint of mischief in his eyes.

"I see what you mean," Annika told Camilla. "He is definitely handsome."

"Let me give you a tour of the villa," Elli offered. "You can choose any of these bedrooms that you like."

The large harem room the girls had expected to see, where all the women lived, did not exist. Nor did they see any eunuchs. Some wives had their own rooms and some had chosen to live together with others. Annika and Camilla chose a room on the main floor with a balcony facing the harbor and city lights. It was not one of the largest suites, but it was comfortable, beautifully decorated and had all the conveniences. All the women wore western clothes.

"Does everyone normally were western clothing here?" Camilla asked.

"Normally everyone would dress in traditional clothing, but we thought perhaps you would feel a little more comfortable if we all were dressed alike," Elli revealed.

"That was thought full of you, but I would like everyone to were whatever they like." No one changed. Annika and Camilla asked Elli about the clothing and she pointed out that all of them had been educated in England and that they were comfortable wearing either western or traditional garb as well.

"I think it would be fun if we could also have saris." Said Camilla. They donned their new outfits and then all the other women switched to their traditional saris.

Dinner was being served on the terrace. It was now dark outside and the view of the harbor area was majestic. A light parade lit up the coastline and the several illuminated ships added to the spectacle.

A four masted illuminated sail yacht was a focus point, but also, was clusters of lights from developments scattered along the hill side adding to the magic.

A mild breeze swept in off the ocean carrying the sweet fragrance from the abundance of flowers. As Camilla and Annika took their seats, Annika was startled to see Torsten Farin sitting at one of the tables on the veranda, looking equally surprised when they appeared.

"Wow, what a surprise!" Annika greeted him. "I knew that Camilla asked if you could join us, but I never expected them to pull it off." She walked over to him.

"This was a pleasant surprise! I had no idea. You must tell me what's going on here. What are you doing here?" He asked. The girls' traditional clothing added to his confusion.

"I was invited here to talk business. I had no idea that I would run into you here. You know, I was looking for you everywhere, I couldn't figure out where you might have gone. Boy, am I glad to see you again!"

"Camilla, meet Torsten. Torsten, this is my friend Camilla, from Gothenburg."

"I heard they addressed you Princess. Are you a real princess?" he asked.

"Not really, but they all insist on calling me princess, so I guess I have to live with it. I have been called much worse," she added smiling.

"That's for sure," Annika interjected. "Wait a minute. I didn't mean that like it sounded. I meant that I have been called much worse things too." They all laughed.

They all were seated, Ali's twelve wives, Camilla, Annika and Torsten. Annika and Camilla filled him in on all the events. A young man provided dinner music on a stringed instrument that the girls did not recognize. It sounded a little like a guitar but with a higher pitch. Their garments hung loosely, and were comfortable in the warm climate.

"That's quite a story. Have you decided on what to do next?" Torsten asked Camilla.

"The only thing I know for sure is that I will go back with the cruiser. Regardless of what happens, I will have to go back home and get the children and settle up my affairs one way or another."

The women found Ali's wives charming. They were all fun to talk to, worldly and had a good sense of curiosity, humor and they all appeared to enjoy each other. Maida explained that, in order to be considered as a wife for Ali, a girl had to be a virgin, unless chosen by Ali. If a wife changed her mind, she could divorce Ali any time she wanted to, if she was not pregnant. Being married to a prince was considered a great honor and it carried many benefits and status, in particular being married to Ali, the Crown Prince. His wives did have to perform sexual favors upon request. Ali's wives did not appear to resent Camilla in any way. It appeared as though their common goal was to make Ali as happy as possible. They all, in turn, had a lot of questions for Camilla about herself and about Swedish culture.

It was late by the time Torsten was driven back to his hotel. He had been invited to stay on, but he had business to tend to the following day, and he chose to be taken back to his lodging. However, he agreed to return the following evening. When Annika and Camilla returned to their room, a red rose lay on each bed.

The following day Camilla and Annika were driven to the shopping district. A limousine followed them slowly as they walked down the street examining the exotic wares in shops and street markets. Elli walked with them, insisting on paying for everything they bought. She charged everything. Elli explained, "it would be inappropriate for you to pay for anything when you are guests of Ali. The Alibassi family fortune was substantial and had Ali been with them, he would have thought nothing of buying Camilla a luxury car or anything else." Elli explained that; "all his wives had unlimited shopping privileges."

Both Camilla and Annika dressed in traditional dress. They could not help but be taken in by their exotic surroundings, by the first-class treatment they received and by having people turn their heads when they appeared. Camilla and Annika stopped for lunch at a restaurant with a view of the piers and the waterfront activities. A powerful aroma, resembling clam chowder laced with garlic, or perhaps curry, greeted them. The group was immediately seated at a front table and waited on by several servers.

"I wish Ali were here," Camilla sighed. "I wonder how he's doing," she added. "We haven't heard anything from Ali, has anyone?" she asked Elli.

"No, not yet. But don't worry; there is not a problem in Jodassy. The problem lies in the neighboring countries, the larger countries with ego problems, that can't get along. Jodassy is sandwiched in between. Both countries like to have Jodassy there, so they don't have to border each other. This crisis will work itself out, just as they always do. Ali is good friends with both countries' leaders," she explained. "The king is getting old and Ali has to perform several of the duties that the king would normally do. The kings on both sides of Jodassy are married to Ali's sisters," she added. "In fact, one of them is married to two of them. They are twins and they went as a package deal," she said laughing. The girls weren't sure if she was joking.

"You mean that they were sold?" Camilla asked cautiously.

"Well, we think of it more as giving a generous dowry. I guess technically it is the same thing, but it sounds better than saying they were sold," Elli explained, smiling warmly. Her perfect white teeth sparkled as she spoke. Her peach skin was perfectly smooth, her eyes were large, dark and expressive, and she exuded femininity. Neither she nor any of the other wives wore veils over their faces. Camilla grew restless and wanted to go back to the villa in case Ali should contact them.

As they entered Maida's office, she looked up and smiled at them. "Ali called. He is back in Jodassy. Everything is fine, however . . ."

"What?" Camilla interrupted impatiently.

"There is a problem with his father. It's not an emergency, but he is not feeling well, and Ali is afraid to leave him right now. His father is seventy-seven and has been having health problems for a while, but it is getting worse. Anyway, he wanted you to call him when you got back. If you go to your room I will try to make the connection for you," she offered.

Camilla had just entered her room when the phone rang. "Hello!"

"You are connected," she heard Maida say.

"Hello! Camilla!" Ali exclaimed. His voice was a little raspy, but she could hear him.

"Ali! How are you?" she asked anxiously.

"I'm just fine, thank you. How are you? Are they treating you well?"

"Like a queen. It's all like a wonderful dream. I'm expecting to wake up any moment and be back to normal."

"Well, I feel the same. I can't stop thinking about you. You are so beautiful and so charming. I feel so bad that I had to take off so suddenly right after I met you, but I didn't have a choice. Then, to make matters worse, my father's health took a turn to the worse. He has been ill for some time and I can't leave right now."

"Of course!"

"He is getting a little old and fragile, and one never knows what could happen."

"How's he doing?" she asked. She sat down on the bed, next to Annika.

"Oh, I think he's doing fine. He should be all right in a few days, but I think he had a mild stroke. I know your ship leaves tomorrow, which will not give me enough time to see you again before you leave. Is it possible for you to change your plans and stay a little longer? I would fly you back, if you like, and you could still be back in Sweden at the same time you were expected. Maida told me that you have your friend Annika staying with you and that her friend Torsten joined you for dinner last night. I'm glad to hear that, I want you to feel at home. As I told you, and I don't want to be pushy, but my dream is that this will be your home too, soon. Have you given any thought to what we talked about?" he asked.

"I have, and I'm intrigued. But things are moving so fast. I do want to see you again, very much."

"Good, that's what I was hoping to hear. Please talk to Annika and her friend, and see whether they can stay a few days extra as our guests, and then fly back with you. In fact, if it is all right with you, I will come with you . . . if I can . . . and meet your children . . . better yet, you come here to Jodassy. You can stay here for two days and get to know me a little better and get to know Jodassy. It will give you a fuller picture of your future life, should you choose to stay with me. Of course, you should bring your friends. Think about it and I'll call you back later, after dinner, to confirm that I should make the arrangements." His voice became more serious. "If you chose to marry me, you will have an exciting life, but it also carries a lot of responsibilities. Frankly, my father does not have much time left and when he passes away, I will be crowned King of Jodassy. Actually, I have already taken over most of the official duties. My point is that if you chose me, you will be Queen Camilla of Jodassy.

"Whoa! I have to admit that I find that thought a little scary."

"Don't. I know you will do great," he assured her. "If you come, there will not be an official welcome, as I think we should save that until you say, 'definitely yes.'"

"Thanks for that vote of confidence and thank you for everything. I love it here and I will ask my friends. Yes, I'll tell you if we can come when you call back. Frankly I would love to, but I won't come without Annika, as I'm sure you understand. I hope to see you soon and I hope your father is better soon."

"God bless you."

Torsten arrived right on time. He brought mixed flowers for Camilla and roses and a jade broach that he had purchased locally for Annika. "Well ladies, fill me in on the latest," he said. He was dressed in a light, off white linen suit and a smartly shaped straw hat. He was trying out new cologne that the sales lady had guaranteed would make him irresistible to women. "Is that new cologne you're wearing today?" Annika asked. "I like it. It has a masculine fragrance."

They took a stroll down to the pier and by the stables while they waited for dinner. There were several children at both places. Elli explained that they were the children of people who worked on the premises and their friends. She said that most of them spoke Jodassy, English, Spanish and French, and assured Camilla that if she brought her children, they would have lots of friends.

"Actually, Jodassy is not that different from Spanish, but the children are encouraged to speak English as much as possible. Ali believes that English will be an international language in the near future." Elli explained.

"How's your business coming along?" Annika asked.

Torsten held the stall door open for the ladies. "I'm done with business. I'm just waiting for the ship to go back tomorrow." He pulled out a long cigar from his breast pocket, and snipped one end.

"Have you ever been to Jodassy?" Annika asked. Her smile revealed that she had something up her sleeve.

"No, I can't say that I have. I don't travel in the Middle East very often. Why do you ask?" He lit his cigar and took a few quick puffs.

"We, Camilla, you and I, have been invited to fly over to Jodassy in the royal "airplane for a two day all expenses paid vacation, living in the royal palace as guests of Prince Ali. We will then be flown back to Sweden. Does that sound like something you would be interested in?" she asked him, her eyes wide with wonder.

"Let me see if I got this right. You are asking me if I want to make this trip with the most beautiful woman that I have ever known?" he asked. "Did that pretty much sum it up?"

"I'll go and call Ali right now and tell him that we're coming. Wow!" Camilla half ran, half skipped back to the villa.

The passengers lunged forward as the pilot reversed the props to slow the plane. It was as if he were testing how much abuse the rivets on the vibrating plane body could stand. For a moment the noise was deafening. Then the plane taxied down the runway to two waiting limousines, parked to the side of the main terminal, before coming to a complete stop. The few minutes the plane sat there before allowing the passengers to disembark felt like an eternity to Camilla.

Suddenly the door opened and Ali stepped into the cabin, dressed in western clothing. He walked over and hugged Camilla kissing her on each cheek. "I'm so glad you could make it," he whispered to her.

"Ali, this is Annika . . . Annika, please meet Ali," Camilla said, turning to her. Annika held out her hand, but Ali ignored it and gave her a warm hug instead.

"Please let's not be formal when we are not in public. I'm glad to meet you Annika. Camilla has told me a lot about you and I know she treasures your friendship. I hope we will also be good friends. A pleasure to meet you," he said, turning to Torsten.

"Oh, forgive me. This is our friend Torsten," Camilla said.

"It's a pleasure to meet you, Torsten. I hope the flight went well?"

"Perfect. It couldn't have been better. It's a great pleasure to meet you Sir."

"Ali please, and I hope you will enjoy your stay here."

"How is your father doing?" Camilla asked.

"He seems to have stabilized. He is doing much better today," he told her smiling.

"He's doing well enough to grab the behind of his nurse." They all laughed.

"Sounds like a good sign to me," said Annika.

"I was hoping you could meet him, Camilla. I would like to show you off to him. I know he would love to meet you. He is an expert on, and really appreciates, beauty."

"I would love to meet him," Camilla assured him. "He sounds like a nice man."

"Let's first get settled in, have some lunch and then we can go from there," Ali suggested. "Unless you would like to do something else?"

"It sounds good to me. Perhaps after lunch, Annika and Torsten would like to do a little sightseeing on their own, and you and I can talk alone. Ali, I think we have a few things to talk about," Camilla suggested.

"Yes, yes of course," Ali agreed.

They stayed at Ali's country estate rather than at the royal palace downtown. It was more private and less formal. Furthermore, at the palace they would constantly have to respond to staff greetings, and be subject to public scrutiny. After lunch Annika and Torsten set out on their own, with a driver, to see the sights. Ali and Camilla went to see his father.

"What about your mother?" she asked. "When will I get to meet her?"

"Unfortunately, she died at childbirth. I'm her only child, but I do have three half-brothers and four half-sisters. However, only three of them live in Jodassy, two of my brothers and one of my sisters. My other sisters live close by. They married royalty from neighboring lands."

"Yes, Elli told me about the twin package deal." Camilla smiled as she looked at him.

"That Elli, she likes to joke about things. It is true, however, that we traditionally arrange marriages. I know that is viewed as a strange custom in the western world, but it works for us. We never force marriages where all parties aren't in agreement. It is also required that the couple spends a minimum of twenty-four hours alone before they tie the knot." He reached over and took her hand, moved it over to his lap and held it gently with both of his hands. Camilla moved slightly closer to him. "It is true that the twins got married at the same time," he confirmed. "I believe they're happy," he said after some thought. "I wasn't planning on moving quite this fast, but, I can think of no more reason to wait." He reached over to a side compartment and retrieved a small package that he handed to her. "Camilla, I have known from the first few minutes I laid eyes on you that you are the right woman for me. You are extraordinarily beautiful. You are very smart and witty. But what is more important, you are compassionate and sensitive, fair and tolerant. It is not going to be long before I will be King of Jodassy. That would make you queen. Should anything happen to me, you would inherit the throne. I think you will be a good queen, a good wife and a good mother. Camilla, will you give me the ultimate honor of being my wife and mother to my children." He looked deep into her eyes.

"Ali, I don't know what to say. Your offer is very enticing, but there are a few small complications. First, I'm already married, at least on paper. I couldn't marry you until I'm divorced. Second, I have my children, and I don't know what will happen in the divorce, whether I will get full custody. I have to think of their schooling, of their future. And what if something happens to you? Jodassy would end up with a queen who doesn't speak a word of Jodassy and who knows nothing about its politics. Besides, you're Muslim and I'm Lutheran.

"I'm also already married. That's not a problem based on Jodassy law, even though you will be the first woman with more than one husband. It has never been done before, but there is no law against it, and it would only be until you get your divorce. Also, in our treaty with Sweden, Sweden has agreed to honor our customs. You'll have to become a Jodassy citizen, but you can have dual citizenship if you chose. We would begin the divorce procedure immediately. I have very capable attorneys who will take care of all that for us. Your children, our children will get the best education possible. You will learn Jodassy fast. They say it's a quite easy language to learn. As far as knowing anything about politics, your elected leaders have no political experience either, when they first get elected. You're very intelligent, you will learn quickly. You will do just fine. We'll get married right away but then we will have a wedding ceremony after you are divorced. I'm a Muslim more by tradition than by faith. I will make no attempt to change your religion. We have many Christians in Jodassy. We have a Christian church. I have already worked out the logistics. What do you say? Will you marry me?

"I would be honored to marry you Ali. Yes, I will." She reached over and returned his kiss. "Everyone at home will be shocked though, that's for sure."

Ali's father was taking a stroll assisted by two nurses when they arrived.

"Glad to see you son," he responded to their greeting, "and who is this lovely young lady?"

"Father, you are the first one to know. This is Camilla and she has just agreed to become my first wife. She is the woman that will carry our family name forward."

"Son, damn it, you've hit the jackpot. Come over here and give your future father-in-law a hug. I know Ali, and I know he will be a good husband. I hope you'll love him Camilla."

"I do love him," she said, looking up at Ali. It was the first time she had professed her love for Ali and she felt comfortable saying it."

Ali's face lit up, and he leaned over and kissed her on her forehead.

"Then you have my blessing. Welcome to the Alibassi family." King Abimi pronounced. He and Camilla hugged and kissed on both cheeks.

"I like your dad a lot," she told Ali as they drove off. "What a charmer. I can see where you got it from."

The following day Ali and Camilla wed in a civil ceremony, with Annika, Torsten, King Abimi and Ali's other wives as witnesses. Thus, Camilla became Princess Camilla Alibassi of Jodassy. She signed the documents for citizenship at the same time.

CHAPTER 23

May, 1949 - Leaving Jodassy

The noise from the plane's engines made conversation difficult. The twin engine planes flew slightly above a blanket of clouds penetrated by tall mountains at some distance. The sun shone brightly through the cabin windows. In one of the planes flew Ali, Camilla, family and friends. Ali and Camilla rode in the main cabin, but sat alone up front. In the other flew the support team. They would land at Torslanda "airport outside Gothenburg in about four hours.

"Tell me about Jodassy's government, the structure and so on," Camilla said. "I have so much to learn."

"Don't worry, you will do just fine, I know. It will all fall into place in time. Jodassy is not a large country. We have fewer than half a million citizens. It is actually an island connected to the mainland by a bridge. We do not have an army, but because of our strategic location, in between two large countries with conflicting interests, it is in both their interests to maintain Jodassy as a neutral buffer zone. Many of our most basic needs are provided by our neighbors, but we could be self-sufficient if we had to. It would just be a little costlier. We are blessed with several natural resources, but we also have a significant manufacturing industry. We are well known for our Alibassi wines. . .."

"Oh, that's where I heard that name before. It sounded so familiar," Camilla interjected.

"And we have a small ship yard and substantial investments in several other countries."

"Who owns all this? This is a kingdom, so does that mean that it all belongs to the Alibassi family?"

"Yes and no. My father and I are working on establishing what we believe is a perfect country. We are looking at the whole country as if it were a large corporation. The Alibassi family is set up as a trust and the Alibassi trust owns fifty-one percent of all shares. The rest belongs to the people. They are like stock holders in the corporation. When a Jodassy is born, he or she receives one thousand shares in the corporation. He or she can earn additional shares by maintaining a certain grade average in school, for an example, and for other good deeds. The shares can also be taken away for misdeeds. The shares cannot be traded. They are our social safety net and pension plan. The proceeds, or dividends, if you like, from the shares are placed in a trust until the individual is twenty. However, they may withdraw capital for specific uses before they are twenty. Health care is provided at essentially no cost to the individual. After you are twenty, you have to pay a small amount for each doctor visit, unless the visit is required by a doctor, in order to avoid misuse of the system. Education is also provided by Jodassy at no cost to the individual. As long as students maintain a C-average, they can continue all the way through a Ph.D. If they cannot maintain the 'C,' they will be taught an appropriate trade. Of course, if they are maintaining a C-average they are not likely to ever earn a Ph.D.," he added smiling.

"That makes a lot of sense."

"In order to keep our 'corporation' in good health, it is imperative that our people are in good health and educated to the best of their ability."

"Sure . . . of course. You sometimes wonder why many countries appear to prefer to have a large part of their population unproductive."

"I know, I have thought of that many times. I guess many are so afraid that some people will get something for nothing that they would rather support a large section of the population at a staggering cost to the country.

Even though most industry is owned by the Jodassy Corporation, several businesses are privately owned," he continued. "Those businesses pay a lease, or taxes if you will, for operating on Jodassy property. There is no personal income tax in Jodassy. We have a relatively simple legal system. Most disputes are solved by arbitration. If that is not possible, we have a court with one judge who determines the facts in the case and who gives a 'legal' opinion. The case then goes back to arbitration. If that does not work out, there is a final court consisting of two civilians and three professional judges. Each party to the dispute may submit a written statement, including adding new evidence. In special cases, including split decisions, an appeal can be made to the Corporation Board. The Corporate Board has the final say on all issues in Jodassy and can raise any issue on its own initiative," Ali explained.

"Boy, it sounds as though you have thought of everything. How is the 'Corporation' set up?" Camilla asked.

"The board consists of five elected representatives who each control ten percent of the votes, and three Alibassi representatives who control the remaining fifty percent of the votes," he explained. "In order for a motion to pass it has to receive a majority vote. The King can break ties. I'm proud of our system, and it serves us well."

"Sounds terrific to me," Camilla agreed. "What does Jodassy base its law on? Do we have some form of a Constitution or Ground Law?" she asked.

"We have what we call The Jodassy Foundation. We do not have absolute laws, because, we feel that each situation should be considered on its own merit. We have several Rules that one would need an awfully good reason to violate, not to get in trouble. For example, if you kill someone, it better be in self-defense. Generally, we apply a three-point test. I guess you could call that our Constitution. First, the degree of carelessness. Second, what is adequate and third what is fair. It is rather basic and seems to work pretty well. We call it Passion, Adequate, and Justice and it is written on our State Shield"

"Good. Let's go back and chat with Annika and Torsten, and later on you can fill me in on the names, and credentials, of all important people that I should know. I would also like to have a lesson in speaking Jodassy."

"Yes, we will begin with the most important phrases like 'ye mona' which means 'I love you,' or 'ye mona lee' which means 'I love you too,' and 'ye mona patso' meaning, 'I love you with all my heart, or passionately."

"Ye mona patso," she told him, putting her hand on his leg and leaning her head against his shoulder. He looked at her with his warm eyes and gently put his lips on her forehead. She looked up and reached for his lips with hers.

"Ye mona lee, patso."

"That is such a beautiful language, sounds more Italian though, than Spanish," she reflected.

"Perhaps, but I think when you hear some more, you will hear the Spanish connection. We will also have to cover our industrial complex and foreign policy another time. I have to say that I'm impressed with how well you comprehend everything we discuss, yes, very impressed."

She leaned over and kissed him, "thank you. I have a great teacher. One more thing, how do you say, 'You are so incredibly handsome, I would love to jump in bed with you,' in Jodassy?"

"Wow!"

"Wow!" she repeated "means all that?"

"Yes, it pretty much covers it, I told you that it was an easy language to learn," they both chuckled.

"I'm going to have to be careful, around here, not to express surprise to people, it could be misinterpreted. I can't wait to get back to Sweden to tell that no good second husband of mine that it is over, to see the kids and have them meet you. I hope they will understand."

"Yes, you will have to break it to them gently. They will still have their father and they can just call me Ali," he suggested. AAll right sport, let's go back to Annika and Torsten and see how they are doing."

"Wow!"

"I'll stay at the Park Avenue Hotel while you go home and get the children. It's probably better for you and Annika to go alone and to break the news gently ... Then we can all have dinner here at the hotel, if that's fine with you."

"I'll give Mamma a call."

"Mamma! Hi! It's Camilla. I'm back in town and I'll be home in a short while. There are so many wonderful things that have happened but I will tell you when I get there. Are the kids all right ... and yourself? ... Is Sven around? ... Really? ... Well, I'll see you in a short while. I love you Mamma. That jerk, he hasn't been there since we left," she grumbled to Ali.

"Kjell and Maria, there is something important I have to tell you. First I must tell you that Mamma and Pappa love you very much and nothing will ever change that." Maria, the two-year-old was more interested in playing with her Mother's purse than paying any attention to what she had to say, but Kjell was listening. "Kjell, I hope you can understand. I had the most wonderful vacation of my life. I went to a beautiful place on a large boat. It was so nice. While I was there, I met a wonderful man who really cares about me and we are going back down there to live. I think you'll love it there. Mamma and Pappa will not be living together anymore. We will still be friends, I hope, and we will always be your mom and dad, but we have discovered that we don't have very much in common or rather, it's like always having to play with someone that you don't get along with all that much. You wouldn't like that, would you?"

"No"

"Well neither do we. Dad has some other friends that he prefers to spend his time with, and now I have also found someone. His name is Uncle Ali and he is a wonderful person. He is a real prince ..."

"A real prince? Kjell asked in disbelief.

"Yes, a real prince, and someday he will become the King of a country called Jodassy. It is a beautiful place surrounded by water and the weather is always warm. There are a lot of young people there and you will have lots of friends. ... We're going to have dinner with Uncle Ali tonight, so you'll get to meet him and some other ladies whom I'll explain more about later ..."

"A real prince?" he repeated. " With horses?"

"With lots of horses?"

"Can Johan come and visit?"

"Sure, if it's okay with his parents." Camilla assured him.

"What about school?" Kjell had just started going to school, and he liked it.

"You will go to school first in Jodassy and then in an English-speaking country, perhaps England or America."

"I would like to go to America, I think. . ... to be a cowboy."

"We're not yet completely sure about what's going to happen, because a judge will have to make some decisions first, but I'm really glad to hear that it's all right with you."

"Are you kidding, a real prince? Wait until I tell Johan."

"We're going to leave in a few minutes to go and have dinner with Uncle Ali. If you'd like to tell Johan you'd better run down and do it right now . . . and come right back! Okay?"

"Okay. Can Johan come with and meet Uncle Ali?"

"I think we can arrange that."

"Mom, I'm so happy!" Camilla put her arms around her mother's neck and tears began to flow. "I was so worried that Kjell would be upset, but he seems to think that it's the greatest thing. I better give Sven a call. I'm quite sure I know who he's with."

"Hello!"

"Yes high Ruth, this is Camilla. Can I please speak to Sven? . . . Hi Sven. I know that you're busy . . . but there are a few important things I have to talk to you about. I have also found someone . . . and I think it is time for us to go our separate ways. Don't you agree?"

"Well..." he paused, startled by the abruptness of her announcement. Finally, "yes, but you know that I can't afford to pay a large alimony for you and the children."

"That's alright. I don't want anything but my personal things, and I won't ask for any alimony."

"Nothing, did you say no alimony?" Sven was speechless for a few seconds. "You got a deal. You will take care of the children and I will not pay anything?" he repeated to make sure he heard right, emphasizing not.

"Yes, you heard me right and I hope that for the sake of the children that we can remain friends and that you will see them on occasion."

"You got a deal. You must have run into a lot of money to make that offer."

"He's doing all right. I'll have an attorney draw up the papers tomorrow then. Could you come to the conference room at the Park Avenue Hotel tomorrow morning at nine, to sign the papers and to make the final arrangements?"

"I'll be there."

"All right then, Mom. We are going for dinner and I have a few things to tell you."

The following morning, Sven showed up right on time, escorting Ruth. There was only one other person in the room besides Camilla, one of Ali's attorneys.

"I have to make it clear to you that I'm representing Camilla and you will have to sign this document, that you agree to proceed without legal representation," the attorney instructed Sven.

"That's all right, I agree based on the terms we agreed to yesterday."

"Regarding some issues that you did not cover, do you agree that you will keep half of your savings, and the other half will be placed in a trust account for the benefit of your children, and do you also agree to make Camilla the legal custodian of the children, and that she will also absorb all costs in raising and educating the children?"

"I do. You mean the cash we have in the bank, right?"

"Right. . .. Then please read through these documents to make sure they reflect your understanding of this agreement and if so, please sign next to Camilla signature and it is all final. Camilla will pay the recording fees," she explained.

"Now I would like you to meet my new husband . . . Prince Alibassi of Jodassy." Sven looked at Ruth in disbelief. She went to get Ali, without awaiting his answer.

"Sir, it's a pleasure to meet you," said Ali, while extending his hand, western style.

"You have the best mannered children I have ever met. You must be very proud of them." Sven nodded.

"I will do my best to take good care of them, and any time you want to see them, please be our guest in Jodassy." Ali shook Sven's hand firmly while looking him straight into his wide eyes. Sven was speechless.

CHAPTER 24

July 1949 - Lisa and John

"Guess what?" asked Lisa as she entered John's office.

"What?" He asked, removing his glasses as he looked up.

"We're going to have a baby!"

"Really? Really?! John shot up from his chair and hugged Lisa. Are you sure? Oh, I love you! . . . But wait . . . maybe you better sit down here on the couch, and rest."

"Don't be silly. I haven't turned instantly fragile. I still have eight months to go, and a few days. Isn't it exiting?! I have to write Camilla and Annika. "Let's invite Billy and Diana over for dinner and celebrate the good news. We haven't seen them for a while."

"You're right. We should make time to see our friends more often," Lisa agreed.

Billy and Diana arrived in their dark blue Jaguar. Normally Billy rode in his chauffeur-driven Rolls Royce when in London, so he would not have to find parking. However, John and Lisa lived outside of London were there was plenty of parking. Besides, Billy enjoyed driving, especially his Jaguar. John and Lisa were standing in the yard as they drove up. Billy jumped out of the car and with a big smile, rushed over to Lisa and gave her a warm, but tender Billy hug.

"Come on Billy, you can do better. I'm not 'gonna' break," she assured him.

"I'm so happy for you, Lisa, and John too, congratulations! I envy you." He shook John's hand vigorously, before returning to the car after a giant bouquet of pink roses.

"Diana, you look great! How's everything?" John greeted her.

"Fine, thank you." Diana returned his hug.

"I'm so glad you could come. It's been way too long. Here, how about a glass of homemade sherry."

"Love to. I remember your sherry, it's really good. You know, you gave me the recipe once, but when I was going to give it a try I couldn't remember where I had put it," she confessed.

"Oh, it's really simple essentially only water, rye, sugar, yeast, lemons and oranges. Let it sit for five weeks and voila! You've got sherry. I'll give it to you again," Lisa said. "Guess what? We're getting married! We'll have a small reception here on Friday after we sign the papers with the judge. I hope you can come."

"I wouldn't miss it for the world." Billy gave her a warm hug and kissed her cheek.

"Heard from Annika or Camilla?" He asked, as they walked inside.

"Well, Annika seems to be having a nice time traveling in the US with that crazy Kurt, after just having returned from a trip to Jodassy. For the world, I can't see what she sees in him," said Lisa shaking her head. "They're not even married, you know."

"I know that, and believe me; I have given it a lot of thought. But she is living as married and she has the children." The faraway look in Billy's eyes gave away the depth of his feelings for Annika.

Dinner awaited them inside. "Can you believe Camilla's adventure in Majorca and Jodassy?! Can you imagine marrying a stranger - a prince of all things, after just a few days? Lisa smirked.

"What a fairy tale, uh?" Diana exclaimed.

"Yes, I agree," said Lisa, "that whole story sounds like a fairy tale to me. I have never even heard of a country named Jodassy, and then again, you are basically married to a prince or a king yourself. Diana. Is there anything in southern England that Billy doesn't have an interest in?" Lisa asked, rhetorically.

"I would have loved to be there when she returned and told her husband, was it Sven? 'Hi honey, you can call me Princess Camilla now . . . I just married a Middle Eastern prince on the vacation. How are things at home?'" John laughed heartily.

"That could ruin a guy's day," Billy agreed. "Maybe someday we can go and visit," he suggested.

"Yes, if we can find it. It's not even on a map. I've looked," said Diana.

"Yes, but that's probably because it's more like a protectorate, like private property that is part of one of its neighbor countries. It's given special political independence, in this case, because of its strategic location. It's somewhat similar to Monaco's relationship with France and Italy. I have actually been there a few times. It is a beautiful place. Ali, its crown prince is actually a friend of mine." Billy explained.

"Yes, or like your property, Billy. Have you ever considered seceding from England, Billy?" Lisa asked smiling.

"Not yet." He sipped on his wine. "You know, I actually know two of Ali's wives, sort of. When I went to Cambridge, I took a class in international law and there were two girls there married to some foreign prince. I remember it well because of the controversy of having more than one wife. I remember having a discussion regarding whether it was fair that a man with two wives was breaking the law, but his wives were not, because they were only married to one man. Anyway, I also remember that they were very smart; in fact, one of them graduated as number one in the class. It's a small world isn't it?" Billy helped himself to the 'cream of mushroom soup' and passed it on.

"Not that I wish anything bad to Ali, but it would be interesting to see what would happen if he was the king and then passed away and Camilla became the queen. Would Ali's siblings stand for that?" Lisa asked.

August 7, 1949
London

Dear Camilla,
I have some great news that I have to tell you first. I'M PREGNANT!!! We just found out. We are completely ecstatic about the news. And we just got married. Now that we are going to become parents, we thought it was high time, so we were married by a justice. We had a small reception afterwards with John's family and a few of our British friends, including Billy Jones, if you remember him, the British sailor that liked Annika. He still does. We are thinking about having a bigger wedding later when I can take some time off from work, perhaps back in Sweden. Yesterday John came home with several toys for the baby. Of course, it will be quite a while before the baby grows into them.

Enough about me, You, crazy girl! I had to make sure it wasn't the first of April after I read the news, that you were not making a fool's joke. Your story is so fantastic that it sounds like a ferry tail. I do agree on the point that Sven is not likely going to recover from his alcohol dependency as he does not recognize that it is a serious problem. Also, the fact that he has been seeking comfort with other women just because you have been busy with your school work is not a good sign at all, and really is not related to his alcohol abuse. It sounds as though Prince Ali is a wonderful, sensible and caring man and you deserve no less.

I hope you are doing well. I miss you so much. We haven't seen each other for six years now. That's way too long, but I don't have a solution right now. After I have the baby, I'll take a year off from work. Maybe then we could work something out. Everything is going well here with us, except that we work too much.

I was glad to hear about your success at the art show, Camilla. I always knew that you were a super painter, especially of portraits. That's an art within itself. I'm sure glad that I got one of your paintings while they were still affordable. I sure hope that you'll continue with your painting even though you no longer need the income. I hope I'll see you and Ali and the kids soon. That's all for now. Give my best to Ali. Love, Lisa

CHAPTER 25

July, 1949 - Going to the USA

When Annika returned from Majorca, only two months remained before the family was leaving for America. She looked forward to the adventure, but she was quite sure that she and Kurt would return to Sweden soon. After all, they still had their apartment, the summer home, Kurt's business, Eva, and Kurt's mother. So even though Kurt talked as though they would stay in America, she was convinced that they would return to Sweden sooner, rather than later.

Kurt rented out the summer house. They packed four large trunks with their personal belongings and on July 26, 1949, they all stepped aboard the MS Saga, the ocean liner that would take them to South Hampton at the southern tip of England. The trip would take three days. In South Hampton they would change ships, to the MS Queen Elizabeth, the largest passenger ship in the world. The MS Stockholm was not available. The Queen Elizabeth would take them to New York in five days. When Annika entered their cabin on the Queen Elizabeth, she found a red rose lying on a cot. The mystery had only deepened over the years. She could think of no one except Kurt who could have arranged to have the rose placed on her bed, unless the ship did so for all its passengers.

The voyage to America was less than ideal. The weather was bad from the start, and the Nobels spent most of their time in bed seasick, as did most of the other passengers. The ship negotiated waves up to fifty feet. All windows were sealed off on the three lower decks. Owing to the constant rolling motion, the bathrooms were the most frequently visited rooms on the ship. Kurt did not appear to be adversely affected by the rolling, but he was rather lonely on the upper decks and in the exclusive dining room in particular. It was a trip they would remember. On the last day the storm had passed, and land was a welcome sight at the horizon. By the time they were greeted by the Statute of Liberty, most travelers had overcome their illness and were up and about. Annika took numerous photos of New York's skyline and harbor as the ship pulled in. Martin had lent her one of his cameras. He had instructed her in the art of photography and had encouraged her to take plenty of pictures. The sky scrapers, including the Empire State building, and the Statue of Liberty were magnificent, much more striking than they appeared in the pictures Annika had seen.

Going through customs turned into quite an ordeal. Kurt's restlessness drew the attention of the customs officials. They apparently interpreted Kurt's impatience with waiting, as suspicious behavior, and searched his luggage with a fine-tooth comb. The family ended up spending all day with the customs officials, mostly waiting. Having two small restless boys along did not help matters. At first, they were fascinated by the dark-skinned people, whom they had never seen before. After the fascination wore off, boredom and restlessness set in, and it was a long day indeed. Annika did her best to entertain the children, but they grew tired and whiny before long, and the time difference added to their sleepiness. Finally, at 5:00 pm they were cleared from customs.

The cab ride to the hotel was nerve wracking. The cab swerved back and forth between the lanes of heavy traffic. The drivers communicated with each other using their horns and sign language. It was hot and humid, and their clothes clung to their bodies. Annika was appalled by the filth she saw in the streets of New York. There was garbage strewn most everywhere.

The kids got a kick out of one of the police officers directing the traffic. He had turned his traffic directing into a well-coordinated dance routine. Throngs of people filled the sidewalks and most of them appeared to be in a great hurry.

The following morning, they took a cab to the train station. Annika and the children were fascinated by the black attendant dressed in a white uniform. One stood in each wagon of the train. The attendants set out a small step stool to assist the passengers in boarding the train. They would then attend to the passengers' needs during the trip, including transforming the benches into beds in the evening. The Nobels had no problem going to sleep to the rhythm of the train's cla-dunk, cla-dunk, cla -dunk . . . as it traveled towards Chicago.

The scenery was magnificent: weathered mountains, lakes and prairies stretching for miles.

"Look at all them cows!" Axel called out.

"Yes, there are probably enough cattle there to feed the whole of Sweden." Said Kurt.

"And over there, the antelopes." Do they farm them? Annika asked.

"Looks like there is a fence around." Kurt noticed.

Cattle, horses, pigs and sheep all looked different from what they were accustomed to. The beauty of the countryside contrasted sharply with the slum neighborhoods of New York and other cities they passed through.

"Welcome to the land of opportunity" Kurt greeted Annika as she stepped off the train.

"How hot is it today?" Kurt asked. "It feels as though my blood is boiling." It had not been so uncomfortable inside the train station, but outside it was scorching hot.

Annika wanted to see were Camilla had lived so Kurt hailed a cab for the tour. What's the temperature today? He asked the cabby.

"It's not bad today. It's in the high nineties. We had 115F three days ago," The cabby informed them.

"That tells me nothing," Annika confessed.

"Well, I think it's close to 37C. It's hot." Kurt explained.

"You have to be careful not to touch the car with your hand. It will burn," Kurt cautioned the boys.

It took a little over an hour in heavy traffic to drive from downtown Chicago north to Evanston, where Sven and Camilla had lived. The breeze from the open window made the drive bearable, but each time they had to stop, the car turned into an oven. The noise from the wind and the traffic made it difficult to hold a meaningful conversation. Annika took several pictures along the shoreline drive. On one side there were parks, beaches and Lake Michigan. On the opposite side stood skyscraper apartment buildings, and closer to Evanston, exclusive mansions on manicured estates. Many had large stone walls and impressive iron-gate entrances.

"How would you like to live here?" Kurt asked Annika as they passed by a particularly large mansion with a gilded gate.

"That would be all right if we had a lot of help to take care of everything. But don't you think that it's a little out of our league?" Annika asked.

"Someday."

The Nobels spent two days in the Chicago area, in more than 100 degrees heat. The second day a terrific storm besieged Chicago, leaving the air muggy and damp afterwards. The storm caused a power outage, and it knocked down several trees, disrupting traffic. Several boats and small aircrafts were destroyed, they heard on the news. Miraculously, no one was seriously injured.

Sven and Camilla's home were nice. Sven had remodeled an old barn into a unique studio, where they had lived and worked. They only stopped briefly as the place was occupied by someone else now. It was being used as an antique shop.

The Nobels decided to take a side trip to Milwaukee for a couple days. Kurt had seen pictures of Milwaukee, and he wanted to see it in person.

"It's too bad the weather is so bad. Last time I was here it was warm and sunny, but not hot. We should have picked a better time of the year to come, I guess," Kurt said.

"Camilla said the winters are really nasty here, cold windy and rainy most of the time. Chicago is nicknamed 'the windy city,'" Annika informed him.

"Yeah, well, one gets used to it."

"Why would anyone want to get used to it?" Annika grumbled.

Milwaukee seemed so much more pleasant. It was clean and nicely set, with buildings and trees sloping down towards the water. However, Kurt was fascinated with the commerce and excitement of big cities like Chicago and New York, and Milwaukee, although a large city, could not compare in that regard.

The Nobels left for St. John, Newfoundland, to see Kurt's friend Peter and family, who lived in the outskirts of St John, with a magnificent view of the Atlantic. Peter and Hilda also had an apartment in Quebec where Hilda's main office was located. Their St John home was spacious and had a sizeable guest room with its own bathroom. Annika had never met Peter before. She was pleasantly surprised at the warm welcome they received. Annika took an immediate liking to him. She thought his wife Hilda was nice, but a little stuffy at first. After she had a chance to get to know her a little better, however, she found that she was anything but stuffy.

"How long will you be able to stay?" Peter asked.

"We were hoping we could stay for a week, if that's okay?" Kurt said.

"That's great. We are really glad you could come. You can stay as long as you like. It isn't as though you come here all the time and we love to have company."

"There is only one thing," said Hilda. "You know I have a flower-gift shop business, and there is a trade show in Quebec in three days that I need to attend. It is an important show where I buy most of my gift items for the entire year. It's only for two days, though, and Peter can take good care of you."

"That's really nice of you, Peter. I'm sure we will be fine," said Annika.

"Kurt, why don't you go with Hilda to Quebec? If you are planning to start a business here, you might get some ideas. It's not only gift items, they have just about everything," Peter suggested.

"Would you mind if I tag along, Hilda?"

"Not at all, it would be fun to have company. You'll love it. They have everything there and then some. If you only go to one trade show a year, this is the one to attend." Hilda assured him. "I will take good care of you, Kurt" she added.

Hilda was from Lillehammar, a popular ski resort in Norway. She had met Peter six years before when they were both working on the Norwegian cruise-liner Stavanger Fjord. She was a perky redhead in her early thirties. A truly "bright' red head, as she liked to put it. Her windblown hair, reached past her shoulders, hanging into her eyes. Her freckles, petite body and bright shiny red lips gave her the appearance of a doll. Her big green eyes were accentuated with mascara. Her fragrance remained in the room long after she had left. She exuded femininity and there was not a man born that would not turn his head when she walked by, nor a woman. She could make even a baggy carpenter's coverall look sexy, like the ones she liked to wear around the house. Her Norwegian accent was still quite noticeable, which added to her charm.

"Do you dare to have Kurt travel with Hilda?" Annika asked. "They might just keep on traveling," she joked.

"And then I would be stuck here with "only you". What a horrifying thought!" he grinned. "I'm not worried about Hilda. I'm more concerned about Kurt, that he is not taken advantage of." They all laughed at that picture.

"Hilda is like a little puppy dog; she gets a little lost at times, but she always finds her way home eventually," Peter explained.

"Hey, thanks for calling me a dog!' she interjected, wrinkling her freckled nose in protest.

"Not a dog, a cute little puppy," he clarified, "with a cold wet nose and a long wagging tail," he added smiling.

"A cold wet nose, well at least that means that I'm healthy," Hilda concluded.

Kurt had known Peter since child hood, when his parents worked at the British Embassy in Sweden, and Kurt and Peter had been classmates. As a child, Kurt was drawn to Peter because of his English skills. They had also traveled together as seamen. Ironically, their friendship had grown stronger when Peter moved to Canada.

Kurt and Hilda left for Quebec two days later, Kurt driving Hilda's brand-new red convertible, a 1952 Ford Crest liner. It was another hot day, and the breeze felt good. The back draft made Hilda's hair fly in her face, until she tied it into a pony-tail with a scarf. She wore a sporty beige suit and matching heels. Her dress slid past her knees when she sat down, making it difficult for Kurt to concentrate on his driving. They drove to Channel where they took the ferry to Sidney Mines on Nova Scotia. They continued across New Brunswick to Riviere and next, to the St Lawrence River where they caught the ferry to Quebec. Strolling around on the ferry, Kurt enjoyed watching the wind play with Hilda's hair. It was calm; however, the ferry created its own wind.

Upon their arrival in Quebec, Hilda had to first stop by her apartment to unpack and to check her mail. It was too early for dinner, so they decided to go to a movie. They searched for one in English being that most everything was in French in Quebec, and chose *Casablanca,* which was playing at a theater nearby. Afterwards they would have dinner, at a place Hilda suggested. Kurt took a quick shower and sat in the living room waiting for Hilda, with a glass of chilled white wine. Hilda had left the door to her bedroom wide open. Through the angle of a hallway mirror, Kurt could see directly into the bed room. It was as if Hilda knew that Kurt could see her at that particular spot, because she changed her outfit right there.

"I'll be ready in a few minutes," she called out.

"No hurry, I'm doing just fine," he responded. "Take your time."

"What do you think?" she asked him as she entered the living room, stopping in front of him and making a full turn, to show off her outfit. She wore a tight skirt split to her knees, a white filmy blouse, and a small black lace hat, tilted down on her forehead.

"Hot, baby, hot," Kurt complimented her.

"Hot, huh?" She responded, striking a flirtatious pose.

"Hot," he repeated.

The theater was almost full even though the film had been out for close to six years. Kurt and Hilda sat in the last row. As the film proceeded and the movie plot tightened, Hilda snuggled close to Kurt. Eventually she reached for his hand that lay in his lap. Hilda could feel him grew. She kept her hand in his lap.

"Did you enjoy the movie?" Hilda asked him as they left the theater.

"Yes, it was good, but I think they should have gotten together at the end. How about you?"

"Yes, I liked it too. But I agree, they should have gotten together." She took his hand as they walked back to the car, swinging their hands between them.

"But I couldn't have had nicer company," Kurt told her, squeezing her hand lightly.

"I'm glad you didn't mind. I couldn't help myself after accidentally having launched it." She replied innocently.

"Hilda, you can launch it any time you like, and I think you know that."

"Yes, I have noticed how easily it takes off. I'm curious about what would happen if I really tried."

They dined in a restaurant that was converted from a railroad car, and then returned to the apartment.

"Help yourself to some wine in the living room while I slip into something more comfortable."

Kurt poured two glasses and brought Hilda hers in the bedroom. She had removed her dress but did not appear to mind his company. "Oh, thank you, that was sweet." She continued undressing, ignoring Kurt's presence. "How do you like this outfit?" she asked, spinning around in front of him, dressed in only her bra and panties.

"Aren't you a little overdressed for the occasion?" he asked her.

"Perhaps, but that's all you're going to get to see. Is there anything I can get you? How about a little ice cream for dessert? and perhaps a cup of coffee."

"I would love some. I'm a sucker for desserts, and coffee I can drink at any time." She pranced into the kitchen to get the treats, followed by an appreciative Kurt. "We probably shouldn't make it too late tonight. We have to get up early tomorrow for the show."

Peter took Annika and the children for a boat trip the day that Kurt and Hilda left. They went up the coast to a small island with an abandoned lighthouse. It was one of Peter's favorite places for swimming, fishing and for picnics. The rocks had smooth ledges that lent themselves perfectly to diving or jumping into the water. There was no wind whatsoever, but Peter's sailboat had a backup engine. They spent all day on the island. When it was time to go, Peter could not get the motor started, and the ocean was like a mirror. "Looks like we are going to be stuck here until tomorrow morning when we should be able to sail home. We should be all right though. Just look at it as an adventure. I have plenty of food and water in the boat, and you can't beat the company."

"It could be fun. Not the first time I've camped out."

"Let's go up to the light house. We'll be more comfortable there. It's always left open just for occasions like this," Peter explained.

They had fresh fish for dinner, grilled on their campfire. They prepared a sleeping area for the children on the lighthouse's upper deck, and went back down for coffee. The aroma from the coffee made the lighthouse feel cozy.

"Would you like to sleep down here tonight, or would you prefer to sleep up there with the boys?" Peter asked as he lit the two oil lamps, which spread a yellow flickering light about the room. He rolled down the wicks some, to stabilize the flames.

"At least it's plenty warm here," Annika pointed out. "No, I'd rather stay here with you, if you don't mind. Would you like to take a little walk outside before it becomes totally dark?" she asked.

"Yes, I need to go down and check on the boat anyway. I think there is a little wind picking up and I have to make sure that Doris is tied up securely."

"Doris?"

"Yes, Doris the boat. We named her Doris after Hilda's mother."

"Oh, that's nice. Do you have anything that's named after you?" she asked. The light wind felt good, cooling on their skin, warm from spending all day in the sunshine.

"Lots! Let's see. . . .. St Petersburg, Peter the Great, Peter and the troll flute, Peter Pan, . . . to mention a few."

"Alright, I meant after you personally, silly."

By the time they got to the boat, the wind had picked up, and bands of white foam formed on the water. The ropes beat against the mast and together with the surf hitting the rocks, it sounded much like an orchestra warming up. The boat was well protected in the small natural harbor. Peter and Annika brought a couple extra blankets with them back up to the lighthouse. They checked on the boys; they were sound asleep.

"Boy, the weather sure changed in a hurry," Annika reflected.

"Yes, it's quite common here, especially this time of year, August-September. It can be completely calm and one hour later you can be in the middle of a storm. We'll be all right here though," he assured her.

"I don't know what it is with you sailors. When Stellan came and spent the first night at Stenongsund, you know Stellan, don't you? Kurt's seaman buddy."

"I've heard of him. Stellan the prankster. But I don't know that we have met."

"Well, we had the worst thunder storm that I can remember, and now this. I hope there won't be a thunder storm tonight. This building is the tallest thing for miles. It seems as though the lightning would love to strike here." Annika reflected uneasily.

"It has been sitting here for at least a hundred years, and it is doing fine so far."

"Yeah, so far. That reminds me of the guy that fell down from the skyscraper and on every floor, they could hear him say, 'so far everything's okay,'" Annika laughed nervously, "the famous last word."

Peter moved two bunks together and spread out the sleeping bag on top as a sheet. He then spread out the blankets on top. They spent much of the night sharing stories. Annika felt comforted by Peter's self-assurance and calm, and she didn't mind when he put his arm around her.

The following morning Annika woke up to the smell of fried bacon and freshly brewed coffee. "Good morning my lady, how about some breakfast," Peter greeted her. "How would you like your eggs?" Peter was whistling 'oh what a beautiful morning, oh what a wonderful day,' as he rushed about preparing breakfast. "The kids are already up. It's a wonderful morning. The sun is shining, and the sky is clear. It smells wonderfully fresh outside after the rain. We're having breakfast on the veranda if it pleases milady?"

"Boy are you perky in the morning. Now how did you get hold of all this food? Did you plan all this?" Annika asked suspiciously.

"Yes, storm and all."

"Well I know you didn't plan the storm. That was probably an extra bonus, but you seem awfully well prepared for it all to be just by chance."

"You know our old Boy Scout's motto, 'always ready.'" His smug smile suggested more.

"Well I don't care if you did, and I'm sure now that you did. This has been fun and the kids are having the best time of the trip so far." Annika walked behind the bathroom curtain to freshen up and soon joined the rest for breakfast. Alex had picked wild flowers that Peter had arranged in an empty milk bottle as the centerpiece. Peter had made French toast for the children. There were fresh fruit and bread and several varieties of jam. "Your scout leader must have been quite a gourmet," Annika commented.

"A renowned connoisseur of fine dining and what's good in life."

"I think he might have been just a notch off though on the principles of scouting. It isn't about what's good for you but how you can do good for others," Annika informed him, smiling.

"Oh, I know. I think he just took the concept to a higher level, based on the system of capitalism and free enterprise."

"Oh yeah?"

"Yes, one is more likely to prepare a nice breakfast if one gets to enjoy it and share it with a lovely lady when it's done."

"Oh, I see. That's the principle of capitalism?"

"You got it. I have some good news. I was down checking out the boat this morning and the engine started right up. There must have just been a little dirt in the fuel line last night."

"Imagine that."

The trip back was uneventful. Peter grilled hamburgers for dinner, by popular demand. The boys, in particular, had developed a strong liking for the American/Canadian hamburger. Annika picked a large bowl of yellow raspberries, a novelty to the children.

"You know, I have an old violin that I purchased at an auction once. I've heard that you're quite a maestro on the violin, how about playing a tune or two for me?"

"Sure, if it's in working order."

Peter fetched the fiddle for Annika and he brought his own guitar. They walked down to the beach, started a bonfire and spent the evening making music and toasting marshmallows.

"Annika, I'm so glad you could come so I got to know you. I've really enjoyed having you here."

"I've enjoyed meeting you too. I hope that we can meet a little more often from now on. If we should move here permanently."

"I sure hope you do," Peter interrupted.

"It's nice to have good friends and Hilda, she's a jewel! She's zany enough that you have to love her."

After Annika had put the children to bed, Peter and Annika continued making music in the living room. Peter was singing a Swedish ballad when he noticed that Annika had dozed off, exhausted from all the events the previous night. He sat there and studied her silently.

CHAPTER 26

August, 1949 - Eva and Stellan

"What's up Eva? How are you doing?" Stellan asked as he walked up behind her.

"Stellan! Hi! I'm just fine, how about you?" Eva was strolling down the path toward the coffee shop at the Botanical Gardens.

"Oh, I just came down to get a break from work and to people watch, listen to the music and have a cup of coffee. I like it here with all the pretty flowers. Are you alone? Well I can see that you're alone, I meant, are you meeting anyone?"

"Yes, I'm alone and no, I'm not meeting anyone. I came for the same reason as you, just to get out a bit. With Kurt being gone, there's not too much excitement around here. A lot of work, but not all that much fun."

"Do you mind if I join you?"

"I'd love to have you join me Stellan. I think we're quite a bit alike you and I. We are both playing second fiddle to the ones we're hung up on, for whatever reasons."

"I think that pretty much sums it up," Stellan agreed. "Well let's try to forget the Nobels for one evening and have a little fun on our own. Okay?"

"Okay."

"What would you like to have?" the waitress interrupted.

"'ll have a cup of black coffee and a piece of princess torte," Eva said.

"'ll have the same please."

" Speaking about princess torte, I have to ask you what you think about Camilla and her prince. Can you believe that?" Eva asked.

"Well, I just hope that it works out for them. I have a lot of respect and admiration for Camilla for daring to take a step like that. I really hope that she will be happy now. Regardless, it will be an experience that the rest of us can only dream of."

"Yes, she's living out our dreams for sure," Eva agreed.

"I know we agreed not to talk about Kurt or Annika, but Eva, have you heard from Kurt? Do you really think they're going to stay there this time?" Stellan asked.

"Kurt? Or even more so Annika?! Not a chance in hell, as Kurt would put it. Kurt likes to talk about it, but he has too much going on here. Kurt just thinks that the grass is greener on the other side. Of course, when he gets there, this becomes the other side. I would be willing to bet you that he'll be back here for the international industrial fair in three weeks. I would bet my life on it," she added. "Brrr, it would be nice if the sun came back. It gets a little cold now in the evenings, if the sun isn't out."

"Well, why don't we go to my apartment after we finish the torte here. I just got some new records that I haven't even heard myself. I just moved in there a couple months ago and it has a really nice view."

"I know, Kurt told me. Okay, but it can't be too late. I have a lot of work to do tomorrow."

"On a Sunday?" he asked curiously.

"All days are pretty much the same for me. Yes, I have a project that I'm working on that has to be finished by Monday. I shouldn't really have gone out tonight, but I decided I needed a break. And I'm glad I did," she added.

"Me too. I'm sure glad you did, and that I did," said Stellan.

AMe too, I mean that you did." Their eyes met and held for a moment, reflecting an understanding.

"What's the important project that you have to complete? Is it something that I could help you with?"

"It's nothing exciting, just tedious work. I have to fold stuff and address about five hundred envelopes. It will take me the better part of tomorrow to get it all done," Eva sighed.

"I tell you what . . . let's stop by your apartment on the way over and pick up the stuff, and I will help you while we listen to the music. Does that sound like a plan to you?"

"Are you sure you don't mind? I do have enough time to get it done tomorrow."

"Sure, I think it will be fun! I'll fix us a light meal later on. You do have the stuff at home? Do you?"

"I took it home."

"Good! Then I get to see where you live."

"It's nothing special . . . just an apartment."

"Yes, except that it's your apartment. That makes it special to me."

Eva was dressed in a pink angora sweater and a white pleated skirt. Stellan could not but admire her shapely legs as she led the way up the stairs to her apartment. Eva had moved after she split up with Bo and she now lived not far from Stellan's apartment.

"I didn't realize that we were almost neighbors," Stellan observed. "I hope I get to see . . . a little more of you, now . . . now that we know where we live.

"Wow, I like your apartment. It's so neat and clean," said Stellan.

"I thought Kurt told me that you're dating Ingrid. What about that?" she confronted him.

"We do go out now and then, but we are just friends. I don't think anything serious will ever come from it. I do like her a lot and I named my boat after her. I don't think that she wants to get serious with a sailor. She lost a close friend to the sea."

"Oh, I didn't know. Anything you would like me to bring?" Eva asked.

"Just that nice smile will be plenty. How about you? Are you seeing anyone?" he asked.

"Not really. I needed some time to get over my divorce from Bo, so, I have been idle for some time."

Stellan had not planned on bringing anyone home and had to make a mad rush to tidy up the apartment when they arrived. "Come on, for a bachelor I think it looks pretty nice here. You even made your bed this morning, not bad," Eva commented as she followed him around, exploring his apartment.

"'ll start a pot of coffee while you get started with the envelopes and then let's snap to it, Okay?" Stellan brought out his record collection and put on one of his new records, a Benny Goodman LP. He asked Eva to dance to a couple of tunes, but returned right away to the project. Eva was easy to dance with, a natural.

Four hours later they were done. They had also finished the warm sandwiches that Stellan had prepared and Stellan was refilling the wine glasses. He put on 'Misty' and they danced slowly without saying a word. He held her tight around her waist and she snuggled up against him, her arms around his neck. After the dance they returned to the couch. Eva was going to finish off the last drops of coffee when Stellan accidentally bumped into her arm, while sitting down in the soft couch, and she spilled the coffee over both her blouse and her skirt. "It will come out, don't worry about it, but why do these things always happen to me? When I met Bo, I also got soaking wet, repairing his sink."

"I'm so sorry, we better soak them in water. I will get you something to put on."

When he returned from the bedroom, Eva was already in the Kitchen. She had removed her stained garments and she was scrubbing them in the sink. "I think it is going away," she reassured him.

"Here you can put this on in the meantime if you like?" He handed her one of his shirts. She slipped it on, but without bothering to button it. Stellan did not have to ask her to spend the night there. It just seemed natural.

CHAPTER 27

March 1952 -- Tina

Just as Annika and others had predicted, the Nobels returned to Sweden in the spring of 1952.

"Of course, the boys shall go to a private school." Kurt insisted. All our friends' kids go to private school. How would it look if we had to send them to public school? Not the Nobel boys.

"But then they have to go downtown, and we are going to have to drive them to school every day." Annika reminded him.

"It won't be so bad. I will drop them off when I go to work, and you have your car, and you always want to go downtown anyway, so then you can pick them up on your way home." said Kurt.

Kurt had bought Annika a Morris Minor, a British car. Of course, Kurt's wife had to have a car, even if it was only a gray Morris Minor bubble.

Annika had the benefit of having a young girl, Tina, living next door. Tina appreciated the opportunity to earn a little money by keeping after the boys. When not in school, or doing school work, she followed them around wherever they went, or perhaps they followed her. Tina spent so much time with the Nobels that she essentially became one of the family. The boys were fascinated by Tina and she had no problems with having them follow her lead.

During the summer they routinely went down to Liseberg's outdoor swimming pool, when they were in town. The boys, at eight, were old enough that they could no longer go with the girls into their dressing room or to the woman's sauna. They now had to use the men's facilities and begin wearing swimming trunks in the pool area. Tina on the other hand, like several other young girls, could use the men's facilities as long as they wanted. Liseberg's Baden was popular and quite crowded, mostly with younger people. The pool grew particularly crowded when they turned on the giant wave machines. It became a sea of appreciative, screaming and jumping bathers.

"Annika!" Kurt called out, as he closed the front door behind him. "Annika, we are going to Sälen in February. I got hold of a real nice cabin there, during the school winter vacation. Almost a miracle."

"What? What happened?" Annika asked. She was folding laundry on their bed.

You know Dr. Falk. They own a cabin right by the ski lift at the big resort and they aren't using it this winter. She happened to mention it to the nurse that they were going to rent it out. Of course, I jumped at the opportunity. Here we will get a whole house with a kitchen instead of just a small hotel room.

The log house featured a rather spacious common room, with the kitchen on one side and the fireplace on the other.

"We will have to bring in some firewood for the fireplace. There is some in the shed over there. Dr Falk told me." Kurt was making himself at home.

Off a narrow corridor were two bedrooms and the bath. The front porch was large enough for the ski equipment and also for a picnic table where the Nobels would have lunch, weather permitting. The view from the porch was stunning. The deep sparkling snow covered much of the surrounding cabins and blanketed the large spruce trees. The mountains across the deep valley were diffused in a pinkish haze.

Tina had joined the Nobels. It was her first trip to Dalarna.

"Here is your room. It's not very big. It just barely fit the bunk beds and a dresser, but it will have to do. Tina, why don't you take the top bunk and the boys can sleep below. That should work out fine." Annika offered.

At bedtime they would all get up on the top bunk to socialize and to tell scary stories, but the daily skiing, the sun and the wind, and the high altitude took its toll and it would normally not be long before they all fell asleep.

In the summer of 1953, the Nobels rented a house at the popular summer community Marstrand, Tina joined them for most of the summer. On a few occasions she stayed alone with the Nobel children when Annika went to Gothenburg. Kurt would come out now and then. He still had his mahogany boat. He had moved it to Marstrand, but he rarely used it. The few times he took it out, they would go down to Marstrand's west harbor inlet, by a tall cliff. Several small boats would typically be fishing there, regardless of the weather. Kurt fished for cod or herring, often adding a large chunk of fish-bait onto the lure, optimistically hoping to catch the big one. He rarely caught anything, however. The boys, on the other hand, took the time to catch and bait their hooks with worms or clams and would normally catch enough fish for the following day's dinner.

In their cottage the Nobels always had a hook-rug sitting out on a table for the whole family, including the boys, to work on. Every Saturday evening, they would listen to an episode of a detective story that played on the radio, as they worked on the rug. No self-respecting child of less than fifteen would miss the program. Annika also wove small rugs and table cloths on her 'Loom'.

During the day the children would hike to their favorite swimming place. There was a mini-peninsula with shallow water on the bay side of the weather-worn rock, while the water was deep enough for diving on the sea side. The area was secluded, and the children could go swimming and sunbathing nude. Tina was past swimming nude with boys around, but she was used to Axel and Alex. The boys had discretely followed her development with increased interest.

During the summer of 1954 the boys spent three weeks at Annika's sister Kajsa's farm, close to Varberg, on the Swedish west-coast. The Brobergs leased the farm from a cooperative, and raised cattle for milk production. They also grew feed for their fifty cows, and two horses, and for their own needs.

"That's Carrot and her name is Pajamas," their cousin Maran explained. "Because she is strawberry blond and Pajamas reminds one about the material in Jonas' pajamas." She explained.

Jonas, at two, was the youngest Broberg. Martha, or Maran, as she was affectionately called. Maran had done nothing particular to earn herself the nickname, which means terror in Swedish. She was sweet as could be and did not appreciate the endearment, but the more she protested, the more others persisted with it. The Brobergs also had pigs and several chickens that ran freely about, laying eggs just about any place. Periodically, the Brobergs would find new nests filled to the brim with eggs. Of course, they also had dogs and several cats on the farm.

The Brobergs lived rather isolated. A small village about a thirty-minute bike-ride away from their farm provided for their essentials. Varberg, the closest city, was more than twice that distance. Maran and Jonas did not have close friends where they lived. It was therefore a treat for them to have Axel and Alex visit. The Brobergs were essentially self-sustained. Kajsa made most of their clothing and they had a large freezer, and of course a root cellar, where they could store their food. Most food was canned or in some other way preserved for storage. A school bus came and got Maran for school. She had to spend close to one hour on the bus every school day.

Getting up before the roosters was the routine for the Brobergs. The cows had to be milked at five am. and the milk pasteurized.

"I will go out and start the starter engine on the tractor. It will take about fifteen minutes to warm it up enough that the tractor will start, and we have to bring down the milk to the collection rack by seven. That's when they come and get it," Mr. Broberg explained.

Alex and Axel loved the farm life, including getting up early. When they opened the barn door in the morning, the cows would greet them impatiently with their "moos." The strong odor of steamy manure inside the barn did not bother the boys. Tomas Broberg would turn on the radio music quite loud, and it seemed to have a calming effect on the critters. He would feed them before hooking up the milk machines. The machine made a slurping sound as the tubes sucked onto the udders, before beginning their rhythmic pumping. The cows acted as though they were completely indifferent to the whole procedure, as they chewed on their breakfast. Tomas would first waste a few drops of milk, milking by hand, a process the cats eagerly awaited, and ready to catch the milk. Tomas had a pretty good aim, and he could fire away a beam of milk straight at a cat's face.

"Let's let the cows out to pasture and then we can go in and see if Kajsa have some breakfast for us. I'm ready for some eggs and bacon, what about you? Mr. Broberg asked.

Breakfast time was when family matters were discussed. The boys loved the smell of the freshly brewed coffee that filled the large kitchen, together with the aroma of baked bread and fried bacon. After breakfast Tomas would return to the barn and the stall to shovel out the manure. The boys would try to run the wheelbarrow, but it was heavy and difficult to balance, especially outside where they had to drive across the manure covered planks. Quite often the boys would lose their loads. After the cleaning, Jonas would go about his daily chores. The boys helped Maran fill the kitchen bin with firewood and to collect the eggs, after which the children would go fishing.

The boys and Maran slept in the guest room in a separate building behind the laundry room. Maran was full of energy, and a true tom-boy, and the boys thoroughly enjoyed her company.

It was known in town that Tomas was awaited other women from their village, creating tensions between him and Kajsa. Still, the boys liked Tomas. He was full of energy and always willing to let them try new things, such as driving the horse wagon and the tractor. The boys also appreciated Kajsa, who was warm and motherly and, as was typical of farm wives, she always worked, baking or cleaning.

"I have a special treat for you today." Kajsa announced. "I have made something I know you like. Ris-a-la-malta."

"Wow! Thank you aunt Kajsa. We love that." Both boys said in chorus.

Kajsa always gave them generous servings. Axel and Alex also loved Kajsa's saffron rolls, in particular when they came fresh out of the oven.

"Can we go for a ride today Uncle Thomas?" Axel asked.

"It's going to have to wait for a while. Ruckels is going to have her calf any moment now. Come here and I'm going to show you a little miracle.

Ruckels moaned in discomfort. A couple legs were already visible from Ruckels' behind. She was breathing heavy and appeared to be struggling. Tommas sat down and comforted her. Suddenly the calf came gushing out, slimy and bloody. Almost immediately it tempted to stand on the slippery concrete floor. It was a female calf and they named her Alexandra.

The boys loved riding the big work horses, and had fun playing with the cute baby pigs. The little pink critters were only a few days old and had not yet opened their eyes. They had to keep them away from the mother so she would not smother them. Both Axel and Alex would have been content staying on the farm permanently, but the summer came to an end and it was time to return to city life.

CHAPTER 28

June, 1954 - Annika moves to Stockholm

During the summer of 1954, after the boys had returned from the Brobergs, Annika and the children moved to Stockholm. Annika had finally decided to leave Kurt. She was concerned that their unorthodox living arrangements would impact the children adversely. Perhaps mostly, she wanted to be closer to Torsten. Kurt was surprisingly helpful. He arranged for an apartment in Solna, a suburb of Stockholm, and he helped Annika move her furniture. She set up a delicatessen with proceeds from her secret account. It was the first time that she had dipped into her special account, except for when she needed to pay for the substantial taxes that were owed on the account. She called her deli "The Red Rose." The shop took up much of her time, but she liked it that way. The boys would stop by after school and have dinner. They would either stay there until six, when she closed and help her to stock the shelves, which always landed some candy in their pockets, or they would ride their bikes back home or to a soccer or hockey game, depending on the season. There was an illuminated ice field in the park next to their house where the boys could play bandy. The park was convenient in that Annika could call the children home from their kitchen window. Kurt had his own apartment in downtown Stockholm, but he did not spend much time there.

During the following summer the boys spent a few weeks with the Brobergs again. The boys were now eleven years old and had not seen Maran for two years. When they arrived, she greeted them with a huge smile, as always, while attempting to calm the dogs that danced around yapping. The boys felt a little unsure about how to great Maran. She was their buddy, but she was an extraordinarily attractive girl. They settled for a simple greeting and returning the grin. It was a warm sunny day, perfect, except for the annoying flies that buzzed around them. Annika would only stay for the day.

After the boys had unpacked their things, the children went exploring. Tomas was "necking" or decapitating chickens. The boys were not comfortable watching, but they could not let Maran know. Tomas would place the chicken's head across a log and chop it off with an axe. He would then let the headless chicken go and it would run quite a distance flopping its wings. One headless chicken flew up on the roof. Afterwards they would collect the chickens and dip them in boiling water so the feathers would come out easily.

"Come! I want to show you something!" Maran said enthusiastically. They got on their bikes and rode down to the beach. "Look, that's our new sailboat." She pointed at a small wooden sailboat anchored a few hundred meters out in the bay.

"Wow!" the boys marveled. "Can we take it for a ride?" Axel asked. He had a hard time keeping his eyes off Maran. She was so pretty and animated. She wore a light-yellow summer dress that was held tight against her by the west wind while flickering like a lose sail on her leeward side. Her smooth skin was golden tan and her long hair blew across her face.

"Sure, we can wade out. It's not very deep, until the very last few meters. Or we can use the small dingy there, but it will only hold two people so we would have to make a couple trips. Oh, let's wade. The water is warm," she suggested.

They all stripped down to their underpants; made neat little rolls of their clothes, tucked them under their arms, and began wading out to the boat. The boys could not but notice that Maran had developed, since the last time they saw her. Maran was right; the water barely came up to their knees until they got close to the boat, where it suddenly dropped off. By the time they reached the boat they could just barely reach the bottom and they could just as well have kept their cloths on, because everything got soaking wet. Maran reached inside the hull for the ladder, making it easier to climb onboard. They rigged the sails, dropped the keel, attached the rudder in the stern and fastened the anchor to a buoy. They were on their way. There was a nice breeze and the boat held good speed. The children hung their clothes up to dry. They stayed close to the bay area which provided good protection from the open sea. As they ventured a little farther out, they could feel the long rolling ocean surfs that had made it through the passage. There were many small islands and they had to be cautious not to run aground on a shallow reef, although, Maran knew the waters well. They stopped in a small bay to go swimming and exploring and soon it was time to turn back.

Dinner was ready when they returned. Annika was still there. The Brobergs ate early, before they milked the cattle for the second time.

"How did you like the new boat?" Kajsa asked. "We just got it."

"It was great," Alex assured her. "It's real seaworthy and it glides easily through the water." he added.

"Maybe if the weather is good, we will take it all the way to town someday," Tomas proposed.

"And who is to care for the cattle while we're gone?" asked Kajsa.

"I'm sure Fredrik wouldn't mind. It would only be for one afternoon."

They had roasted chicken for dinner, but for some reason, the boys were not very hungry.

CHAPTER 29

February, 1957- Annika and Torsten in Mora

Annika was now seeing Torsten on a regular basis. During the February school winter vacation, Annika made arrangements for her and the boys to meet Torsten at a ski resort in Dalarna, one day's drive north west of Stockholm.

"Oh my God!" Annika yelled in panic. She realized that she was driving on a single lane railroad bridge as she heard the planks clap under the car. It was snowing heavily and she could only see a few feet in front of her. She could not see the ground or water below the bridge, through the massive side rail. She stopped the car. "If a train comes, just jump out," she screamed to the boys.

"Don't stop here Mamma; we had the green light," Alex calmly pointed out.

"Yes, we did," Axel agreed.

"Are you sure? I didn't see any light!" She was beginning to calm down and proceeded to drive along the bridge. They were on their way to Mora Tourist Hotel. It was pitch dark at only six in the evening, and her headlights turned the falling snow into a white curtain in front of them. They had been driving since early that morning in Annika's Morris.

Annika expected to arrive in Mora within the hour. The landscape was rather flat, sloping gently toward Lake Siljan below. Mora was not a resort for down-hill skiers, but it was excellent for cross country skiing. There was a giant old mining pit in the middle of the city that provided all the downhill challenge the Nobels sought. There were several ski trails around the community marked in different colors, depending on the expertise of the skier. Several ran past historic sights and small shops, where hot lemonade, homemade pastries and souvenirs were available.

The blizzard delayed Annika's arrival time by an hour, and Torsten was pacing the lobby when they finally arrived. An anxious but relieved Torsten greeted them.

"I must admit that I was getting quite concerned," he told Annika. "This weather, it must have been treacherous driving in this blizzard." He was, of course, worried about Annika's driving in the storm, but he also could not shake the thought that perhaps she had gotten wet feet and decided not to come. They had not seen one another for more than two months. Torsten had been away on a business trip to San Diego.

Torsten and Kurt had met, and amazingly, they got along fine. Kurt was impressed by Torsten's several key positions in prominent business and social organizations. Torsten liked Kurt's spontaneity and ingenuity in finding new business ventures to explore. They were both slightly self-absorbed and liked to share stories. They were two completely different personalities, yet, shared several traits.

Annika and Torsten embraced warmly as she got out of the car and the boys engaged in a snowball fight.

"The dinner hour has ended, but they prepared some sandwiches for us before they closed, beef soup and there is hot chocolate." Torsten explained. "Let's go into the dining room first so we can fill the tummies and warm up. I'm sure you will like the crisp rye bread that's a specialty of the Lake Siljan area."

After the boys had gone to bed, Annika and Torsten joined the other guests in the lounge. A dance band played to a good-sized crowd. Other vacationers, who rented rooms around town, as well as locals, would gather there in the evening. Torsten and Annika both enjoyed dancing, but the limited floor space restricted the creativity in their performance. The band played a variety of dance numbers and would occasionally play more funky styles, like the Bunny Hop, the Charleston and, of course, the classic Shottis, Mazurka, Hambo, Cha-cha, Polka and Tango, Torsten's favorite, and the Vienna Waltz, Annika's favorite. Torsten glided across the floor and Annika followed his firm lead easily.

After a pause, Annika returned from the lady's room to find Torsten dancing with a young blond girl in a revealing dress. Torsten explained that the girl had asked him to dance on a lady's choice, but this explanation did little to ease Annika's jealousy, even though she, herself, had danced with other gentlemen. What annoyed her was that the girl was dressed so provocatively, and she was giving Torsten a come-hither look. Torsten claimed to be oblivious to these details.

As for Alex and Axel, they were in love. Upon their arrival they had seen a blond girl, the most beautiful girl they had ever seen. Unfortunately, she appeared to be a year or two older, and she had already been noticed by some older boys. They could not believe their luck when they found themselves seated at the table next to Birgitta's for breakfast. The previous evening, she had been dressed like a princess in a white lace dress, white anklets and slippers. She had worn a pink bow in her long straight hair. In the morning she tied it back into a pony tail. She wore black ski-pants, boots and a red angora sweater. Her face was shiny from Nivea sun screen. Her fragrance, Lilly of the Valley, reached the boys and drove them mad. When she turned and said good morning to the boys they reeled.

"Hi, I'm Birgitta. Did you guys just get here?" Her smile could melt an iceberg but these boys were already warm. "I'm from Stockholm. Where are you from?" she continued, her voice singing in their ears.

"We're from Gothenburg," Alex managed to respond. "How come you're here this week? Didn't Stockholm have their winter break last week?" he continued. This performance exhausted Alex's courage, and he looked away from her eyes. But Axel looked straight into her eyes, transfixed.

"They did, but one of my brothers was sick then so we couldn't go . . . so, my parents took us out of school for one week, so we could have our vacation."

'Lucky us,' they were both hollering inside. "Where are you going skiing today?" Axel asked.

"We're taking the blue trail that ends by the pit and then we will do a little downhill there. What about you?" She had the sweetest voice the boys had ever heard.

"We don't know yet . . . Mamma, where are we going today? Could we go to the pit?"

"Yes, this afternoon we can."

"Well I'll probably see you there then. How do you tell each other apart?" Birgitta asked.

"It's pretty easy, Axel is always the other guy," Alex quipped.

"Yes, and Alex is the other guy," Axel added.

"It must be fun to have a twin. What class are you in?"

"Fourth," said Axel. "What class are you in?"

"Fifth grade. I'm in the fifth. I've been to Gothenburg," she continued. "We stayed at Marstrand for two weeks last summer. My dad likes to sail, so we sailed down. We stayed there for two days. It was very nice."

The boys could not believe that she kept talking to them after finding out that they were fourth graders, and with enthusiasm no less, as if she were interested in them. They later learned that she was in fact the same age as they were, but that she had skipped one class in school. The boys were so taken with her angelic looks and charm, it did not occur to them to be impressed with her intellect. "Do you sail?" she asked.

"Well, yes, we have an optimist-jolle. We race every Thursday during the summer," Alex explained.

After breakfast the boys ran in to Birgitta again in the lobby and she cheerfully greeted them by their names. "How did you know who was who?" Axel wondered?

"Actually, I was only guessing, but I think I can tell you apart," she said. "I bet that when I get to know you well, before we go home, I will be able to tell you apart."

"Yes!" the boys shouted to themselves. There were several other children at the resort including sixth grade boys who did their best to win Birgitta's favors; but Birgitta enjoyed the company of the twins and spent most of the vacation with them, including dancing in the evening.

The third evening Birgitta invited the boys up to her room. "My parents are playing bridge in the lounge," she told them. They're not coming back until late. Do you like to play some game?" she asked.

"How about a game of card? The looser have to pay a penalty." Axel suggested.

"What kind of penalty?" Birgitta asked.

"Well, if you lose you have to kiss the winner." Alex proposed.

"You mean like this." She suddenly turned to him and kissed him on his cheek.

"No, that won't do. It has to be a kiss on the mouth." Axel insisted. "Have you ever kissed a guy on the mouth before?"

"Of course, I have. I'm not a nun."

They didn't mind sharing her. They were used to sharing everything. Besides, neither would have been willing to give her up. It was a quick kiss, but it was on the lips and it was fantastic. The following evening, they all went on the traditional sleigh ride. Birgitta rode in the same sleigh as the boys. She fit snugly between them, covered by fuzzy thick bear hides. They were each given a live torch to hold. There were seven sleighs all together and the perky bells on the horse-harnesses rhythmically announced their presence as the horses trotted about the village.

"Life could not possibly get any better than this," Axel pronounced.

"I agree," Birgitta joined in. She gave both of them a light jab with her elbows.

That evening Torsten proposed to Annika and they made wedding plans. Torsten had prearranged with their waiter to bring in the dessert, on cue. Annika's dessert was decorated with the engagement ring. Torsten had also made arrangements to have the band play the tango Red Roses which had a special meaning to them. Annika was not totally surprised with the ring, as they had discussed the subject on several occasions. Still, she could not help weeping with joy. They would hold a small ceremony when they returned to Stockholm. Torsten's wife would get custody of their children.

Kurt was ecstatic. He would no longer have to support Annika, and he could tie the knot with Eva.

Torsten and Annika lived a good life. They traveled frequently and entertained lavishly, but Annika became increasingly jealous, owing to Torsten's flirtatious personality.

"Torsten, how about taking a walk if you absolutely have to smoke those stinking cigars?" Annika asked him. "The crystal chandeliers get so oily from the smoke."

"I'm standing on the balcony."

"Standing by the door doesn't help much. All the smoke comes right in."

"I don't have time to take a walk. I have to submit the tickets for Solvalla by six."

"Well there is another habit of yours that I have a hard time identifying with. I'm sure you lose a lot more than you win on the horses." Annika lectured him.

"Well, a guy got to have some fun." These were the simple things that gave Torsten most pleasure. He would sit nearly all day on Saturdays to figure out his betting systems for the Sunday races. He would roar with satisfaction if he won, but he would never say a word when he lost.

"You know, when I was eighteen I won ten thousand crowns on the Swedish state lottery. It could happen again." This early windfall likely contributed to his continuous fascination with gambling. Torsten also invested in the new Swedish fighter plane the "Wiggen," built by Saab. This investment did not pan out, though, and Torsten, and many others, ended up losing sizable sums.

PART V

CHAPTER 30

July 1958 - The boys being boys

In the summer of 1958 the Farins rented a small summer home on idyllic Marstrand.

"You realize that I can only stay there for two weeks, the first and the last. You will be on your own the other three weeks, okay?" Torsten asked.

"We will be fine. The boys will have such a good time, and I will be all brown when you see me again." Annika ensured him.

Each day was spent essentially the same way.

"Wake up boys if you like to have some breakfast. It's seven and the sun is shining." Annika prompted them.

They packed their swimming gear and lunch snacks and hiked across the island, up past the old bazillion, past the regatta signaling tower and an old lighthouse and down to a favorite swimming hole facing the open sea. The island mainly consisted of smooth weathered granite rock, but there was also a network of gorges with various cliff formations, vegetation and ponds where one could walk protected from the sometimes ferocious winds. These gorges also lent themselves perfectly to hide and seek games. It took a good two hours to walk the trail around the island. There were several choice spots for swimming, which they chose, dependent on the weather. They always sought to avoid the wind and with it, the jelly fish. If it looked as though a storm was brewing, they chose a location closer to the cottage. Each afternoon they dressed up and had dinner at the same restaurant where they had breakfast. The boys would pass time in the harbor admiring the many yachts that were tethered at the piers, while waiting for Annika to get ready. Many boats carried foreign flags. Some boaters had to jump across several boats to reach theirs. There were also the coast ferries and a few military and customs ships, all mixed with small motor and sailboats.

"Does anyone know what country that flag is from?" Annika asked them.

"Danish," Alex tried

"That's a good guess, but don't you know the flag of our next-door neighbor? It is red with a full white cross. This one has a small white cross in the middle. It is from Switzerland" Annika informed them.

"Yes, ok, If we are going to split hairs," Alex conceded.

"That's silly," said Axel. "Switzerland isn't even by an ocean. It is up in the mountains."

"So! They have a big lake. Lake Geneva." Said Alex.

"Perhaps, but it would be a challenge to move that big boat all the way from there." Said Annika. "I suppose it's possible for someone from Switzerland to raise their flag if they own the boat but keep it someplace else," Torsten elaborated.

"It looked like Danish," Alex persisted, "red and white."

After dinner, the family strolled down the harbor to people watch, and perhaps listen to the band playing in the park. They always walked down to the restaurant at the east entrance of the harbor. They would have coffee and sodas and cake and listen to the band play while watching the sun set, turning the sky orange above the late arriving boats.

"I will miss you when you leave tomorrow," said Annika.

"I'll miss you too. But the time will go real fast for you. It's so nice here. Three weeks will fly by and then I will be back again." Torsten comforted her."

The boys set out for the castle, where they could find other children playing games or otherwise passing the time. The castle was illuminated and so were several of the trails surrounding the castle, but it still felt a little spooky, knowing that in the past the castle had served as a prison and a fort. The youngsters would group into teams, normally with two boys and two girls on each team, and play hide-and-seek. Often the hiding part was the highlight of the game. If a team had a great time hiding, it might not even return. Axel and Alex had a favorite cave to where they liked to bring their team. The girls were fascinated with the boys' being twins, handsome and quite mature for their age.

That fall, in 1958, when the boys were fourteen, they took a school trip to the Middle-Ages town Visby on Gotland, a large island on the Swedish southeast coast. The class took an overnight ferry from Stockholm. The teachers had their hands full attempting to keep the boys from getting into the girls' rooms and vice versa. This was probably the worst age to take them on the road, or on the sea. There was not much sleeping that night on the ferry. Instead, most of the travelers slept soundly the following morning as they traveled by bus through the idyllic sites on their way to the hotel in Visby. Visby was fortified all around with a twenty-foot tall stone wall. One had to enter the city through gates in the wall that barely accommodated the busses. The bus made a hissing sound as it traveled down the narrow, winding, cobblestone streets. Ivy, climbing roses or bougainvillea covered the old buildings and colorful flower baskets hung from most balconies. The scent of the flowers penetrated the bus.

The hotel was not really a hotel. It was more like a private home, except it was not particularly private. Six of the boys shared Alex and Axel's house, and there were no adults there. A teacher chaperone came by at night to count heads. After organizing the daily field trip and counting heads at night, the chaperones mostly left the students unsupervised. The group spent time at the Snäckargårds Baden's beach, an exclusive Visby resort, and enjoyed a festive lunch at its restaurant.

Afterwards, the hardy amongst them returned to the beach for a swim, even though it was quite windy. The cold water did not seem to reduce their testosterone. Swimming under water they would occasionally try to pull down each other's swim suits. The girls were just as good as the boys in executing this game, perhaps even more aggressive. The group took a trip to a horse farm where they all rode the small Gotland ponies. Trotting around, bareback, on these miniature horses was quite bumpy, but the youngsters had a great time. They rode the horses straight out into the water. Afterwards, it took a while for those with no riding experience to work off the pain in their legs that developed when trying to remain on top of the horses.

One group of girls got hold of some girlie magazines that they secretly shared with their co-travelers. Axel and Alex were invited up to the girls' room for a peek at the pictures and they ended up engaging in some fairly innocent petting.

Big Barbro was the main attraction. She was well developed and proud of it. Smoking was another fascination that several of the children tried for the first time. The students gained more experience during this school trip on the subject of autonomy; however, most of their learning took place outside the teacher's lesson plan.

In the winter of 1960, Annika and the boys traveled to Salen, a popular ski resort in central Sweden, to spend their February ski vacation. Torsten was not willing to travel together with a group of high-spirited young people confined in a bus all day. He would arrive two days later on the train. Annika and the boys traveled by bus as part of an organized tour package that included four busses. The travel guide did her best to entertain the travelers, including playing guitar and singing popular songs. All the young people sat at the rear of the bus while the parents sat up front.

There were several teenage girls onboard, and the boys took a liking to two girls in particular. Gina, a dark-haired exotic looking girl appeared to be of Asian heritage, while Lena looked very Swedish with light strawberry blond hair and large blue eyes. Lena exuded warmth and her smile made her audience feel important. They were quite different in their appearances. Gina was tall and slender, probably an inch taller than the boys, while Lena was shorter and more curvaceous. Although everyone came from the Stockholm area, neither Gina nor Lena lived close to the boys in Stockholm.

Emma, one of the tour guides, had everyone introduce themselves and name their favorite tour guide. Emma won the most popular tour guide title, unanimously.

During the next phase, Gina announced that her favorite animal was a dog. She liked sailing and skiing, romantic movies, adventure books and meatballs. Her favorite color was pink and she would like to be a veterinarian someday. Lena's favorite animal was the horse. Sailing and skiing were her favorite sports. She liked romantic movies and adventure stories. Her favorite food was *Lappskojs*, she liked to sew her own clothes and wanted to become a fashion designer someday.

"Hi, my name is Alex. I'm seventeen years old and like sailing, skiing and adventure books . . . and adventure movies. I chose the eagle, and spaghetti for favorite food. I want to be a movie director," he revealed.

"Can I star in your movie?" Lena asked. Slightly embarrassed, and surprised at her own forwardness, her cheeks reddening.

"Sure, but maybe you should first find out what the story is all about," Alex suggested.

"Oh I trust you. You look so nice you wouldn't do anything bad . . . would you?" she asked.

"Everyone say Ahh!" Emma directed.

"Ahhhh!"

"He also likes to impersonate me," Axel added. "Well, my name is Axel and I'm sixteen. I have the same favorites as Alex, except for the animal. I chose the tiger and I would like to be an architect."

"Now wait a minute!" Gina interrupted. "How can you be seventeen, Alex, and you sixteen Axel when you are twins? Were you born at midnight on January first?"

"No, no, it is simply a matter of interpretation. We are sixteen and ten-months old. By every mathematical standard I know that is seventeen when rounded to an even number," Alex explained.

"Alright, that's, pushing it, but alright," Gina agreed.

"Now tell us why you made your choices and Gina goes first. Why did you pick the dog of all animals?"

"I have a dog that I love. He's a Golden Retriever. He's smart and great company."

"Axel, right?" Emma hesitated for a minute, unsure of weather she was speaking to Axel or Alex.

"Yes, I chose the tiger because then I don't have to worry about becoming the supper for the other animals. Also, the tiger is powerful, not easily trained, slightly lazy but will step forward when necessary and get the job done."

"Boy, that was a powerful statement," Emma noted clearly impressed.

"I bet I can train you," Gina suggested daringly.

"Me, too," voices joined in.

"Yea, many have tried and failed," Axel responded.

"What did you do then? Have them for dinner?" Lena asked. Everyone laughed.

"One girl thought that she had me trained once, but it turned out to be my brother," Axel joked.

"Yea, right," said Alex.

"And Gina, why the horse?"

"I love horses, they're so powerful and full of spirit. And they're easy to train," she added for Axel's benefit. "Some trainers start by breaking down the animal's spirit before they build it back up. I don't go that route. I train with rewards, positive incentives."

"Wow! You can train me any time you like," Alex offered.

"And why an architect?" Emma continued.

"I want to build things, create new landmarks, taking construction to the edge of what's possible." Axel had stood up as he spoke, and suddenly the bus veered for a rabbit. Alex lost his balance, falling and landing in Gina's lap. "Sorry," he said looking a little bewildered. "Are you all right?"

"I'm fine, no problem," said Gina." Although I must say that it went much faster than I expected to get you down on your knees."

"Very funny!"

Sandwiches and hot tea awaited the group when they arrived. It was late by the time boys got to their room, and the beds were inviting. The following morning, they met with Gina and Lena. They decided to take it easy the first day and settle for the green, easy trail, in the morning. It was not clear in what direction the weather was heading. It was sunny and quite warm, right around freezing but rather windy. Annika chose to go with the guided tour group, as did Gina's and Lena's parents.

The boys helped the girls waxing their skis. The warm temperature would make the snow stick to the bottom of the skis.

"I brought some candles to wax the skis with," said Lena. That's what we use at home."

"Well, that works fine if you're going downhill, but it gets too slippery for going cross country. You don't get enough traction, unless... perhaps, if you only do the front half of the skis. This red wax is better though. It's made for this temperature," Alex explained.

After having rubbed on a generous layer of red, warm weather wax on the skis, they departed on their first of the season ski venture. They began their tour by slowly climbing the mountain, thereby providing for mostly downhill skiing on the way back. Axel led the way, followed by Gina, Lena and finally Alex. The well-used track had become quite icy in the warm weather and even with the red "glue" wax on their skis, they all had problems climbing the gentle slope. They removed their anoraks and tied them around their waists as they grew warm from skiing. They made frequent stops to rest and to chat. The group had not made it very far before the sun disappeared behind dark clouds, the wind picked up and it rapidly turned colder. They decided to return to the hotel.

By the time the four reached the hotel, the beautiful morning had developed into a full storm and they could barely see each other in the swirling snow which was rapidly building large drifts. They learned that the tour busses had taken the guided tour group into the village, but because of the weather, it was not clear when they would return. It would not be for lunch, and perhaps not even that night.

Axel, Alex and the girls, together with a few others who had stayed behind, spent the afternoon playing games in the social room, in front of the large fireplace. They did not bother dressing up for dinner, as was customary at ski resorts, as there would be few guests for dinner. The intensity of the snow increased toward the evening and it was now clear that the busses would not be able to return that evening. Annika and the girls' parents called and were relieved to learn that the teenagers were all fine, shortly before both power and telephone connections went out. Fortunately, the resort had emergency generators and was able to restore limited power. The guests began to retire to their rooms.

"Any suggestions on where we spend the night?" Lena asked. I'm not going to sleep alone here," she declared.

"Me neither," Gina agreed. "Shall we stay here or go to a room?"

"Let's stay here by the fireplace. It's kind of nice here by the fire," Alex suggested.

"Yeah, let's," Axel chimed in. "We can get some pillows and blankets and camp out here. It'll be fun." They returned shortly and prepared for the night. They all stayed by the fireplace until early morning playing games and talking. Then they returned to their rooms to get ready for breakfast.

The girls had to knock hard on the boys' door to get their attention.

"Hey guys, it's almost noon and lunch is served," Gina yelled through the door.

"Come in, it's not locked," a sleepy Axel responded.

"Are you guys planning on sleeping the whole day? We got a little worried when you didn't show up for breakfast," Lena said.

"I guess we fell asleep, eh?" Alex responded

"I guess you did," said Lena.

"Have you heard anything about the road? Is it passable?" Alex asked.

Lena walked over to the window and pulled away the curtain, instantly brightening the room. "Yes, no. I mean, the road would have been passable if it weren't for an avalanche in the pass. It's a pretty bad one. It's going to take some time to clear. They don't know how long it will take. At least they don't think that anyone got caught in it, because the road was closed when it happened."

"Boy, you guys are up early," Axel commented. He squinted up at Gina noticing that she was wearing her ski pants with walking shoes.

"t's not that early, and if we are going to get out while there's still daylight, we better get moving," said Lena. "Maybe it would be fun to go sledding after lunch," Alex suggested. "I saw some people yesterday being pulled up by the ski lift on their sled."

"I talked to Mamma and they are all fine, so it's just a matter of waiting it out," Gina told them. "The roads are not going to be cleared until tomorrow at the very best. The good thing is that we have plenty of food. In fact, lunch is served right now, so why don't you guys come down and we can eat together?"

The girls were right; there was no shortage of food. After lunch they all took a walk outside to burn off the heavy lunch they had eaten. They built an igloo, or actually more like a hole in the snow, made snow angels, and engaged in a snow ball fight before returning to the lodge and meeting in the pool. After dinner they returned to the boys' room for more games.

"What shall we do?" asked Lena. "Who would like to play cards?"

"All right, I know a game" Gina offered. How about truth or consequences? Or a little friendly strip poker?"

Again, it was early morning before they fell asleep.

CHAPTER 31

1961 - Ali in Salen

Annika's tour group stayed overnight at the Bassi Ski Resort. She had to share a room with three other women, including Gina's mother Jenny. They were fortunate to have found a room in one of Sälen's most luxurious hotel. It was spacious and had a grand view from the large picture window of the downtown area and the valley and mountain range beyond.

They were told that they would have to stay there at least until the following morning, so they decided to go shopping. None of the women had brought anything suitable to wear for the evening. Shopping for an evening dress was not an imposition on the ladies and they had a grand time scouring the several small boutiques in the resort for the just right outfit. Eventually Annika found a dress that she liked. It was dark blue with small red polka dots. It was tight around her waist but quite wide at the bottom, with a ruffle at the hem and around the short sleeves. The dress fitted her perfectly, nicely accenting her figure.

All four women were married yet traveling alone with their children on the vacation. They were all easy going and spirited, and they all got along well. After a delightful dinner Annika returned to her room to call Torsten and the boys, before joining the girls in the social room.

"Everything was fine. It was raining in Stockholm," Annika told them, "and it was really windy there too."

"We sure lucked out with getting our room. The whole town was fully booked. I understand that it was an Arab sheik that had reserved several rooms, but when he heard about the avalanche he agreed to let go of some of his rooms," Jenny told them. "From Jodassy, I think they said."

"From where?" Annika flew out of her chair. "From where did you say? From Jodassy? Is that what you said?"

"I'm pretty sure that's what they said," Jenny responded, taken aback by Annika's reaction.

"They're here, I can't believe it." As Annika turned around to go to the front desk, Ali and Camilla walked toward her with open arms.

"Annika, I can't believe it's you. You look fabulous," Camilla greeted her.

"Ali, wow! I can't believe it." She gave him a warm tight hug. "How have you been? . . . oh, excuse me ladies, these are my dearest friends Prince Alibassi of Jodassy and Princess Camilla. Please meet Jenny, Sara and Anna. Camilla is a dear friend from home, and she recently married Prince Alibassi, well almost ten years ago now. Please join us. You have to fill me in on everything that has happened since the last time I saw you. Gosh, I can't believe that it's actually been ten years since the last time I saw you. By the way, remind me about telling you what 'wow' stands for in Jodssy," she smiled and reached for a second hug.

Camilla and Annika reminisced, filling in the gaps of the past ten years. After having married Camilla, Ali had begun making investments in Sweden, including in this hotel in Salen that he had built. Ali and Sonja were there "alone" celebrating their tenth anniversary. Ali's father had passed away a few years ago and Ali was now the king of Jodassy. However, he had decided to keep his prince title in order to bring as little attention to himself as possible. He felt his country was better served with continuity and with the royal family's taking a lower profile. For the same reason, they had decided not to have an elaborate formal wedding. Regardless, he was now the king of Jodassy and Camilla was the queen.

"The Bassi Resort. I didn't make the connection. Alibassi . . . oh well." Annika confessed.

Camilla and Ali acted like newlyweds. Ali would do small things like have the waiter place a rose by Camilla's plate, and he would light her cigarette for her. He opened doors, and stood up when a lady was standing, even now as the king, but that was the gentleman in him.

"Annika, I have to tell you!" Camilla said with enthusiasm, I have had three more babies since I saw you last, three boys, triplets! I had to have a caesarean delivery. And something else, I have met your puppy love sweetheart from England, Billy. Is this a small world or what?"

"Wait a minute," Jane interrupted. "If you had triplets by caesarean delivery, then they would have seen the light at the same time, so who would become the crown prince?" she asked.

"We tossed a coin," Ali joked. "No but that is an interesting question, and we have not decided yet. At least for now they are all three crown princes. Perhaps one of them will be more interested or perhaps better suited than the others to take over. We'll just have to wait and see." He ran his hand through his hair, for no particular reason.

"This was another dilemma we had, in not wanting to bring too much attention to the royal family," Camilla interjected. Camilla was looking sharp. She wore a tight light beige business suit, with matching shoes, over a champagne colored silk blouse and a bright silk scarf. She had a nice tan and she looked healthy and fresh.

"What about Billy?" Annika asked impatiently. Tell me!" Annika held on to the table rim with both hands and looked straight at Camilla.

"Well, I don't know when you saw him last . . ."

"It's been close to twenty years. Billy was a British navy officer that I met in my youth right as the war was escalating and I cared for him a lot," she explained to the other women. "So how is he doing? Is he married?" she probed.

"He's doing fine, no he's doing well, no, and he's doing fantastic, financially that is. He was married but lost his wife to cancer just recently. He does not have any children, and I know that's a huge disappointment to him. But he's now running an industrial empire, doing business all over the world, including in Jodassy. In fact, he has a home in Jodassy and he has become one of our closest friends. We often talk about you and he seems to know a lot about what you are doing. We were just talking about how I met Ali and he told us that he knew you. I had forgotten all about that night at Liseberg and that we had actually met before. You know when he speaks about you, it sounds as if you were, and still are, his big love."

"It would be fun to meet him, but I have Torsten now and it wouldn't feel right. Still, I have to admit that I have often thought about him, about what he might be doing and about what could have been." Her Mona-Lisa smile ended with her twitching her eyebrows and changing subject.

"Tell me more about yourself, Camilla. How is it to be a queen? How are the children doing? Everything, tell me everything!"

"Wonderful! I'm so happy. Ali is such a wonderful, considerate, intelligent, devoted husband. I count my blessings every day. I still can't really believe that this has happened to me. The children are doing great. Kjell, is attending medical school in South Africa of all places and Maria is attending college in England."

"You look fantastic. You're more beautiful, more vigorous, than ten years ago, and you looked fantastic then!" Annika enthused.

"I agree, she looks better every day," Ali interjected.

"And you too, Ali, wow!" said Annika. "Your gray hair is very becoming. Obs, I hope wow is not a bad word in Jodassy?"

"Not at all, it's quite a compliment. Thank you, Annika. Not only are you very generous with your compliments, but, well, you are the one who should be complimented. You look great, just as I remember you. You haven't changed a bit. There must be something in the water here in Scandinavia that makes all the girls look so youthful," he said, extending his compliment to all the ladies at the table.

When Annika had a moment alone with Camilla and Ali, she asked her.

"How is it working out with Ali's other wives? Are you all getting along?"

"Oh yes, they're the greatest. There are only six more wives now, and I love them dearly. You know, I understand that it can be difficult to the non-initiated to understand, but I look at it a little like being a doctor's wife. He does all sorts of things at work, but it is how he acts when he gets home that matters. Besides, call me a little kinky if you like, but I sort of enjoy it. Perhaps I'm bisexual, I don't know, but I get turned on by having a little company in bed on occasion. It just makes love making a little more interesting, and I never have to worry about Ali going out sleeping with someone who might have a venereal disease."

"That would work for me," Jenny offered. "Where do I send my application?" she asked jokingly.

"I'm afraid that all positions are filled. Although, there is one Jodassy girl whom Ali might have to marry, as a courtesy to her family. She's a cute little thing and it could be fun," said Camilla, winkling her nose.

"Shame on you Camilla, you behave now," Ali lectured her, but making it clear that he enjoyed the little devil within her.

After dinner Ali had to tend to business and Camilla wanted to go to their suite to freshen up.

"Come with me up to the room Annika. We must change to evening gear. I have so much stuff and we are about the same size. Perhaps you would like to try something on?" she offered.

"Alright, we see you all at the social room in a little while." said Annika.

Camilla's and Ali's suite was huge. Camilla's closet alone was larger than most people's bedroom. There were several outfits to choose from, but Camilla took Annika's advice and selected a dark blue velvet wrapped skirt that was split up her right leg. She wore a white blouse with ruffled collar and sleeves, under a matching vest. She looked royal in the dress, and sexy.

Annika tried on several outfits and eventually settled for a red dress that reminded one of a sari.

A small band played dance music and the social-room was quickly filling. Ali and Camilla had a table reserved for themselves. They moved over some chairs and invited Annika and the stranded women to join them. Other gentlemen frequently asked all the girls, including Camilla, to dance. Ali did not mind, and in fact, he also danced with the other women. However, he performed best when dancing with

Camilla. Clearly, they had taken dance lessons together. They floated around the floor as a finely synchronized unit. It was a pleasure to watch them dance. Their company soon moved over to other tables conversing with their new-found dance partners, but Annika did not accept invitations to do the same. She had so much to talk to Camilla about. Eventually she followed Ali and Camilla to their suite for a night cap before they called it a night.

Torsten arrived the following day and the couples had the opportunity to spend some time together. The road was opened that afternoon but Torsten and Annika chose to stay with Ali and Camilla for one more day. The boys did not mind having one more evening "alone." Camilla insisted that Annika promise to come to Jodassy to visit.

When Alex graduated from business college in the spring of 1961, he went to work for a small movie company in Stockholm. His job was to send out the advertisements and posters to the theaters that were running their movies. The nice perk that came with the job was that he could view any movie he wanted for free. It was a fun job, although with modest pay. The job kept him occupied until he had to enter his active military service in 1963. Alex remained in Stockholm close to a year when he moved to Gothenburg, helping Kurt while awaiting the service. Axel helped out Annika in her shop for close to a year before he also moved to Gothenburg to work for Kurt.

CHAPTER 32

1962 - On the road

On the boys' eighteenth birthday Kurt helped them purchase a car. The first one was a fifteen-year old Volvo with major rust problems. The motor did not run predictably, or rather, predictably it would not run. A couple of weeks later they sold it to a junk yard and bought a five-year-old Pontiac. It was a dream-come-true for the boys. It was sky blue, had a built-in record player and lots of shiny chrome. The boys could not get enough of driving the car, and it was perfect for picking up girls. The problem was to feed it. It had a tremendous appetite, and most of the boys' earnings went to gasoline and other car expenses.

Axel and Alex would drive down to the town square where the young folks with cars gathered, sitting around the parking area visiting or cruising down the main street. Sometimes they would all join, caravanning to popular places along the coast. Most of the boys were well behaved, with common interests in automobiles and girls, but there were always some rotten eggs in the bunch that had to make a nuisance of themselves. Those misfits would drive like fools, and others were annoyingly loud and obnoxious.

The boys would cruise down the street until they saw a couple girls. After a brief conversation, perhaps they would invite the girls to go for a ride. If it clicked, they would drive to some interesting place, a coast community or a folk park. The boys had a good repertoire of jokes and could entertain the girls for hours. They would, of course, play their favorite records . . . if they hadn't forgotten them on the dash of the car, and parked in the sun, causing the records to warp and no longer work in the record player. This mishap often befell their favorite records.

If things were still going well, they might drive somewhere to Aenjoy the view". If it was cold outside, they would have to start the car every now and then to keep it warm and to defog the windows. On occasion the boys drove south to Copenhagen. They enjoyed driving fast and could do so in the countryside, where there were no speed limits. On the freeway going north to Kungälv, a road of choice for the boys, the car would literally go airborne on some of the larger bumps. Kurt also liked to drive fast and would often race the boys. On the weekends, after work, they would compete on who would be the first one out to Lindome, their country home that Kurt had built on a lot, separated from Eva's parents' farm.

Kurt drove his cars like he lived his life, on the edge. On one occasion when Kurt was racing the boys to Lindome, he was ahead of Axel in his new Studebaker, Silver Hawk. Kurt was getting ready to pass cars ahead of him in a long sweeping curve. There was always a lot of traffic leaving town on Saturday afternoons, people going to their summer homes. Eva sat next to Kurt cheering him on "go, go Charlie!" as she often called him. As Kurt floored the accelerator to get the car to switch into low gear, the rear axle popped and the wheel, with part of the axle rolled across the road and down a field. The Studebaker spewed a cascade of white sparks as it sped down the road on three wheels and a gas tank. Luckily Kurt did not meet anyone right then, and he was able to keep the car on the road. On a different occasion, when Kurt was pushing his Studebaker up around 180km/hour, air entered between the steel roof and the inside ceiling liner, pushing the ceiling down on Kurt's and Eva's heads. Again Kurt avoided an accident.

The boys began delivering coffee and other merchandise from Kurt's store, doing several routes around the country side. The boys would finish their routes in one fourth of the time of what the previous drivers had spent. They participated in a couple orientation car rallies, where they had to find designated locations on a map and get there within a specified time. They commonly placed right in the middle of the field. Kurt and Eva seemed totally oblivious to the dangers involved.

In the spring of 1963 the boys were called upon to serve their country. Like all other Swedish males, they would participate in military service for one year. After a few years, they would have to return to update their training. Alex and Axel chose to enter the school for airborne rangers, an elite division of the army that demanded exceptional physical endurance. The rangers were trained to go behind enemies' lines, to sabotage and to cause distractions. The rangers did not have to stand guard, with the exception of providing the honor guard one weekend at the royal palace in Stockholm. Further, the rangers ate better than the regular army soldiers and were excused from kitchen duties. They did, however, have to keep their own rooms dust free, and the standard for beds was that a crown had to bounce back when dropped upon the tightly made bunks. Axel and Alex spent countless hours spit-shining their shoes and cleaning their equipment. Their training was intense. They had to run several miles a day, often in full combat gear and while negotiating obstacle courses. They practiced quick marches and often played the role of the enemy, when exercising with the regular army. Things could get ugly when the rangers would overrun a camp of regulars, in the early morning, steeling their food. Such training exercises did not sit well with the older soldiers who did not appreciate having to be there in the first place, having to take time off from work to spend a couple weeks in a camp, upgrading their military skills.

The boys' favorite activity was to blow things up. At the practice range, they would dig a hole under a large tree, prepare the charge, and send large trees flying. It was a privilege and honor to wear the burgundy berets. They certainly made the boys stand out in a crowd.

The training was divided into two segments. First was the summer training at Karlsborg, which also included several demonstration jumps during various festivities. Summer training ended with a demonstration where a couple squads of rangers were dropped over an abandoned air strip on a mission to blow up a fake missile site.

"What are we going to do this weekend Axel?" Alex asked, as he held out his thumb for a passing car.

"What do you think about driving down to Copenhagen, now when we have an extra-long weekend?" Axel asked.

"Maybe we'll have better luck if we stand and thumb alone, to catch a ride," Alex suggested. He had now stopped holding out his arm and was resting against a guard rail. It was hot, standing in the sun in their buttoned-up uniforms. However, they knew they would have a much better chance to catch a ride in their uniforms.

"If they got the car fixed that is, or else, we're going nowhere." Axel tossed a small pebble into a nearby creek in frustration, thinking of the unexpected expense.

"Perhaps we could fly from Landskrona to Kastrup airport in Copenhagen. It would cost less with a military standby than taking the car on the ferry plus the gas."

"Do we dare to take that chance of going standby?" Axel asked.

"What if there are no return seats available . . . and we would be late back to base? But I suppose . . . that's a relatively small risk to take for Swedish airborne rangers, the best of the Swedish armed forces," he added.

"If worse comes to worst, we will just have to pay regular fare, or take a cab to the ferry," Alex reasoned. "If real men ride ferries," he joked.

"Sure, but let's first see if we even make it to Gothenburg . . . if the car is fixed," Axel suggested. A light tan Chevrolet convertible with two young girls drove by. The boys changed their thumbing to plain waving as they knew that the odds of two girls stopping in a 1956 red convertible in the middle of nowhere was less than zero, and probably an enormously large negative number. The car slowed down but did not stop. "Boy, if they stopped wouldn't that be something," Axel mused. A little farther ahead the car came to a stop and began backing up. The boys grabbed their packs and ran toward it.

"Where are you fellows going?" a sweet voice asked them, emerging from the angel like creature behind the wheel. Her blond curly air resisted her effort to move it out of her face. The girl next to her was a little younger, perhaps fifteen, and looked quite a bit like the driver.

"To Gothenburg. What about you?" Axel asked.

"To Gothenburg, get in, if you don't mind the wind in the back," Ann Marie offered.

"Not at all, thank you. We were beginning to think that we would have to walk all the way home." 'You got to be kidding,' Alex thought, 'as if two rangers would reject a ride out in the middle of nowhere, from two gorgeous girls driving a shiny convertible Chevrolet . . . because there may be some wind involved,'

"Well we can't have that. Good thing we came along."

"You can say that again, and we really appreciate you stopping," said Alex sincerely.

"Well, we almost didn't. I don't normally stop for hitch hikers but I thought I'd make an exception today being that you're wearing uniforms. We just came from Karlsborg. Dad was one of the officers jumping into the lake this morning, so we just came up to take part in the festivities. We live in Gothenburg. This is my sister Rebecka. She convinced me to stop."

"Ann-Marie, that's not so," Rebecka protested her face turning light pink.

"Well we are forever grateful," said Alex. "I love your car, is it . . ."

"Yep, I have this thing for convertibles and especially American cars," she interrupted. "This used to be dad's car and he gave it to me when I graduated," she explained.

"Wow, that's quite a graduation gift," Alex reflected.

"It's nice, but it uses a lot of gas, and I'm thinking of trading it in for a smaller car," she explained.

"Alex and I have a 1956 Pontiac, so we can identify with that. On top of that, we just had to install a new, or used I guess, transmission. It gave out on us last weekend," Axel said.

Ann Marie turned into a small roadside cafeteria featuring a giant ice cream cone on the roof. "Anyone for an ice cream?" She asked.

"Yes, but it will be on us," the boys insisted. They sat down at a table to finish their ice creams. They learned that Ann-Marie had recently returned from New York where she had worked as an au pair for one year. She went there to improve on her English and enjoyed her stay very much. She said she loved New York. She now worked for her mother who owned a chain of women's apparel shops on the west coast. She was a year older than the boys and she did not have a boy friend. She agreed to see the boys later in the evening, putting an abrupt halt to their Copenhagen trip. It was an easy choice for the boys. Ann-Marie would also bring her friend Bibi.

The Pontiac was waiting for them at home when they returned. Eva had picked it up from the service station. She had also filled it with gas. She said that it was a present for the boys for having successfully finished the first phase of their ranger training.

The girls were ready when the boys pulled into their driveway. They lived in Longedrag, not far from where Annika was reared. The boys would have preferred to take Ann Marie's Chevy, but did not ask. Alex drove, and Ann-Marie moved in next to him up front. Her friend Birgitta, or Bibi, slid in next to Axel in the back seat. Bibi was pleasant looking and had a warm and friendly smile but was slightly round. She was definitely attractive but had the disadvantage of being compared with Ann Marie. Bibi also worked for Ann-Marie's mother. She was a year younger than Ann Marie, and both girls lived in what had been Ann Marie's grandmother's apartment downstairs in the family home. Bibi was from Östersund, where the boys would go for their winter training. She would not be there at the same time as the boys, but she gave them advice on things to do and places to see.

First, they strolled down the boat harbor in Longedrag. The girls pointed out where Ann- Marie's family boat was docked. Both girls enjoyed sailing and they agreed to go sailing the following day, even though it was a little late in the season, weather permitting. Next, they drove to Kungälv. After hiking around the old fort, they continued to the folk park, at the other end of town, and danced for a while to a popular local band. They changed partners a few times while dancing, but the original random selection seemed to have taken root. The park was crowded and festive and the couples walked about, now holding hand. They tried their luck at a wheel of chance and won two small teddy bears. After having a late supper at a hot dog stand, they returned to the Longedrag harbor enjoying each other's company in the car until early hours.

Later that day, the weather turned drizzly and the group spent most of the day in Ann Marie's boat, playing Monopoly and other games, cuddling and discussing world issues. The cabin was large enough to sleep eight people. Ann Marie folded up some of the cots and replaced them with air-mattresses, essentially turning the floor into a large mattress.

The boys had just two days before they had to leave for Östersund, for their second training stint. The couples spent every precious moment together until the girls drove them out to Torslanda airport. They agreed to keep close contact and to write often.

The winter training in Östersund would end with a ten-day forced march on skis across a mountain range where the rangers would camp out, and dig sleeping caves in the snow. It would be a little challenging, as the clothing, wet from sweat and melted snow the previous day, would freeze stiff overnight, like panzer shields. The group started out with two hundred soldiers; it was not long before the number would be cut in half, owing to attrition. Only seventy-five rangers would emerge, including Axel and Alex.

CHAPTER 33

1964 Axel, Alex and Ann Marie to the US

Ann Marie was a prolific letter writer. Alex received one letter from her every other day and he answered as often as he could. She wrote about anything and everything. It was as if she sent him the pages from her personal diary. She sent him her graduation picture and he carried it with him at all times. He would often pull it out and stare at it. Alex was in love.

Axel and Bibi also corresponded regularly. Axel would write about his interest in moving to America when he got out. Bibi was a little more cautious.

Alex and Ann Marie also discussed the proposition of moving to America, and they both found the idea intriguing. They decided to move to Ballard, a Scandinavian section of Seattle, and open an apparel store there specializing in Scandinavian fashions. They would call the boutique Annie's fashions. Annie was Alex's nickname for Ann Marie.

"Kurt?" Annika asked, as someone answered the phone.

"Hi, Annika! How's it going?" Kurt responded. He leaned back in his chair and put his legs up on a chair next to his desk.

"Great! I don't think I've ever been better," she teased him, about what he was missing.

"That's hard to believe. Not that you aren't great, you always have been, but that it's possible that you could be even greater," he flattered her.

"Well thank you . . . I think. I just wanted to talk to you a little about the children. The boys, oh, how is Eva?" Annika asked. She had developed a cautious but close relationship with Eva. She liked Eva who was always very positive, to the point that one wondered sometimes whether she was sincere. Annika also could not completely forget that Kurt had left her for Eva, even though it helped that she, Annika, took Kurt from Eva in the first place. Regardless, they got along fine together.

"Oh, she's doing just fine. She's doing whatever Eva is always doing and she's doing it well. And how is Torsten?" Kurt courteously replied.

"He is doing great, at the top of his game."

"Alright, so from now on it's going to be all downhill for him?" Kurt asked jokingly.

"I don't think so, I think he will stay at the top for quite some time," Annika said, somewhat defensively. "Anyway, you know the boys are talking about moving to the US.

They must have inherited their America fever from you."

"Not totally impossible. I wouldn't mind moving there myself if I could get away from everything here. Things are getting so bad here in Sweden with the socialists. That damn Sträng, taking everything, one earns in taxes."

"I didn't think you paid all that much taxes. Seemed to me that you always had enough deductions to cancel out your taxes . . .

"Perhaps, but those deductions are costs . . ."

"But let's not get into a discussion of that, let's talk about the boys," Annika interrupted, frustrated by their getting off the subject. Rearranging the cord, she sat down at the kitchen table. "You know it's only two more weeks before Alex and Ann Marie are getting married, and I haven't even met her yet."

"Don't worry about them; she's really nice and capable. They seem so much in love, always holding hands and teasing each other. I'm sure they'll be just fine," Kurt assured her.

"Well that's nice to hear, but there are other things. Are you going to help them out, to get started in the US?" Annika asked bluntly.

"Well, I hate to have to tell you this but I'm currently in a terrible financial bind. I don't know if you read about it in the papers, but I'm the one that is building the new office complex downtown. That is, was, until they found some historical artifacts there during excavation. I had everything that I could get my hands-on liquid, so I could invest in this project and here we are sitting doing nothing for close to six months now. The bank is refusing to advance any money until they know for sure if the project will be stopped permanently," Kurt sighed.

"Really? I had no idea. Now when you mention it, I did read about finding the artifacts but I didn't put it together with you," said Annika.

"In fact, I haven't been able to make the payments on some of my other loans because of this, including my Mamma's home which we used as collateral. We just got a notice from the bank that if I don't pay within two weeks, it will begin foreclosure proceedings on Mamma's home. Can you believe that? She's lived there all of her adult life. It seemed such a sure thing. I have the building almost full, in pre-signed leases. So, you can see the fix I'm in."

"Well it couldn't have happened at a worse time that's for sure. Is there anything that I can do to help out?" Annika asked.

"Well thanks, but no thank you," Kurt chuckled. "I need quite a bit more than what you could provide."

"Well, you are, after all, the father of our children and I don't want them to have to worry about this. How much do you need?" she repeated her question.

"I told you I need more money than you will ever see, several hundred thousand crowns."

"How much would you need to clear the mortgage on your mother's house and to get by until this is clear?" she persisted.

"Annika, I appreciate your concern but we're talking real money here, at a minimum I would need one hundred and fifty thousand crowns to get out of the immediate bind."

"I will let you borrow three hundred thousand for six-months at 10 percent, and you will have to sign over the title to the buildings in my name as security. And . . . you will have to sign an agreement that you never use your mother's house as security for a loan again as long as she lives. Do we have a deal?" Annika took a deep breath. She had surprised herself with how boldly she had presented her offer. "You can have the money in three days, will that be all right?" She continued, as Kurt apparently had lost his ability to speak.

"Wait a minute, is this some kind of a joke?" a perplexed Kurt asked. "From where would you possibly get that kind of money? And you would do this just to help my mother, who has only been mean to you."

"Oh, I didn't think you ever noticed. Yes, I will, and perhaps to let her know that she was wrong about me and perhaps for the children's sake. I'm not sure, but all the same, the offer stands, and regarding where I got it, that is my business."

Six days after Kurt received Annika's money, his development was cleared to proceed and he promptly returned the loan. His mother never uttered a word in gratitude.

Annika traveled to Gothenburg one week before the wedding and helped out with the final arrangements. Ann Marie's parents had rented the dining room in Tjölöholm's Castle for the wedding. It was about an hour's drive south of Gothenburg. The storybook castle was molded onto a small hill with a grandiose view of the ocean on one side and the castle's park on the back side. The castle was now owned by the community, which rented it out for special events. It was a perfect setting for a wedding. Alex and Ann-Marie spent the weekend in a luxurious resort in Båstad, a location that is best known for hosting the Swedish Cup tennis tournaments.

Two weeks later Alex and Ann-Marie were off to Seattle. Axel now had the Pontiac to himself.

Axel worked for Kurt another six months before he decided to move to the US. Working for Kurt did not promise much of a future. Kurt made it clear that he might, at any moment, sell out everything and move to the US, himself.

Axel saw Bibi only occasionally. She was not prepared to leave Sweden permanently, so Axel decided to go on his own. He left in the fall of 1965, 21 years old, with a one-way ticket to New York. Mrs. Greenberg had agreed to sponsor him, as was needed for him to get a green card and to be able to work. Axel had advertised for work opportunities in a US newspaper and he received a few answers just before he left.

He took a job at a livery stable on the north side of Chicago. He cared for horses and managed the high school riding program. He picked up the students at their schools, brought them to the stable, and back. Eventually he also began teaching riding classes.

A year later, Axel received a draft notice. He contacted the Selected Service Office and explained that he did not speak much English and thereby managed to have his service delayed a year. America was engaged in an effort to defeat communism in Vietnam. Axel was not eager to serve.

It was not a prestigious job, but he enjoyed the atmosphere there, at the stable, and helping the many cute little girls solving their riding problems. The stable also boarded and trained horses, and it participated in jumping and hunting shows.

Axel now had less than a year before he had to report for his military obligations. He lived in a small house on the premises, although, he dined with the owners in the main house. Most of Axel's students were more adept at English riding than he was, but Axel purchased a book on the subject, and he would read one chapter at the time, and then teach what he had learned, to the next class. The classes always included riders of various skill levels. If there was something he didn't know, such as the name of some equipment, he would ask a question of one of the advanced students and repeat the answer, with approval, to the class. Such resourcefulness would serve Axel well in the coming years.

Several girls were frequent visitors to the stable and Axel got to know them well. The girls tended to fall for Axels accent, his old-world chivalry and his Nordic features. They left no doubt that they accept a request for a date, and Axel didn't disappoint them. As the number of students requesting riding lessons from Axel grew, he stopped caring for the horses and devoted all his time to giving lessons. He bought an old De Soto from one of the patrons, and soon learned what *drive in movies* were all about.

Now that Alex had wheels, he would go dancing as time permitted. But he did not pursue a serious relationship with any of them because he knew he would be called in to the service soon. With America fully engaged in Vietnam, Axel would have to agree to serve or leave the country. By this time, he had decided that he wanted to stay.

Axel dated several girls he met at dance clubs. Pat, or Patricia he dated on several occasions, going dancing or to a drive-in movie, or just sit and talk for hours. Pat was cute and spunky and she was infatuated by Axel, however, she had a small child and with Axel leaving for Viet Nam, most likely, in only a few months, Axel could not see a future in the relationship, although he enjoyed her company, and he felt a strong attraction towards her.

In July, Kurt came to visit Axel. He stayed with Axel in his cottage for a week. Axel's Desoto was giving out on him, so Kurt, always somewhat extravagant when it came to cars, bought him a brand-new Camaro convertible, yellow with a black top. Kurt told Axel that It was a loan that Alex could repay when he could.

In the fall of 1965 Axel began going on extended rides with Sunny, the president of the North West High School riding club. They often would ride to a creek where they might take a dip and then linger for another hour or two before returning to the stables. By mid-November the rides had expanded to movie dates and other activities. By Christmas they were talking about marriage, but Axel would be leaving soon for military service, so they decided to postpone the wedding. His advanced individual training, together with the basic training, would take close to a year.

The Army informed Axel that would first go to Ft. Leonard. Wood in Missouri for his basic training, and then on to Ft. Mammoth New Jersey for his advanced individual training. He did not know where he would be stationed after that, but Vietnam was the most likely destination. After he was inducted Axel signed up for an extra third year of service in order to attend a school for transmitter repairmen. The basic training was a cinch for Axel after recently having completed his service as a paratroop ranger in the Swedish army. Being a few years older than most of the other men also worked to his advantage. He knew the rules well. If it moves salute it. If it doesn't move, paint it. Axel was immediately promoted to platoon leader and was thereby spared from general cleaning duties. It was hot in Missouri during the summer training, but Axel was in good physical condition and kept up with the physical demands easily.

Axel's next assignment would be Ft Wainwright in Fairbanks, Alaska. This was much better "over-seas" duty than Vietnam, though his was a combat unit, and could be called to Vietnam on short notice. Axel and Sunny agreed that she should stay in Chicago until Axel settled down in Fairbanks. Upon leaving Ft. Mammoth, Axel was promoted to Specialist E-4, the same grade as corporal.

CHAPTER 34

1970 - Sunny, the Wilders and Katrina

Axel's flight to Fairbanks on Alaska Airline was a unique experience. The cabin was decorated like a saloon, and the stewardesses wore saloon-girl outfits complete with net stockings. The friendly crew served complimentary wine from a Russian Samovar. The warmth in the cabin contrasted starkly with the weather outside when they arrived. At -65F at the airport, Axel found it difficult to breathe, and he coughed from the shock to his air way. The thick, pinkish ice fog obscured his vision. The frozen ground crunched under each step as he walked to the terminal. The military passengers were bussed to the reception center at Ft Wainwright.

Axel spent a few days getting organized, including being issued his winter gear and a military driver's license. Six days after his arrival, his company left for Jack Frost winter exercises and Axel camped with six other young men in a tent for two weeks. He spent much of his time sitting guard, bundled up in the dark, guarding a transmitter truck from no one in the middle of nowhere. Surprisingly, though the temperature dropped to -70F Axel was not cold. His inflated bunny boats kept his feet warm and his thick parka and other equipment worked well. He would spend his time, on guard duty, studying the busy northern lights, at times racing across the sky in pinks and greens.

Axel thought of Sunny, of some of their best moments and some of their worst. He thought about Alex and Ann Mary and how close it was that she would have been his. He thought of Annika and Kurt. They were both living so lavishly, but neither seemed to give a damn how he was doing. Why did they never ask? When he had children one day, surely, he would not be as self-absorbed and uncaring as Kurt and Annika were.

Axel thought of Sunny. Would she want to come to Alaska when she learned how cold it was in winter? Was she even waiting for him? Did he want her to wait for him?

Axel knew that he needed more education if he was going to get ahead in life, as long as he was in the service, he could not go to college. Perhaps he could expand on his electronic knowledge, but he was already highly specialized. How much of a demand could there be for fixed station transmitter repairmen?

Maybe it would be easier to return to Sweden, but what awaited him there? There was no future for him in Kurt's coffee business. And he did not have any other marketable skills. No . . . America was still the best land with the best future for Alex. He just needed a plan.

His thoughts were interrupted by the reality that he had to start the trucks and fuel the generators every two hours to keep the oil from getting so thick that the engines would not start at all.

Axel was relieved to get back to his room in the barracks when the Jack Frost maneuvers were over.

Soon Axel was promoted to Specialist E-5, the same rank as a Buck-Sergeant. Being quite resourceful, he developed a reputation for being good at finding supplies and parts for repairing equipment and remodeling buildings. He had developed some skills while working on Ted's farm, after all. Though these projects were outside his work description he did not mind, because they gave him quite a bit of freedom. At times he was doing projects for the battalion and at other times for the company. Both units worked mostly independently and therefore, most of the time, no one knew where he was. He avoided morning formations and several unpalatable duties. If anyone needed equipment, supplies or remedy that was out of the ordinary, Axel had a source for just about everything.

Sergeant Ernie Wilder and his wife Jenny became close friends with Axel. Wilder was a lifer, a carrier soldier, and he took soldiering substantially more seriously than did Axel. Ernie was an airplane mechanic and also a pilot, flying his super cub whenever he could. Axel, however, aimed to get out as soon as his three years were up. Ernie took life in general more seriously than did Axel, except for his rather eccentric after-hours lifestyle. Ernie Wilder was fairly short and seemed to have a bit of a Napoleon Complex. He could be quite stern at times, but also quite silly when he was in the mood, especially when he had too much to drink, which was not uncommon. His relationship with Jenny was strange, at best. Jenny's attraction to Ernie mystified Axel.

Ernie loved to talk about their sex life in graphic details, and Jenny just raised her eyebrows when he did so. Ernie claimed that he completely dominated and Jenny was his sex slave.

"I've her trained well," he told Axel. "One time we went to a strip club in Atlanta together with some friends, and they announced that they would have an amateur strip contest with a $200 first prize. I told her to sign up, and I tell you, she could be a pro any time she likes. She's good!" he added.

"Really, Jenny? Did you strip on stage?" Axel asked her. The image of Jenny as a stripper did not fit with her sweet and innocent look.

"Sure did, butt naked, and I got the first prize, too, out of eight contestants," she declared. "And a lot of tips," she added, "about $30.00 in tips."

"But how did it feel to undress in front of a bunch of strangers? Weren't you embarrassed?" Axel asked in wonder.

"Sure, but that's what makes it exciting, that you're doing something that is taboo, but you can get away with it," she responded.

"Well you can strip for me any time you like," said Axel. "I sure wish I would have been there."

"We'll see, maybe later," she replied.

"Jenny," Ernie said in a stern voice, "our guest would like to see some skin. Take off your dress."

"Yes, Ernie," she said, unzipping her dress and letting it fall. Dressed in only her panties and bra she continued to set the table as if nothing unusual was taking place.

"Jenny, why do you let Ernie treat you that way? Why don't you just say no?" Axel asked, as Ernie went to the bathroom.

"Because I like it. It turns me on. I guess I'm a born exhibitionist and when Ernie tells me to do things that give me an excuse to actually do it, to live my fantasies, it's like playing a roll," she explained. "Do you mind?"

"Of course not. I just felt a little bad for you, being treated like that."

"Don't. I'm having a ball."

"You're incredibly sexy. Will you do anything he asks you to do?"

"Anything. It's up to him how far we go. It makes it incredibly sexy when you don't have control over what's going to happen," she explained.

Ernie returned from the bathroom, wobbling as he walked. His speech slightly slurred, he continued to speak openly about his unconventional demands on Jenny.

"One time I told her to deliver a best wishes card naked to a friend who was getting married."

"Yeah, and some of his buddies were there, and they invited me in and took pictures of me and Steve," Jenny added.

"A couple times when we ordered pizza, I had Jenny go to the door, without a stitch on, to get the pizza."

"Yeah, and the first time it was a girl who came," Jenny filled in, giggling.

Alex, Ernie and Jenny moved to the living room. Ernie was now quite drunk. "Pussy, we're having pussy for desert. How would you like yours served?" he slurred. "Take it all off baby," he commanded, as he fell into a deep sleep.

"Yes Ernie," said Jenny as she wriggled out of her tiny under garments and she stood in front of Axel completely naked. "What would you like me to do Axel? I know that Ernie wants me to please you."

"What's the specialty of the house?" he asked daringly.

"I'll get the handcuffs and show you."

Axel found a small house in downtown Fairbanks, a charming log house, but in need of some improvements. The payments would be no more than paying rent. The lot was nicely wooded, great for Sunny's dog Sherry, a small white spits.

In May of 1971 Axel flew to Sunny in Chicago. Sunny would join Axel in Fairbanks to see how well she could adapt to the far north, before they decided whether to marry. It was not the strongest foundation for a relationship, but Axel was lonely. They purchased a trailer to take their belongings to Fairbanks. They took their time driving to Alaska, stopping often to walk Sunny's dog and for sightseeing. They stopped at The House on the Rock, and Sunny was equally impressed as was Axel. Of course, they stopped at Walls Drugstore, which had signs up all over the countryside, hundreds of miles before they arrived. They drove through the badlands, and they stopped at Mt. Rushmore. They stared in wonder at the monument, which was much larger than they could have imagined. They crossed the Canadian prairie up to Dawson Creek, which marked the beginning of the Alaska Highway. Driving three hundred fifty miles a day it took them five days before they finally pulled up to their home in Fairbanks. They were fortunate, having avoided flat tires or a broken windshield, the usual rites of passage, on their trip up the Alaska Highway.

It was after 10:00pm when they arrived, but the sun was still up.

"Well, what do you think?" Axel asked a bit anxiously. Sunny walked through the house opening all doors.

"It's nice. It's larger than I thought it would be. And the yard is nice. Are you going to finish the basement?"

"Yes, eventually. It would make a nice family room or guest bedroom if I installed a window."

A week after their arrival, after Sunny had settled in, Axel invited the Wilders over for dinner. He was not sure how to prepare Sunny for the Wilders' eccentricities. It was impossible to predict what would happen when the Wilder's arrived, though he did provide a few hints that they were somewhat unconventional.

The Wilders arrived precisely at 6:00 and smartly dressed.

"What's so eccentric about them?" Sunny whispered in the kitchen when she and Axel carried out the dinner dishes. "They seem really nice and quite normal."

"They are nice, but you never know what they will do, especially after a few drinks." Sunny and Axel returned to their guests, having put on the coffee. Ernie's language was becoming more vulgar as his conversation began to focus on sex.

"Sunny, last time I was over for dinner at the Wilders, Jenny told me that she once participated in an amateur striptease contest. . .."

"Really, did you really, Jenny?" Sunny asked in disbelief, but sounding less shocked than Axel expected.

"I sure did, and I won the first prize, $200.00."

"What about you, Sun, have you ever done anything wild and crazy?" Wilder asked.

"Not that wild and crazy. I played strip poker with some friends at home once, but I didn't get naked. There were six of us, three guys and three girls. One of the guys got naked and two of the girls, but not me. I probably would have, though, if I had lost," she confessed.

"But only if the others did. I don't think I would have the nerve to be the only one naked in a room."

"You never told me about that," said Axel, his estimation of Sunny moving up two notches.

"You never asked."

"Ernie and Jenny like to play sex games where he is the master and she is the slave, and she does whatever he tells her to do," Axel continued.

"That wouldn't work for me," Sunny declared. "If I was going to participate in a game like that I would want to be the master and Axel would have to be the slave."

"Well that's not likely to happen," Axel announced.

"'ll let you borrow my slave if you want, Sunny," Ernie offered. "You can have Jenny for your personal slave for tonight. She'll do anything you tell her to do. That is my wish."

"Doesn't Jenny have anything to say about it?" Sunny asked, doubtfully.

"I'll do whatever Ernie tells me to do," Jenny responded almost mechanically.

"Let's move into the living room," Axel suggested.

"Have you ever been to a strip club Sunny?" Jenny asked, "It's a lot of fun. Of course, I'm probably more of an exhibitionist than most. I love to have guys drool over me and I love to have an audience when I undress. I could be a professional stripper, if it weren't for the late hours and all the drinking involved."

"I heard they dilute the girls' drinks," said Axel.

"Perhaps, but if you drink enough diluted drinks, you're still going to get drunk," Jenny responded.

"No, I haven't been to a strip joint," said Sunny. "But I wouldn't mind going. Do they have strip joints in Fairbanks?"

"Yes, Tellons, and one more . . . or two more," Ernie offered. All right, let's go. This will be Sunny's first strip joint night, tonight."

They drove out to a small place on South Cushman Street. There was a small stage and perhaps twenty tables in the room. The room was dimly lit and quite smoky. The smell of stale perfume lingered in the air. The room was half filled with mostly younger men, probably military. A waitress dressed in a mini-dress cowboy outfit came to their table to take their orders. The jukebox played a rhythmic version of The Great Pretender. A middle-aged woman came out on the stage, dressed in a formal red gown covered with glitter. Her low-cut dress exposed most of her breasts and the high split on the side allowed her to move freely to the music. She danced looking at the audience with a mysterious smile. Suddenly she made a quick turn and the dress slid down to the floor. She kicked it over to the side.

"What do you think Sunny? Isn't this a turn on?" Jenny whispered. "Ernie and I have our best sex after we've been to a place like this."

"Yes, but is she going to take all her clothes off?" Sunny asked.

"Everything," Axel assured her. "What about it honey? Do you think you could do that?"

"I don't know . . . maybe?" She began humming along with the music, moving with the throbbing rhythm, as the stripper removed one garment after the other, until she was completely naked. She was amazingly athletic, bending over backwards and gyrating to the music.

"I'm not sure I could do that though," Sunny concluded. They stayed through a few more acts before they returned to Axel and Sunny's house.

"Well, what did you think of that?" Axel asked as he settled in to the over-stuffed couch.

"Pretty hot," Sunny responded. "I got really horny watching the girls dance, that's for sure. Could I do it? Well only if I was really drunk and others were doing it."

"What about doing it together with Jenny?" Axel asked.

"You wouldn't mind if I stripped here right now?" she asked Axel.

"Mind? I'd love it. I'm getting hornier than hell just talking about it."

"I'll try, but I'm not going to promise that I'll go all the way."

"Do you want me to do it with you?" Jenny asked.

"No, I'm horny enough to give it a try alone right now." Sunny took a double swallow from her wine glass. Axel had already selected the music. She began moving to the music and lifted her dress high enough to expose her long shapely legs.

"Higher baby, lift it higher baby," Axel encouraged her.

"Yeah, take it all off baby," Wilder chimed in.

"Go, Sunny, go," Jenny chanted.

Sun raised her skirt more exposing her white panties and a little of her midriff, dancing with her eyes closed.

"Take it off baby, go Sunny, take it off," Axel encouraged her. She pulled the dress over her head and threw it at Ernie.

"Way to go, baby, way to go." She danced around the floor stroking herself up and down her body with her hands sometimes bending forward and letting her hair fall in front of her, then swinging it back and forth, as she had seen some of the strippers do earlier.

"Go baby go, take it all off, way to go baby," Axel called out. Axel was also being affected by the alcohol and the atmosphere.

She reached back and after a couple tries unhooked her bra. She left it on hanging loose, her breasts still in the cups. She reached for the edge of her panties and began moving them down, when suddenly the music stopped and so did Sunny.

"Wait a second and I'll put on a new record," Axel offered rushing over to the record player. Sunny walked over to the table to sip on her wineglass.

"I don't think I can continue now," She announced. I lost the momentum when the music stopped.

"Well you can't stop now, baby, now that I'm all worked up. Take it off baby," Axel pled.

"Wait, you have to be in the mood," Jenny explained, "otherwise it's not right and it doesn't look real. Let me help you Sunny, I'll do it first, and then you can join me if you like." Jenny stood up and began dancing.

Sunny joined her, raising her arms over her head stretching while dancing on, "love it." She bent over backwards and touched the floor behind her. "I knew I could," she said triumphantly, walking around the floor in her compromising position.

The following week Sunny set out to look for a job. She quickly found one as a teller at the savings and loan and began work a week later. Sunny was both talkative and flirtatious in nature and she easily made friends. She and a loan officer at the bank, Steve, quickly hit it off. Steve was married and had just adopted a baby girl. That didn't dampen his interest in Sunny. Sunny found that they had a lot in common, and two months later they left their partners and move in together. While Axel was at work, during his last week in the army, Steve came home and helped Sunny move out, taking everything that was not nailed down.

Axel's house had increased in value, owing mostly to his remodeling effort, which included finishing the basement. He made a tidy profit when he sold it. Recognizing that his carpentry skills, combined with his creative abilities could provide the basis for career in designing and building houses, Axel purchased a lot close to town with a spectacular view of the city. On a clear day one could see Mt McKinley, two hundred miles away. He secured a construction loan and began building a three-bedroom home.

Finally, Axel felt as though the future had something to offer him. Through hard work and building on his innate talent he could make a life for himself in Fairbanks.

In late July Axel stopped at the Frontier Lodge for a cup of coffee while buying building materials. The girl behind the counter caught his attention. She wore her waist long caramel colored hair in a ponytail and Axel found himself fixating on it as it swung softly back and forth as she attended to her duties. Her brown uniform topped with a yellow apron fell several inches above her knees, revealing her long shapely legs, which Axel couldn't help noticing.

"Hi, can I have a cup of coffee please?" he asked, as she looked up at him with a warm smile.

"Sure, one cup of coffee. Anything to go with it?" she asked. Her voice was sweet and friendly. "We have fresh donuts."

"No thanks. Just a cup of coffee, please"

"Sugar and cream are over there on the end table," she informed him. "Thanks," he said, and proceeded to the sugar and cream, where he emptied three packets of sugar into his cup. She observed him stirring in three small bags of sugar into his coffee.

"Boy, you have a sweet tooth, don't you?" She watched him, mildly shocked, as he casually stirred his coffee.

"Yup, I like it sweet. Hey, since there's no one else here, how about joining me for a cup?" he asked her.

"I'd like to, but I'm the only one here and I have to get the potato salad ready, and some other things, before my shift ends in one hour," she said.

"You get off in one hour?" he repeated, reading the information as a vague invitation to try again.

"Yes, I do."

"Could I talk you into going out for dinner with me then? By the way my name is Axel." He held out his hand to introduce himself.

She took his hand smiling. "I'm Katarina. Do I detect an accent? Where are you from?" she asked.

"I'm from Sweden. I came here a few years ago. Actually, I was on my way to Australia, but that will probably never happen now. I like it just fine right here."

"Just fine?" she repeated, mimicking his accent with a flirtatious smile. My name could be Scandinavian too, or perhaps Russian. I don't think that I have any Swedish blood, but one never knows. Would you like a refill?" she asked, avoiding his dinner invitation.

"What about it? May I pick you up here at seven, when you get off, and we have dinner together?" he repeated.

"Well," she stammered, I can't go anywhere. I'm not dressed to go out. I can't go anywhere in this uniform. . . ." she said unsurely.

"Alright, I'll pick you up at seven and then I'll run you over to your house, so you can change, and then we'll go to dinner. How does that sound?"

"Are you sure you don't mind? . . . Well, okay then, that sounds nice." Axel returned in only one half an hour, bought another cup of coffee and watched Katarina as she straightened up the café before closing.

After driving her home where she changed out of her uniform, freshened up, and put on a cream – colored dress which again showed off her legs, the two drove to the Club 11, eleven miles east of Fairbanks on the Richardson Highway, where they ordered the house specialty, prime rib. Though Katarina was barely eighteen, and Axel was now twenty-six, their conversation fell into a natural rhythm. She was charmed by his accent, old world good manners and worldliness, and he by her youthful innocence and having been raised in the Alaskan frontier. Despite the differences in their backgrounds, they found they both enjoyed cooking and music. They both enjoyed discussing world affairs, and despite having been raised on different continents, they shared similar world views. Both of their fathers had been in private enterprise and both having been raised with middle-class values.

Katarina had the weekend off and they agreed to spend the following day together. Axel would pick her up and take her out to his house and then Katarina would prepare one of her specialty dishes for them. The house was still unfinished on the inside, but Axel had a camping stove where he did his cooking. The drywall was finished but it was not all painted yet and he had not yet begun to do the finishing work.

"Yesterday it was really scary . . ." he said as they entered the house.

"What happened?"

"Nothing bad, it was just that I got the electricity installed and I didn't know if everything would work. I built the whole shell and insulated it and did the drywall before I could get the electric hookup. I was really worried that once I got the connection and flipped on the lights that nothing would work. Can you imagine what a nightmare that would have been if switches didn't work, and I had to trace every wire back to the entrance panel to see where I'd left a wire dangling? It was a great feeling when I turned on the circuit breaker and all the lights came on."

"Yeah . . ." Katarina responded, not fully appreciating the risk Axel had taken.

"But that wasn't all . . . "Axel continued.

"What else happened?"

"We drilled the well here earlier this summer, but I never dropped the pump down into it, because I couldn't use it anyway without power. Well, this morning when I dropped it down, it only went about twenty feet. I figured the well had caved in somehow. It's one hundred forty feet deep, and has six-inch steel well casing, so I had a hard time seeing how it could have caved in. So, I called the driller and he came out and it turned out that the well had frozen from sitting inactive most of the summer. So, he thawed the pipe, and the pump slid right down and we now have fresh thirty-three degrees well water."

"Wow! That must have been scary, I'm sure glad it wasn't anything more serious."

"Yes, you have to be careful with permafrost here, even though we're on a south slop. The neighbor is actually taking his house down and moving it to a different lot. He'd built directly over a frozen ice river, and he put in a swimming pool with a fireplace at one end. Well, somehow the combination of the heat and the weight from the rock fireplace made the house sink more than two feet. First the doors wouldn't close, then the windows broke and before long, not a wall in the house was plumb."

"Ouch! Didn't they test for permafrost before building?"

"Sure, they did. They drilled in several locations. Unfortunately, this is not regular permafrost where the ground is frozen in general. These are Ice Rivers or creeks and if you don't hit them right on, they go undetected until it's too late. I found an underground river like that on this lot when I was cutting down the bank back there, but fortunately it was not under the house."

"Does that mean that every time the well sits for a while it will freeze?" Katarina asked, looking skeptical.

"No, we'll put a heat tape down the casing that can be turned on if needed. It's just a pain to have to deal with, that's all," he explained.

CHAPTER 35

1973 – Firefighting, Molly – Tracy, Kurt

Axel's home was almost finished when his construction loan ran out. The loan officer had told him that the bank could extend him an additional $10,000, given the equity Axel had created in the house. Processing the additional loan would take about two weeks.

"Honey, BLM is advertising for fire fighters for a forest fire not far from Fairbanks.

The pay is pretty good so I'm going to sign up. Okay?"

"Sure, but how long will you be gone?" asked Katarina.

"It will only be for a few days. It will give me something to do while we wait for the loan to clear. I'll be fine," he assured her as she looked at him worriedly. "It's good money, and I can't get any more done on the house until the loan comes through anyway." He gave Katarina a quick kiss and jumped in his truck.

Two busloads of men and a hand full of women were brought out to the fire base camp. Axel, four more men and two of the girls were flown to the front line in a large helicopter. Heavy equipment, for making firebreaks, awaited them. However, Axel, Molly and Tracy were driven out to replace a crew on an all-terrain-track-vehicle. Axel was to walk in front of a bulldozer, and lay out the trail to be cleared, seeking the most level ground to travel. The women followed the caterpillar, starting backfires and putting out fires that jumped the line. Axel guided the cat operator along a creek down a gently sloping hillside. Their walkie-talkies did not work, which left them without communication with the main camp.

Soon it became clear that they were walking straight into the fire line. The fire was not intensive, but it produced sparks that initiated new flare-ups on the wrong side of the firebreak. Recognizing that they could not continue on the same path, Axel made a ninety-degree turn clearing a trail up the slope toward where he estimated they would run into the highway. They followed a small almost dried out creek. Axel quickly realized that they were about to become overrun by the fire. The caterpillar operator, coming to the same conclusion, jumped off the cat and ran back down to the larger creek for protection. Sparks were now raining heavily around them. The women did their best to put out spot fires on the wrong side of the firebreak, but new fires started faster than they could put them out. The fire was creating its own wind, and it was intensifying.

Not wanting to abandon the caterpillar, Axel was able to drive it over to a small rock formation ahead with a beaver dam at its base. He began clearing the land next to the water to create a clearing where they could best ride out the fire. The brush was rather low, the area apparently having been cleared by another fire recently. They set camp beneath the rock. What forest was left from the last burn provided plenty of fuel for the current fire to spread. The dry branches on the moss-covered black spruce trees seemed to invite sparks and created a dramatic rocket effect when the fire took hold. The flare-ups sounded like a passing freight-train and the heat instantly intensified around them. They soaked a blanket for protection but did not have to use it.

Axel had no idea how long he had been working. The midnight sun and dense smoke didn't leave much of a clue. The fire passed by Axel and the women, so they had lost that battle, but they had not lost the caterpillar and they were all safe, dead tired, but safe. They spread out a canvas on the ground and all three fell into deep sleep within a few minutes.

Axel awakened to the sound of the laughing women swimming in the beaver dam. The sun was up, the smoke had cleared except for some tree-stumps that were still smoldering, and it was a beautiful morning.

He watched the women play in the water, apparently oblivious to anyone watching them. The previous day they had look more like men in their bedraggled clothing and Bermuda-hats. Now, they had let their hair down, and he could see clearly that they were not men. Their clothing was neatly stacked on a rock next to the lake.

Axel decided to make his presence known and stood up and the girls called for him to join them. He dressed down to his shorts and waded into the water, which was much warmer than he expected. The girls teased him about leaving his shorts on, but Axel did not feel comfortable taking them off even though the girls did not were theirs. When they emerged from the water, they all decided to wash their clothing, and they hung it to dry in a small stand of trees that miraculously had been spared by the fire. Axel tried to start the caterpillar, but the battery appeared to be dead. He told the women that they should stay by the cat until the others came looking for them. "I wonder what happened to the cat-skinner," Axel said. "If he returned to the big creek, he should be all right."

"Have you done this before?" Molly asked him.

"No, this is the first time for me. I heard the call for help on the radio, and I had some time, and the rest is history. How about you? Done this before?" he asked.

"A couple times, but this is the first time this year. We're building a cabin, a log cabin, and haven't had time," Tracy told him. The girls had put on their panties but left rest of their clothing on the tree to dry. The fact that Axel was a man and a stranger didn't seem to bother them the least.

"Nice that there are no mosquitoes. The fire must have chased them away," said Molly.

"Where are you building?" Axel asked.

"In the Gold Stream Valley, not far from the University." Molly said. "We are making good progress."

"I'm also building a house," he informed them. "A log cabin, though, that sounds interesting. I wouldn't mind building a log cabin someday. There's something romantic and Alaskan about log cabins."

"Well you can come and build on ours if you like," Molly responded.

"How long have you lived in Fairbanks? And where are you from?" Axel asked.

"Three years now this fall. We're from Texas. It was getting a little too crowded there so we came here for some breathing room."

"What do you do when you're not fighting fires?" Axel asked.

"We study to be journalists, at the university, but we also mush dogs.

We're building as we go. We don't have a loan. We just build as we earn a few dollars. You should come and visit. We love to have company. But be careful, we might just put you to work," Tracy said chuckling.

"I'd love to. How long are you planning on staying out on this fire?" Axel asked.

"As long as the fire is burning and we have the job," Molly responded.

Axel was sitting on the cat in the middle of his clearing when a helicopter came by. There was enough space for the chopper to land and pick up Axel and the women. Axel had been out there for four days. He had lost track of the time as it was daylight both night and day. He decided he had enough of firefighting and caught the next ride back to Fairbanks.

A filthy and exhausted Axel trudged up the hill toward the house. Katarina saw him from the window and ran out to greet him.

"Boy, am I glad to see you! I was so worried! Did you hear about the helicopter that crashed at the fire? The fire you were at. I was so nervous . . . so scared that something had happened to you. Come in. You need a bath! I'll fill the tub."

"Thanks, I'm glad to be back. Then I need to get some sleep. Didn't get much sleep out there."

"Guess who's here? Your dad!" Katarina burst out. "He came yesterday with no warning. He called from the airport, and I had to run out and get him. He was lucky that I was home. I've been staying with Kajsa while you were gone, because I didn't want to stay up here on the hill alone, when you weren't here. I think he's taking a nap now. You know, he still hasn't adjusted to the time change."

"Was James there?"

"Of course, he's Kajsa's brother and he lives there."

"Yes, and your former lover. . ."

"I chose you, didn't I?"

"yes, but just barely. I had to do some fancy talking to convince you. Are there any news from the bank?"

"Yes, Mr. Bradley called from the bank and he said that the money is available."

Inside, Axel got out of his dirty work clothes. "I met a couple fun girls, fighting fires. We sort of got isolated for a while but a chopper found us. They were real neat and are building a log cabin down in the valley. I offered to give them a hand, so I can learn a little about log building. I think you would like them, even though they are a little bit on the wild side, and I think they're lesbians."

"What was that supposed to mean, that I would like them because they are lesbian?" Katarina shot back.

"No, no, I meant that you'll like them because they're nice and uncomplicated."

"Well, being lesbians can be quite complicated."

"Hi Dad." Axel said, giving Kurt a hug as he emerged from the bedroom.

"Nice to see you again, Axel. Boy, this house is looking great. I'll have to take a lot of pictures so I can show everyone."

"Did you come straight here or?"

"No, I've been in America for a couple of weeks. I stopped by to see Peter and Hilda in Canada, and I stayed a couple days in Chicago. I also stopped by and saw Alex and Annie in Seattle. They're going full speed ahead opening new stores all over the place. They were even talking about taking their company public, listing it on the stock market. I was hoping I could stay here for a week. I can help you build," he offered.

"'ll put on the coffee while you take a bath, alright?" Katarina suggested.

Axel slept for twelve hours straight. It was ten in the morning when he finally got up.

"Good morning," he greeted Katarina and Kurt that sat at the homemade kitchen table.

"Good morning sweetheart. Did you sleep well?" she asked, greeting him with a kiss.

"Like an ox."

"I didn't know that oxen were known for being great sleepers," Katarina teased.

"Is that hypnotist still at Starlet?" he asked Katarina. "Maybe it would be fun to go there tonight?"

"Are you sure that's a proper place to take your dad? It's a strip joint," she reminded him.

"Oh, that's all right. Dad has seen things like that before . . . I'm sure." Axel reached for some coffee cake.

"I heard some guys talking about it. It sounds like it could be fun," Axel insisted. "Hey, this is good."

The Starlet was packed, but they managed to find three seats by adding chairs to someone else's table. A girl was stripping on a small stage on the side, when they came into the poorly lit, smoky room. After she had finished her act, an enthusiastic emcee entered the main stage and introduced "The Great Montello." He greeted the audience, told a couple jokes about the Watergate scandal and asked for twelve volunteers. Katarina stood up with a little persuasion from Axel, and joined the other brave victims on the stage. Montello encouraged everyone in the audience to participate as he went through his 'going to sleep' routine. After the victims had 'gone to sleep,' the lights were turned back on and Montello walked around the audience. As he snapped his fingers while touching individuals, more victims fell under his trance, and obediently went to the stage. Montello ordered his participants to do various harmless things, and it appeared to Axel that he had full control over them. He ended his act by taking Katarina and stiffening up all her muscles before placing her straight between two chairs, her feet on one and her head on the other. Then he, all 180 pounds, stood on her stomach while she remained completely stiff.

"How do you feel?" Axel asked when Katarina returned to the table.

"Fine, I feel great," she responded.

"That's weird. Did you not know what was going on when he was standing on you?" Axel asked.

"Oh, I sort of knew what was going on, but it was like it was happening at a distance, as if it wasn't real somehow," she explained.

The following morning Katarina complained of some soreness in her back, but she was remarkably unscathed.

"So what are you kids planning on doing next, when you got the house finished, and sold," Kurt asked at breakfast. Are you still thinking of going to Seattle?"

"Yes, that's the plan. We're going to open a hardware store with the money we earn from this house."

"Well I'm proud of you Axel. You have made it on your own and you sure seem to be doing well," Kurt responded warmly. "How about you Katarina, you don't mind moving away from here, from your family?"

"Oh, I'll miss my friends here but I will go wherever Axel goes."

CHAPTER 36

Jul. 1973 To Seattle -- Switching rolls

Axel and Katarina found a super deal on a three-bedroom home not far from where Alex and Annie lived. The previous owner was transferred, and Boeing, his employer, would pay for all closing costs. The monthly payments would be $200/month. It was a two-story home with a family-room and a two-car garage, and in a very nice neighborhood. They found a space in a new shopping center and soon they had opened the doors to Axel's paint and hardware. Business was good, but mostly from Axel's contracting, painting and remodeling.

The shopping center was located close to a country club residential area. Many of the upper middle-class home owners were widows with too much time on their hands and plenty of money. Axel was convinced that some of the women hired him simply because they enjoyed his company. He would spend hours sitting and talking to these lonely women, but because he was paid by the hour, he was happy to oblige.

Axel and Alex thoroughly enjoyed spending time together again. The two couples spent two or three evenings a week together, usually having dinner and playing bridge. Annie and Katarina had much in common, especially their interest in interior design and in fashion. Both of them could have been runway models, though Katarina was more inclined to wear jeans, while Annie preferred high fashion. The two women could stop traffic when they were walking down the street.

Axel and Alex decided to have a little fun and to see how well their girls knew them.

"Would you care to place a bet on whether they will notice?" Axel asked.

"Well, I don't think that Katarina would be able to tell that I'm not you. She has gotten us mixed up before. I'm less sure whether Annie would be able to tell." Alex elaborated.

"Funny, I feel the opposite. Who hasn't got us mixed up? Well then how about $10 says that Katarina could tell but not Annie," Axel proposed?

"Let's make it $50 or $100 to make it a little more interesting," Alex suggested.

"$100 it is," Axel agreed, and they shook hands.

"How long will we do this?" Alex asked.

"It would have to be for at least twenty-four hours to be a true test," Axel suggested.

"You don't mind if I spend the night with Katarina?" Alex asked, to make sure he understood the rules.

"Not if I get to spend the night with Annie." Axel replied. "I've always wanted her."

"Really," as if he did not know, "well, I've always wanted to be with Katarina," Alex confessed. "Wow! This is going to be fun."

That evening, before dinner, they changed roles. Axel and Alex traded clothing, briefed each other on issues that they would have to understand to pull it off, and then they joined the others for supper. There were no physical differences that would give them away, but on closer examination, perhaps personality traits differed.

Dinner at Alex and Annie's place went fine. Katarina greeted "Axel" with a kiss as he entered the kitchen and Annie slapped "Alex" on his butt. Neither of them appeared to notice the switch. Both Axel and Alex helped out with the dishes so the girls would finish sooner. From time to time they gave their "wives" tender pats and expressed their devotion. The girls looked at each other somewhat skeptically. After dinner, they had coffee in the living room. "Axel" and "Alex" slid down next to their girls and put their arms around them while watching the evening news.

After the news, "Axel" was anxious to go home. "I have a lot of things that need to be done tonight. So whenever you are ready."

When they got into their car, "Axel" could not find his keys. "I bet "Alex" got them. He had to move the car before and probably just put the keys in his pocket by mistake. When he returned with the keys Katarina moved over and kissed him before he pulled out from the driveway. She sat close to him while he was driving, resting her hand on his leg. "I really need to concentrate on my driving here. The street - light is not very good and it would be nice if they painted the yellow lines so one can see where the road ends. It's hard to see where to go.

As soon as "Axel" and Katarina left, "Alex" turned to Annie and took her in his arms.

"Let's raise some hell tonight. What can we do that's really wild and crazy?" he asked.

"Is that an invitation to some mean kinky sex?" she asked, her cheeks blushing slightly.

"Baby, you have a standing invitation . . . pun intended."

"Well, we could go streaking in the shopping mall," Annie suggested jokingly. She cuddled up to him as they stood by the door, feeling his erection.

"I think I'd rather stay home and spend the night with you alone. What do you say about getting into the hot tub and bringing a bottle of wine . . .?" She quieted him when she raised her chin to meet his lips. "Let's put on some nice music . . ."

"How would you like it if I put on a little show for you?" she asked. You always seem to like when I dance for you. Actually, I have something I'd like to show you".

"Honey, I'd love for you to dance for me."

"All right, go into the living room and I'll get ready. Put on some good music." A few minutes later she returned, gliding across the floor to the beat of the music. Her dress was cut low and accented by a fluffy white/blue boa. The dress was not buttoned in her back and slowly slid down as she walked and fell to the floor. Clad in nylons, black panties and a black bra, her spike-heel shoes and a seductive smile, she asked him "What do you think? We got a shipment of these panties in yesterday and I thought you'd like them. Do you think that we should carry them in our stores? They are made in Sweden by someone your mom knows."

"Of course, I love them. The question is more if we should start a store where we only sell sexy underwear rather than mixing it all into one store," "Alex" responded. "Are there more styles?" he asked.

"Yes, just sit there and I'll get them." She tried on several styles of lingerie. Some were cute and others wild. "What do you think about these? They have little messages on them, like here in the heart it says Love . . . and we would add any name."

"So, you give your undies as a gift after an encounter?" he asked, smiling at the thought.

"I guess you could, or it could just be a message to the one you love, like on this one, 'I'm ready,' or, 'I'm hot,' or here, when you're not ready, 'Rain-check please.'" They both laughed.

"I like them, they're unique and fun. How about men's underwear? There could be one saying 'Standing ovation,' he chuckled.

"We'll see. Anyway, people could come up with their own messages, up to six words, and we would sew it on for them. We have a machine that can do it automatically."

She took off the panties and modeled several bras before they got into the shower, and then the tub. "Alex" helped Annie rub in soap on her whole body and sponge it off, and Annie returned the favor. They got into the hot tub and Annie snuggled up with "Alex".

As soon as "Axel" and Katarina arrived home, they ripped off their clothes and fell into bed together. Following an hour of lovemaking, they had a warm shower together, followed by more love making and a second shower. They returned to the living room where "Axel" gave her a full body massage sitting on his knees in front of the couch. Annie loved every second of it. As he moved toward her most sensitive areas, Annie suggested they move into the bed room. It was four in the morning before any of them went to sleep.

Katarina and Annie met for lunch later that day.

"So, how's your love life?" Katarina asked as she responded to Annie's hug.

"Great. It's never been better. Last night was probably the best ever," Annie responded, grinning broadly. "How about you?"

"Fantastic. It's never been better. We made love for six hours last night. I can't believe that they are so stupid that they think that we would not realize that they switched on us," Katarina reflected.

"Well, I thought it was great fun and I don't think we should tell them that we know. To me it was like making love to Alex but a new revised Alex full of energy and desire. These guys are so unbelievably alike, everything, voices, and they even think alike. They both have that dry humor," Annie concluded.

"I know. It is almost scary at times how much alike they are. You know, there were moments when I wasn't sure if they had actually swished or if they were simply acting as if they had," said Katarina.

"Really? That's funny. I felt the same. I was really comfortable with Axel, as if we'd known each other for a long time." Annie shared, offering Katarina some more coffee.

"Well, they both would pass that test. It's funny, they both mispronounce the same words, and they mix up their w's and v's and their y's and j's. But I love their accent and I hope they never change. Like; I yust came back from Havaii. and the veather vas very varm," said Katarina, mimicking the boys with her best Swedish accent.

"I hope they do it again," said Annie. "It was really fun. I modeled a new line of sexy under garments for him and now I'll have to find a way to do it for Alex also, to get his opinion, but based on Axels' enthusiasm, it's a sure thing. Did you and Alex do anything that I should know, not to expose their game?"

"Nothing beyond the regular stuff. Although, he really enjoyed his massage."

Axel and Alex met for lunch and decided to go back to their own identities, but they agreed to do the switch again from time to time, to put fire into their relationships. They concluded that no one had won the bet, as neither of the girls had recognized them. That night they had some of their best lovemaking ever with their own girls.

CHAPTER 37

1975 - Back to Fairbanks

Axel and Katarina decided to take advantage of the equity they had in their home. They sold it and rented an apartment next to their new hardware store while Axel looked for property suitable for constructing a single-family home. Eventually Axel found an old milk farm that had been subdivided. The lot consisted of a six-acre parcel that, in addition to the old milk house, hosted a large barn and a stall. Before long, he was fully occupied with remodeling the milk-house. It was ideal for remodeling; in fact, it reminded him some of the home Axel had worked on in Spring Green. Katarina, who wanted to change careers, began attending nursing school in the evenings. She still tended to the store during the day, and she had plenty of time there to do her homework.

Axel was fully occupied between house painting contracts and remodeling the farm. As he had finished the inside, Katarina and Axel moved in. There was still landscaping and outside painting to be finished. Axel had bought fifty chickens shortly after he bought the farm, and had been feeding them everything and anything that was eatable. He soon realized that he had made a mistake in purchasing fryers instead of egg layers. Not only did they seldom lay eggs, but they grew huge. He began necking some of the roosters, which turned out to be an unpleasant experience. The chickens had been around long enough that they had turned into pets. The roosters all had their unique personalities and some even had names. Katarina refused to eat any of them, and when Alex and Axel tried one, they learned that chickens taste a lot like the feed they eat, which in this case was a little of everything. Further, it appeared that they waited too long to neck them, or they had been getting too much exercise. They were so tough, they were virtually inedible. Eventually Katarina and Axel found a neighbor who was willing to take them off their hands.

Oil prices soared, and it would take up to an hour standing in line at the gas station. The recent oil crises seemed to have slowed commerce. It was different in Fairbanks. The Alyaska Services Corporation was building the Trans Alaska Oil Pipeline.

Katarina and Axel decided to return to Fairbanks that fall. Katarina would continue her studies at the University in Fairbanks. Katarina and a young couple, who had been their neighbors before they moved to the farm house, would drive up ahead in the delivery van. Axel would come later, once he had finished up all business ventures in Seattle.

The drive to Fairbanks was rather uneventful for Katarina and her friends. Axel, on the other hand, met with more challenges during his trip than he had bargained for. He needed a trailer in order to bring everything that they had accumulated in Seattle with him. Eventually he found a boat with a trailer for less than he would have had to pay for the trailer alone. It was a lake boat, with propeller drift, rather than a jet river boat that would have been more useful in Fairbanks. The tandem-wheel trailer seemed strong enough to carry the load. It was designed for a large sailboat. Axel filled the back of his pickup truck on which he had built a camper box, and the boat, with supplies. He had a lot of building supplies left and he did not want to waste anything that could be of any use in Fairbanks. He even tied supplies around the outside of the boat and covered it all with a tarp. He was loaded to the brim, and the trailer shocks appeared to have bottomed out, but Axel figured he could make it as long as he drove slowly. On front of the boat he had propped a wheel barrow with the handles pointing forward giving the whole package the look of a prehistoric monster with two large horns.

Axel first realized that he had overloaded the trailer when he drove down the hill in Renton onto Highway 907. He could not get the truck to stop on the steep hill. Fortunately, he met green lights at both intersections he had to cross. At his first opportunity he stopped and left some of his heavier items behind on the roadside, conjuring up images of nineteenth century wagon train travelers on the Overland Trail.

Axel made it into Canada before he hit a nasty bump in the road that separated him from his right bumper, and that was probably also when the axle on the trailer bent, causing him to drive on the inside edge of the tires rather than where the thread was. This in turn led to one flat tire after another. Axel destroyed a total of eight tires and had to repair three additional flats on the drive to Fairbanks. His biggest challenge was to find the proper tires. In one case he had to drive close to a hundred miles to Fort Nelson to purchase a replacement tire and then back to get his trailer. Half way to the Fireside Inn he lost the remaining fender, and the stabilizer bar between the axles was coming loose, forcing him to tie the axles together with a chain and some wire. Those who drove during the day and slept at night could see this "monster truck" parked alone, *sans* its driver, at different places along the highway as they headed north. They would pass the truck as Axel sought spare tires during the day, and then he would pass them at night, having replaced the flat, only to have to park the truck the next day as he again sought a replacement tire. Axel did not sleep more than an hour at a time. He was too busy getting tires to sleep.

Finally, after four days, he reached the Alaskan border.

The customs officer was friendly and passed him right through. Axel then noticed that the chain holding the axle together was coming loose and that the bracket on the other side was also falling apart. He returned into the customs office and asked an officer if they had a piece of wire that he could have for tightening his chain. Not having slept for four days, with the exception of a few catnaps, Axel's Swedish accent was stronger than usual and the customs officer asked Axel to show his naturalization papers. He did not know where he had put his papers, not having anticipated having to show documentation at the Canadian border.

"I'm an American citizen; I didn't think one needed to bring a passport going through Canada," Axel explained.

"You have to show that you are an American to come into the country," she declared.

"I'm already in the country. I was cleared by that other gentleman. I just came back to ask for a piece of wire," Axel explained.

"You will have to show me your papers," she insisted.

"Look, I have my Alaskan driver's license here. Will that do?" he asked.

"No I want to see your naturalization papers. Anyone can get a driver's license," she noted.

"Here is my military ID. I served two years at Fort Wainwright in Fairbanks, at the 272nd Signal Company. You can call the company and verify that I did," he suggested.

"It's not my job to prove that you are who you say you are. I need to see your naturalization papers."

"So, you are going to make me unpack everything in my truck to find the stupid papers?" Axel was losing his patience with the bureaucrat.

"If that's what it takes. You will not proceed without showing me your papers," she insisted. Axel started unpacking the truck, looking where he thought the papers would be, but to no avail. Eventually he found his box with important documents at the bottom of the boat. He showed the officer his papers. She thanked him and attempted to explain something about how she was only doing her job. Axel walked away from her as she was still speaking. At least he had found some more wire, and a second chain in the process.

Katarina was staying at her parents' home until Axel arrived. She was sitting at the window, on a Sunday morning, looking out; having calculated that he might arrive that day. A heavily loaded pickup truck pulled up in front of the house. It was pulling a strange looking trailer. Everything was covered with mud. A man got out of the truck and walked unsteadily up the driveway. He was also covered with mud. Suddenly Katarina realized that it was Axel. She ran outside, but shrank from hugging him, filthy as he was. Katarina never less greeted him tearfully and urged him into the house, where she prepared a hot bath and a meal for him. Then Katarina encouraged him to lie down in her girlhood bed, where he promptly fell asleep. Twelve hours later, he was not sure if he had been dreaming. When he opened his eyes, he realized that he was now back in Fairbanks.

CHAPTER 38

February, 1976 Going to Europe

Katarina's parents had an apartment in their basement that needed some remodeling, but that was straight up Axel's alley. Katarina and Axel could live there while doing the work. In the meantime, Axel bought a hillside lot and drew up plans for a house. He procured the necessary permits, secured financing, and was all set to begin construction the following spring, as soon as the ground could be excavated. It was mid-December and Axel thought it would be nice to make a trip over to Sweden during the winter to show Katarina his birth-land and to show her off. Katarina was getting a full month off from her school during Christmas and extending into January. This would be the perfect time to go.

They flew from Fairbanks to Anchorage with Alaska Airlines. "They changed a lot here," Axel noted, after having placed his hand luggage in the overhead compartment. "The first time I flew with Alaska Airline was when I came up here with the military. Then the cabin was decorated like a saloon and the stewardesses wore cancan outfits, net stockings and all."

"Yes it's too bad that they don't hang onto fun traditions like that," Katarina agreed.

Axel had a lot to show Katarina during their short stay in Gothenburg, including making a trip out to Kungalv's Fortress, and to Marstrand, where Axel had spent a lot of time growing up. The weather was not inviting. It was windy and cold, and they cut their stay on Marstrand short. However, they did take the time to hike up to the Bastille and to see the cave where Axel had played, as a child, and where he had discovered that there was more to girls than silliness. They slowly drove past the home where Axel had spent several summers. They drove past a textile factory that had been a brewery, when Axel was a boy. There was a large sign by the guarded gate that identified it as Yvonne's. "Hey, I remember you told me about her, being a friend of mom's."

"I never told you that. But I recognize the name from some underwear I got in Annie's shop."

Suddenly Axel remembered that it was actually Annie who had told him about Yvonne's business during his and Alex's identity switch.

"It's amazing how clean it is everywhere. Everything seems so well maintained and groomed, the forests, the farmer's fields, people's yards. It's like being in a park." said Katarina. "Look there! White picket fences and how neatly trimmed the hedges are." There was no old equipment sitting around like one would find in many yards in Fairbanks. Fairbanksans were very sentimental about their old cars and equipment and would proudly display them in their yards.

Katarina and Axel had decided to meet friends from Fairbanks in Stockholm. Ernie had left the army, against all odds. Unable to resist the lucrative offer extended by an airline he accepted a position as a commercial pilot. Therefore, was able to fly standby with his wife Jenny for next to nothing. They all stayed at the Lord Nelson, a small but nice hotel in Stockholm's old town. It was conveniently located in the middle of the tourist district, and close to the subway.

"They said on the radio that a passenger plane had crashed after takeoff yesterday in England," Axel informed them, while enjoying his hard-crusted breakfast rolls.

"Do they really have to explain that to the Swedes," Katarina teased Axel. "It really couldn't crash before takeoff, could it?"

"Funny, funny." Axel returned to his continental breakfast.

"Isn't it beautiful here?" Katarina asked no one in particular.

"Yes," Jenny agreed," but what is this that the Swedes can't spank their children, that it's against the law?" Jenny asked curiously.

"Yes, it's a bit absurd. The concept is that one should not intimidate children, that they are people, too, and should not be belittled or spanked. Yet they have a big problem with juvenile delinquency. For some reason they don't seem to see the relationship there," Katarina mused.

"What's the point in being a child if you can't be belittled?" Ernie asked.

"Well, I think they are mainly trying to avoid child abuse," Axel explained.

"Well, they go much further than that, though. One can't spank a child at all, or even make the child feel bad."

"It's true. I agree that they got a little carried away with that one," Axel agreed.

"That's really weird," Jenny replied. "It is a lot nicer for everyone, and safer for the children if they are firmly told not to do some things, like touching a hot stove, and giving them a light spank on the fingers surely is better than the child's getting burned."

"You're not getting any arguments from me," said Axel, now finishing of his breakfast with a warm, flaky, Danish sweet roll.

"Yes, and they do the same thing with their prisoners. They're not to be punished, only rehabilitated," Katarina explained.

"Do they have a lot of crime here?" Ernie asked.

"They have a fair amount of crime considering that the living standard is high for everyone. They don't have many murders, as guns are not common here. They have white collar crimes and domestic crimes and some robberies and break-ins. It's pretty easy to get off, though. To get convicted one almost has to admit to the crime. If two people robbed a bank and one fired a gun and each blamed each other, both would go free rather than taking the risk of punishing the innocent."

"That just goes to show you," Jenny concluded.

The two couples toured Stockholm for a couple more days before taking the train to Gothenburg for two more days of sightseeing. They continued on the train down to Hälsingborg where the train rolled onto a ferry that carried them over to Hälsingör in Denmark. They stayed on the train going to Copenhagen where they spent a couple days sightseeing, touring the Carlsborg Beer brewery and, of course, they strolled down the promenade street down town. Ernie was especially amused by exit and entrance signs. In Swedish or Danish they read 'infart' and 'outfart.' Ernie insisted on having his photo taken by one of the 'infart' signs. He could understand an 'outfart,' he said, but he just could not picture an 'infart.' Axel's statement that he favored driving south through Europe on the German Autobahns because they had 'free fart', sent Ernie into a fit of laughter.

In Copenhagen they took the city tour by bus and saw some amazing architectural feats. They saw Copenhagen's harbor, home of the little mermaid who sat on a rock. Unfortunately, the famous statue had been vandalized, decapitated, and workers were preparing for an operation to reattach her head. The group continued to the royal palace to witness the changing of the guard. The serious young men, in their red uniforms, marched in their tall black bearskin hats, lifting their legs high like toy soldiers engaging in an elaborate process each time they changed direction.

The Tivoli Gardens was closed, but the couples strolled to the red-light district of Newhavn. There were many people out on the streets, most young adults and appeared to be drunk. Axel speculated that these were probably Swedes who had come over to benefit from the more liberal Danish liquor policy. There were numerous bars, tobacco shops and strip-clubs, massage parlors and tattoo parlors, all advertising their services outside the buildings.

The "punks" were decorated in every imaginary way. Most of them had partly shaved heads with rest of their hair standing straight out, in all the colors of the rainbow. They had chains and rings going through ears and noses and other creative places. Their clothing matched their hairstyles and jewelry perfectly. The punks added color to their surroundings, and there were plenty of them. Frankly, their behavior was less intimidating than that of many of the rowdy drunken Swedes that had crossed the sound for the cheaper Danish alcohol.

Ernie and Axel wanted to visit a strip club. They entered the Kitty Katt Club were large pictures of beautiful nude or sexily-dressed girls covered the walls in the entrance. The girls performed on a small raised stage in the center of the room, right next to their table. The girls were beautiful, in their early twenties and probably of Asian heritage. They were naked except for a silk scarf that they played with. The Asian girls were followed by three white girls. They were all beautiful and had perfect bodies. They entered dressed in schoolgirl outfits and pranced around the floor before beginning to undress each other.

"Don't you have an outfit like that Jenny?" Ernie asked. "It seems like you used to."

"I used to, but I don't think that I saved it. It didn't look quite that sexy on me, if I remember right."

"Well, you better look for it when we get home," Ernie advised her.

Two girls dressed in mini-dresses, halter tops and high black boots came out in the spot light. They followed the same routine, undressing each other.

"I wonder if these performers are couples, or if they only get together for the act?" Jenny whispered.

"I bet they are couples, lesbians for sure," Ernie speculated. They seem a little indifferent to what they are doing." They all laughed, before being asked to be quiet during the show.

Later the two couples went to a club called the Tomahawk. Here they also had male performers. The young men wore Indian outfits and removed their garments to the beat of Indian drums. The dancers would remove all their clothing on the stage, but with little interaction with the other dancers. Most acts were single performance acts. The girls got a kick out of seeing the male strippers, and the guys enjoyed watching the girls' reaction. Otherwise Ernie and Alex preferred the first place they went to.

"I would have expected the guys to have a hard on," Katarina commented.

"Maybe for the first five hundred times they did," Axel suggested.

"I know that I would, if I was doing it," said Ernie.

"Me too," Axel agreed.

"Well, who wants to go and watch a bunch of limp limbs?" Jenny muttered, shrugging her shoulders.

The couples stayed at the Club Tomahawk until they called it a night and returned to their rooms.

The following day the couples boarded the ferry to Amsterdam. They spent most of the day playing bridge on the upper deck. "Well how do you feel today?" Axel asked. "We stayed up quite late last night."

"Yes, or early this morning," Jenny replied.

"Well, did Denmark live up to your expectations?" Axel asked.

"Yes, I liked Denmark, in particular the lesbian strip show," Ernie grinned. "Wow."

"Yes, not bad at all," Axel agreed.

"We had some of our best sex ever after we got to our room," Ernie announced.

"I came four times." Jenny confirmed.

"Really Jenny?" Katarina blurted out. Everyone laughed.

"We did pretty well ourselves. I open with one no trump," Axel bid, proceeding with the bridge game.

"What show did you like the best Jenny?" Katarina asked. "It's your turn Ernie."

"Well, the Tomahawk was not bad. I would have expected the guys to be larger than they were though," Jenny confessed.

"Me too," Katarina concurred. "I would have expected at least a foot long." Everyone laughed.

"A foot long . . . they were guys, not bulls," Axel protested.

"Well length isn't the most important anyway, right honey?" Ernie asked.

alright, dear," Jenny responded in a patronizing voice.

"It's how you use it that matters, right?"

"Yes honey."

"What about the lesbian show? Any comments?" Axel asked.

"I loved it," Ernie responded.

"I knew you would, but I was more thinking about the girls. Katarina, what did you think? Did it turn you on?" Ernie asked.

"Well yes, it did. Right in front of you like that. Yes, it did. The girls were so cute and they really seemed to enjoy their work. Imagine having to do that every day."

"In Amsterdam's red-light district they have live sex shows," Ernie informed them, "boy, I can't wait to see one of them. Two diamonds. I bid two diamonds," he repeated.

"How could it be more live than what we saw?" Katarina asked.

"A man and a woman having sex on stage," Ernie clarified.

"What about you Jenny? What did you think about the lesbian show?" Axel asked, raising his eyebrows.

"Well, it was interesting. Yes, I got turned on when she laid down in front of us. I was fantasizing last night about how it would feel to be in her place. Two hearts," Jenny bid.

"Now wait a minute someone is lying, there aren't that many points in a deck that we can all bid like this," Katarina declared. "Four clubs. You know, I've been to strip clubs before, but not like they did it there. It was definitely a turn on. I think at that point I was ready to strip myself," Katarina chuckled.

"I know," said Jenny. "What about you Axel? Would you strip in front of a bunch of cheering ladies?"

"In a heartbeat. If there was a bunch of females who wanted me, whom I was turning on, I would do a rain dance that would open the sky."

"Me too," Ernie chimed in. "That would be the ultimate turn on."

"Well you can strip for me any time you like," Katarina volunteered.

"No, that's not good enough. You also have to want me," said Ernie.

"I want you sweetheart," Jenny assured him. "Pass"

"I know, honey, and I love you too," Ernie replied affectionately. "Five clubs."

"But how do I know if you really love me or if you just like to show off that you have good taste?" Jenny asked jokingly.

"I guess that will be my secret to insure that I will never be taken for granted," Ernie responded.

Upon their arrival, they took a bus to the central station of Amsterdam. Their hotel was close by. It was an older building, like most buildings down town, but it had all the modern conveniences, including bathrooms in their rooms. They walked down to the canal and joined a city tour canal ride. It was darkening outside. They found a nice restaurant with sidewalk tables where they had their dinner, and enjoyed watching the variety of people walking by. There seemed to be even more punks in Amsterdam than in Denmark. These young people did not subscribe to the theory of "the less makeup, the better."

After dinner and a catnap, the group was ready to do the town. They walked over to the red light district, only a couple blocks from their hotel. It was everything they had expected. The girls were sitting in rooms with large windows facing the street. The rooms were illuminated like display windows in department stores, exposing the merchandise. Some girls were sitting around talking to friends, or reading books while others were knitting. When the girls got a customer they simply pulled the curtain shut. Some of the lightly dressed woman also stood outside, flirting with passersby.

Several strip joints featured live sex on Stage. They chose one place that had pictures of the performers on display. They seemed young and attractive. The "theater" was not large; perhaps thirty chairs were lined up in three rows before a small raised stage. The audience was firmly instructed to remain completely silent during the performance. A young couple entered the stage. They were both blond and shaved. They went about their act without excessive emotions. The whole show took perhaps ten minutes.

A second couple did a strip act before having sex. They entered the stage in street clothes dancing to soft music. The girl had her arms around his neck and he began unbuttoning her blouse while still dancing seductively. He unhooked her skirt and let it drop to the floor. She wore nothing underneath it. She was now dressed in only a black bra, still dancing. He removed her bra, and they kept dancing, he fully dressed and she naked. They finished their act somewhat mechanically it seemed. The final act involved two couples. They started out sitting on a couch necking, and then unbuttoned and removed their clothing. They completed their act after having swapped partners.

Ernie wanted to go to another place but Katarina was worn out and ready for bed, so the couples split up. Ernie and Jenny continued their evening on town, while Katarina and Axel returned to their room.

The following morning, they met for breakfast before Ernie and Jenny flew on to Greece.

"Well how was your evening? "Axel asked as he buttered a piece of toast.

"Fantastic," Ernie grinned. "We went to a couple more shows, it was great. We even stopped at one window where there were two girls sitting and we had our own private show. They did whatever we asked them to do. It was absolutely fantastic."

"What did you think about it Jenny?" Katarina asked.

"It was really exciting. I think it is healthy to be really bad sometimes, and this was bad," she confessed. "And I enjoyed watching."

"Wow," Axel stuttered, "your lucky son of a bitch!"

"Then at one place they had an amateur contest. Ernie and I entered and, you are not going to believe this, but we won."

"You're kidding, you must be . . .," said the perplexed Axel.

"No, no, no. We got up there and we borrowed the act from that dancing couple we saw together. We first danced together while Ernie began to unbutton my blouse and unhook my bra. Then he undid my belt and let the skirt fall. Boy, I was getting hot. I could have had sex right there on the stage right then. He removed my blouse, bra and my underpants, it was a little awkward to get them off while we were dancing, but we managed. We danced for a while, I was stark naked, and Ernie was still fully dressed. . . well you have seen the act, you know how it goes."

"I can't believe you did that in front of an audience . . ."

"The audience was very appreciative and supportive," Ernie explained.

"We were offered a contract to stay and work there. The pay wasn't the greatest, but the fringe benefits were great."

"Now I know that you're putting us on," Axel laughed.

"Coffee anyone?" Katarina offered, passing the thermos.

"So now you've been to Sweden, to Denmark and to The Netherlands. What country did you like the best?" Axel asked.

"Hard to say. Amsterdam is definitely a fun city. It's international and I appreciate all the freedoms here . . . and it's pretty," said Ernie. "But Copenhagen was really nice too, but not quite as fun as Amsterdam, and not quite as beautiful as Stockholm or Gothenburg."

"If I was going to choose a place to live in, I would probably choose Sweden," Axel responded, "but if I were going to choose a place to have fun, Amsterdam would come first, and Copenhagen second. If I chose a place for its food, either Denmark or Sweden would win."

"I would choose Sweden for sure," Jenny concluded.

"I agree. Sweden for sure, especially if you have a family," Katarina interjected.

"Yes, if you don't mind a bunch of spoiled undisciplined brats running around," said Axel.

"Well, you didn't turn out too bad," Katarina reminded him.

"Touché," Axel replied. "But that's only because you like it when I'm bad," he said suggestively. They all laughed.

Axel and Katarina had only four days left of their vacation and had decided to travel to London to visit with John and Lisa. Not so much because Axel was all that fond of them. He hardly knew them, he had not seen them since he was a toddler, but he had heard about Lisa from Annika. It was also nice to have a place to stay. The hotel costs were cutting into their travel budget. The cheaper hotels often did not have bathrooms in the rooms, and especially Katarina did not appreciate going down the hall to the toilet in the middle of the night, not knowing who she would encounter.

They boarded the train to Calais, where they caught the ferry to Dover. They had called Lisa and John and were expected. When they got off the ferry, they were paged to come to the ticket counter where a chauffeur-dressed gentleman was waiting for them. He introduced himself as Roger, the driver for Mr. Billy Jones, a friend of Lisa and John, and explained that he would take them to Lisa's and John's place and/or wherever else they would like to go. He explained that they were the guests of Mr. Jones. He helped them with their luggage and showed them the way to a shiny Rolls Royce. The car was beautiful inside and out. The seats were made of soft leather and it was black and silver color. Soft music came from somewhere behind their head rests. The ride was smooth and quiet. The driver explained that he would be at their disposal as long as they were in Britain. He said that his employer was a good friend of Lisa and John and that he also knew Annika way back in time, before Axel was born. He told them that his employer, Mr. Jones, would be out of the country for two more days but was hoping he would get to meet them before the left.

CHAPTER 39

1976 – Lisa and John and Billy

John and Lisa lived in a beautiful Tudor home in Covey, not far from London. Lisa and John were gracious hosts and did everything they could to make their guests feel welcome and enjoy their stay. Of course, they enjoyed listening to Axel's stories about what he had been doing and about how the family was. Axel and Katarina met Margarete, their daughter and Prince Charles, their Siamese cat, or PC as the family called him.

"So you have only been here for two days and you are already beginning to speak like a true Englishman," Lisa commented.

"Thank you, I think. Actually, I don't think that I've developed much of an American accent yet. If I have an accent, it's probably Swedish. You sure have a lovely home here. It's absolutely beautiful," said Axel.

"Yes, we like it here. Unfortunately, our schedules don't permit us to spend as much time here as we'd like, but we love it here whenever we can be here. How do you like Alaska?" John asked, adding, "It's so far away from everything and everyone, don't you think?" John asked. "I wouldn't mind visiting there but of all the places to live, I don't think that it would be among my top choices. What is it that attracts you?" he asked.

"I'm not sure," Axel responded, "Well besides the obvious, having the most beautiful girl in the world living there," he winked at Katarina, "I like the open spaces and the more relaxed attitude of the people who live there. I like the climate in that there is almost always sunshine. We have a desert climate, being protected by mountain ridges around us. I don't like when it is hot and that is not a problem in Fairbanks."

"Yes, but what about the cold?" Lisa interrupted.

"It is really not that bad because it's a dry cold. We seldom have any winds there and therefore the cold there is normally easier to take than, for example, the windy raw cold in Seattle that goes right through you no matter what you put on."

"Do you fish or hunt?" John asked. He passed the tea pot.

"No, not really. I don't care much for sweet water fish. They all have too many bones in them, and some taste quite fishy on top of that. I do like salmon, if it's not fishy. The problem is that by the time they come to the interior, they're already half dead and the quality is not the best. They taste really fishy. I do like sea fishing though. Halibut is my favorite. No bones about it and it doesn't taste like fish."

"Yes, I've seen movies about people catching halibut that are larger than themselves, and sometimes as large as seven, eight hundred pounds. That would fill up a freezer in a hurry, wouldn't it?" John concluded. "Perhaps we'll come to Alaska someday to go fishing."

"If you do, make sure you come and visit us. Our house is nothing compared to this, but we still have plenty of room."

"Who knows, we just might," Lisa responded.

"We also have another seafood specialty," Katarina contributed, "the Alaska King Crab. They get quite large, more than four feet."

"Boy, how would you like to meet one of them when you go swimming?" Lisa asked.

"Well, they hang out in the Kodiak Island area where the water is rather frigid and not real inviting for going swimming," said Katarina.

"There is something special about that area that makes everything extremely large. Their brown bears, or grizzlies, as they are known, are the largest bears in the world. They are more than twice the size of our interior grizzlies," Axel explained.

"Sounds like the setting for a science fiction movie," John suggested.

The guest room, like the rest of the home was exquisite. It was tastefully furnished in light oak furniture including a king-size round waterbed. The waterbed took a little to get used to. Each time one of them moved the other would move along for the ride, including having to listen to the clucking sound of swishing water.

"Well what do you think so far?" Axel asked Katarina as she plunged into the bed, almost tossing Axel out on the other side.

"Careful, he cautioned her, we wouldn't want the bed to burst. That would be quite a disaster."

"Could it really? Boy, I would hope not . . . I love it here and Lisa and John are so nice. This is living. They must be doing quite well living in a mansion like this," Katarina speculated.

"Well, they are both doctors, but wait until tomorrow when we go to see Billy's place, I understand he lives in a palace."

"It will be fun. What was that Lisa said about Billy and your mother?" Katarina asked, while turning off the light.

"Well I'm not really sure, but I know John and Billy came to Sweden on a British war ship and met Mom and Lisa and Camilla at Liseberg. The following day they were supposed to meet again, but because Germany attacked Poland, their ship left early and they have never met again since. John told me that Billy still has a thing for mom, after all these years."

"Boy, she must have left a lasting impression on him."

"You know what else he told me? But you will have to promise not to tell anyone."

"Of course."

"John told me that he is sure Billy is the one who has been sending Mom a red rose every month for the last twenty years. He said that no one knows that he knows, besides Lisa. He said that he is sure Lisa has helped him pull it off. He said that he has no clue about why Billy doesn't come forward, but . . . he thinks it's too bad because he knows how much Billy loves her. He also said that he is tempted to set a trap to get them together."

"That is so sad. Billy has everything that money can buy but he can't have the one thing he wants the most, Annika's love," Katarina sympathized.

"Yes, it is strange, because Billy could not possibly have got to where he is without pushing some weight around at times. Still he does nothing to make this wish come true."

"Perhaps that's the reason, your romantic fool. He can buy or arrange anything he wants, but a love that is bought or arranged is not a true love and has no meaning. Perhaps he is still hoping that by some miracle their time will come," Katarina speculated.

"Perhaps."

"He asked me if Annika was happy with Torsten. I didn't know what to say. You know Annika complains about a lot of things Torsten does, but at the same time she looks up to him. He treats her well, but in a businesslike manner. You rarely hear him say anything affectionate to her. And the same goes for her. I have never seen her do anything affectionate toward him. As opposed to us, we like to cuddle and neck at every opportunity, right?" he teased her.

"Right," she said while reaching over to pinch him.

"She often makes these little romantic evening sandwiches and wine for the two of them, but it always seems so formal. They sit on each side of the table with everything in its proper place. Then they go into the living room for coffee and Torsten always sits in his favorite chair until he falls asleep. They never do anything spontaneous. They never neck on the couch or anywhere else, either, I would guess. I guess Mom was a little wilder when she was younger. Anyway, is that love or is it a convenient relationship? I'm not sure, but it would not do for me," he concluded.

"Me neither," Katarina agreed. "To me it's important to feel loved and to feel needed and desired. And it's important to do something spontaneous now and then. Routines may be good for a lot of things, but not for your love life."

"Yes, I agree," said Axel.

"They are comfortable with each other, but they don't seem to be in love. There is no passion in their relationship," Katarina concluded.

"There is no guarantee that a relationship with Billy would offer anything different. Although, sending her the red roses for over twenty years certainly is a positive indicator of healthy passion, at least on Billy's side. That's not to say that I would want to take part in rearranging her marriage," said Axel.

"Of course not, but one can always let the spark glow, just in case. Things could change," Katarina suggested.

After they had passed the main gate to Billy's estate, they had to drive another ten, fifteen minutes before they came to the main building. It was a castle indeed and an impressive one at that. There were three other Rolls Royce's and a few sport cars parked on the side of the road. Billy came out to greet them. He gave both a warm hug and he seemed a little choked up when he hugged Axel. "Welcome, welcome," he greeted them. "It's jolly good to see you. I hope Roger has been taking good care of you. I must apologize for not having been able to see you before. It was a matter that could not wait."

"Please Sir . . ."

"Please, just call me Billy. I don't care much for a lot of formalities. As I'm sure you know, your mother and I are very special friends, and I hope we can be too. You must feel like you are at home here, and if there is anything you need or would like to have, please help yourself or ask someone for assistance."

"Well thank you so much, you have already been more than generous . . . chauffeuring us around London, and Roger insisting on paying for everything."

"It only makes me happy if I get to do something for Annika's children. She has a very special place in my heart, and you are part of her. So please do not mention anything about the bloody cost. It's not a factor. I'm very happy that you could come."

"Well, so are we," Katarina interjected.

"I'd like to get to know you and I would enjoy it if we could have dinner together tonight."

"Of course, that would be very nice," Axel replied.

"Oh, excuse me. This is Li and Amy. They are my right hand and stay with me most of the time. Ladies please meet Axel and Katarina. Axel is one of Annika's sons," he explained.

"Nice to meet you," Axel grinned and gently touched their hands.

"Would you like to have supper here tonight? Perhaps you are tired, or would you prefer someplace else? There are many nice establishments to choose among."

"Whatever you like will be perfect for us," Axel assured him.

"Well there is this place in Seaford, close to Brighton, that is pretty nice. All right, how about a cup of tea on the veranda, then you could rest for an hour and we will leave from here at 5:15. Would that be all right?" Billy asked.

"That will be perfect," Katarina and Axel confirmed. They followed him through the main building and out on the veranda. The veranda had an exclusive view of the city of Worthing and the ocean beyond. Billy told them about that evening in Gothenburg with Annika and about his experience as a prisoner of war for four days. Axel and Katarina told him about Alaska and other things.

"The reservation is confirmed, and the flight plan is filed," Li informed Billy.

"Thanks Li." He also told them about some of his more interesting business affairs. They had a good time together and Billy also gave them a quick tour of the estate. At 5:15, there was a helicopter waiting in the front yard.

"It really isn't that far to where we're going, but I thought you might enjoy a sightseeing tour from a bird's view."

"Super, thank you very much, it will be great fun," Axel assured Billy. He bent forward slightly as he walked under the blades even though they were not yet spinning. Axel and Katarina were joined by Billy and his right hand. Billy told them about everything they flew over. He was well informed, but then again, he probably owned much of it. There was a dock by the restaurant where they landed.

"This place has the best fish," Billy informed them, "but they also have terrific steaks, but nothing like your Swedish hotdogs," he joked.

"You're a hotdog fan like me? That's funny. That's one thing that I miss in Alaska, the Swedish hotdog vendors. They have nothing like it there," said Axel.

"I was sold that night when I met your mother in Gothenburg. I remember it well. I had a full special with two grilled hotdogs on top of creamy mashed potatoes served on a bun, and topped with their special mustard and catsup and a heap of sliced spicy pickles." They all laughed at his enthusiasm about the hotdog.

"Now you made me really hungry," Katarina confessed.

"Good."

The hostess greeted them at the door. "Good evening Mr. Jones. Your table is ready." She also smiled warmly at the others. "I put two bottles of Chardonnay and a carafe of house Alibassi burgundy on your table, will that suffice?" she asked. Amy handed Billy a slip.

"For now, yes . . . Thank you. Amy, tell the ambassador that I will see him on Thursday. You know, one place where I often go, serves La Garonne as their white house wine. It is one of the cheapest wines on the market, but I think it's one of the best. Not too sweet and not too dry. Normally I only drink Alibassi wines, because I have some personal interest in the winery."

Billy had aged to his advantage. He was in good physical shape. His white wavy hair was neatly combed backwards and contrasted with a deep tan. He had friendly eyes and a warm smile. He carried himself with self-confidence and seemed to be at peace with himself. "It is too bad that you are leaving so soon. I have a couple temperament full Arabians at the stable that you might enjoy taking for a ride. How about tomorrow morning? Would you care to join me?" Billy asked.

"I'd love to. I haven't been on a horse for a while, but there is a funny story, I actually inherited six horses that I cared for when I worked at a stable in Chicago. The owner, an older widowed lady, gave me her horses at her passing. I had to sell them as I did not have the resources, nor the need, to keep them."

"That's great," Billy chuckled. I will have some riding clothes at your room by the morning. What size do you take in boots?" Billy asked.

"Size twelve."

"Hmm... that's impressive." Li made a call and nodded affirmatively.

"Have you ever been to Alaska?" Axel asked.

"No.... not yet. Seems so far away. I'm not much of a hunter or fisherman," Billy confessed. "I have some interests in California and a modest operation in Seattle. I have been to Victoria, a real beautiful city on Vancouver Island, but that is about as far north as I have been on that side of the globe."

"May I ask why you haven't kept up the friendship with Mom when you clearly have some special feelings for her?" Axel asked. He refilled his wine glass, as well as Katarina's.

"Well that is the problem. I do have special feelings for her and I do not want to do anything that might add confusion to her life."

PART VI

CHAPTER 40

1977 Annika and Billy

The spring came early, and Axel got a good start on his construction project. He finished the first home in mid-August and started a second home that he completed during the winter. He found a newly developed south slope subdivision, which was free from permafrost. The area had been cleared some thirty years before by an eccentric owner that intended to raise buffaloes on the property. The property had a beautiful view of the city and of the Alaska Range beyond. The lots were perfect for his purpose. He chose a prime lot for his and Katarina's own home and commenced construction.

"Axel, what do you think about getting a dog? My sister, Angela, just got a German Short Haired Pointer, and she is so cute. They have one more female that needs a home. What do you think?" Katarina asked while sitting down for breakfast.

"Sure, if that's what you want, but you realize that it will be a lot of work and she will make it more difficult for us to travel," Axel cautioned her.

"Angela can take care of her if we go somewhere. Or perhaps Molly and Jenny would like to. They might even like to house-sit, so they can use our indoor plumbing."

"Perhaps. What are we going to call her?" Axel asked. "How about Starlet?"

"There is no way that I will call her after a strip joint. She shall have a classy name, in case we want to show her. How about naming her . . . Karenina, after Tolstoy's Anna Karenina? That's a cool, classy name."

"I'm not sure it sounds like a dog's name, but . . . whatever. How about Sweet Anna Karenina?" Axel suggested.

"It makes her sound a little like a racehorse, but I like that name. OK. Sweet Anna Karenina is, or Kanina for short."

"How about naming her 'SAK' for short?" Axel inquired, jokingly.

"Kanina," Katarina declared, giving him an "are you for real?" look.

"Why don't we run by Molly and Jenny's place tonight?" Axel proposed. "We haven't seen them since we got back from Europe. Let's pick up a basket of chicken and go out to see them. If they aren't at home, we just have chicken tomorrow also."

There didn't appear to be anyone there when Axel and Katarina pulled up their long driveway, but their golden mini-truck was there, and several dogs were barking. They walked around the back side and saw steam coming out of the new sauna. Axel knocked on the sauna door and Molly called out "who is it?"

"Hi! It's us, Axel and Katarina." Axel opened the door and was hit by a burst of steam. It was a spacious sauna. There was easily room for ten adults.

"Hi guys, you're back already? How was the trip?" Jenny wrapped a towel around herself and stood up to give them a welcome hug. "Why don't you join us for a sauna?" Molly offered. We just got in. What do you think? We finished it up today. This is the first time we've use it."

"Well, it seems to work just fine," Katarina replied. "It must be one hundred and twenty degrees in here, at least. All right, sure why not, Axel? We'll be right back." They went inside the cabin to undress. They wrapped themselves in towels and returned to the sauna. Molly was splashing water on the hot lava rocks, steaming up the sauna and making it even hotter. The bleachers were too hot to sit on, bare skinned, but it was all right sitting on the towel.

"So how was the trip?" Molly repeated, "you had a good time?"

"It was great. We had a wonderful time. We met up with the Wilders in Sweden, you know Jenny and Ernie. Yes, the other Jenny, and spent a few days together with them in Gothenburg and Stockholm, and then we took the train to Amsterdam, stopping at Copenhagen on the way down. It was a once-in-a-lifetime experience," Katarina explained enthusiastically. "I loved Stockholm! It was so pretty there! Copenhagen was neat too. A little wilder than Sweden."

"What do you mean, wilder?"

"Oh, we went to Newhavn, the red-light district of Copenhagen, and we saw a few live sex shows and boy, there was no holding back there. You guys would probably have liked the lesbian shows. They did everything imaginable, a few feet in front of us." Axel explained, lifting his eyebrows.

"Maybe," said Molly. "Were they pretty or old and . . .?"

"Pretty, they were gorgeous," Axel assured her. "And sometimes there were several of them at the same time."

"And Amsterdam was even worse, or better, if you like. They had live sex shows with males too. It was pretty hot," Katarina explained. "Yes, and the girls were lined up, sitting half naked in their display-windows, waiting for customers."

"Yea, those Amsterdameans, and also the Germans have always been quite liberal both with sex and with drugs. My kind of people," Molly added. "Did you see the hot tub behind?"

"Yes, it looked very nice. You guys have been busy," Axel noted.

"Are you ready for the tub?" Jenny asked.

"All right," Axel agreed. The warm water poured over the rim when all four got in to the steamy tub.

That fall, in 1978, Annika called Axel, Alex and Annette to let them know that Torsten had suffered from a stroke and was in intensive care. They all rushed to Stockholm, but by the time they arrived, Torsten had already passed away. The boys helped Annika with the funeral arrangements and after much discussion they decided that Annika would move to Alaska. Axel would add on an apartment to his house. Two weeks later, whatever of Annika's belongings that she had not offered for sale at an auction or given to charity, was packed into a container and on their way to Fairbanks, Alaska, USA.

As it turned out, Annika would not receive Torsten's pension. It would go to his first wife. Although the document stated that the pension was to go to Torsten's spouse, Torsten had neglected to change the names in his policy when he divorced, and the policy had his first wife's name on it and she was therefore found to be the rightful benefactor. Annika would have been in dire financial straits had it not been for her Guardian Angel. As it was, Annika was financially independent. She also received a modest pension from the Swedish state.

Annika stayed in one of Axel and Katarina's guest rooms until her apartment was completed in the spring of 1979. In the winter of 1979-1980 Axel and Katarina decided to get a motor home and drive down the Alaska Highway, down the west coast to San Diego and Mexico.

Axel and Katarina realized that they took a big risk bringing Annika along on their motor home trip, but they did not feel that they could leave her behind either. The plan was to leave her with Alex and Annie in Seattle on their way down, and to pick her up on the way back. Alex was reluctant to have her stay for two full weeks, because he knew that Annika was not particularly fond of Annie. She was a career woman, rather than staying home and taking care of Alex and children, and she always dressed too provocatively, according to Annika. Alex also had to work, which would mean that Annika would be spending a lot of time on her own, but it would have to work out, he figured.

It was five degrees below zero, when they left Fairbanks. By the time they got to Delta Junction, one hundred miles straight east, it was twenty below zero. A hundred miles later, at Tok, the temperature had dropped ten more degrees to minus 30 degrees. And at the Canadian border it was minus 40F. [and C, as the two systems meet there]. Axel was hoping that they would make it to Whitehorse, in Yukon Territory, the first day. They would spend the night there at a motel because it was too cold to sleep in the motor home.

They had gotten off to an early start from Fairbanks, but it was a fourteen-hour drive to Whitehorse and they did not expect to arrive until nine in the evening, if all went well. In order to save time, Katarina was standing at the stove, warming taco meat, which she had prepared at home, on the motor home stove, while Axel was driving. Suddenly a rabbit ran in to the road, hesitated and turned his head back and forth, trying to decide which direction to turn as Axel sped toward him. Axel hit the breaks to avoid hitting the rabbit, causing Katarina to lose her balance and the taco meat pot to go "airborne, coating much of the interior of the motor home, including the shag carpet, with taco meat. The motor home was not designed for the extreme cold of the north and not much functioned. The gas pedal would stick to the floor making it necessary for Axel to stick his foot in underneath to lift it. The windshield defroster did not work and Axel continuously had to scrape ice of the windshield to see out. The poorly insulated walls began to build ice layers at the corners, and other spots where the insufficient heat did not reach. The taco sauce froze on the walls, ceiling and floor. The steering had become stiff, requiring both hands to turn the steering wheel. It was stressful driving, but they made it to Whitehorse only an hour off schedule.

They now had to make an important decision. They could continue to go south for the next four days under similar driving conditions, or they could double back to Haines Junction, about one hundred fifty miles, and cross the mountains over to Haines, in Alaska, where they could board the ferry and have a nice trip down the Alaska coast. The problem was that the ferry would leave the following day at 5:30. If they missed that one, there would not be another one leaving Haines for one week, and they would lose two days going to Haines and back to Whitehorse, after which they still have to drive four more days to Seattle.

They decided to try to make the ferry. The temperature had dropped to -55 degrees by the time they left Whitehorse. The condition of the motor home had not improved under the night. If anything, it had worsened. They were relieved to hear the motor home start up in the morning. The outlet had functioned as had the heater on the motor home. Otherwise the oil would have been as thick as molasses and the motor would not have turned over. The sun was shining bright, which was uplifting, but it reflected on the frozen windshield making it next to impossible to see out. The first part of the trip went rather smoothly, in spite of the driving conditions, but when they approached the higher elevations, crossing the mountains between Haines and Haines Junction the weather turned bad and heavy snow was falling. Travelers checked in at several check points between Haines and Haines Junction, and plow trucks continually drove back and forth to clear the road. Stakes, like slalom poles on either side of the road helped Axel see where to drive in the whiteout conditions. The wind-built snow drifts in only a few minutes so one had to drive fast enough not to get stuck in a snow drift. To add to stress, on a few occasions when the snow let up some, they could see that they were driving close to a steep drop off on their starboard side. They were also driving against the clock.

Shortly after they reentered the US, as they drove around a sharp bend in the road, they encountered a rock slide. There was no way Axel could avoid hitting the rocks and they ended up crushing the muffler. The weather had turned dramatically warmer on the coast side of the mountains, and the snow was turning to slush. The wet snow splattered onto the engine, and somehow blocked the exhaust, making the engine sputter. It was an exhausted and relieved Axel who finally drove up to the ferry terminal, making his presence known with his broken muffler, fifteen minutes before the scheduled departure time.

The three-day trip on the ferry down the Alaskan and the Canadian coast was heavenly compared to the previous two days of driving. The ferry ran close enough to the shore that they could observe the wildlife on shore. They also saw several killer wales, seals and dolphins, playing games in the wake from the ferry. The captain announced each time there was something special to view. It was a relaxing trip; Annika was occupied with her knitting and Katarina and Axel read a couple books. Axel and Annika also passed the time solving Swedish crossword puzzles, with some clues found in pictures. They had made copies of the ones they found in Annika's Swedish magazines, and they would compete to solve the puzzle first. Axel was convinced that these puzzles, wildly popular in Sweden, would catch on in America, too, and he was creating a set of them. He was hoping to publish them someday.

They went ashore for a few hours in Alaska's picturesque capital, Juneau, even though it was raining heavily. They also disembarked in Sitka, the former Russian capital of Alaska, and saw the main attractions in a couple hours from the windows a tour bus.

In Seattle the first order of business was to service the motor home. Besides the muffler needing replacement, they now also discovered several plumbing leaks from previously frozen pipes. The previous owner obviously had not done a very good job of winterizing the unit in the fall. It was nice though, to be able to see through the windows again.

The following morning Alex told Annika to get ready to go to the airport to pick up some business associates, and he and Annie wanted Annika to come along. Katarina and Axel would stay home. Alex had not told Axel whom they were picking up. Billy was one of the first passengers off the plain, having traveled in first class. He was smartly dressed in beige slacks and a maroon club jacket with a matching tie, and he was escorted by two business-like ladies and one young man. Annika did not recognize him. She had not seen him for forty years.

"Mom, perhaps you remember Billy Jones . . ."

Annika paused for a moment in stunned disbelief.

"Oh my God! It's not, no . . . can it be . . . no, is it really you, Billy? Annika stammered.

"Hi Annika, great to see you. You're looking better than ever." He walked up to her with open arms and a wide grin on his face.

"Billy! Is it really you?" Her eyes teared up. They embraced in a long silent hug. "How do you know Alex and Annie" she asked, when they finally let go.

"Well, I got their address from Lisa. When Axel and Katarina came and visited last summer, they got me thinking, and then when I heard that you lost your husband, I contacted Alex . . . It was actually a mistake first. I intended to get the address to Axel and Katarina, but all the same, I found out that you were coming here to Seattle. That was only three days ago, and I hurried to make the arrangements to come and visit with you."

"You came all this way just to see me? I'm awfully glad that you did." Annika hugged him again warmly.

"I hope you don't mind, but I have arranged for three suites at the Sheraton. Oh, excuse me, this is Li and Amy, and this is Leo. They are my assistants. Please meet my dear friend Annika. If you would like to stay there you are welcome. Of course, I understand if you rather stay with Alex and Annie. I know you don't get to see them very often."

"Well, they have to work, so I won't see them all that much anyway. Of course, I do want to spend some time with them, but I'm also eager to get reacquainted with you."

"Well, how about if you take the suite at the Sheraton and then we could all have dinner together. How would that be?" Billy asked.

"Alex, would that be all right?" Annika asked

"Sure, of course. That will be great. Are you going to need a car?" Alex asked.

"I have made arrangements for a limo with a driver. Leo could drive, but I think it is nice to have a local take us around. So, would you like to ride with us, Annika and we will follow Alex to get your things, then we could go over to the hotel and get settled in, and, perhaps at 5:30 we could come and pick you all up for dinner. How does that sound?"

"That will be great."

"I hope Axel and Katarina can also join us for dinner. They are still here, I trust," said Billy.

"Yes they're leaving tomorrow morning for Mexico. They are going to drive all the way down in a motor home," Annika informed him.

"Sounds exciting. I'm looking forward to meeting them again. We had a really nice visit when they came to England. They are the sweetest couple."

Axel and Katarina were surprised to see Billy and his entourages come home with Alex and Annika. They visited shortly before moving on to the Sheraton Hotel, which was constructed on a pier in the down town harbor. Annika sat close to Billy in the limo, his Old Spice cologne brought back a flood of memories. She felt as though she were 19 again. He held her hand the whole way. They both had a lot of questions, a lot of catching up to do.

The suites were huge and each had two bedrooms. Billy offered Annika her own suite, but Annika chose to have her own bedroom in Billy's suite. Therefore, Leo took Annika's suite for one night. The following day he would take the extra bedroom in the girl's suite. It was already two in the afternoon, and Billy suggested they all take a quick nap so they could be alert in the evening. The time difference was taking its toll on Billy. But Annika was not tired. She was too excited to relax. She went down to the lobby, bought some post cards and wrote to friends.

Billy awakened at 4:00, took a quick shower and appeared a few minutes later in a dark blue suit, white shirt and tie. Annika's eyes moved over him in approval. Billy was of course, much older than when she had seen him last, but the years had been good to him, and he filled his shoes well. Annika had put on a midnight blue dress, cut rather deep in front, with a short vest jacket. She looked like a million dollars. He greeted her with a kiss on the cheek and complimented her on her dress.

They pulled up to Alex's house exactly at five. They were all ready, waiting. Billy asked the limo driver to give them a condensed tour around the downtown area, Pioneer Square and the Pikes Market. There were quite a few people out and about, even though it was a week day. They drove past the Space Needle and out to Ballad to take a look at one of Annie's shops. Finally, they drove along the piers to the boat landing hosting the yacht where they would dine. It was a large ship capable of serving two hundred guests. It was trimmed with lights around the edges and across the guy wires. A few other guests were already onboard; friends of Leo, Li and Amy, Billy, Annika and the boys and their girls had their own table.

The trip in Puget Sound took a little more than two hours, and it was dark when they returned. Seattle looked inviting with all its illuminated buildings, the Space Needle and bridges. The dinner was first class and Billy had made arrangements so everyone got their favorite dishes, prepared the way they liked them. Several waiters served them, enough for everyone to have his or her own attendant. After dinner they were treated to Baked Alaska dessert, a tribute to Axel and Katarina, and of course Annika. Annika felt comfortable with Billy. Several times she would reach over and touch him during conversation and she would even tease him.

"Is there any chance of your moving to the US, Billy?" Alex asked.

"No, I don't think so. I'm happy in England and I have the center of my activities there. But I do like to travel on occasion, and I like my place in Jodassy, too, when I need to get away for a bit," he explained.

Annika stayed with Billy, and Axel and Katarina took off for Mexico.

Annika and Billy had a marvelous time in Seattle. They spent the day Axel and Katarina left, mostly catching up on the past. In the evening they chose to have dinner alone, in their suite. By pure coincidence, Annika had found a dress in the hotel boutique that was very similar to the one she had worn the time they met at Liseberg. The collar was slightly different, and the hem was shorter, the resemblance was unmistakable. The material was almost exactly the same. She did not wear the dress for dinner. Instead, she wore another dress that she had found in the boutique, a one-piece dress, cut low in the front, and slit up her right leg. It was made from faux suede and fit her perfectly, flattering her still youthful figure.

After his usual evening shower, Billy dressed in navy trousers and a white polo shirt. They had agreed to dress casually for dinner. Room service had set up their dinner table formally with a white table cloth, and there was a bottle of champagne in an ice tub. The bottle was cold, and when Billy took the bottle to serve, a small cloud of fog arose from it. They raised their glasses by interlocking their arms and looking deep into the others eyes. "Cheers," they said in unison. "To us," Billy offered a second toast. "To us," Annika repeated. They enjoyed their dinners and wine and moved over to the couch for coffee.

"Annika," Billy said seriously. "There are a few things that you should know and I'm not sure how to say it. I'm afraid that you may not see it as it was intended, and that you will be offended."

"Try me. I don't get offended very easily. What is it?" she asked uneasily.

"When I first met you, I fell completely in love with you. My feelings for you helped me through many hard times, but it has been an impossible love that has also been hurtful many times when I have been thinking about you, missing you."

"Well, I'm not offended yet," she responded.

"As may be apparent, I was fortunate to do well in some business ventures and one thing led to another and eventually I managed to build quite an industrial empire."

"I'm still not offended."

"Good. When I learned that you had married I was deeply disappointed, but at the same time I was very happy for you, that you had met someone whom you loved. And I was very happy for you when I heard that you were pregnant. I only wished that I had been the father. Regardless, I have kept up with you all these years, like a common stalker, having a person following you everywhere just to let me know what you were doing, so I could be a part of your life. I'm sorry for what I did, but then again, I would probably do it again." Annika sat quiet waiting for him to finish.

"You're the one. You are the one who has been sending me all the roses, aren't you?" she asked.

"Yes. I just wanted to do something nice for you, even though I couldn't be with you in person."

"And you are the one who has been putting all that money in my account, aren't you?" Her voice was shaking.

"Yes. I just wanted to share some of my success with the woman I loved."

Tears were now running down her cheeks. "Nothing but a common stalker," she repeated. "You silly fool. I'm not insulted. I'm deeply flattered. I only wish I would have known that it was you. I thought that it was some eccentric person picking my name randomly in his testament."

"I didn't want to interfere with your life."

"How did you possibly know where I was going before I was even there."

"Here, read this." He handed her a letter addressed to Lisa.

September 7, 1941

Dear Lisa

I expect that John is there now. Please give my best to him. Thank you so much for passing on my letter to Annika. She wrote me back, as I'm sure you know. Although I'm thrilled to have heard from her, I'm saddened to learn that she is no longer available. She appears to have married a good man, and she is carrying his child. She asked me to remain her friend. As much as I would like to be a part of her life, I'm concerned that my friendship with Annika would interfere with her relationship with her husband and cause hardships. I have only one desire, and that is for Annika to be happy and well cared for. If destiny has decided that we are not to be, however sad it makes me, I'm willing to stay in the background and watch her from afar. She will always remain a big part of my life.

I'm going to ask you for an enormous favor because I know that you're her best friend, and a true friend, and you, like me, are only interested in what is best for Annika. I have been fortunate to acquire substantial wealth and nothing would make me happier than if I could share some of it with the woman I love more than anything. Again, I don't want to do anything that directly interferes with her family life but I would like to be her safety net and benefactor whenever possible. She must never know about this arrangement. This is where you come in. I need someone who lives in Sweden to help me accomplish this. I need someone with exceptional judgment who shares my love for Annika. I'm setting up a trust fund for Annika in an American bank that works through a Swedish bank, in order to protect the trust against an adverse outcome of the war. I will give you full control to administer the distribution of the trust earnings. You will not have to be concerned about managing the trust itself. You will be expected to charge the trust for all expenses relating to your administrating the trust, substantial or trivial, including compensation for your time. It is imperative that Annika will never know about her benefactor, and if she should ever attempt to trace her guardian angel, any possible trail should end with you. You are not to guide her life, only to makes things easier for her. You will be expected to keep in touch with me and inform me about what is going on with Annika. I intend to write her a last letter and then I will withdraw. I'm including a check for immediate expenses with having the baby, until the trust is set up.

Thanks a million. Your friend Billy.

"Oh Billy, I'm so overwhelmed! You've loved me and provided for me all these years. Wait a minute. I have something for you. Just wait here and I'll be right back." She went into her room and put on the special dress. Then she went into the shower and showered with the dress on before coming in to Billy, soaking wet, in the living room. "What do you think? I thought we'd continue where we left off."

Annika did not go back to Fairbanks. Instead she flew with Billy to Las Vegas where they were married, and then on to England.

CHAPTER 41

1983 Three-day party in Sweden.

In August of 1983 Axel and Katarina decided take a sabbatical year in Sweden. They leased out the house and flew to Sweden. They planned to stay in Kurt's summer house in Lindome. The idea was to live through a full year in Sweden and experience the various Swedish traditions. Hopefully Katarina, would also pick up some Swedish. They settled in to the house in Lindome, which was really much more than a summer cottage. They got a kick of the "school bus" that came to pick up the neighbors' children. It was a Mercedes Benz with a school bus sign up front. Not bad for a school shuttle. Of course, a large vehicle would not have made it across the narrow bridge and up the winding hillside road.

Axel contacted some of his old friends and invited them out for a reminiscing party.

Axel and Katarina were in turn invited to a crayfish party the following weekend by a couple that Axel knew from his child hood, Patrick and Aina. They had lived in the same apartment complex as the Nobels. They were dating then, sort of, dated through school, a little on and off, and eventually got married. Aina ended up being Axel's lady for the evening. Aina was cute and perky, and easy to converse with. She spoke freely on most subjects and had an endless supply of risqué jokes that she did not mind telling. In fact, she seemed to enjoy shocking her audience. She was great on the dance floor and more flirtatious than Axel had found American women to be.

"You'll have a good time at our party, I promise," "Aina told Axel. "We'll have a lot of fun and I expect there to be a good crowd. I know of thirty people who will come for sure. I think you'll know some of them that lived in Johanneberg when we grew up."

"Sounds great! You think that I will be able to find it all right?" Axel asked. It is right before we get to Gottskär, right?"

"You won't have any problem finding it. We will put out signs and balloons so it will be easy to find. Are you sure there is nothing we can do to help out?" Axel offered.

"For sure, we have already made all arrangements. The only thing would be if you like to drink anything other than beer, wine or Aquavit, you could bring it. And come prepared to stay over. This is a three-day party . . ."

"What?! A three-day party?" Axel asked.

"Yes, most will stay through the scavenger hunt that begins at four in the morning. Well, it will be Friday morning and it will end at high noon on Sunday, making it a three-day party," she explained.

On the day of the party, Axel allowed for a little extra time to make sure he could find the place all right. It was easy to spot, just as Aina had said. The drive-way, besides being festooned with balloons, was also marked with live torches. The house was tucked into a small private bay, protected from the weather while still having a formidable view toward Tjolöholm Castle. There was a lawn in front of the house where they had set up a large tent, the type often used for revivals. The front side of the tent was removed. They had also erected several small tents on the side, apparently for those sleeping over. Several of the guests arrived at the same time as Axel and Katarina. There was plenty of parking in and around the fruit orchard. Aina and Patrick greeted all the guests personally.

Axel got pared with Maria. Axel had not recognized Maria at first. After all she was only two years old the last time he had seen her, when they were neighbors in Johanneberg.

"Maria, I can't believe it's you. You've changed so much," he added.

"Yes, it has been a few years," she acknowledged.

"The last I heard was that you moved to some country . . ."

"Jodassy," she helped him.

"Yes, Jodassy. Your mother married the King of Jodassy? right?"

"Yes she did."

"So does that make you a real princess?"

"Yes . . ."

"So, what are you up to now days?" Axel asked.

"Well, it's a long story," she began.

"I have lots of time. Fill me in."

"Well, as you know my mother married Prince Ali of Jodassy, who shortly thereafter became King Ali. They had triplets, three little boys that were technically all crown princes. I went to school in England. My older brother Kjell went to medical school in South Africa."

"Yes, Kjell, how is he doing?"

"Fine. Just fine. He is now a physician practicing in Jodassy. He recently got married and has a little girl. Anyway, my three half-brothers did not live to be three years old. They all ate of a rare very poisonous mushroom, when they were playing in our backyard, of all things."

"Are you serious?!"

"Unfortunately, yes. Then Mom had a daughter with Ali and she died from a hornet sting before she was one."

"Boy, that's the strangest thing I've ever heard."

"The doctor told mom that she should not have any more children because of a special condition she has. So Kjell became the crown prince. Well, to complicate things farther, Kjell has no interest whatsoever in ruling a country. He's all into his medicine. So, do you know where that leaves us?" she asked.

"You! You mean you are the crown prince, or princess of Jodassy?"

"You're looking at her. The one-and-only."

"Wow. That is quite a story."

"Yes, so I'm here in Sweden to get briefed on some of our holdings and interests here," she explained. "It was really nice to be invited here to get away from work for a few days. How about yourself? Mom told me about how she ran into you guys up in Sälen a few years ago, and about the avalanche."

"Yes, that was quite a vacation," Axel recollected. "Well, I sure lucked out getting to have you as my partner. Whom did you come with? Are you married?" Axel asked.

"I came . . . Do you remember Ragnar, on the third floor in Johanneberg? Well, I have remained good friends with his sister Lena and I needed a date so I asked him to come."

"I bet you didn't have to ask twice," he said.

"It was not a sure deal. We've known each other for so long, and always through Lena, so I think he looks at me more like a sister than as a date. Besides I had to compete with an important soccer game being played this weekend."

"Well it looks like you won that contest with flying colors," Axel concluded. He offered his arm and escorted her to their seats.

Katarina was pared up with a dentist named Stig. She peppered him with questions about the latest treatments and Swedish practices. The party proceeded with the usual speeches and toasts.

"So how do you like Alaska?" Marie asked Axel.

"Not bad. It can get a little cold at times but. . .. Actually, it's worst for the cars. Everything gets thick, stiff and cracks. When you start driving your car in -30, the bottom of your tires, which got flat standing on the ground, remain flat for a while until they warm up and turn round again. We call that driving on square tires. It really isn't all that bad though, as long as you plug in your car's heater, and you don't mind it being dark most of the time, in the winter."

"Seems like you're a glutton for punishment . . ." she said.

"Actually, the summer makes up for it when it's sunshine all the time. Our flowers and vegetables grow enormous there thanks to the midnight sun."

"Have you ever thought of moving south or back to Sweden?"

"I don't think so. Katarina was born in Fairbanks. She is my girl friend who's here with me.

"You are not married?"

"No, we never saw a point in doing it. Neither one of us is particularly religious and in the US you actually have to pay higher taxes if you are married so . . . I can't see her living anywhere else, permanently. Katarina is rather involved with her work in Fairbanks. She is a nurse for a dentist and she is almost married to that office. We have talked about it though, especially recently, after my mother married this British gentleman Billy Jones. . .."

"Billy, you're kidding. Billy got married? To your mother? Boy, this is a small world. Billy is a good friend of the family," Marie revealed. "He has a home in Jodassy and I see him often. Annika? I never saw the connection. So, it's your mother that he's been talking about."

"Anyway, it was probably a good thing that we never married, because I feel that we are slowly drifting apart. It's a small world," Axel agreed. "So, you're not dating anyone, that's difficult to believe."

"Not currently. I have dated a few guys in the past but not Mr. Right," she confessed.

"I take it you have been on one of "Aina's scavenger hunts before?" he asked.

"Everyone for the last five years. It's a lot of fun."

Axel asked Marie to dance. She was a good dancer, and had no difficulties in following Axel, even when doing the jitterbug. Maria snuggled up tight when the music slowed down. Axel noticed how nice she smelled. Eventually "Aina announced the rules for the scavenger game.

"Thank you all for making this evening special. Most of you know the general rules, but for the first-time contestants I will repeat them. I'll give you a list of items to bring back. Some of them are next to impossible to obtain and you are not really expected to bring back all items, but points will be given for the best effort. You have until Sunday noon to return here and be scored. You can do whatever you like to get your items, within the law. It's all up to you. The winner, as always, will receive the honor of winning. There is a revolving prize and next year, this year's winner will have to give up the prize. There will also be a second-place winner. In case the first-hand winner for some reason cannot fulfill the obligations that go with becoming the winner, the second-place winner will become the first place winner with all the duties and benefits that go with the title."

"Are you ready for the list?" she asked. "As usual there are twenty-five items on the list and here we go: 1. An airline ticket with an airline other than SAS and ideally to a foreign country. 2. A red Danish polser (hot dog) 3. A G-string. 4. A ticket to an Opera. 5. Five condoms of different brands. 6. A tube of red ski-wax. 7. A hotel match box. 8. A licorice rope, one meter long. 9. A match book from a strip joint. 10. A sea shell. 11. A receipt from a ski-resort. 12. A net T-shirt. 13. A red lip imprint on a napkin. 14. A receipt of a purchase from a tax-free shop. 15. Five wine corks. 16. A shampoo bottle from a hotel. 17. A black beret. 18. A miniature Eiffel tower. 19. One man's magazine featuring a nude female on a front page. 20. One girl's magazine featuring a nude male on front cover. 21. The strap from a cigar. 22. A get out of jail free card from Monopoly. 23. A miniature French flag. 24. The original autograph from a famous person, and finally, 25. A curl of black curly hair. I will be the judge and all decisions are final. If more than one team has collected all items, the effort exerted and the quality of the items will determine the winner. See you here on Sunday at noon, or earlier. My official time right now is five minutes after four a.m. May the best couple win.

"Boy, that was quite a list," Axel commented. How many items did you come up with last time?"

"About half. But the guy I was with was not very imaginative. It should not be too hard to beat that number. Would you like to take a rest first or just get going?" Maria asked.

"Well, I'm not very tired right now so why don't we get on our way, if you're alright."

"Good, let's get our things and get going then," Marie said enthusiastically. "We have one- and one-half days to get it done. Do you have any of the items on the list?"

"I may have a few. What about you?" Axel asked.

"The same, I might have a few. Do you want to stop by your place first, since it is almost on the way to town, and then we can stop by mine and see what we can come up with, and make a plan for getting rest of the stuff?" Maria suggested.

"That sounds good."

Katarina and her partner Stig was already at the house in Lindome, and had taken the red ski wax Axel knew he had.

"Did you hide rest of the ski wax, Katarina? I was sure we had three tubes left."

"I guess you were wrong then," Katarina said in a voice that suggested that she knew more. "Good luck. See you Sunday. Stig and I are on our way to Denmark. Bye, Bye."

"Boy, did she turn competitive all by the sudden. I know she hid the wax but I also bet I know where she hid it." They went down to the basement to the laundry room and looked in the cabinet where they had chemical products, and sure enough there were two red ski wax tubes sitting there. "I knew it. This is her favorite hiding place. That was one down, and twenty-four to go. There is probably no point in looking for her black beret. I'm sure she took it."

"Well, what about girly magazines? Do you have any?" Maria asked.

"I do, but somehow I got a feeling they are also gone. We're probably wasting our time here. Looks like Katarina either took them or hid them."

"That's all right; we can get one from other sources. Let's stop by my place and see what we can come up with there."

Maria's apartment was in reality the penthouse of a downtown hotel, owned by her family. It was spacious and had a wonderful view of much of central Gothenburg. "Let's plan how we're going to go about this. We could drive down to Malmö or Hälsingborg and take the ferry over to Denmark. We could probably get most of the things we need there. Or, if you're up to a little more excitement, we could take the plane to Paris or Amsterdam and perhaps Copenhagen on the way back . . ."

"Sounds like a plan to me. How are we going to get the signature of a famous person?"

"Let me take care of that." She called down to the lobby. "Hi Kelly, it's Maria. I need a favor. Do we have any celebrities staying at the hotel today?"

"Margaret Thatcher is here."

"Really. Margaret is a friend of mine. Will you please ask her for an autograph for me when you see her. Tell her that it's for me and I will explain later. Thanks a million. I will get it from you either tonight or tomorrow morning."

"It's nice to have connections," Axel commented.

"For sure," she responded. "Let's see what else I have." She pulled out a couple magazines featuring two muscular excessively oiled male bodies on the front page."

"Perfect," Axel reacted.

"I'm not sure about perfect, she joked, but not bad. Not bad at all." She flipped open to the center page. "Yes, not bad at all," she repeated dreamily. "Twenty-three to go," she added. "Oh no! It says nude males or females on the front cover. I don't think this will do. They aren't nude on the front cover. Well, we'll have to get some later."

"Oh, yea," Axel grunted. "I would agree with fair." They both laughed.

"I have a condom, do you?" Maria asked.

"I have three, but they are all of the same brand."

"Boy, you came prepared didn't you," she smirked. "Well, we better run out to Torslanda and see what plane we can catch. There will be things in the souvenir shop for us to get. Let me take a quick shower first though, okay?"

"Of course, I better have one, too, if I'm going to sit next to you on a plane for four hours. My deodorant is just about to give up."

"Fine, and we can't have that, can we? . . . and I would like to make one thing clear now. This trip is on me. I have a corporate credit card and this is nothing for the corporate coffers."

"Are you sure?" Axel asked politely though he knew she was correct. He gave her a light kiss on her cheek. "Thank you very much. I'm having the time of my life."

"Good! Me too. Come to think of it, I would have a receipt from a ski resort at home. The corporation owns a resort in Sälen, as you know. I still have my receipt from my last stay there."

"Great, looks like we're doing quite well," he said optimistically.

"Let's do the lip stick now also. That's an easy one." She led the way into an enormous bathroom. It was all tiled and marble and featured a Jacuzzi on one side and a brass and glass shower next to the bidet. It had a double sink marble counter, and one wall was all mirrored with a brass bar running across, like ballet dancers use in training. It also featured various exercise equipment and a big screen TV.

Maria pulled out a bright red lipstick puckered up and went to work. Axel studied her applying the red cream and working it in with several lip-puckering/rolling motions, being careful not to get any on her teeth. She had a sweet, yet mature and sensuous appearance. Enjoying her audience, she turned to him smiling while still working her lips. "Well, are you ready for a sample," she asked suggestively.

"Sure." He walked over to her and took her a little with surprise when he kissed her right on her mouth. "Hmm, and it tastes good, too."

"Actually . . . I was more like suggesting testing on a napkin," she stuttered, "but what the heck, thank you, I needed that." She reached up and returned the kiss, this time with more feeling, smearing her lipstick on his mouth.

"Now I'll need a shower for sure. Do you mind?" He turned his back toward her and dropped his clothes. This time it was Maria's turn to study Axel. Axel had the strong muscular build of an athlete. He carried himself with a confidence that was reflected in his walk.

"Now that's perfection," she said boldly. He turned around smiling at her, before stepping into the glazed shower stall, still observed by the slightly surprised Maria. She was not used to having men undress in front of her and step into her shower. And what a man. She was also surprised at her own candor and her feeling comfortable with the situation. While waiting for Axel to get out of the shower, she disrobed herself and slipped into a white fluffy robe. She turned on the Jacuzzi. She handed him a towel when he got out and invited him to wait for her in the Jacuzzi. She dropped her robe and stepped into the shower.

Axel slipped into the warm, bubbling water. The steamy glass obscured his view somewhat, but he had a good view of Maria when she got close to the glass. She had a slender, well-proportioned body. Her legs were unusually long; her buttocks were softly rounded; her abs were tight. Her waist reminded Axel of a cello. Her breasts were firm with the erect nipples pointing upwards. She had the body of an eighteen-year-old. In fact, she looked a lot younger in her birthday suit than he had imagined her the night before.

She did not bother to put her robe back on after her shower but walked straight over and joined Axel in the Jacuzzi. She sat down next to him and placed her hand on his muscular leg. Axel put his arm around her shoulders, avoiding touching her inviting breast.

"I think there is a plane leaving for Paris at seven something, let me see." She opened a small trap door and pulled out a phone. "Yes, hi Kelly, it is me again, Maria. Can you please check on when the next flight goes to Paris? Any carrier but SAS. Air France, at 7:15, that's great. Will you please make two reservations, first class, and have a driver ready in half an hour? Thanks a million."

While they waited for their flight, they were able to pick up both the magazine, and two more condoms of different brands from automats in the restrooms. Maria did not know that Axel was doing the same at the same time, so they ended up with dual supply of condoms. However, they still needed one more brand. They got both the flag, cigar ring, and Eiffel Tower in the gift shop. They got the tax-free receipts and purchased the tickets on Air France. Before the plane had left the runway, both of them were sound asleep, leaning against each other.

Katarina and Stig had a pleasant trip to Helsingborg. They had stopped by Stig's apartment and found several of the trivial items, including the airline ticket and ski resort receipts. Axel was right, Katarina had taken his magazines and her black beret. Stig had a tennis ball that was signed by Bjorn Borg. He also had a men's net T-shirt. They put Stig's car on the ferry and during the short trip they were able to buy candy and a cigar in the tax-free shop. Stig was nice company. Katarina could not get enough of his stories from medical school and from his practice. He was highly intelligent and possessed excellent social skills. He was attractive, although slightly overweight.

"You're still not tired after having stayed up all night?" Katarina asked. "At least I slept for three hours in the car. I don't know how you could stay awake."

"I don't normally get tired when I drive, and with all this extra excitement, I had no difficulty staying awake, even though I admittedly am beginning to feel a little sleepy now."

"Well why don't you go down to the car and take a nap now. I will finish the shopping and we should be in Hälsingör in twenty minutes," she suggested.

"Perhaps I will, so I can be a little more useful later."

When Katarina returned to the car, Steve was deep in sleep sprawled out in the backseat. He mumbled something inaudible when Katarina got into the car but he did not wake up. Not even the ship's loudspeaker's warning passengers to return to their cars, or the ferry's bumping against the pier, or the semi-truck's noisy diesel engine rumbling next to them awakened him from his sweet dreams. Katarina moved over, into the driver's seat, and drove off the ferry. The customs agent simply waved them through. After stopping briefly to pick up a few things in Hälsingör, Katarina took off for Copenhagen. She chose the scenic coast route driving through a park like landscape and impressive estates. Three hours later she had found a nice older hotel by the Tivoli Garden, in the heart of Copenhagen and not far from Newhavn, the red-light district. She shook him hard, and he was still out. He looked so peaceful, cuddly. She reached over and kissed him and suddenly he opened his eyes.

"I was trying to bring you back to the living. You were out so cold that I thought I better try some artificial resuscitation," she explained.

"I guess I woke up just a little too early then. Then again, if I was asleep, what good would it do?" She laughed at his comment.

"We're in Copenhagen now. It's about 11:30, in the morning," she added, "and it's Saturday. I respond to the name Katarina, and we are on a scavenger hunt," she reported.

"Funny, funny. I'm not that far out of it."

"We're parked outside a nice hotel in a central location and I thought this might be a nice place to set up base. I thought at least that we should make some plans . . . have a discussion about how to reach our goal," Katarina suggested.

"Excellent. I'm really sorry that I pooped out on you. You must be really tired too. You only slept for three hours with several interruptions. I hope I'm not appearing presumptuous, but would you mind if we got a room here and rested a bit more before we proceed with our hunt? Then we could return to Gothenburg tonight."

"No, I was actually going to suggest the same thing. I could really use a shower before I'm seen in public," Katarina countered.

It was a spacious room, tastefully decorated and clean, in an older building with tall ceilings and cornices around the walls. The bathroom was clean, and had apparently been remodeled recently. There were two beds in the room and Katarina threw herself down on the closest one, before kicking her shoes off. She was tired and the only thing that kept her awake was the excitement of being in a hotel room with a stranger in a foreign country.

"If you would like to take advantage of me, this would probably be the perfect time," she offered. "I would have no energy whatsoever to resist."

"Well, I do not intend to take advantage of you, however tempting that sounds." He sat down on her bedside and played gently with her hair while talking. "That would be a shame," he added. Perhaps we should make an assessment of where we're at. We still need to get a girly magazine, opera tickets, get-out-of-jail-free-card, polser . . ."

"No I got one in Hälsingör," Katarina interrupted, "and the licorice rope and the sea shell. I found a shell by the ferry, a pretty pinkish one."

"Boy, you have been productive. I'm impressed. The biggest challenge as I see it right now will be to get an opera ticket. We will just have to go down to the opera house and see what we can do. Perhaps if we catch the people getting out of the opera, we can buy, or get a used ticket. We will have to find out when it's over."

"How about a two-hour nap before we get going?" Katarina had barely finished the sentence before she was asleep.

Stig laid down on his bed for a while but he had difficulty falling asleep. He was totally awake now and was reflecting back on his life while looking at the peacefully sleeping Katarina.

He wrote her a note telling her that he would be back soon, and he drove over to the opera house. The ticket office was open, and he asked to buy a ticket to yesterday's performance, hopefully at a discount. The young girl did not understand his unusual request, assuming there was a language miscommunication, she vigorously attempted to explain that the yesterday tickets did not have any value today. She did not understand the words treasurer hunt, until he explained the whole thing in English. She gave him a free ticket.

When he returned to the hotel Katarina was not in her bed, but he could hear her taking a shower. She was also singing, seeking the high notes to Hosanna David's Son. She came out undressed, not expecting anyone there, and was startled when she saw Stig laying on his bed.

"Oh, excuse me, I didn't expect you here. I'll go back for a towel," she said.

"It's all right. I'm a doctor. I work with naked bodies all day long. You don't have to get one for my sake."

She stopped and turned around, hesitating, standing there naked, trying to decide whether it was too late to go back for a towel; whether it made any difference now when he had seen her anyway; whether it made any difference since he was a doctor. But a dentist . . . not exactly a gynecologist, whether she would look prudish covering up for a doctor, whether this was any different from taking saunas with Molly and company, and finally whether it was alright because of Axel . . . and because she was also feeling some excitement about standing there exposed before him, and she liked it in a scary way. But then again, who knew what Axel was doing with that pretty blond he was so friendly with. She concluded that it was not worse than when they took saunas with Molley and Tracy and their friends, and it was Axel's choice not to get married. "I guess we are both adults and this game is supposed to be a little wild. Who knows what Axel's doing, so, if you get a thrill of looking at me, that's just fine." She held out her hands as if to emphasize her position.

"It's true that I work with bodies all day long, but none like yours," he admitted. "You're absolutely gorgeous. You have the sexiest legs I have ever seen. I love your cute little feet. Your bottom is perfect . . . "she turned around to give him a better look. Your flat stomach is perfect, and I love your naval. It's perfect for kissing." She gently moved her hands over the areas he described as to feel for herself if he was right. "Your waist is like an hour glass, couldn't be nicer. Your chest, large without being droopy and your nipples are just right. It's amazing, to have breasts like that. She shook her torso to show him their firmness. Your face is perfect, youthful and mature at the same time, sweet but still a little devilish at times, and you have that little devilish smile that will drive a guy crazy with desire. A ten-plus-plus for sure. Besides, you are intelligent and witty at the same time. Unreal."

"Don't stop, I love it, tell me more."

"Well, come over here for a closer examination. Lay down here next to me. Great. Well, your hair is soft and flows so softly through one's hands. I love to touch your skin. It's soft and clear and you smell so good. Your soft rosy cheeks are so touchable, kissable and bitable. Your shoulders are soft and tan. And your breasts are showstopper quality. I would give them 'best in show' every time. They're screaming out to be touched. Your erect nipples are perfect for rubbing, playing with, sucking, and nibbling on. These breasts were made with men in mind. They're just the right size for touching and squeezing, to be manhandled. Your stomach is perfect, tight yet womanly soft. Your legs belong at an exhibit of fine art, displayed as the main feature. They are masterpieces, long slender, yet muscular. Absolutely perfect."

"Thank you, you're so sweet. Perhaps we should do our shopping and we can continue where we left off later. We paid for the room for the night, so we'd just as well use it."

A company driver was waiting for Axel and Maria at Charles de Gaulle airport in Paris. He took them first to Maria's apartment and then on to the opera house, for the ticket. They had no difficulty procuring one, but at a prime price.

"Well, we have a choice tonight; we could go to the opera, we have the ticket. True, only one, but we could arrange for one more. Or . . . we could go to a strip joint. We need to stop by one regardless. Perhaps that will be enough with having dinner some place too."

"Yes, I'm not much of an opera connoisseur anyway. There is a lot of beautiful opera music that I love and can play over and over without ever getting tired of them, but I don't care much for all the scale singing in-between the arias."

"I agree, so the strip joint it is. If it's alright with you, I'd like to show you one of my favorite restaurants here in Paris. It's not the fanciest, but it has that great Paris atmosphere. It is right by the Seine. Very romantic. We should probably get our shopping over with first."

They stopped at a department store.

"Bon jour, Monsieur, Mademoiselle"

"Good afternoon. We're looking for a G-string, please."

"Is it for a guitar, Sir?"

"No. A swim suit."

"Is it for you or the lady, Sir?

"It isn't for either of us, we just need one."

"Oh, it is a gift?"

"No, it's not a gift, we just need one."

"Well, I need to know if it is for a male or for a female."

"Give us one of each," Maria interrupted. "Where are they?"

"The males are up one floor and the ladies are on the fourth floor."

"Thank you. Do you have condoms here, please? No . . . never mind we have all we need, don't we?"

"Actually, we need one more," Axel reminded her, "Most of what we have are of the same brand."

"Oh, you have a collection, Sir?"

"No I just need one more."

"Right, over there, Sir."

"What about Monopoly games?"

"You're in luck Sir, we have them on sale right now in the game section on the fifth floor."

"Thank you."

They found the G-strings and purchased a matching set. Hers was only half the size of his, and his was tiny, just barely big enough to be functional . . . at a relaxed state. They also got two net T-shirts. In the game section they purchased the game, opened it and asked for help finding the get-out- of-jail-free card. The young man attempted to explain that it was only a game and did not really work. They did not have the time to explain the details to him.

"Well now we are down to seven things. We need the wine corks, the match book from a strip club, a sea shell, a pölser and the black curly hair. Oops! we didn't get the black beret yet either. They will probably have one here though," Axel suggested.

"The challenge now will be to come up with the black curly hair. But I have an idea," said Maria.

"I was never worried. I knew you would come through," Axel said. "So, what is your plan?"

"Just wait and see. Why don't we go back to the apartment and rest up a little for tonight? It's going to be late. By the way, there is a wine store close to the apartment."

Maria's apartment was modest compared to her penthouse suite in Gothenburg, but it was still spacious by most standards. It was located on the west bank of the Seine, a district mostly occupied by artists and other eccentric or colorful individuals. The restaurant they were going to was within walking distance. Axel watched her carefully as she unpacked. She was lovely in every way and she walked with such grace and confidence. She wore a permanent smile which intensified with eye contact.

"How about a glass of wine?" Maria asked. "We only had to bring the corks, not the whole bottle. By the way, the reason why I got two of everything is that I noticed an invitation to a party of one of my neighbors. These are some of the more eccentric people on the block, but they do know how to have fun, and they are all French. I thought that if you thought it would be fun, we could drop by for a short visit later on and then we could wear our new outfits. The net T-shirts, G-string and the black berets. We will probably be the most conservatively dressed couple at the party. Some of them can get a little carried away. Besides, that's where we can get our black curly curl"

"Love it. Absolutely. Cheers!" he proposed, lifting his glass.

He laid down on the bed to rest and continued to observe Maria poking around in the apartment. He had the radio on.

"Did you hear that?" he asked.

"Hear what? about Reagan's being reelected? she asked.

"Yes, probably not a big surprise to anyone."

"Did you vote for him?" she asked.

"No, I didn't. I normally vote for the independent candidate just to keep them on their toes in Washington. Besides, I could not support anyone who supports our Federal Reserve policy of limiting growth to less than three percent. I think it's criminal."

"You are a man of strong convictions, I can tell," she said, unable to resist a smile.

She had dressed down to something resembling a short night gown. It covered the essentials except when she bent over. Maria refilled their glasses and lay down next to him. Axel had gotten warm and had dressed down to his shorts. She poked on his groin and suggested that maybe they should have got a larger size on his G-string.

"I don't see how all that is going to fit in that tiny G-string," she said. "How can you walk around with all that tucked in like that?" she asked. That can't possibly be comfortable."

"Well, a man's got to do what a man's got to do. She moved up sitting on top of him. She could feel him glide inside her. She made a slight moaning sound of pleasure, while slowly moving up and down.

Axel lifted her gown over her head. She helped him by raising her arms but without stopping her rhythmic moves for a second. He reached behind her, pulling her buttocks toward him to increase the force of his trusts.

It was close to 8:00 when they woke up from their rest. Maria got into the shower first and Axel joined her a few minutes later.

"Do you have room for one more in here?" he asked politely.

"Sure, there is always room for one more, right?"

"Well I'm not sure about that, but I will make myself small. Here, let me do your back."

"All right, but back only, otherwise we'll never get going," she cautioned. "We can dress casually, it's not a fancy restaurant we're going to."

Axel and Maria walked along the Seine River to the restaurant. The sidewalk was lined with street vendors, selling everything from art to astrology. The vendors were at least as colorful as their merchandise. Numerous street performers did everything from drama to playing music, both classical and abstract.

The restaurant was mostly outdoors, and there was a courtyard in the middle and balconies around. It was beautifully decorated with plants, thousands small light bulbs, and pictures of famous people. Checkered table cloths covered the tables and the waiters wore berets and colorful scarves. The waitresses wore short black dresses over black stockings. Their white bodices were highlighted with black bow-ties. Each also wore a flower in her hair. A violinist played gypsy music. Maria was right, this place oozed Paris.

Maria and Axel were seated by the river's edge down in the court yard, slightly above the path of the walking traffic. The view of the street venders and performers' and the people walking by added to the festive atmosphere. They arrived at 9:00 p.m., right when the restaurant opened for dinner. The place was filling fast. Many of the patrons were younger couples seemingly deeply in love and acting affectionately. A young handsome waiter came over to their table and handed Maria a red rose. "Mademoiselle Maria, welcome back to Paris, the city of love and red roses." He also placed a basket of *du pain* on the table

"Thank you Pierre. Please meet my close friend Axel from Sweden."

"It's a great pleasure to meet a friend of Mademoiselle Maria."

"The pleasure is all mine. This is a marvelous place you have here, very romantic."

"It's the city of love," he repeated.

Their dinner was superb. They danced to Edith Piaf's, *Je ne regrette rien*. It offered a smooth, slow, soothing sound perfect for a lovers' dance. Maria easily followed Axel's lead, including an occasional deep dip.

After dinner, Maria led Axel to the red-light district. There were sex shows and cabarets, restaurants and paraphernalia shops all intermixed. They chose a smaller place, the first one they saw. It was dark and smoky inside. A small round stage filled the back of the room. It was sparsely surrounded by a few other patrons. Suddenly the music came on and four girls came into the room dressed in only some fluffy leg bands and a feather crown. They danced on the stage, flirting with the onlookers and exposing their assets. Axel ordered wine for himself and for Maria. They stayed through a second dance even though the joint did not have its name printed on its match boxes. The second show consisted of two naked girls singing and playing a French folk-song on flute. Axel and Maria needed their match box and moved on. They chose another strip joint that appeared to be larger, from the outside. The music was loud as they entered the room and the smoke was heavy. Axel and Maria chose a table a little back from the stage. Yes, there was a match book in the ashtray with the name of the establishment printed in front and some personal pictures of performers on the inside of the cover. The show was more of a skit and neither Axel nor Maria understood much of the plot. Regardless, the performers all ended up naked.

They decided they had enough and to stop by their friend's party, after first stopping by Maria's apartment to put on their outfits. Axel had difficulty keeping his hands of Maria. She looked like a bombshell in her tiny G-string and net T-shirt that came short of her navel. The apartment below was packed with people. Maria was right. Their outfits were conservative compared to the other guests that were mainly dressed in body paint, applied to accent their assets. It was a predominantly young crowd. Friends were openly expressing their affection for each other all over the place. They returned to Maria's apartment around three. They made love for one and one half hour, shaved some curls, showered and were at the airport at 6:00 a.m.. At 9:00 they touched down in Copenhagen, getting the pölser and the sea shell. At 10:30 they landed in Gothenburg. Half an hour later they stopped by Maria's apartment to get the waiting signature and a few other things and at 11:15 they were on their way back to Aina and Patric's place. No, they didn't win. They were five minutes late and were disqualified.

Katarina and Stig had a glass of wine and walked over to Nyhavn to check out the stores. They needed to consume at least one bottle, as they could only bring four bottles to Sweden without having to pay duty. They found most of what they needed visiting the small shops. They found a G-string, shaped as a tiny heart and the magazine with the nude male on the cover. They returned to their room with the bags, spread out all the items on the bed, went over their list and concluded that the only thing left to get was the match book from a strip joint and the black curly curl.

"How about modeling the G-string for me?" Stig asked.
"Are you kidding? There's nothing there."
"I bet you would look great in it."
"It doesn't have a top."
"You can put on the T-shirt. What's the big deal? I have already seen you naked?" he asked.
"Well, that was an accident. I didn't know that you were there, and then I don't know what came over me. I got carried away."
"Well, I'm glad that you did. You're gorgeous."
"Don't be silly, look at those girls," she said, pointing to their magazine. "Look at those."
"They're too large, out of balance and disproportional. Yours are perfect. Nicely rounded, with no sag, perfect."
"Then how about her, clearly she has a more voluptuous body than I?"
"She's nice, but a little too heavy. If she was leaning forward, her breasts would sag and so would her abs. Also, you have to remember that these pictures have been retouched. They've removed every little wrinkle and rash. You don't have any to remove." Katarina took the T-shirt over to the mirror, removed her jumper and bra, and with her

back turned to Stig, ignoring her reflection in the mirror, she slipped into the T-shirt. She turned around taking a pose. "t's pretty sexy, isn't it?" she asked. "It doesn't hide much, does it?"

"Yes and no. It is very sexy and it doesn't hide much. That's what makes it sexy."

She turned to the mirror again and dropped her pants and panties and slipped into the G-string. She turned around. " It's too small."

"It's not too small, it's perfect. You need to shave a little to wear it, everyone does. By the way, we need some curly black hair. That would be perfect. It was clearly the intention of "Aina and Patrick that we should return with some pubic hair. Anything else will deduct points."

"My hair is not black. It is dark. . . . brunet."

"It is dark enough; besides we don't have any darker, alright?"

"All right, but you'll have to help me. I don't want to get cut there."

She removed the G-string and laid down on the bed, putting her bottom on a pillow to give Stig better access. Stig returned with his shaving equipment and went to work.

"You sure changed your mind in a hurry. A few minutes ago, you did not even want to model the G-string and now I get to shave you. What happened during those minutes to make you change your mind?"

"Well, I decided that, what the heck. Besides, I kind of liked it when you described my autonomy, and I like when you like to look at me."

"Baby, I do. Believe me. Very much." He shaved her clean. She felt with her hand.

"Boy, that feels funny, but I think I like it."

"Well, I like it. I think it's sexy," Stig told her, also feeling the smooth area.

"What strip joint shall we go to? Look here in the paper there is a lot to choose from."

"Believe it or not, but I happen to be an expert on strip joints in Nyhavn. Not long ago we, Axel and I came over to Sweden together with a couple we know from Fairbanks and, of course, we visited several places. It was pretty wild but quite a turn on."

"What type of place do you prefer?" he asked.

"Last time we were here there was one place where two beautiful girls were having lesbian sex right in front of our table. That was really naughty."

"Have you ever had sex with another female?" Steve asked.

"No, that was as close as I ever have come. I prefer men, but it was still a turn on for some reason. What do you like best?"

"Oh, my favorite are those places that have amateur striping contests. It is almost like making love with a virgin, watching them strip for the first time." She nodded, agreeing.

"I noticed a place earlier today that advertised amateur stripping contest close to the porn shop we went to earlier," Katarina recollected.

"Me too. I was hoping we go there."

"Fine."

As always, it was dark and smoky inside. The contest had already begun. There were eighteen girls participating in the contest. First price was $100 second price was $50 and third price was $25. About half of them looked like they were semi-professional but the rest of them looked like they walked straight off the street. A blond cute little girl was getting up on the stage. She was dressed in jeans and a halter top. She was laughing nervously looking over at her friend. She began moving slowly with the music. She unbuttoned the two top buttons on her jeans exposing her white panties. She moved up to her top, lifted it up over her stomach, hesitated some, then pulled it off. She undid rest of the buttons on her jeans before reaching back to undo her bra-strap. She let her bra hang lose for a short moment before taking it off all together. The audience was eagerly cheering her on. She let her pants fall, almost falling herself, getting tangled in her jeans leg. She danced in her panties for a few moments walking back and forth on the stage, finally stopping facing away from the audience, and she removed her panties. She turned around dancing nude until the music stopped.

"She was kind of cute, wasn't she?" Katarina asked.

"She did pretty well if that was her first time," Stig agreed. "She was cute enough."

The next two girls were professional. They had the usual outfits and moved around the stage with full confidence. They were followed by another amateur. A slightly older lady, perhaps in her mid-thirties. She wore a skirt and blouse. As soon as the music began, she dropped her skirt. She did not wear panties. It did not take her long before she had also removed rest of her clothing. She was in a big hurry to get naked. They watched all the girls do their routines. Then they did one number when all the girls stripped on the stage at the same time. Afterwards they narrowed down the field to five contestants, by letting the audience vote with their applause. The five finalists did their routines a second time. This time they added a few more risqué moves, a little more bumping and grinding. The winner, an apparent armature with long black hair and beautiful long slender legs was dressed in a dress. She began by removing her panties. She would then tease the audience by flashing the audience as she did her routine.

They tried a couple more places; one Katarina had been to before. They had different strippers this time, but they did a good job. Katarina was resting her hand on his leg during the performance increasing Stig's sexual exuberance. They got the match book and returned to their room. Katarina filled their vine glasses and turned on the radio music.

"Well, what do you think?" Katarina asked. "Did you have a good time?"

"Yes, it was quite an experience. And I couldn't have had nicer company. I would rather have been watching you strip though. At that amateur place we went to first, I was thinking about you stripping there. I know you would have won."

"I couldn't strip before a large audience like that. I would feel so naked. In a way it would be a turn on, but I just couldn't. Not in front of that many people."

"How many people could you strip in front of?" he asked.

"I don't know. Depends on who they were and how much I had to drink. Do you really think I would have done all right?"

"I know you would."

"Here, sit down and watch me and see what you think." She started to move with the music lifting her skirt to show off her legs. She gracefully removed her panties, lifting her skirt to tease him. She let her skirt drop dancing only in her bra and blouse. She opened the blouse, dancing with it hanging loose. She removed the rest of her clothing dancing naked in front of him. "Well, what do you think? How did I do?"

"Honey, if you had done that on the stage you would have won for sure. There is no question in my mind. You are so beautiful, and you move with such grace. I could look at you all night. If you like we could go back down, and you can give it a try, it's only a five minute walk. The contest is over, but they do pay ten bucks per dance if you would like to know how it feels."

"You're crazy! But I admit that it would probably be the ultimate turn-on. Its one o'clock there is probably not going to be very much people there now. Yes, I saw the sign, ten bucks a dance."

"What would you ware? In a way it would be neat to put on your cool G-string and net shirt, but that almost looks like something a stripper would ware. It is more fun for the audience, I think, if you ware regular street cloth so they can tell that you're an amateur. The skirt and blouse that you just had on were pretty neat and the panties and bra were fine too."

"Are you sure, should I really do it?"

"That's completely up to you. But if you think that it will be the ultimate turn on, then I think you should try it. You will probably never have a better chance. Here no one knows you."

"Let's do it, damn it, let's do it. You don't mind."

"Mind, I think it will be fun. I love it"

There were fewer people there now than when the strip contest was going on, but there was still thirty to forty people left. There were a few couples and even a couple girls in the audience, but most were middle age men, except for a group of younger boys, probably soccer players. One of the in-house strippers was performing when they arrived. She was doing her routine by the brass bar. When she was done the bartender asked for dancers from the audience and Katarina walked up to the small stage. She got enthusiastic applauds, cheers and whistles when she came on stage. She walked up to the microphone.

"Hi, my name is Molly and I like to dance for you."

The music started, a soft rock tune with a strong beat. The bright stage light came on almost blinding her for a few seconds. She stayed with the same routine as when she stripped for Steve, starting by slipping out of her panties. She danced around the stage lifting her skirt at times. She stopped before the soccer players and lifted the skirt all the way up to her waist. The guys were cheering her on. She turned around, bent forward and flashed the soccer team. The audience began throwing money on the stage. She let the skirt fall and unbuttoned her blouse, danced some more and removed her bra and blouse. She continued the dance completely nude. When done, she collected the money and her cloth and returned to the table where she got dressed and they decided to return back to the hotel.

"How much money did you make tonight? Stig asked.

"I haven't counted it yet, but it's quite a bit. Let's see. I made one hundred and ten dollars for those two dances, not bad. And I would have done it for nothing, for the thrill of it."

"Well how was it? By the way, you did a marvelous job. You deserved every penny of that. Well, how about one last dance for me, then we should probably take a short nap before we return. We are going to have to leave in about one hour to make it back in time. They returned to Gothenburg five hours late and were disqualified from the savage hunt.

CHAPTER 42

1983 Alex meets Corina

Alex and Annie's business were growing with leaps and bounds. They had expanded their inventory and they were starting new stores on a monthly basis. They had also started a chain of Scandinavian restaurants and bakeries. They were on the road most of the time and did not see each other much, but they both liked to be busy and they both enjoyed their independent lifestyles.

In the spring of 1983, Annie turned seriously ill. After seeing a doctor for constant headaches, Annie learned that she had a tumor in her left breast. An operation was performed to remove the breast. The morning before the operation Annie took several Aspirin for her headache. The Aspirin had a none clogging effect on her blood and she would not stop bleeding. She died the following morning.

Axel engaged himself completely in the business to help him deal with his loss. He continued to expand the business and arranged a trip to New York.

Being unfamiliar with the city, and Alex not wanting to have to spend more time away than he needed to, he contacted an escort service for a lady familiar with New York. For two hundred dollars he got his guide. It was a young redhead girl dressed in a rather suggestive outfit that came to his door just fifteen minutes later. He excused himself for a minute to use the facilities before they left. Apparently, he had not made his attentions clear to the girl, because when he returned from the bathroom, Connie, his escort, had removed most of the little she was wearing. She was sitting on the bed dressed in her silk underwear. She was a beautiful sight. Her long red hair hanging down over her shoulder. Her full bust attempting to escape her captive. She had a lovely body, a slender, narrow waist rounded bootie and long slender legs. Her bust seemed disproportionably large for her body.

"I'm sorry, I did not make myself clear, I actually need help with escorting myself around town. I need you to help me find places. Alright Connie let's stop by a store and get you a different skirt. Even though you look very sensuous in that short dress, it will not be appropriate for our appointments. I think we better get you a blouse to. With a build like yours you would look vultures even in a set of old coveralls. But we better try to neutralize you a little anyway. I also have a few other things I would like to do while you are here to help me out if that's all right with you."

"Sure. You have paid for twenty-four hours and I'll do whatever you like," she responded with a very service minded attitude.

"Good. They had a lady store down in the lobby, and still do actually," he corrected himself, "why don't we check it out first and see what they have. Would you also mind wiping of some of your make up before we leave? I think any makeup on your pretty face is an overkill."

"Well thank you mister."

"One last thing, I would prefer if you did not call me mister. Alex will do fine."

"Okay, Alex."

They found several nice outfits in the boutique and Alex let her choose two. They also stopped by a shoe store and got Connie a pair of walking shoes before making their first appointment. The gentleman from A.G. Textiles greeted them in a large plush office. Alex introduced Connie as his assistant. They soon reached an agreement, placed the order and got on their way. It was late in the afternoon and Alex suggested they go dining. Connie picked the place. It was modest but nice.

"I used to work here," she told him.

"Really, what did you do? Hosting? Cooking?" he guessed.

"All of the above, I managed it."

"So, the obvious question, why did you quit?" Alex asked.

"Thank you for assuming that I quit. I was actually fired. The owner had a lot of personal expectations that I could not accept," she explained.

"Really, so you joined an escort service instead?"

"I know it may sound a little strange, but I don't have to go to bed with any of my customers if I don't want to, or anyone else. I get paid for providing company, that's all. If I go beyond that it is because I like to. When I worked here, the owner would call me at any time, night and day, for favors and when I refused, I lost my job."

"So why did you choose this place now if you can't stand the owner?" Alex asked curiously.

"I have friends that still work here . . . and I thought it would be nice to come here when I'm dressed nice and in company of such a gentleman. I guess I'm showing off." They got seated in the rear of the restaurant. The decor was pleasant in soft pastel colors. Soft music floated in the air. There was a distinct savor combination of garlic, grilled meat and some pine like incense.

"So, tell me a little about Connie. Who is Connie, where are you from and what are the highlights in your life?" Alex asked.

"It's not a real interesting story, but my name is actually Corina and I'm twenty-six years old. I was born in Nebraska on a farm there. I moved to New York when I was eighteen, right after high school. I have a master's degree in performing art. I was unable to find work in music. I majored in vocal opera, but I never seemed to be right for any part. I'm now pursuing a master's in business, mostly by correspondence. I work for the escort service when I have some free time. I enjoy the escort work. I get to meet a lot of great people like you."

"Well thank you. Boy, that's a different story than I had expected. Do you date anyone seriously? if I may be so bold to ask."

"No, not right now."

"Well, I'm here to look for suitable property here in N.Y. to open a few restaurants so I will stay here until Sunday. How much more will it cost me if I switch to your weekly rate?" he asked.

"I don't really have a weekly rate, but I'll make an exemption. You can have me until Sunday night for eight hundred dollars. That's a bargain."

"I give you four hundred and that's a generous offer."

"I will make a special exemption because I was going to quit and go back to school on Monday anyway. Six hundred, that's my final offer."

"Five hundred," Alex tried.

"Five hundred it is. And just to make sure there are no misunderstandings later, it is five hundred on top of the two hundred we have already agreed on, right?"

"Right." Alex had to smile at her savvy.

"And it is until Sunday night at ten p.m., and includes room and board, and there will be no sex unless I want to, Okay?"

"We have a deal." Alex held out his hand to consummate the agreement.

"Agreed."

"I have to ask. I'm deadly curious. What is my prospectus for sex at this time, in percentage?" Alex asked. He got a kick of her business-like attitude.

"About 110%," she admitted.

"Do you care to elaborate on that?"

"Well, it means that I think I will have to work on you some for it to happen, and I will, I'm normally really good at convincing."

"I have noticed that."

"What do you have in mind for after dinner?" she asked.

"Well, I would like to make you a proposition."

"Oh yea."

"I would like to offer you a position getting a few restaurants started here in New York. You would have to come to Seattle to get initiated. The training process will take up to three months. I will prepare you to find the best property, negotiate deals and set everything up. I will be right behind you if you'll need help. I will send a construction supervisor that will help you with getting the property ready. We will start you out at fifty thousand a year plus benefits. It is not as much as you are making at the escort service, but it is a lot safer. I like what I have seen, and I think you will do an excellent job. It will be based on one condition, that you will finish your master's in business within three years. I will pay for your educational expenses. Are you interested?"

"Interested, are you kidding. I'm esthetic. Of course, I'm interested, and I would love to. This is more than I ever dreamed of. Thank you so much." She reached over the table for his hand. He responded with a warm hug.

"You're quite welcome and thank you."

"When do I start? I could use another month here to finish up my degree and . . . How about May first?" she asked.

"That would be perfect. May first it be. Here is one of my cards. Call Shelly at the office and she will help you make all arrangements, OK? Well, enough about work for tonight. What would you like to do?"

"I think you know what I would like to do. I would like to take you back to the hotel room and seduce you." She looked at him while tilting her head.

"Well I'm flattered but it is early, and I was more thinking if there was a place you would like to go to, or a play that you would like to see, or a movie."

"Anything is fine with me. The Phantom of the Opera has very beautiful music but I'm not sure how easy it is to get tickets. But we can try. It would be a heavenly experience."

Unfortunately, they were not able to get tickets and ended up going to see Forest Gump at the movie instead. It was raining hard when they got out of the movie theater and by the time they got back to their room they were soaked. The room had two beds and Alex laid down on his, turned on the TV, offering Corina to use the bathroom first. She came out dressed in the bath towel. She carefully hanged up her cloth to dry. Alex took his turn getting ready and when he was done, he came out dressed in a silk pajama. Alex slipped into his bed and Corina to hers and they turned off the lights. After having laid there for a few minutes, Corina whispered, "Alex, are you awake?"

"Yes."

"Can I come over?" she whispered.

CHAPTER 43

September, 1983 - The accident

What was first intended to be a one-year sabbatical year in Sweden for Axel and Katarina, became a four-year stay. They benefited from a favorable currency exchange rate and purchased a mansion in Särö, an upscale community outside Gothenburg. The house was in poor condition, but the structure was good and the large lot was worth the price alone. Sitting on a small hill, it offered an undisturbed view of the ocean, the golf course and the lower lying homes. Axel planned to restore the building before they returned to the US.

Axel purchased a sailboat, so he could participate in the Thursday night regattas, but he never placed well. Even though the boats participated on a handicap point system, Axel felt the larger boats had a distinct advantage. The winds would normally calm down around 6:30 p.m., when the race began, and the taller ships not only blocked the wind for the smaller ones, but they could also reach the higher winds.

Katarina had a more difficult time adjusting to Sweden. She missed her friends and work in Fairbanks.

One August evening when Axel came home from sailing, Kurt called. He was going in for heart surgery in the morning and wanted to touch base before. After all Kurt was seventy-seven and anything could happen during an operation. He asked Axel to look after Eva if something should happen to him. He recovered from surgery the following day but shortly after the operation he got worse and a few hours later he passed away. Ironically, it turned out that he, like Annie, had taken Aspirin for headache the evening before the operation with the same devastating result, causing him to bleed to death after the operation.

Alex and Annette came the following day.

"Ironically Kurt never moved to the US," reflected Axel. "He was the one who was always so enamored of America, yet, just about everyone he knew moved over there including mom, but not him."

They drove past a kiosk where the newspaper headlines screamed that Prime Minister Olof Palme had been shot walking with his wife in Stockholm. Killed. Everyone was shocked.

"Sweden is becoming just as bad as America," Axel commented, "people being shoot down on the streets."

"So, you guys are going to see Mom and Billy in England on your way back?" Axel asked. "You will like it. It's quite a place he has there. He makes the Queen of England look like a poor woman," Axel suggested.

Billy and Annika married in a quiet ceremony with only Annette, John and Lisa attending. At seventy-four, Billy was still active in his work, even though he had transferred several duties to his assistants. Billy and Annika settled in England, dividing their time between his country estate and the London suite. They also spent time in Spain, were Billy had a vineyard and in Jodassy where Annika could visit with her old friend Camilla. Billy and Ali had much in common both privately and professionally. Billy pressured Axel to come and be initiated into his business suggesting that Annika may need his help someday. Axel made a couple trips to England, to see Billy regarding business matters.

On July 11, 1989 Axel received a call from Annika. Hearing his mother's voice, he expected her to wish him Happy Birthday. But

Annika was crying and incoherent. He eventually understood her say that Billy had crashed in an airplane, together with King Ali, and she needed him to come right away.

Annika met Axel at the airport. She was dressed in black.

Ali had picked up Billy in his plane, and they were going to check out a project together.

"The weather was good, and the control tower did not receive any emergency messages. The plane just disappeared," Annika explained tearfully.

Axel drove his mother back to the London suite, allowing her to speak uninterrupted most of the way. Upon arriving at the apartment, Axel poured each of them a drink.

"So, you inherit everything from Billy?" Axel asked with disbelief in his voice.

"Everything."

"So, what will you do? How are you going to proceed from here?" he asked her.

"I have no idea. I don't know the first thing about running a business, much less an industrial empire. Axel, I need your help desperately."

"Why me? Alex has as much experience as I do, or even more," he asked.

"Alex would do fine, but he is so involved in his own affairs. Besides, Billy told me to ask you for help if anything should happen to him. You must have made a strong impression on him. You know it's strange, but it's almost as if though Billy knew that something was going to happen. During the last month he has been doing a lot of preparing just in case this should happen. He's been signing over a lot of his assets to me. I have no clue on what I've been signing, but recently I have spent most of my time signing documents."

"Well, we'll take a look at it. We'll set up a meeting with his top directors to sort things out. Do you have contact with Camilla?"

"I talked to her once, and she told me that she would call as soon as she heard anything more. That poor thing. She's now the Queen of Jodassy!" Annika sighed, looking past Axel, her thoughts drifting.

"Well, I don't see her situation as being that much different from you more or less becoming the Queen of England."

The car phone rang and Annika answered. "Hello! Really. . . Nothing more? Thank you for calling. Axel is here now and will help me out. I'll call you later. Please call if you hear anything more. Thank you." Annika turned to Axel. "That was Camilla. They think the plane went down over the water, but there is still no sign of it," she whimpered. "It has now been missing for three days."

The doorbell rang and Axel opened the door. Two agents from Scotland Yard and one from Her Majesty's Secret Service stood at the door. They had several questions for Annika. Unfortunately, Annika could not help much, as she knew little about Billy's activities other than that he had told her he would be home two days ago. They told her they did not suspect foul play as of now, but they were aware of threats that Billy had received.

Axel and Annika invited Amy Whittenberg, Billy's right hand woman, over for dinner and for a general briefing. Axel knew Amy from his previous visit. Amy informed them that Annika was already the owner of all Billy's holdings for two months back. Billy had taken the role of vice president. She told them that the empire consisted of some thirty corporations all operating independently under the umbrella company and that those thirty corporations were currently directed by her and her staff. She offered to remain operations director for as long as she was needed so that Annika could concentrate on personal issues for right now. Amy told them that Billy had made all preparations to bring Axel in as the chairman of the board. She agreed with Annika, that even though Billy was always well prepared, it seemed to her that he was anticipating his departure.

Amy explained that they could not have a funeral for Billy until they found his remains or until they obtained a court order declaring him deceased. She dropped off several binders with information on their corporations, including what they did and their financial status. Axel was impressed with her vast knowledge on all issues and with her professionalism.

"I guess there is no reason for Alex to come here now, until they find Billy or something," Annika said tentatively. "Can I count on you helping me out Axel? I don't understand what all those English documents say, and even less what they mean."

"You can count on me, Mamma. I will help you. I don't know what Katarina will say about this, but I'll do it regardless. I would suggest that you call Camilla and make arrangements to go down and see her for a few days. This must be very difficult for her also."

"Yes, but she's such a brain. She understands these things a lot better," Annika responded.

The following day Axel was brought to B.J. Ltd's administration building. It was a six-story building located in the outskirts of London. Amy greeted him when he arrived. She gave him a quick tour of the building and introduced him to several of the key personal. She showed him Billy's plush office that would now be his. It was conveniently connected to Amy's office, and it was well suited for the frequent meetings that he anticipated.

"Thank you, Amy. I looked at the documents you gave me yesterday and it looks like were involved in just about every industry in the books."

"Yes, Billy believed in being diversified."

"Are all of them profitable?" he asked.

"Yes and no. There are some that are showing a paper loss because of making major capital investments, but that put aside, yes, they are all generating revenue. Our gross revenue was more than six billion U.S. Dollars last year. We grew with 18 percent and our net profit was over 700 million US Dollars. Of that about half was onetime income from selling a steel plant. We have a solid operation. We have liquid assets at the tune of half a billion. We have operations in most parts of the world. Our most, or rather, least stable investment right now is probably in China. We have some telecommunications interests there and after the recent Tiananmen Square incident, it's difficult to predict what will happen there."

"What's your salary?" Axel asked.

"I make $75,000/year. We do all transactions in US Dollars because we have operations in several countries; it is easier to work with a common currency, so dollars it is. Billy started this policy during the war, in case the Great Britain lost."

"When was the last time you had a raise?" he asked.

"Actually, not that long ago. Billy raised me from $68,000 only two month ago."

"Well, for me you are worth more than you were to Billy. For me you are priceless. Assuming that I take over tomorrow, we will improve on that."

"Well thank you very much in advance." She smiled at him warmly. "May I ask what Katarina is thinking about you staying here?"

"Not much. She doesn't like the idea of moving here, even if we'll be living in a palace. She's working in Fairbanks as a nurse for a doctor whom she apparently admires."

"Oh . . . Here is a list of Billy's personal assets, outside of B.J. Ltd. He has seven residents in various places. He has a very nice estate in Jodassy. It was one of his favorites. Of course, he and King Ali were close friends."

"What happened to Li? Did she quit?"

"Oh, you didn't know? Li was traveling with Billy when the accident happened. If it was an accident."

"You don't think it was an accident?" he asked.

"I'm not convinced. Billy was receiving threatening letters for some time and it's possible that he was assassinated. It is also possible that it was King Ali that was the target. Probably we'll never know. That is one thing that you should consider now, to stay out of the public eye as much as possible so you are not recognized. Billy never had security guards, other than at some of the estates. He thought it was better not to call attention to himself. 'I'll be fine with my pepper spray,' he used to say."

"I'd like to take a look at those estates. Will you please make a list of pressing issues and then make arrangements to travel to all headquarters and to all the estates? Thanks again Amy." He raised his hand for a high five. "I will enjoy working with you."

"Thanks, me too. I will get right to it."

King Ali's and Billy's funeral was not large, considering that it involved royalty. Perhaps five hundred guests attended. After the service the caskets were driven through the business sector and to a grave yard on the Royal Palace ground. Billy was to be buried with his old friend. A reception area was set up in the great hall. Maria was there, but Axel did not see her, or recognize her under her Veil. However, he did speak to her briefly the following morning at lunch arranged by Queen Camilla. Maria was friendly but subdued. Amy stayed with Axel at all times, though she frequently had to take calls on her cell phone. Billy's guests, including John and Lisa, were all staying at Billy's estate, but Annika stayed with Camilla at the palace. Amy and Axel were also joined by a woman who was the director of Billy's operations in Jodassy. Sandra arranged for a dinner at Billy's estate that evening. It was the last day there for most of the guests. Annika would stay with Camilla for the time being, and Axel, Amy and Sandra would tour the Jodassy operations. Later, they would also tour the operations in France and in Seattle. While in America, they made a trip to Fairbanks so Axel could see Katarina and tie up some loose ends.

Katarina and Axel had agreed to separate so that Katarina could see the doctor with whom she worked, and Axel could return to England. Katarina got to keep the full Fairbanks estate.

CHAPTER 44

1984 -- Maria

Having renewed her friendship with Camilla, Annika moved to Jodassy permanently. Most of the time she stayed with Camilla. She took no part in running the business.

"Axel! Hi it's Mom! How is everything? Listen, there's something I need to talk to you about. This is going to sound crazy to you, I know, but it's very important. Camilla, as the new Queen of Jodassy takes on a position similar to mine, as the chairman of the board for the corporation. However, she is having some medical problems and is preparing her daughter Maria to take over the reins of Jodassy. Maria is pregnant, but she won't say who the father is. The problem is that it will not work for Maria to become the queen, being pregnant and not having a husband. So, we were thinking, Camilla and I that, we should try to arrange a marriage between Maria and you. You're not seeing anyone, now are you?" Annika asked.

"Mom, I don't know what to say. I'll talk to Maria. At least I'll promise that much."

"Not only is it important for Camilla and Jodassy, but Camilla tells me that it will improve the business positions enormously for both parties. If we move our headquarters to Jodassy, then all the taxes we pay would go to our selves, more or less. You know, arranged marriages are common in this part of the world, and most of them seem to work out fine. Besides, Maria is an angel."

"I'll talk to her."

Axel asked the driver to stop at a flower shop on his way to see Maria.

"Can I help you Sir?" a young woman with a cheerful voice asked him from behind.

Axel turned around. "Yes, I would like to have a bouquet of roses for a beautiful lady," he said, "but I'm debating about what color to choose."

"Well, if she is a lady of virtue, innocent and sweet, a bouquet of white roses would be appropriate. She would appreciate the gesture for sure. However, if she is an untamed spirit and passionate, a bouquet of red roses will keep that fire burning," she suggested.

"Well she is sweet, and a lady of virtue for sure. I will have a bouquet of white roses, please." The girl prepared the flowers for wrapping. "Excuse me miss, if I should be completely honest, lets add one red rose, please."

"I'm so sorry that I had to drag you into this," Maria said awkwardly. "Mom and Ann . . . I was going to call . . ."

"Shhh . . . "he put his finger on her lips to silence her, wiped a tear off her cheek, leaned over and kissed her. "You little dummy. You don't really think that I would do this just as a favor, do you? Sweetheart, I've never been able to get you out of my mind since we first met. I'm in love. I love you, I looove you," he repeated, embracing her tightly.

"Maria," he gazed deep into her emerald eyes. "I think I know who the father of your baby is. It seems as though the timing coincided . . ."

"I was going to call you when this mess happened," she interrupted him.

"Ye mona patso."

"Wow!"

THE END.

P.S.

This tail continues in my next novel; *Connie*